A
MILLION
NIGHTINGALES

ALSO BY SUSAN STRAIGHT

Aquaboogie: A Novel in Stories

I Been in Sorrow's Kitchen and Licked Out All the Pots

Blacker Than a Thousand Midnights

The Gettin Place

Highwire Moon

A MILLION NIGHTINGALES

Susan Straight

PANTHEON BOOKS
NEW YORK

Pantheon Books and colophon are registered trademarks of Random House, Inc.

Library of Congress Cataloging-in-Publication Data

Straight, Susan.
A million nightingales / Susan Straight.
p. cm.
ISBN 0-375-42364-8
1. Racially mixed people—Fiction. 2. Plantation life—Fiction.
3. Teenage girls—Fiction. 4. Women slaves—Fiction.
5. Louisiana—Fiction. I. Title.

PS3569.T6795M55 2006 813'.54—dc22 2005050052

www.pantheonbooks.com

This is a work of fiction. Names, characters, places, and incidents either are the product of the author's imagination or are used fictitiously. Any resemblance to actual persons, living or dead, events, or locales is entirely coincidental.

Printed in the United States of America
First Edition
2 4 6 8 9 7 5 3 1

For my mother
and her mother, Frieda
For Fine, Callie, Daisy, Alberta, and those unnamed
the other foremothers of my own daughters
and all who came before them

I have a million nightingales on the branches of my heart
singing freedom

—From a folk song adaptation of the poem
"Defiance," by Mahmud Darwish

CONTENTS

A
Million
Nightingales

One AZURE

In late summer, I collected the moss with the same long poles we used to knock down the pecans in fall. I waved the pole around in the gray tangles and pulled them down from the oaks on the land beside the house, not far from the clearing where we washed and sewed.

I couldn't take the moss from the two oaks in front of the house, where the windows faced the river, because Madame Bordelon liked to look at that moss. It was a decoration. She watched me from the window of her bedroom. Everything on the front land at Azure was Madame's, for decoration. Everything in the backlands was Msieu Bordelon's, for money.

And me—she stared at me all the time now. She stared at my hair, though she couldn't see it. My hair was wrapped under the black tignon my mother had made last year for me, when I turned thirteen. I hated the weight on my skull. My hair was to be hidden, my mother said. That was the law.

The cloth at my forehead felt like a bandage. Like it was holding in my brain. A brain floated in Doctor Tom's jar, in the room where he always stayed when he came to treat Grandmère Bordelon, for her fatness, and where he stayed now to treat Céphaline, for her face. The brain was like a huge, wrinkled, pale pecan. One that didn't break in half. Swimming in liquid.

When I came for his laundry, he sat at the desk and the brain sat on the shelf, with the other jars. He said, "You can hold it."

The glass was heavy in my hands, and the brain shivered in the silvery water.

"I bought that brain in 1808, yes, I did, and it's been two years in the jar after spending several years inside a skull. You seem unafraid to hold it or examine it, Moinette," he said in English. He was from London, and his words made his thin lips rise and twist differently from Creoles. "Your lack of fear would indicate that your own brain is working well." Then he returned to his papers, and I took his dirty clothes away.

How could brains be different? I measured heads the same way Mamère had taught me to measure a handful of fat to throw in the pot for soap, cupping my palm; the heavy handful had to reach the second bend on my fingers. The other side of knuckles—the little pad of skin like oval seed pearls when a person held out a hand to get something. I stared at my palms so long, clenching and straightening them, that Mamère frowned and told me to stir the soap.

At the edge of the canefield when the cutters were resting, I hid myself in the tall stalks and fit my bent fingers over their heads. The grown people's heads wore hats and tignons, but the skulls were nearly all the same size under my curved hand. It was not exact, though. I made a loop of wire from a scrap and measured Michel's head when he was in the cane. He was a grown man, same as Msieu Bordelon.

The cutters held very still when they rested. Their backs were against the wagon wheels and the trees.

When I took clean laundry to the house, I stood near the dining room and quickly measured those heads at the table. The same loop for Msieu's head, the only time he didn't wear his hat, while he was eating.

All our heads were the same size according to our age and sex: mine and Céphaline's, Mamère and Madame's, the men cutting cane and Msieu Bordelon's. Under their hair, all their skulls were the same, and so the pecan brains floating inside that bone would be the same size unless the head was wrong, like Eveline's baby who died. The baby's head was swollen like a gourd grows in summer when it's watered too much and then splits.

By September, I pulled down the last moss from the side-land oaks. They were the most beautiful to me. Their branches lay along the earth so that I could walk on the bark. The bark was almost black, damp under my bare feet.

I could hear the field people working in the cane near here, when someone shouted or laughed, the hoes hitting a rock now and then. They were weeding the rows. The cane was so tall, everyone was invisible. I piled the moss on the little wagon we used to take laundry back and forth from our clearing to the house. I pushed down the springy gray coils with my palms.

When the bell rang for lunch, I pulled down one more dangling clump, and then Christophe was behind me.

"Boil it and kill it and then it look like your hair. Then I sleep on it."

He hated me now. He had always pulled my hair when we were small, but now that he was sixteen, he hated me. His hair was damp and separated into black pearls on his head, from the heat. His faded black shirt was white with salt around the neck. We wouldn't get new clothes until Christmas.

He held up his torn sleeve. "I got a girl on Petit Clair. She sew it. You useful for nothing."

I shrugged. "We can't sew for you. Only Bordelons."

He imitated me, shrugged much more dramatically. "Cadeau-fille," he said. Gift girl. He always called me that, adding, "Yellow girl only good for one thing, for what under your dress. All you are. Don't work. Don't mean nothing till he give you away."

"Your head looks small," I said, moving back so I could hook my fingers into a circle, like the wire, and measure.

But he moved forward and pushed my hand down.

"Somebody come for you soon. Just like your mother."

"Close your mouth."

My mother had been a gift for one week, a nighttime present for a visiting sugar broker from New Orleans. I was what she received. But Cadeau-fille was not my name.

I pulled the wagon down the path from the side yard toward the clearing near my mother's house. The moss had to be boiled.

Christophe followed me. He spoke low and constant, like a swarm of bees hovering near my shoulder. He said he was a horse, at least pure in blood and a useful animal. He said I was a mule, half-breed, and even a mule worked hard. He said I was nothing more than a foolish peacock that les blancs liked to keep in the yard to show people something pretty. Then he said, "And the men, you are only there so they can think under your . . ."

At the clearing, fire burned low under the pots, but my mother was not there. I threw a bar of soap at him. I didn't want to hear it again.

He picked up the soap and threw it from the clearing. "Go in the cane and get it. Then cadeau-mère can't see you. You have to lift up your dress when Msieu pick someone for you. Lift it up now. Hurry."

In the heat and my anger, my eyes felt underwater. He'd told some of the men I went in the cane with him. Just to let him look. The women had told Mamère.

"We're all animals," I said. "Hair and skin are like fur." I had nothing else to throw at him.

He shoved me against the pecan tree where we hung our washline, and then ran into the cane. The stalks shifted and then stayed still.

I found the soap. The bar was soft and wet from Mamère's using it all morning. I worked off the dust with my fingers, underwater.

My mother and I made the soap for Azure, and each bar was measuring and stirring, to me. Christophe was a man, so he didn't think about his clothes being clean or the soap washing the cane juice from his hands. He didn't think anything except cane was work, and he hated my face and especially my hair.

My hair fell to my waist, in the same tendrils as the moss from the branches, but black. But now no one ever saw it except my mother. On Sunday nights, she washed it with soap made from almond oil and boiled gourd, rinsed it in the washtub, and formed the curls around her fingers. We sat near the fire. When my hair was dry, she braided it so tightly my temples stung and covered it with the tignon.

Hair only protected my scalp. The thin cover protecting my skull. And my brain. My hair was only a covering. Céphaline Bordelon's hair, too, like every other human.

But hers was thin and brown, her braid only a mousetail down her back. Her eyes were bright and blue, and I knew inside her brain was perfect, because she learned everything each of her tutors taught her and even questioned the lessons. But her pale skin was speckled with crimson boutons.

Madame had to marry Céphaline to someone with money, and for weeks, she had cried until her own blue eyes were rimmed as with blood. None of the men who visited could see Céphaline's brain. Only her face, and her hair, and her mouth never closed or curved in a smile. Her mouth always talking, arguing, reading to people from her books.

The moss was soft in my hands, in the basket. I liked to look at each strand and feel the covering, like the velvet of Céphaline's brown dress. My mother would be angry if she saw me studying the moss. She wanted me to boil it and lay it out to dry. It was not a lesson. It was stuffing. Every fall, we made new bedding—this year, seventy-two pallets for slaves and five mattresses for the Bordelons.

We lived between. Le quartier was one long street, houses lining the dirt road to the canefields and sugarhouse, but a grove of pecan trees separated the street from the Bordelons' house. Tretite, the cook, lived in the kitchen behind the house, and Nonc Pierre, the groom, lived in the barn.

But my mother's house was in a clearing near three pecan trees at the edge of the canefields. A path led from the main road to our yard. Madame Bordelon could see us from her second-floor gallery, could see what color clothes we hung, or whether we had washed the table linens, but she couldn't hear what we said.

Under the trees, my mother spoke to me every day, but only when she had something to teach me and only when we were alone.

When I was young, I asked her the same thing many times, until I understood.

"Mamère."

"Oui."

"Who do I belong to?"

"Me." She never hesitated. "You are mine."

"No one else?"

"No."

"Not Msieu?"

"No."

"Not God?"

Then she would pause. I watched her pour another dipper of water onto the wood ashes held in a wooden trough over the big pot. The gray sludge dripped into the boiling water.

"No," she said then, stirring the lyewater. I knew to stay away. One flying drop could burn the skin. Brown to pink. Pink and shiny-raised as mother-of-pearl buttons on my mother's forearm. Like she had sewn them to her own skin, as if she had finished mending the Bordelons' clothes and then decided to decorate herself.

"No!" My mother's voice rushed from her throat, harsh like she was chewing coffee beans. "Here on earth, you belong to me. If you died, then you would belong to God. Là-bas." She lifted her chin to the sky above the pecan trees. "Eh bien, I would die, too, because I would need to be—gone with you."

"Gone?"

"There. Not here. Là-bas—with you."

I wouldn't look up. I didn't want to see that sky, là-bas. I looked down, at the fire under the pitted black iron of the washpot, until I could speak. "God would kill you, too? Because you let me die?" I whispered.

"No!" My mother's eyes were fierce and slitted under the tignon covering her hair and forehead. The cloth had slipped up, so a stripe of gleaming undusted skin showed above her brows. "God will not kill you, or me. No. My only work here is to keep you alive." She spat into the boiling water and stirred; her arm disappeared in the steam so that I was frightened for a moment. "This is not my work. This is how I pass the time while I keep you."

When I was small, and she said that, I would fling out my arms and spin under the fine muslin cloth hanging to dry in the low branches of the sweet olive. She had patched the torn mosquito netting from Madame's bed, sewing in newer, whiter muslin, and my mother's work floated like tiny clouds above me.

My mother's throat would calm again, and she poured more water over the ashes, her face a mask under the sweat and dust. She took a turkey feather from her apron pocket and dipped it into the bubbling lyewater. After a few seconds, she pulled out the quill, like a stripped white bone.

I watched the blue flame under the pot. "What is my work?" I used to ask, before I understood that my work would be every moment.

"You wash and sew and be cautious. You do what I say, exactement."

"But I am a mule. I will carry things, no?"

She turned with the feather like a toy sword. "What? A mule!"

"Christophe says I am a mule. And he is a horse. He is better."

"He is orphée. He is angry that you have a mother."

Christophe was cutting cane already, living with three other men. I didn't understand the mule yet. I touched the clouds in the muslin and said idly, "How would you get there? Là-bas? With God? With me?"

My mother stepped away from the pot and wiped the gloss from her forehead. "The way I do everything else," she said, angry, and I took my hands from the cloth and backed away. She spat lye steam from her mouth, fixed her eyes on me, and didn't smile. "Myself. I would do it myself."

I believed her. I was all she cared about, except for the coffee she loved so much she hoarded the beans inside a special tin in our room. She counted the beans during the night, before she came to sleep, when she thought my eyes were closed.

But before she held them under her nose with her palm flat, her nostrils almost touching the dark beans, she prayed, and I listened. She lit two small candles, ones she kept hidden because we weren't supposed to have them. She made them for herself when we dipped all the others for the Bordelons. She poured a sip of the day's coffee into a tiny blue dish on the washstand and laid one bean on a piece of cloth so blue it was almost black. She put one gold piastre on the cloth, too, and a circle of my hair braided like a bracelet.

She glanced at me, and my eyes were closed.

She prayed in French, and African words crept in. Words I knew she had learned from her mother, but words she never said to me. She prayed to all the gods, of water and earth, and to God above, mon Dieu, that I would be healthy in the morning, alive all day, protected until the next night, when she would ask again.

When she was finished, she blew out the candles and laid them on their sides next to our wooden plates, and they looked cold and small. Then she put them with the cloth scrap, the bracelet of hair, and the piastre in a pouch inside the kitchen safe, where we kept our spoons and cups. If anyone ever came looking, they wouldn't think that collection of things was special to anyone. They might take the piastre, but they wouldn't know the rest was her church.

She slept in her chair for much of the night. I would wake to see her slumped against the rush backing, her right cheek propped on her bent hand. The night was far gone, the fire lessened to ruby chunks.

Toward morning, she would be beside me in the bed, her breathing rough like the file rasp the men used to sharpen their cane knives. She woke me before dawn, when she stirred the fire. She roasted her coffee beans in the black pan and then ground them in the metal grinder she clamped to the table's edge. She poured boiling water on the coffee, in the dented pot, which was one of the first things I ever remembered seeing as a baby. Then she reached into her basket of rags for the tin cigar box. From inside, nested in brown paper, she took out the hard cone of white sugar, which glittered in the firelight.

Green cane crushed and boiled and brown molasses drained out and then the sugar bleached white and formed into a cone hard as a cowhorn by some magic in some faraway place. Slaves had molasses, measured out in pails during the week. Tretite, the cook, had stolen the sugar for my mother weeks ago, in exchange for a white wedding dress. Only the Bordelons had sugar.

My mother cut two large pinches with the ancient sugar scissors. She stirred the hardness into her coffee and opened the wooden shutters. She stared out the window at the pink or gray of day, and her throat worked as she swallowed the black.

The smell rose like bitter strong dirt. I didn't understand how she could drink that liquid, how she could chew the beans during the day. And once when I said that, she told me her own mother used to chew something that made her teeth orange. A nut or seed.

"In Africa."

"Did the nut taste good?"

She shrugged. "Never taste it."

"You were in Africa?"

"I was little child on the boat. Only remember the boat."

"But how did she die? Your mother?"

My mother lifted her chin at me, exactly as she did to Madame and everyone else, and for a moment, she didn't even see me before her. Her lips were pressed together so tight they disappeared, and her face was like something floating in Doctor Tom's room, like the air was a silvery sharp liquid.

But then her eyes dropped back down to me, and without a sound of breath, her bosom rose high and then fell.

"She die from the smell. Soldier blue. That indigo."

Today when she turned from the shutter, the sky was still dark. She put her cup on the table and tightened her tignon. From the tin, she took out my peacock plate.

My mother had exchanged fine soap and cloth to a bayou trader for the small plate. I was seven. She told me if I ate my biscuit or cornmush, a whole world would appear underneath.

A tree with dangling branches. A gate, and past it a river with a small boat. And on the gate a peacock, his head crowned, his tail a dragged flourish.

Faint voices rose all the way from the street. The work bell would ring soon. She wrapped the cone of sugar in paper and closed the tin, against ants and rats. Just then, someone tapped at the shutter, and my mother whirled around with a look on her face as if she'd seen a snake.

Nobody came unannounced to visit my mother. She went to see women in le quartier, sometimes bringing favors for trade, but even Tretite the cook always let my mother know beforehand that she was coming.

"Marie-Thérèse," an urgent voice whispered near the opened shutters. "C'est moi."

Eveline. I propped myself on the bed. The sunrise was only a silver breath over the trees. Two women stood at the door.

Eveline came inside, but the other woman, a stranger with scars high on her cheeks, stayed in the doorway. "That monthly visitor come when I was out in the field by Petit Clair," Eveline said. "So far to walk my whole dress gone."

My mother opened the bundle, and I smelled the blood.

Eveline sighed and looked over at me braiding my hair. "I know Moinette get her monthly now, too. I know you have so much wash, Marie-Thérèse. I bring you something from Michel for thanks."

She opened a cloth bag at her feet and showed the gleaming head of a duck, its bill yellow green. Bone? Was a bill made of bone?

Her husband, Michel, trapped on the weekends and traded the rabbits and birds. Eveline and Michel cut more cane than anyone else on Azure. Eveline straightened again. She was round in the arms and face and stomach, from all five children, she said, leaving behind their baby fat on her. But Eveline's neck was the most beautiful part of her, when she lifted her head. Her throat was long and perfect as a vase with three etched lines of decoration, three lines of paler brown skin from where she bent at the cane all day and at her cooking all night.

"We come in so late. Say maybe a freeze coming. Can't wash, and can't leave the dress in the house. That smell bring rats."

My mother winced. "I do it today," she said. Then she lifted her chin toward the doorway at the strange tall woman.

Eveline said, "She new. Buy for the grinding. Want to see you."

When Eveline left, the new woman stepped inside and stopped politely. My mother lifted her chin again, like she did to everyone. Her jaw and chin were most of my mother's language, how she slanted her face to indicate anger or curiosity, how she raised that shelf of bone directly toward someone to show she was listening.

The new woman's face was narrow and dark, like Mamère's, but her eyes were surrounded by more lines. The two scars on each cheek were raised and shiny as oval inserts of satin. She leaned against the wall.

"Just get here," she said in English. "Me and my children." She held up four fingers.

My mother nodded. "Speak little English, me. But she speak some." She moved her chin toward me.

"M'appelle Hera," the woman said.

"Marie-Thérèse."

Hera's eyes moved quickly from the bed to the chairs, from the washboards hanging on the wall to the three mattress tickings we had finished sewing last night, to me.

"Someone leave you a bright hardship." She studied the hair I hadn't finished braiding.

Mamère didn't answer. She moved the mattresses toward the door. We had to take them to the house.

"Him up there?"

I bit my lips. Mamère hated this part, and so did I. When people saw us for the first time, traders or new slaves or visitors to Azure, they tried to establish who we were, where I had come from.

"Non."

Hera was quiet, having heard the anger in Mamère's answer. She rubbed her arms and glanced at my sewing. A sleeve of Céphaline's.

Hera was staring at us. Seeing what we had. Measuring, the way humans measure one another all the time, every minute. She wanted to see what we looked like, what we owned, compare it to hers, think of how to get us to give some, or take some, or trade something for her own room, on the other side of Eveline's. She had nothing, maybe. Or more than we did. No. Look at her eyes. Like Madame Bordelon's when she evaluated the carriages and coats and china of other women.

Then Hera looked at me again. "Your only?"

My mother glanced up. "Take but one candle to light a room," she said.

Hera nodded and rubbed her arms again. I could smell the blood from Eveline's clothes.

Mamère put down the washbasket with the black clothes and said, "Quoi besoin?" She frowned at me. She wanted the English words.

"What do you need?" I whispered, to both of them.

"Not me," Hera said.

"What they need?" My mother meant Hera's children.

"Say you sew."

My mother moved her chin up an inch.

"Say you trade."

She lifted her brows.

Hera said, "My girl fifteen. She need a dress for the New Year. I hear he only give black dress. She need pretty dress, to find someone and set up." She nodded toward me. "Mine ain't bright, like that one. How old?"

Her tribal scars shone—she was from Africa, I knew. How old had she been when someone cut her? Had her own mother done it? Cut open her daughter's skin?

"Just turn fourteen," I said.

"Not long," Hera said. "Bright one like that, someone come for her soon."

"Long enough," my mother said, her eyes slitting to nothing. She opened the door. The sky was silver now, and Hera shouldn't be walking outside the quartier unless she walked in a line toward the canefields. "That bell ring soon."

But Hera paused. "You think on a trade?"

My mother inclined her head to the left, and I hoped Hera saw that meant possibility.

My mother put the duck in a basket hung from the ceiling. She put a piece of yesterday's cornbread on the plate. Inside the yellow, she had placed a sliver of sugar. It melted on my tongue.

When we got to the kitchen, Tretite would slip us meat and biscuits with the bundle of laundry. And coffee beans. Mamère never ate anything but meat and biscuits, and all day, she chewed coffee beans.

She stretched the blanket tightly over our mattress, though she had lain there only a few hours. The moss had sunk to fit my shape on one side, by the window.

"Why don't you come to sleep early?" I asked her when I was small.

"Because the bed is too soft."

Today I said, "Will you sew for her?"

She shrugged.

"Aren't you tired? Why sleep in the chair? Not the bed?"

This time Mamère's face was different. She said, "Because then I would be comfortable. Lying down on the bed is like flying. I couldn't get up if I felt like that all night."

I looked at the wool blanket over the empty place that was mine. "Comprends?" she whispered, staring at me. "It is frightening to be so rested."

I nodded, but I didn't understand.

The wooden wheels of the small cart creaked. Mamère kept one more pinch of sugar in her apron pocket. But the sugar was all around us, canestalks that made a wall along our clearing. Nine feet high. I measured it with my palm up. Once Doctor Tom had said to Msieu, "Your biggest slave Michel must be an impressive six feet tall," and I had backed away until my stiff hand was equal to Michel's height.

The cane was Michel plus half of his body.

"Stop," Mamère whispered. "You look like you are waving."

"To who?"

She pushed my hand down to my side.

"To anyone."

We waited at the back gallery for Tretite to bring us the bundle. Her face was a fallen cake under her red tignon, her cheeks flat and wide and shiny with sweat, her eyes and nose and lips all gathered tightly in the center.

When I was six, she saw me staring and whispered, "I sleep on my face when I petite like you. I mash tout." Then she put my fingers on her tiny chin, the glossy red brown of dripped molasses.

She nodded this morning and said, "Dorm bien?"

Mamère shook her head. It was what they said. Sleep well?

Behind Tretite in the pantry were large jars of olive oil lined against the wall, and candles to be trimmed.

"Tête bien?" Mamère held the bundle and looked up at Tretite, who shrugged. Tretite had headaches every day. She pointed a stubby finger toward the roll of dirty napkins.

"Merci," my mother said. Inside the initialed squares would be our breakfast, and ten coffee beans. Tretite would steal for Mamère forever, because of the white muslin dress Mamère sewed for her from an old mosquito barre.

Tretite was forty, had no husband, but loved wedding dresses.

She had belonged to Madame Bordelon since she was twenty, she told me, and was never allowed to marry. "She don't want me distract by no man or no baby. Then I couldn't cook so perfect. I don't want the man, me—just the white dress. I had the man once when I was sixteen, and too much trouble. My house is my house. My fire is my fire."

She witnessed Madame Bordelon's wedding to Msieu, and cooked the elaborate feast, and all these years, she had wanted a white dress. She wore it on Sundays to visit in le quartier. "A dove and you starlings," she said, but the people only laughed because she laughed, too, and they could leave their black clothes behind on Sundays.

I picked up the laundry basket and turned back toward our place.

From the back gallery, you could see the stables and barns, Tretite's kitchen off to the side and her room attached. Then down the road, our three pecan trees, our clearing like a cave, almost, though Madame had the branches trimmed so she could see us.

They could see everything.

Farther down the road, the slave street lined with houses and catalpa trees. The chimneys each with smoke thin as threads now rising into the sky, like God pulled up the dark skeins for himself.

Now that I had turned fourteen, I had to stay in our one room or in the clearing. I couldn't even walk in the cane, or at the edge of the ciprière swamp, where the ancient cypress trees rested their roots in the black-glass water. I couldn't linger by the river because someone might steal me. Tretite said, "We too far south from New Orleans, and Lafitte men come up the river or the bayou. Look for someone to sell. They see you, they take you that fast."

"Lafitte's men won't come in the cane," I said, angry. "Privateers don't want grass."

"Slave stealers take anyone. Took that little boy from Petit Clair while he fishing. His mother lost two now. She scream so loud, I hear from our yard. Lafitte men sell a girl like you for—"

My mother said, "You stay where I see you. All the time."

"There's good moss in the ciprière," I began, and my mother said, "Lafitte men know every bayou, every ciprière."

"Lafitte men know under your dress," Tretite said. "They keep girls look like you down there in Barataria, where they stay." She pulled my tignon down tighter over my forehead.

My hair was hot under the tignon. Under my dress, and on top of my head. I was tired of hearing the words. What would they do with my hair? Pull it out of my head? Turn it into a rope to strangle me? Simply stare at it?

My hair was soft as the gray moss when it hung from the branches. But we boiled the moss in the washpots, then hung the dripping curtains of black along the fence palings and low bushes. After a time in the sun, the moss was black wire, tangled and stiff. Mamère and I pushed the dried moss into the new cotton tickings we had sewn for the Bordelons.

I took one new mattress at a time on the cart, and Félonise, the housemaid, helped me lift it upstairs to the bedrooms. She smiled dreamily at me.

Félonise rarely said anything, to anyone. She stared only at the thing just in front of her—the table she polished, the vase she dusted, the floor she washed.

One day when I was ten, she took me into Msieu Bordelon's room to clean the furniture. Félonise gave me a small rag sprinkled with lemon oil, and my hand followed hers circling steady on the armoire. She hummed above me, the hum vibrating in her throat, falling down to my scalp and entering my skull as a shivering. The lemon oil disappeared into the wood, leaving behind a sheen. It turned my cloth translucent, and when we were finished, Félonise had still not said a word, only hummed so long that my ears felt tender. She took my hand in hers, our fingers shells of glaze, Félonise's hand sealed to my own when we left the bedroom.

Now we carried a new mattress to Grandmère Bordelon's room, on the women's side of the house. Grandmère was very fat, and she sat in her chair before the doors that led to the gallery. She had a spyglass, and she watched the river. She turned to us and said, "You—don't forget to roll it well. Always roll a new bed."

The rolling pin rested in notches atop the mahogany headboard. We put the mattress on the ropes and lifted down the rolling pin, polished and heavy. Back and forth, smoothing the stubborn lumps of moss, and while we worked, Félonise's eyes crossed until I knew she saw nothing, not the cotton ticking or my own fingers on the other side.

All day and night, Grandmère Bordelon spoke to her and moved her about the house to bring and take and hover. I was afraid of Grandmère Bordelon's huge trembling cheeks, which hung below her chin as if her face had melted; fat was under our skin, fat like the waxy white smudges under the rough skin of ham.

Grandmère was Msieu's mother. She had lived in the first small house, amid the oaks on the side land, and after her husband died, she could not be alone. Her slave Marie-Claire was told never to leave her side, even when she slept. But once Grandmère awakened alone. She screamed, but Marie-Claire was in le quartier with a fevered child.

Grandmère had Marie-Claire tied down. Two days she was staked in the side yard. Tretite said that from the gallery, Marie-Claire looked like a doll forgotten on the ground, and no one could go near her.

When she was released from the stakes, Tretite saw bleeding holes in her cheeks. "Rats," Marie-Claire said, and didn't speak again for weeks. The rats came every night to Grandmère's house, where she kept a store of sweets and nuts.

That first old house burned down from a cooking fire, and now nothing was there amid the oaks.

I could smell Grandmère's breath. When we had made the bed with the white coverlet I had bleached so many times to take out the stains, Grandmère held my skirt with her finger and thumb.

"Sang mêlé," she said, lifting my pale wrist—mixed blood—and letting it fall. "I forgot about you."

Her black crepe dress smelled of sour wine and onions and smoke.

"And you are old enough now. In New Orleans, les mulâtresses are the best for dressing the hair." How could mules be good with hair? She nodded decisively. "Today. Today you will learn about the hair. Whether she is forced or not, Céphaline needs a maid now to dress properly." She peered up at my face, her eyes blue like Céphaline's but murky around the edges, as if someone had stirred cornstarch inside.

I went back to the kitchen. Mulâtresse. "You a mule, but mule don't breed," Christophe said once. "You only work for pleasure."

Babies. I couldn't have babies? Félonise stood near the table eating a fig. Her skin was the pale gray of washed-too-many-times shirts. Her eyes were the same. She took her fig and disappeared into the parlor, and Tretite came inside.

"Tretite," I whispered, knowing that this was something my mother didn't want to teach me yet when we were alone in the clearing. Maybe my mother didn't know. "Tell me the name for Félonise."

"Comprends pas," she said, shrugging, sorting the purplish figs.

"Mulâtresse, c'est moi," I said. "Me. And Félonise?"

Tretite looked up sharply, her tiny mouth pursed to disappearing under her draped-down cheeks. "Pourquoi?"

I lifted my chin and felt my mother inside my skull. Then I lifted my chin higher and said, "Grandmère Bordelon said mulâtresse must learn to do hair."

Tretite put the figs in a blue bowl and then rested her fingers in a fan on the table's edge. "Oui. Mulâtresse. So. Félonise, c'est quadroon. The mother, like you, the father, c'est blanc. Eh là, Félonise had a girl, and the father blanc. In New Orleans. C'est octoroon, that baby. They take her away when she is two, and Félonise is sold down here. That baby—so white, like Céphaline, but black, black hair and black, black eye."

Félonise's fingers were tight on mine, that day, the lemon oil glossing our palms.

Tretite said, "And other way—that is Eveline. Griffe. The mother mulâtresse, the father nègre. Eveline's enfants call sacatra—griffe mix with nègre. So."

I heard Mamère with the cart, bringing up Céphaline's new mattress, and I stepped outside. My mother was African, Singalee, but her forehead shone not pure black under her tignon—brown and red, too. Her palms always wrinkled white from washing. Her tongue pink when she stirred. Her eyes nearly purple when she looked into mine. And a stripe of golden dust on her cheek, where she'd rubbed.

How could you do numbers as on Céphaline's lessons, but inside someone's blood? Félonise came behind me to help lift the next mattress into Céphaline's room.

Céphaline sat at her desk writing. Her hair was lank and tied with a dirty ribbon. She did not look up at me. The letters and numbers were so small and close together, the page seemed covered with black lace. I had been learning to read her words since I was small. I could make out only a few of these—*coeur, cheval, écrire, ordinaire*—when I walked past slowly, to get down the rolling pin from her headboard.

Heart, horse, write, ordinary.

I wouldn't tell my mother yet that I would leave her for the house. It was still early. I shook the bottles of our cleaning solutions, to see if any had gone bad.

The tablecloth was stained with many colors, spread out on the worktable in our clearing. Wine spill like a red tongue. That must have come from Msieu Lemoyne, the very old man who lived alone next door at Petit Clair. His hands always shook at Sunday dinner.

The Bordelons had entertained two families from down the river yesterday. That meant Céphaline would have had to smile and speak to sons, and today she would be as bitter as the smell from this bottle for oil stains.

Mamère tied different colors of thread around the neck of each bottle to show what they were.

The grease from the ham made windows of clear in the linen, made the cloth shimmer so the table's wood was visible underneath, and I pressed my fingertip to the fat. How did the pig's fat enter the threads? The same fat we boiled for soap, how did the ashes change the grease to the—what did Céphaline call it, in her lessons with Mademoiselle, when the Auzenne girls were laughing at her concentration, the way her forehead wrinkled? The agent. The agent to erase the grease?

And how much fat and grease was under my own skin? I wondered, pinching my arm. Mamère caught my fingers.

"Get the grease out, you use green one."

"I know."

I shook the bottle gently. White soap shaved very fine, soft rainwater and salt, two yolks of fresh eggs, cabbage juice and bullock's gall, and salt of tartar from Tretite's kitchen.

I rubbed the liquid onto the golden spots.

"What?" She knew a question circled in me.

She saw me looking at her forearms and wrists, wider than the part above her elbow, and she said, "Wash toujours, every day, the arm so."

"No. Not your arm."

"What?"

I couldn't ask her. She hated the questions I brought from Céphaline's room with dirty clothes, when I'd heard her reading or arguing with her governess. How do you measure the grease in a person? I pushed in my own cheek. Was that fat under the cheek? Not muscle?

She never wanted to discuss the lessons about brains and bones and books, so she began her own teaching quickly with one word when we were alone.

"Blood." She pushed Eveline's black clothes into a pot of water that did not steam. But then she handed me a white pillowcase with brown freckles. Céphaline's pillowcase. She had scratched her boutons again, the bumps on her cheeks.

"White thread."

White soap shaved fine, a pound of alum, tartar, and rainwater. Mamère soaked a white flannel rag with the liquid and rubbed it onto the dried blood.

Since I was small, she had always begun with one word. "Blood. Cold water and be careful. Blood stay forever, like it grow in the cloth."

"Gravy. Get it out, you use that bottle with the brown thread."

"Mud. The bottle with the black thread."

"Wine. Red thread."

Soap for the perspiration stains under the arms of Madame's chemise and Céphaline's, which smelled of salt and worry, Msieu's white shirts, which smelled of smoke and grass, and the huge pantalettes Grandmère wore under her dresses—rancid meat and rosewater.

How did yellow egg yolks and sour cabbage juice take the fat from the threads? The bottles held their murky fluids. Blood and saliva and tears were inside us. What made the tears?

We boiled the white clothes and rinsed them in bluing. Before noon, I hung them on the lines strung from the pecan branches, with the wooden pins Eveline's husband, Michel, carved for Mamère long ago. Flared out at the ends like dancing ladies, I thought when I was small, only playing with the pins. Now they looked like faceless men straddling the clothes.

It was so warm, the white clothes dried quickly, and they seemed alive against me. The air was inside them. I took down Céphaline's first, the same size as me, and it was as if we were walking together down the line. Her chemise was full with the wind, leaning into me. And Msieu's shirt twisted away.

Madame Bordelon came out onto the back gallery and put her hand over her eyes, like she did all day. Her fingers a goose beak, her wrist and forearm a long curved goose neck. Like a secret signal to someone, even though she couldn't actually see any slaves except us. She could almost always see us.

"White?" she called loudly to Mamère. "You washed all that white and not Grandmère's dress yet?"

Mamère didn't look nervous. Madame came halfway down the gallery stairs that led to the yard. The kitchen and clearing were her charge—not the fields. Madame's eyes were a dark stripe of shade, but her mouth was a glittering stripe of teeth when she lifted her lip to help her squint. To see.

Mamère wasn't supposed to wash clothes for field people. They had to do their own laundry. We washed only for the Bordelons and their guests and Tretite. Eveline's black skirt floated in the pot.

"Madame dress next." Mamère raised her voice but not her face. She never seemed nervous that Madame might come down into the clearing.

But Madame didn't turn yet, as she usually did. "Moinette."

"Madame?" I called back. My mother stopped rubbing clothes on the washboard, the sluff sluff ceasing.

"You'll come at noon bell, Moinette." Then Madame turned on the stairs. "Marie-Thérèse," she shouted. "Don't forget to take off the buttons . . ."

"They jet buttons from Paris," Mamère finished softly.

Fig leaves boiled in water—what we used to take the stains from Grandmère's black crepe dresses. She had worn black for ten years, since her husband died and left Azure and all the land to her. Since that day, everyone else had worn black as well.

She liked to say, Easy to see black crows in the cane. See if they steal. See if they sleep.

Sleeping was stealing. Stealing time. I cut the button threads.

My mother looked up at me now. "Noon bell?" she asked. "Today?"

She held up the pile of cloth, black as charred paper, but the wash water ran dark red. Eveline's blood. Under her dress. "You going up there just for today?" she asked.

The jet buttons glittered on the table like bird eyes. I said, "Don't know." My mother was afraid. She was afraid I was going to have to sleep inside the house, away from her.

Then horses' hooves rasped on the shell road. Madame Auzenne was here with her daughters. They came every week for lessons, but today they brought their hairdresser from New Orleans to prepare Céphaline for winter season—dinners and dances and men.

Mamère listened to the carriage wheels. "Céphaline feel about her lesson for marry like you feel about sewing?" she asked.

She knew I hated making my stitches smaller and smaller, like they were supposed to be. I smelled the always-wet place at the edge of the cane where we poured off the dirty wash water, the mossy smell of bluing and damp, and suddenly our clearing felt crowded, like Tretite's armoire when I hid in it as a child. My head felt much too large under the black scarf. The Auzennes' voices came through the leaves like tiny hammers on iron. Laughter high and chattering. My mother's face so small and dark under her tignon.

The clothes wrapped damp sleeves around me. I couldn't go into the cane and find a stalk to chew, couldn't wander along the riverbank looking for what the current brought. I had to stay here, so close to the washpots their heated iron breathed on my arm.

"Not her lessons," I said. "Not the lessons you think about."

I thought I knew what would happen, I wanted to say. I knew the cleaning liquids, the way clothes had to be ironed and sewn and folded, the places to get moss, the way the tallow smelled when we made soap. I thought I knew where I belonged. To Mamère.

But I wanted to see Céphaline's room again, to glimpse her words on the paper and the words in the books, to hear the words she spoke for her own lessons. Last year, when Madame argued with Céphaline over the corset and my fingers tightened the laces, my eyes kept moving over Céphaline's papers. Pages covered with fine writing, numbers, drawings, and poems. I learned to read some words from listening to her lessons and seeing her children's books. I knew my numbers because I loved them as a child, arranging pecans in circles and multiplying them the way Céphaline did her ink dots on the page.

"My lessons from you I understand," I said now to Mamère, because Madame Bordelon came out onto the gallery and put her hand to her brows. She was looking for me. "Céphaline's lessons from books she understands. But her other lessons, to become wed to someone with money, she refuses to hear."

Then I left Mamère amid the clothes, and she turned away without a word.

I waited in the yard. The carriage had been put away. The governess's voice was steady as a trail of ants while she read. Lines of words with no object to avoid.

Mademoiselle Lorcey was the second governess to live in the room beside Céphaline's. The first one lasted a long time, with her thick spectacles like tiny ponds of clean water over her eyes. Céphaline loved her. She taught Céphaline about the numbers and how they could be multiplied and divided forever.

I entered the house like a fly, back then, when I was eight and ten and twelve. I landed in each room long enough to deliver clothes, to clean shoes with blacking, to touch a few tables and the closets with my fingers while I put away linens.

I heard the lessons. That governess, Madame Lustgarten, was a widow from New Orleans who had never had children. "You are nearly like my own," she said once to Céphaline. "Your mind is so quick. And girls—they never love numbers as you do. They are afraid of science. But not you. I have never had a pupil like you."

I listened while lost to everyone's sight in the long hallway where the floor gleamed like a molasses river and the portraits on the wall stared at one another and not down at me.

"Rust. Iron oxide. Look at the elements."

Mamère knew the mixture to take rust away from the white shirts of Msieu, if he'd been inspecting machinery from the sugar mill.

"Look at how the elements must react if we put this nail inside a jar with a few drops of water."

Now, on the back stairs, I remembered listening to them both. Mamère and Madame Lustgarten. Varnish and lemon oil. Rust and metal. Soap made of tallow and ashes.

But Msieu sent that governess away after three years, because Céphaline spent all her time in her room, with her papers. She would not sew or play the piano or dance. She would not speak to Grandmère Bordelon at all, only stared—not even at a person or wall or window. When I saw her eyes focused on the very air in front of her, I knew she was doing sums and experiments inside her brain.

After Madame Lustgarten, no one came for a long time. We were thirty miles south of New Orleans, Madame Bordelon used to fret. "No one of any stature wants to live in Plaquemines Parish now."

I remembered when Céphaline learned the names of the bones.

Under my dress was nothing but my ribs and skin and stomach. Céphaline had told me about the body while I hung up her clothes. Last year, in winter. It was as if she had to tell someone of the lessons, after Madame Lustgarten had been sent away.

She said we were bones and ligaments and tendons and fat and muscle and organs. She said to look at the pig's body when it was killed; we were the same except for measurement.

"Of what?" I asked, setting down her shoes.

"Of those things. Of brains, bones, stomachs. Mammals have almost everything in common. Look—" She was at her desk. "Mammals give birth to live young. Reptiles lay eggs. Fowl, too. Look at the classifications." Her book had gold-edged pages.

She knew I couldn't read all those words. But from her child's picture books, I learned other words quickly. *Chat, cheval, chien.* Cat, horse, dog.

That day, she was putting animals into columns. Cow. Pig. Horse. Snake. Turkey. Chicken. "Where is mule?" I asked.

She frowned, and pushed her finger across the columns. "A mule is the offspring of a horse and a donkey. It's a hybrid."

Madame called me now. I carried the pressed table linens, wrapped with red ribbon. Mamère always tied the clean clothes in square bundles with ribbons, at first so I knew whose were whose, but then because Madame liked it.

Madame and Msieu were leaving the table. The small splinter of wood between his teeth.

"That's why she is valuable," Madame said, glancing at the linens in my arms. I was thinking of the words. *Mammal. Hybrid.*

"That one?" He stared at me.

Cold trickled across my back. Your shoulder blades, Céphaline had told me. Not angel wings. That is foolish. They are bones. We are humans, not angels.

"No," Madame said, taking the bundles. "The mother. Marie-Thérèse. She does the laundry perfectly and sends it back tied up beautifully like that."

He looked not at me but at the ribbon. He said, "It is clean. How laundry is delivered is not important."

Madame sounded impatient. "It is the presentation of beauty," she said. "It is more important than you know."

"For who?" His voice was louder now. "For you?"

Her voice was soft as steam. "For the women who come here and see tablecloths and napkins and judge us. The women who have sons. Unless we can spend weeks in New Orleans this winter, we have only the Desjardins and Auzennes to think about for husbands. Don't you see them looking at this house? At her?"

Her was Céphaline. I had to learn to make her beautiful.

"Moinette," Madame Bordelon called from the dining room. "Take the gingercake and tell them I'll be in shortly. I don't know where Félonise has gone. She's getting so old she can't move." Madame Auzenne, her curls like caterpillars along her cheeks, her dress maroon silk, studied something on the buffet.

I carried the platter into the parlor, where the girls had to play piano for an hour after lunch.

The Auzenne girls were on the settee. They were twelve and fourteen and sixteen. Their hair was black and curled at their temples, their cheeks white and smooth as the curve of eggshells. They sat like the dolls on Céphaline's shelf, heads erect, hands still during history lessons, and when Mademoiselle Lorcey asked them for the name of a governor in New Orleans or a king in France, they didn't move anything but their eyebrows and shoulders to say they didn't know and didn't care.

Céphaline took a piece of gingercake right away. "Ginger is a root, not a bean like vanilla," she said, and the Auzenne girls smiled politely as if she'd stumbled on the grass.

Céphaline's boutons glowed on her cheeks and jaw like tiny berries inserted under her skin. I waited near the door, thinking of the cloves Tretite slid under the collar of the ham.

"Lessons are finished for today," Mademoiselle Lorcey said, and the Auzenne girls smiled faintly. But they didn't reach for the gingercake until their mother came in and said, "Yes, petites."

Mademoiselle Lorcey sighed. "At least the names of royalty would help you make conversation with someone at a dinner."

The oldest Auzenne girl raised her brows again. "Must Céphaline play the piano today? Perhaps the hairdresser could *help* her now. With her—toilette. Then we wouldn't get home so late."

Céphaline's mouth was set in a thin line like a nail scratch of blood. She had rubbed scarlet geranium petals on her lips, as her mother had told her. "You cannot be *helped,*" she hissed, and moved her skirts around me when she left.

Madame Bordelon watched, her own face unmoving. "Moinette,

come upstairs," she said. The hem of her dress collected cake morsels Céphaline had dropped.

Last winter, to prepare her for the winter season of dinners and dances in New Orleans, Madame showed me how to dress Céphaline and style her hair. Céphaline should have had a maid before, but she wouldn't let Félonise touch her. She refused to wear her corset and pulled her hair into a ball at the back of her head.

She was always hunched over her desk. Back then, I practiced putting on her corset and pulling the stays, and her curved back would lift. But her hair began to fall out—a bird nest of dull brown in the brush, strands on her pillowcase—and Doctor Tom came from New Orleans on his horse. He brought tonics and medicines, as he always had for Grandmère.

Msieu told Madame, "I don't trust him—an English doctor. No one wants the English here. Maybe we should take Céphaline to Paris."

Msieu had looked anxiously into the bedroom where she lay. He loved Céphaline, even though he never smiled. His face was dry and chapped under his black hat, from riding the canerows.

I curled up on a pallet in the corner, but she wouldn't sleep, her head down in the dandelion-ball of light from her candle while she read. "I can't study while you breathe," she said at last. I let my air in and out, only my own air, my cheeks pressed against the plaster where the walls met. But she had sent me to the kitchen for milk and then locked the door and refused to let me or anyone else in. No one could touch her anymore, she'd said. No poking and lacing.

Now she read at her desk, her back bent like a heavy shawl weighed on her shoulders. She turned when I came inside the bedroom.

Céphaline's eyes were glowing blue as the lowest flames, the cooking fire under Tretite's pine knots, and inside the blue were bars of black like wagon-wheel spokes. Her eyes were like nothing anyone had seen.

But the skin around her mouth and the edges of her hairline was red and swollen with boutons. Her hair was thin at the temples and dull brown as faded pecan shells. Not Creole black like the Auzenne girls, thick and lustrous down her spine so we could gather and pin and curl it—so that a man could unpin it.

The hairdresser from New Orleans was named Zerline. She carried two bottles, cut glass decanters as if for brandy and cognac, but smaller, with wider mouths.

She was paler than me. Which of Tretite's words fit her? Quadroon? Hair straight and shiny black as bootleather, pulled so tightly into a knot it was as if she had no hair at all.

"The smell goes into my brain," Céphaline said without looking up. Then she lowered her head onto the pages, and when her mother lifted her, smudges of oil were left on the paper.

"The price of beauty," her mother said softly. "In France, our hair was so heavy and high, we knelt in our carriage. Be grateful you have only the curls on the sides to arrange."

The curling tongs sat next to the lamp, sharp as black scissors.

"This comes from New Orleans, madame," Zerline said in her soft, pinched voice. "Made special for the ladies there, for the balls and parties. I will send it on the boat, if you approve."

She dipped a silver comb into the bottle, and the black liquid clung to the teeth until she pulled the comb slowly through Céphaline's hair. The strands stood alone, tiny black canerows, until she smoothed her palms over the hair, pushing the color into a glossy helmet.

"So, là, wait some time. The skin is next." From the other bottle, she poured liquid into a bowl and made a paste with alum from the kitchen. The smell of camphor rose from Céphaline's hair, and her cheeks and forehead were covered in the white mask.

She stared at me, her eyes fierce. I turned away. Someone was supposed to pull our hair from the pins, put his mouth on ours, and then reach to move our dresses.

What was supposed to happen then, I didn't want to know.

"Nothing Céphaline say help you. When you were nine, she say cane is a grass, and you cut the little grass near the house and mash up and boil. Then you throw up."

My mother was angry. I had no words for her. I had said the word *patella* aloud to myself, while sewing.

Who first ate the grass, in India? Céphaline said the sugarcane had come from there. Who saw a tall, waving stalk and thought to grind it green in his own teeth, to find the juice sweet?

What if he had died?

"She say the names of the bones. How that help you?"

Clavicle. Femur. Cranium. The bone around the brain.

"I like to know the words."

"You know nothing yet." She moved the needle into the sleeve. Now that the mattresses were done, we had to sew new coats for the men, for Christmas. The coarse cottonade was already dyed black.

"Doctor Tom said fingernails and hair grow but they are dead. They are not living. That's why it doesn't hurt when you cut them or burn them. The curling tongs are hotter than your iron." I had to make Céphaline's hair into black spiraled curls. Curls just larger than mine.

"You don't be in the room with that doctor," she said. "Nobody trust Englishman with voice like that. Old and no house. Just a white horse and all them bottles. You don't listen to him."

Doctor Tom had two eyes in a jar. When I hung his clothes in the armoire of the guest room, and he was gone to help old Msieu Lemoyne, whose breath was not working, I lingered to see the jars and books.

What made the disk of color on the edge of the white ball? I didn't touch the glass. Whose eye, this murky green? Whose brain? What was the pale fist in another jar?

In a dish lay teeth, their whitish roots like thorns, which he kept to show slaves who didn't believe teeth should be so hard to pull.

"You wouldn't believe those were from a child," he said behind me, and I dropped the packet of white shirts.

"I'm sorry," I said, but he laughed.

"I need a clean shirt," he said, pulling salve-stained fabric away from his body. "It took me all night to calm Lemoyne's lungs."

I untied Mamère's ribbon around the shirts. "Are the lungs white, like that?" I pointed to the jar with the pale fist, hoping he would say what that was.

Doctor Tom spread his hands on his own chest. "Lungs are large and grayish pink, guarded under the ribs," he said. "Lemoyne is old-fashioned like all the French. He believes that when the grinding begins, the vapors from the sugarhouse will clear his lungs. A lovely Creole superstition—when the first cane is cut, all will be well."

"Maybe if he believes it will cure him, he will be correct," Madame Bordelon said coldly from the doorway, tilting her head to study me. My fingers raked up the dirty laundry from the floor.

Doctor Tom rode his white horse between New Orleans and the houses south along the river, the only doctor willing to come this far down the Mississippi. Msieu paid him to take care of Grandmère and Céphaline and any slaves who were sick or hurt, and as Azure was large, he stayed here while he worked. At the next place south, Bontemps, Msieu LeBrun raised hunting dogs: some for deer and fox, some for slaves. At LeBrun's hunting parties, men would get shot accidentally or fall off their horses and break a leg. "I am the stolid, dull repairer of drunken French-Creole carelessness," Doctor Tom would say, showing me the blood on his pants leg from a hunter's bullet wound.

Mamère hated his balding head and dirty blond sideburns, his jars, and especially the things he told me. Every day now, I worked at the house, and at night, I tried to explain the body to my mother.

"Lungs?" She gripped the needle. "He show you a chest? I tell you the other words." When I turned away from her rasping tone, so tired from the way I held myself at the house, the constant listening, she said, "No! My work is I tell you. Your work is be careful."

"Skin? He say the skin protect the body?" She slammed the heavy iron onto his shirts as rain swirled in the pecan branches outside. My fingers hurt from the pastes and the washing and the needle. My mother asked angrily, "Why the skin soft so? Why les blancs have boutons? And fur on the face and arms?"

I put my head down over the stitches in the coat. How could the red bumps only appear on Céphaline's face, not her feet or hands or her stomach? Not a pox.

Then, for the first time, I saw my mother not sure. "Hair," I said. "You taught me how to hide my hair under the tignon. They teach me how to put Céphaline's hair into curls. All for nothing. Hair is dead. Like the wreath in Madame's room, the wreath with her mother's hair."

"*Moinette,*" Mamère said, hard as if she spat out broken pecan shells.

"All the hair is dead. That is what Doctor Tom talks to me about. He says hair and fingernails are like fur and claws. We use them the wrong way. He doesn't look at me as—under my dress. He looks at me as—a body. A brain. Men or women. Animals." The ants of my stitches walked around the sleeve. "Why should we try anything if we are just going to be like animals in the end?"

My mother said, "Don't ask me that. Don't ask." She turned away and lifted the next coat, heavy and shapeless without arms.

The woman named Hera slid her voice through the closed shutters, and my mother let her in.

I had been asleep, my mother sewing in her chair. She had hung an old tablecloth from two nails to shield the bed from the fire, so the light wouldn't keep me awake. The grease spots were like islands of gold water in the light, and I could see Hera near the door.

My mother said softly, "Where you get that name? Don't hear that, jamais. Never before. Hera."

I had never heard her ask questions of anyone.

"Name of a queen. He tell me something like that. Name us all from a book. My girl Phrodite."

"Where?"

"South Carolina. Come here last year to grow sugar. Should stayed in the rice like before. He got fever. Die in one week." She held her arms out for a moment, her neck bent while she studied them. "Sugar more dry than rice. But smoke and sharp. People get cut."

My mother nodded. "Toujours. All the days." She picked up her sewing again, dismissing the woman. *Dismiss*—that was the word Céphaline used on her mother, who hated it. You can go now. You are dismissed.

Hera slid down the wall, so slow it was as if she were drying a line of liquid with her back. She squatted on the floor, leaning her head back, and then her hands went to her cheeks, fingers spread out like a fan. Between her fingers, I imagined her sparkling scars.

"Him up there, he buy us at the death sale. Buy for the harvest. He sell fast?" she whispered.

"No," Mamère said, gently now, to my surprise. "He keep."

Hera dug her fingertips into her cheeks so hard she lifted the skin toward her eyes. "Phrodite. They tell her only black clothes on this place, but on Sunday wear what you want." She nodded toward the black coat in Mamère's lap. "That all they give here. But she need a dress. Something pretty, so she can find her own man. A place. If I go, she can take care my three little ones."

"Go?" Mamère said.

"What I see here—Louisiana—how easy to go."

"Parti?" My mother was confused. "Leave?"

"Go die."

Now my mother stood up and held out her hand so Hera would sit in my chair. This woman thought a dress could solve everything, that beauty and cloth could make her daughter safe.

"Them scar," my mother said.

Hera put her feet apart and rested her hands on her knees. "Here they say them scar Singalee. My mama say Bambara. She pass when I was nine. You don't get the marks until you get the blood. When I was fourteen, an old woman do them."

Then my mother said something in the same African words with which she prayed. I recognized a few words. *Ni. Dya. Faro.*

Hera drew in her breath.

My mother said, "Mine pass when I eight. But no one to do the mark on me. Like on her."

Hera said, "I can't mark Phrodite. They don't like the Africans here. Want Creole nègre. Ask me always am I Creole nègre. Can't do nothing for Phrodite." She breathed hard, close to crying, and her breasts fell and shook. "You can't mark your bright light."

My mother said, "No. No mark for Moinette."

My eyes were closed because I knew they would study my sleeping form and lower their voices. Hera said, "Not him up there?"

She was asking again about my father. But my mother wasn't angry. She said, "Sugar buyer come to see the crop. Tretite the cook say, He see me in the field, he like my face. Call me petit visage when he come here." My mother cupped her hands around her cheeks.

Small face. The man who was my father. But what he wanted—

"And her," Hera said. "Small face, them eyes like honey. All that hair. And so bright—"

My mother shook her head. "No. Don't say it."

"Who look?"

"Nobody," she said. "Nobody see her. But now she up there." My mother lifted her chin toward the house.

"Bright girl—" Hera began to speak again, but my mother interrupted her.

"Say you trade hair."

Hera said, "Do her hair?"

"Mine."

Neither of them moved. Then my mother said, "I make a dress. Blue. For Sunday nights."

She was already outside when I woke in the morning.

She was cutting up one of Céphaline's old linen pillowcases. The rectangles of cloth were sleeve size. She was going to make a dress for a girl she didn't know, for a woman she had only met twice.

A woman with marks like my mother's mother. Their voices soft and braided as woven grass.

The blacking was a raincloud on Céphaline's pillowcase every morning. Madame had given me white linen to make seven new pillowcases, one for each day.

We soaked the black stains in the white solution. Then my mother said, "Go on to the house now. Madame call for you."

I was dismissed.

I applied the white paste with the back of a spoon.

"My face is so cold," Céphaline said. "And the iron is so hot."

Zerline had shown me everything. I made the paste with egg whites and rosewater and alum, made the blacking with lead and camphor and a drop of almond oil. Zerline had told me if we ran out of lead to use lampblack, but lead was what they used in Paris.

I understood how Mamère felt when I sat in her chair. I didn't want to lie down. My arms ached from all the wash, from the combing and holding the irons over the fire, from keeping myself so careful not to hurt Céphaline that my shoulders burned.

Then Hera stood behind my mother's chair and took off her tignon. My mother's hair was newly washed. Hera took the comb and began to section off the long shoals of hair that sprang from around my mother's forehead.

She always washed her hair at night and combed it herself, after I was sleeping. She kept it in a rough bun under her cloth.

But Hera made it into patterns of braids that swirled away from my mother's face as if a strong wind blew her hair into rows.

"Because you don't know how," she said. "You comb Céphaline hair. Not mine."

"Why are you angry? Where are we going so late?" The night bell had rung.

"Angry?" My mother walked quickly. She carried a small bag with a knife and a rag. Her words were ragged. "I am nothing. Qu'est-ce—the word?" She looked down the street toward le quartier, where the shutters were closed and houses dark. "Useless. Like fingernail. Pas animal to kill with a claw."

She had been crying while I had come back late from Céphaline's room. The edges of black in her eyes were blurred into red.

We hurried down a path toward the side land. Franz the overseer would see us on his rounds. "Are we running?" I whispered, and when my mother didn't stop walking, I pulled at her arm, as I had when I was a child.

We were just near the edge of the canefields. The blackened outline of the small house, where Grandmère Bordelon used to live, was beneath our feet. Then Franz rode toward us on his horse, and a small figure appeared from the low fence surrounding the family gravestones.

Marie-Claire. Grandmère Bordelon's old slave—her cheeks marred with pink rosettes from the rats, the only thing I saw for a moment in the darkness. Like fistfuls of flowers approaching. Then the rest of her, mouth surrounded by wrinkles that danced when she smiled. "Marie-Thérèse," she whispered to us. "And her girl."

She held up a gourd. "I make my water every night, me, and carry over here. I pour little on his gravestone. Pee on his name. The rest where they bury her when she time. Old and fat. I make the ground soft for her. When she gone là-bas—" Marie-Claire flicked her fingers like sprinkling water on cloth for ironing. "Moi, I still here. Then I pee on her head every night."

She turned as Franz rode up to us. She said, "I finish stretch my old bones, Msieu. Merci."

She walked toward le quartier. Franz said to us, "You ain't old. Where you going?"

My mother, as always, didn't look nervous. "Gather herb for take out stain from Mademoiselle pillowcase. Her medicine."

"Thirty minutes I be back," he said. "Stand here and wait until I see you. Or I get the dogs."

We slipped into the canerows. The rustling stalks were high above us, lit by the moon into silver ribbons. Ribbons for dresses. Mamère swung the cloth sack and said, "Thirty minutes. And I finish."

Her narrow back and tignon were like black smoke ahead of me in the light. The canestalks brushed sharp against my face until I covered my cheeks with my sleeves. My new dress—an old dress from Céphaline's rag pile. Calico print of yellow and pink.

We came out at the headland road that separated Azure from Petit Clair, and my mother headed toward the ciprière, the swampy backland that was not cultivated. Somewhere deep in the ciprière was a bayou where the privateers and river traders met. Christophe said he'd watched them in secret. My peacock plate had come from that water.

I could smell the sharpness of coming frost deep inside my nose and throat. The cane cutters would have to start tomorrow or the next day, before ice ruined the sugar.

When we came to the ciprière, my mother panted while steam blew past her face. She turned and a single tear glittered down each cheek.

"Hera get this dress and give to her girl. Madame and Grandmère buy dress for Céphaline, make her beautiful. And me—" She swept her hand along my skirt. "Nothing from me. Only words from me. Words you don't want. You get words from the doctor. He can take you with him when he go, and I never see you. Jamais! Never! I have nothing!"

I tried to embrace her, but she turned so that I was draped along her back like a cape. I held her tightly, and she shook under my arms. I knew she was forcing everything back inside her. Then she wiped at her eyes and said, "Thirty minutes until Franz look for us. The old plants in the trees."

The black water stood like coffee around the cypress stumps in the swampy area, but we turned down a weed-choked trail into the forest itself. I had never been here before. The half-moon lit my mother's neck when she bent her head and pushed through the growth. This had once been a road wide enough for a wagon.

"You are not finished," I said to her back. "I always listen."

"Won't matter."

"Just tell me. Or why did you bring me?"

We stumbled through bare vines like gray threads for a giant's shirt. My mother fell and the knife skittered into the leaves. She put her face into her knees and cried again, and I could only kneel beside her. "I never leave you alone," she said. "I always sit in my chair, wait for who send for me. Or for you. But now I see no one come for you. You go to them." She clutched the sack. "I make this dress for Hera girl, and she find someone. Maybe Christophe. She stay by Hera and have her baby. But Céphaline find someone and go. She take you with her, and I never see you again."

She laced her fingers behind her neck and pulled so hard that her knuckles swelled for a moment. When she stood, she cleaned her face with her sleeve. Salt in the cloth, I thought, touching the wet.

"Nonc Pierre and the men cut this road," she said, her voice lower. "Cut the cypress for Msieu house. Singalee men know the wood."

"When?" I found her knife in the leaves, and a stumbling of tiny feet rushed away from us.

"Time pass. When they first come, Bordelon and Lemoyne. From

France. Everyone from somewhere else. Except them Indian used to live here in the ciprière."

We pushed through to an open space in the trees. Brick walls draped with vines—two large square vats. Four iron pipes pierced the wall of the higher vat; they must have let the liquid drain into the lower vat.

"Far from the house because that smell," my mother said, her voice nearly dead. "When they make the indigo."

She always said the word like poison. I breathed carefully but smelled only cold standing water and the musk of a fox den.

"Where the cane grow now, all indigo. They pick branches and pile them up in the first pool and soak with clear water. Then the leaves go rotten and make that smell. Drain the water into the second pool, and the women have to put up the dress and stand in the water and beat with a stick. Get the blue, have to beat the water. The blue settle on the bottom. But the smell go inside the skin. In the body."

A vine hung like a necklace from one of the pipes. The second vat was filled with dried leaves and brackish mud. Nothing blue.

"Cane cut you," my mother whispered, soft as soap foam on the wind. "But indigo go inside. Tout mort."

"All die?" Brick crumbled under my fingers.

She nodded. "Nonc Pierre and the men build the house and barn, but the women make the crop. Four, five years. Then they bury."

The back row of the slave cemetery was a line of wooden crosses with arms nearly touching. No names. But my mother left pieces of broken blue bottle there once a year. And she said the name Amina.

She bent to the ground. "Grow wild where all the seeds fell," she murmured. Plants as high as her knees grew in patches, the small leaves shaped like fingernails. She covered her palm with the rag and pulled an entire plant from the dirt. I smelled nothing but damp earth and bitter green when she put it inside the sack.

"Franz wait there," she said. "Walk fast."

"Will it make us sick?"

My mother pushed air through her nose in disgust. "I ever let bad touch you? You think I let a maringouin land on your arm, I see it?"

Even a mosquito in our room couldn't escape her eyes and ears. She used to sit beside me in bed and wait for their warning.

The freezing air hurt my earlobes, the only part not covered by my tignon. "You aren't finished," I said. "I do listen. I heard you talk about the *ni* with Hera. And *dya. Faro.*"

I thought that would stop her, but she shook her head. "What you listen, don't matter. You are not Bambara. You are patella. You believe the hair is dead."

"How can it not be?" I shouted into the wind, but then we smelled the smoke.

Two | FARO

A leaf. A leaf rolled and left to fire.

Not sweet. Not cane. When we came out onto the headland road, we saw a smear of red light in the distance. Not Azure. Msieu Lemoyne's house—Petit Clair.

We ran through the cane toward the place where Franz was not waiting. He had already crossed our fields to ring the work bell, shouting for the slaves to join him with buckets.

Over the cane that glistened in the wind, the house burned somehow small and red, like the fireplace of God behind a grate of tree branches.

By morning, Msieu Lemoyne's house was smoldered coals between brick piers. From where Mamère and I stood with the others from Azure, we could see pieces of iron like spider legs.

"Smoke a cigar and forget where he put it," Tretite said. Blue smoke twirled from the ashes. "His cook, Nonnie, in my bed now. Shiver all night. She finish her pantry and go upstairs, and he sleep, and the fire start on his desk. Nobody else to help, and he so heavy, and she so old. She only get him to the stairs and no more."

His body in there? Like the tallow for our soap? Wood ashes and skin ashes? Cigar—leaves of tobacco Msieu Lemoyne grew special. A plant burning into paper and then wood. Bones and hair.

"They believe Nonnie? Msieu and Madame?" I whispered. We had heard her ragged sobs inside Tretite's room, the hoarse gasping again and again.

Tretite shrugged. "She burn her hands, try to get him out. Don't you believe she try? But tonight she have to tell his people come from New Orleans. Maybe they don't believe."

When we returned to Azure, my mother walked toward the clearing without speaking. I cleaned the ashes from the gallery railings and even the tops of Doctor Tom's glass jars. Cane ashes we saw every day during harvest, splintery black needles. But these ashes—floor and carpet and skin and money—were gray flakes and dark cinders and white trembles of powder that melted when I touched them.

These ashes made the Bordelons anxious. Azure would host the Lemoyne relatives from New Orleans who came to pay their respects to Msieu Lemoyne. "Seventeen ninety he build it," Msieu said to Madame, his sideburns black with soot. "Nothing saved. Nothing. But I can run the sugar mill with Franz. We won't have to break the harvest."

Madame moved purposefully through the rooms, adding flowers to a vase, nudging right the portrait of Msieu from France. Madame's fingers skated on the shine of her long dining table. She loved her house as if it were a person; my mother touched her own things this way, like Eveline touched her children's heads and shoulders.

Upstairs, she said to Céphaline, "You have to make an opportunity from tragedy. The Lemoynes will bring so many people from New Orleans, and they will stay here." Then she turned to me. "Moinette. Go get your things. Céphaline needs to be prepared. You will stay in her room from now on, whether she prefers it or not."

Mamère was not at the washpots when I got to the clearing. She wasn't inside the house, when I put my other dress and other tignon into a bag. I touched the chest, her altar, which held only the daytime ornaments of wooden plates and carved forks. The bone comb lay on the mattress.

She wasn't finished with me. Not with her words and lessons. Gravy. Blood. *Faro. Ni.*

I was afraid to sleep there, in Céphaline's room. I was afraid to break something, to burn hair. The cook Nonnie had fainted away. "Her heart so fear it might stop," Tretite said. What if I pulled on Céphaline's hair and more fell out?

Who would comb my hair now? Even though I shouldn't remind Madame that I had hair, maybe I could slip away to my mother, at least for a moment.

Her skin was still white, but there were holes in Céphaline's nose. Tiny black holes. And the boutons had moved from her cheeks to her jaw and forehead, like nail studs painted red.

I went to the kitchen for the alum. Tretite's face was ringed with silver tracings of dried sweat. She was so worried and busy cooking for the guests, she hadn't had time to wipe her forehead.

"Msieu and Madame talk. Lemoyne daughter, she sell Petit Clair. She don't want the land. But Msieu want the land. And the sugar mill. He grind his crop over there. But right now, he has no money."

When the Auzennes needed money, they sold field hands. They always talked about it during Sunday dinners. "Always extra chickens or pigs or Pierres," Msieu Auzenne had laughed once.

"Who will he sell?" I whispered. Her fingers sorted tiny stones from the rice.

"Céphaline," she whispered back. "She marry the money, Msieu buy the land next door, and build a new house for them. Watch to see the husband treat her right. What Madame say. Say Céphaline fragile."

The chicken meat on the cutting board glistened pink. The breastbone was splintered, and marrow welled up in the tiny holes.

She handed me a small bowl. "Egg white. Go."

I applied the paste to Céphaline's skin. If the yolk, with its red speck, was the beginning of the baby, what was the white?

Her eyes stayed beautiful. Doctor Tom had left eyebright to erase the red. She would not stop writing at night. I tried to look inside her eyes, for the veins, but she closed them.

"Now we're supposed to embroider, and I'm meant to tell you secrets," she said. "But I have none."

"Oui," I said. My hands were in my lap.

She spoke through the white shell on her face. "You have to sleep here now. But we are not friends. And we are not like sisters. The

Auzenne girls pet their maids and say they are like sisters. My parents have no other child."

"I understand."

"My mother says in France women wear their hair up so high, people at the opera cannot see past the styles. She says the medicine is coming from Paris. For my face. Then we won't have to use this."

I sponged off the paste, and her boutons glowed. She opened her eyes. "Lemoynes and Auzennes tonight." She said their names as if they were diseases. "Your foolish lessons of beauty will be judged, but no one will ask of my own."

I shook the faceted bottle and dipped in the comb, careful not to let too much liquid collect on the teeth. The camphor smell was sharp. Black as mine, her hair, when I pulled the teeth gently from her forehead over her skull. Like rows of the thinnest grass, with her scalp the earth between. The blue veins near her temples, the pinkish irritation at her nape, the tiny red puckers where she'd had sores and scratched them.

Under the scalp was the white bone and the swimming brain. Inside the folds and valleys, where were the words and recipes and numbers? How did a man's brain decide he wanted under the dress? How did a woman's brain learn to measure the pictures painted on a dish?

"You can smell the smoke even up here," she said drowsily. "Grand-mère said this morning it smelled like Haiti when she was small. They grew sugar in Haiti until the revolution."

She closed her eyes. Somehow, her voice sounded like her grandmother's now, repeating a story in exactly the same way.

From up here, the tops of the canefields were gold and brittle, and the cane fires licked the distant fields, and the sugar mill at Petit Clair sent up black veils of smoke. All that grass from India turned into money. Then a burning leaf of tobacco erased it all.

Her hair was black, thicker from the liquid, and when the strands had dried, I heated the curling tongs over the lamp.

"I don't mind the combing," she said suddenly. "It makes me drowsy. But the curling I hate. Don't burn me, Moinette. Don't."

"No."

The black spikes of iron separated, and I clasped the end of the first section. I twirled slowly, as Zerline had shown me. The sweet almond oil in the hairdressing hissed a bit, and I went as close to her temple as I could. She winced, and I said, "Don't move. Please."

When I opened the tongs, my hand trembled. The curl fell fat and shining to her shoulder. I let out my breath. Voices downstairs.

"If God had invented a particular torment for me, he couldn't have chosen better," she said.

For me as well. If I burned her, would Msieu burn me, in the same spot on cheek or neck? A boy groom at Auzennes' had let the youngest daughter fall from her horse and her arm was broken. His was broken, too. Who had taken his arm and snapped the bone?

Céphaline's voice was bitter as fig leaves but her breath too sweet as it rose toward my face, almost as if she'd been eating candied orange rinds. But she hadn't. Not since last year.

I held the tongs over the lamp again, and she said, "It is damaging my brain. I know it. Every time you put the heat so close to my head, I feel it burning inside."

"I would never touch you with it," I said carefully. I hadn't come any closer than two fingers' width to her head—measuring with my eyes. My throat filled with saliva—the word Céphaline used, saying men spit tobacco and saliva—and some liquid of fear moved through me.

Félonise handed me coffee and cakes and cold meat. Msieu Lemoyne's daughter, from New Orleans, and her husband. The Auzennes, without their girls. They spoke of the fire, the slaves, the sugarhouse that Msieu would run while they decided what to do with Petit Clair. They didn't mention Nonnie.

Then Msieu Lemoyne's daughter said, "Céphaline! You are not a child any longer but a lovely young woman! We will bring my husband's cousins tomorrow, and they will be so glad to meet you."

Céphaline's hair glowed. Her boutons were covered with fine white powder, but what remained were tiny dusted biscuits all along her cheeks and jaw. She knew. She stared at her mother, and her mother stared back.

———

I could hardly sleep on my pallet in the corner of her room. Céphaline read by candlelight, and Madame came in twice to tell her to stop. Finally, Madame blew out the candle and took the book.

My mother lit her candles now. Prayed. Did she stare at the empty bed? Did she eat from the peacock plate?

I had slept away from her only once. I curled on my side and saw everything in the clearing. My mother's skirt, near my face when I was small, a bleach spot like a cloud in black sky. Shiny pink scar on her forearm from a burn. Cast-iron pots, with craters like healed skin. Clothespins lined up to dance in the sand. Washboard silver but veins of rust like washboard blood.

Even the sweet olive bush seemed to watch me, and the cane was taller than the sky. When I was small, our clearing was my mother's own earth, no one else's, and as long as I could touch her skirt every now and then, I never wanted to leave.

She came in the morning with the clean ironed clothes in the cart, and I met her in the shade. "Mamère."

She lifted her chin. She couldn't dismiss me. We had just started. "Dorm bien?" I whispered.

Her lips were held tight like a grain of rice was between them.

"I asked Madame if I could bring the clothes down to our place. But she said I have to dress Céphaline now."

Mamère took the basket of dirty linens. Fifteen coffee beans were inside the napkin blotted with remoulade. I had hidden them there, but I couldn't tell her that.

Her eyes swam with light, and she turned away.

"Even their conveyance is impractical," Céphaline said, looking out her window, and her mother frowned.

"The new carriages are like that," Madame said.

I tied the ribbon close to Céphaline's forehead.

Downstairs, I helped Tretite clear the table from the huge company breakfast. The Lemoyne woman had gone back to New Orleans, and the husband stayed here, to help with the slaves at Petit Clair. I took coffee to the office, where Msieu and the husband opened the ledgers.

"Why does he keep those grisly things in there?"

"He's a doctor," Msieu said. "They study the body. Me, I don't want to know what is inside. Just my stomach feels well, I'm happy."

"He's an Englishman?"

"Better than American." Msieu ruffled more papers and said, "Lemoyne had forty-five slaves over there."

"What if some of them run? No one's there but your driver Franz?"

I heard Msieu turn pages. "Franz is good. The sugarhouse is full speed. Nobody runs much here, as LeBrun has those dogs. Chiens de nègre, chiens de renard."

Dogs for blacks, dogs for fox.

"Fox more fun."

"Only bozals run—those new Africans. You can tell by the scars they came on the boat. I have only a few bozals. Mine are Creole. Mine don't run. I'll ride your place all day and send Franz over there at night."

"It's not my place. It's hers. Until she decides."

I measured nothing here. I moved the flat silver tool along the tablecloth scraping the crumbs. Saving the rice grains, the edges of cornbread for Tretite to take to her chickens. Conveyance. Tretite carried the food to the chickens, and then she'd kill one and carry it back here for the pot. Coffee from beans, sugar from grass. Swallow and wait for it all to pass from your body. Take off the clothes and wash the gravy and sweat and stains from where the food passed through you and into the privé.

The armoire was filled with Madame's dishes from France. So Céphaline could live and a man could take her from here and put their money together and build a wooden house and buy dishes from France and have children who wanted dishes.

I took the crumbs outside to the kitchen, to Tretite's wooden bowl.

The cane cutters were in the field just past our clearing. Mamère was not there. The cane knives flashed like whirling birds. The wagon waited for the stalks. Conveyance. Hera's girl needed a dress so she could live and a man could take her into a different house and join their tools and tables and have children who wanted dishes.

I wanted to tell her I understood what was wanted for them, but I didn't understand at all what she wanted for me. Mamère.

"Did you see the brain in his jar?" Céphaline asked me. "I heard you in there."

"Yes," I said. I had gone into his study to put away papers he'd left in the dining room.

"That brain belonged to a man who died of gunshot. They cut open the skull with a saw and took out the brain to examine it."

"He said that?" Doctor Tom told me when he first came that the brain was from a black baby found by the road. He'd said, "And your mother loves you, and didn't leave you by the road, so you should do everything she says, isn't that right?"

She walked past her father's office, where the huge desk and ledger book faced the gallery doors and the river, and then into the guest room next door. "Céphaline," I said. "We shouldn't—"

"Look." She whirled around, pointing to the big jar with the floating brain. "It is still perfect because he was shot in the heart. But something is making my head hurt. The curling tongs and all the combing. I can't swallow sometimes. The smell of your paste."

Her eyes were fierce on me. Could I contradict her? "It is Zerline's paste," I said softly. "The skull—the heat cannot enter bone, no? Just your scalp hurts."

"No. My brain." She twisted the jar until the brain swam. "Inside the bones is marrow. Like a cow's bones. But the only thing wholly encased by bone is the brain."

What was I allowed to say? That I hated touching her? "I wish I didn't have to curl your hair."

"But that is your lesson. My lesson is to learn foolish things and forget important things." She put her hands on her temples. "My eyes are not the same as anyone's. But whose brain did I receive? Not my parents'. And Grandmère Bordelon knows nothing but herself and the parts of her body. Her mouth and stomach and feet."

I never knew whether to answer or listen. Tell the truth or lie. I didn't know what Céphaline wanted. No one knew what she wanted.

"I must have inherited a brain from someone in France. A man. Or maybe I am not from these people. Do you know where it is formed?" Her voice was faster.

"The brain?" My cloth moved slowly over the low table with the curling legs.

"The baby."

Should I say that in another jar, the womb was a white fist angry and clenched, and Doctor Tom had said behind me, "When the womb is alive, it is red with blood and stretched around an infant so tightly that it splits like a grapeskin when cut?"

Besoin. What you need?

Céphaline said, "You aren't required to know. Only to perform."

With her palms, she flattened her hair against her temples. Her eyes were not sky. They were not flowers. No cousin would say such.

"You mustn't look offended," she whispered. "I am required to perform as well. I am making no distinction between our tasks."

Her eyes were not azure.

In the dish near her elbow, the child's teeth were gray as old chalk. Her hair smelled of metal and oil and perfume. The curls limp, her scalp red and flaking. A cap of pain—worse than the heat of my tignon each night when I tried to sleep and the sweat crawled on my own scalp? Madame saw me take it off the first night, and she said, "The law! You are to keep your head covered!"

I used to tear off the cloth as soon as night came, the air on my head where Mamère said the skull was once soft—when I was a new baby.

Céphaline could not take off her scalp. She lifted her eyes to mine. "Say it."

"What?"

"What you are holding in your mouth."

I said carefully, "A new baby has a soft place on the head."

She stood up quickly. "But you don't know how it is formed."

I wouldn't talk to her of what my mother had said. The four lips. Their passage.

"I am not meant to know," she said. "Only to produce a mammal. A son. My mother couldn't. And you are meant to produce girl mammals. Monsieur Lemoyne always said girls like you are worth more than boys."

My shoulder blades were not angel wings. They were bones. Cold. What did she know about animals like me?

She pulled my arm, took me to her father's desk. "I am making no distinction between us. I am supposed to meet the Lemoyne cousin, the Auzenne nephew, and mate with someone. You mate with someone else. I can read Latin and Spanish, and it won't change my task."

She opened the ledger and ran her finger down the words on a list. I tried to read quickly.

Two armoires—twenty-five piastres. Silver dessert spoons—eleven piastres. Preserve dishes—five piastres.

She turned the page. Another list, Msieu's writing, the letters slanted as if facing a strong wind.

Esclaves. The list of us.

Hera—Senegalese, 32. Aphrodite—Creole nègre, 15. Apollo—Creole nègre, 10. Janus—Creole nègre, 9. Romulus—Creole nègre, 7. (En famille—nine hundred fifty piastres.)

The newest purchases, written last.

Her finger moved past their names quickly. "An infant," she said.

Michel—Creole nègre, 30—one thousand piastres. Eveline—griffe, 26—seven hundred piastres. Bat—sacatra, 10—three hundred piastres. Alphonse—sacatra, 8—three hundred piastres. Séraphine—sacatra, infant—fifty piastres.

"Look, there's a baby. Do you see? The moment your mammal breathes, it will be worth money."

I was tired of lessons, of all the words—*sacatra, mammal, patella, dahlia.* I said, "And our tasks do not differ?" Then my face flushed with fear at my angry voice. If she told her father—

She closed the ledger before I could find my own name. Or my mother's.

"My task is to make money by marrying," she said, looking out onto the gallery. "The moment I agree, my father makes money. But then I must lie down and receive the formation of a boy. Or everything will be lost. That's what they whisper in the hallway."

She turned to face me. "When you put burning solutions on my face and head, I tell myself you are completing your tasks, and I am completing mine. I try not to hate you."

We heard a boat passing on the river. I couldn't hate her. When she went with the husband, she might take me. How much was I worth? I opened the ledger again to the same page. Marie-Claire—Senegalese, 60—five piastres.

The woman who had stayed awake night after night with Grand-mère Bordelon—until rats tasted her flesh.

Céphaline closed the book.

"I try not to hate you as well," I said softly, then waited for her to strike me, but she was hardly listening. The words Tretite had told me measured the blood. Mulâtresse after my name. And a number. My lessons. I said, "Your father's list will say the name of my mammal. Your father's Bible will say the name of your mammal."

Céphaline looked past me. She said, "The cousin or nephew will say, Your eyes. Creoles don't have such eyes. That is what they all say. I want to say, They see. That is what I always say."

I couldn't tell my mother the words and numbers. Marie-Claire spinning in front of her house all day, fingers shiny as polished wood. Five piastres. Less than spoons.

I couldn't see my mother at all. The house was full, with the Lemoynes from New Orleans, daughter and husband, three aunts and cousins, all worried about Petit Clair and the sugar mill.

Félonise's eyes moved like gray wood lice, hurrying over each table setting, but her hands moved slow like a hunting cat when she arranged things. Squab—twenty of them, laid out on serving platters, and then their bones ringing on the plates like a game.

Céphaline was silent, even when a Lemoyne aunt said sweetly, "I heard you are writing a book."

Madame said quickly, "No, she is painting. Birds and flowers."

But Céphaline said nothing, didn't eat her squab or ham. She touched the tail of the fish on the platter. Her hair was perfect, the blue ribbon around her forehead matched her eyes, and her skin, from a distance, was white. But the scabs made a map under the rice powder.

"So far south of the city," Msieu Lemoyne's daughter said, holding her fork delicately. Her wrist bones moved like peach pits under the skin. "No opera, no schools. I prefer to stay in our other house. And the lawyer wants to inquire quickly about possible buyers."

Her husband was fair and balding, the sweat at the back of his neck disappearing into folds when he lifted his head from the fish.

Msieu was silent, moving his rice on the plate. He needed money. He wanted the sugar mill. I stared at one fish scale shining, curled, on the tablecloth like a fingernail pulled from an angel.

I hated the coffee. What if someone moved the cup and I burned the hand? Their fingers moved too much. Tretite said the daughter's husband had sold Nonnie, Msieu Lemoyne's cook. It wasn't her fault he'd forgotten his cigar, but she was sold at auction in New Orleans.

I held the preserve dishes, waiting for Félonise to bring the dessert.

Where had the river trader got my peacock plate? Pink rosettes in Marie-Claire's cheeks, these dishes worth more than her bones. Là. There. I would be with you là-bas, Mamère had said. She was in her chair, praying I wouldn't drop this dish.

"Dahlia," Madame said, lifting the figs in their syrup. "My favorite dishes."

The next morning, I made certain to be downstairs when my mother came. And when I met her on the back gallery stairs, she didn't slide her fingers inside the laundry bundle for coffee beans. She said, "You ask why do we try if we are only animals? Because even a rat feed her babies and work hard to get my sugar and cornbread. Even a rat sit up at night and look at the dark. When the babies sleep." She pointed to the side land and said, "Rat eat Marie-Claire cheeks and turn that blood into milk for her babies."

Madame was shouting upstairs. My mother turned and walked away.

"We think the books cause the boutons!" Madame said angrily. I took them from the parlor shelf and stacked them in wooden crates.

Céphaline took two volumes back from my hands. "I don't put my face into the pages."

"You don't sleep! You don't go outside! The Auzenne girls ride every day and make bouquets for the parlor. They have the flush of health. You are always reading and making yourself nervous."

Céphaline said evenly, "You are nervous. I am reading."

These were Grandmère Bordelon's husband's books, from France. I touched the spines.

Madame sighed. "The Lemoynes will decide the sale of the land after the grinding. We will order dresses from New Orleans for winter. It is your task to think of pleasant conversation. Not from a book."

Nonc Pierre, the groom, his hair silver gray as fog rising from his forehead, took the books to the barn. Madame had me polish the mahogany bookcase with lemon oil, and on the shelves, she arranged vases and Spanish lace fans.

Céphaline laughed. "I will continue to write my own books," she said. Her fingers were purple, her sleeves stained with black.

What if no one reads them but you? I wanted to ask her. Are they still books then?

But I was silent.

The next day, she had pages and pages hidden under her mattress. They whispered when she moved, calling out for water. When she took the glass, her face looked as if it floated in a dark, rain-heavy cloud on her pillow, and her breath rose sweet-hot as sugared brandy.

But her book gave me back to my mother, if only for one morning.

"Look at the ink," Madame fretted. "Céphaline is too ill for lessons today. Take those dresses to your mother to treat the stains."

Céphaline slept, eyelids traced with lavender bayous like her maps. In the kitchen, Tretite was assembling a basket. "Your mother say white beet for ink. The leaf, too. Six eggs. She say bring salt."

I hurried to our clearing. The cane was still high here. The cutters would approach the rows closest to the Bordelon house last, near Christmas, presenting the final stalk tied with a red ribbon to Msieu.

"Mamère."

She was drinking her coffee at dawn, sitting in the chair. I knelt before her and kissed her circle-bone knees through her dress.

I couldn't tell her how much I missed all her words, even though they had frightened and angered me when she pressed them into my ears. With her hard thumbs on my forehead, but her eyes watching mine.

And now, she waited.

"The eyebrows," I said. "That's how I know what they feel. To be careful."

She nodded.

"Madame's and Céphaline's are the same. Tadpoles kissing and leaping apart." I clasped her legs and sat. "Msieu's are wild like his hair on his head. He even has hair on his fingers. So angry. He wants to buy Petit Clair. He needs money."

Mamère loosened my tignon and pulled out the heavy plait. Her hands were warm and dry against my neck. Out the open door, the sun sent golden needles into the clearing. I had even missed the clothes flying empty and clean and silent. Sleeves flat under the iron and no faces springing from the collar to speak.

"Céphaline not ready yet?"

"No. Madame is waiting for medicine from Paris. But Céphaline is sick again today. Her head."

Mamère nodded. "Write, write. Oui?" She studied the stained dresses

I'd brought, sprigged calico and pink muslin, blue-black ink stains along the cuffs and sleeves. "Get that out, make a cake. Like the one I show you, when the doctor first come. He bring that India ink. Bring you all them words."

She said nothing after that. She began grinding the beet leaf with her pestle, releasing the bitter juice. I wanted to lie down on my bed, but a dress lay on the blanket. Pinned together, not sewn. Skirt of stained tablecloth. Sleeves of pillowcase.

"I have never seen Phrodite," I said.

"She been in the cane since the day she come. All day." I sat next to the dress. Someone I had never met slept in my place. Strips of cottonade for trim were arranged at the waist and neckline.

"She look like her mother. Bambara. But no scars," Mamère said. "Same animal. But you are a different animal from me. No scars for you. But you are half mine. Your hair is not dead."

"Then how can I burn Céphaline's and she doesn't scream?"

My mother shrugged as if giving up. "Doctor know. He and governess know. Céphaline know. I only know other words."

She began to unwrap something at the table. "A mother never governess because she always wrong. Toujours. But them scar? On Hera? My mother tell me four lips. Two on your mouth, two under your dress. Doctor don't tell you this."

I didn't want to hear about under my dress. She raised the tiny biscuit of indigo. A cake of twilight.

"Old woman show me this. My mother already gone. Show me to shake the bucket, indigo settle on the bottom and you make enough for one cloth. Say in Africa, indigo grow wild and people make just enough for their own cloth. Say my mother cry and tell her, indigo was good luck in Africa. Someone from Africa bring it here and grow so much it kill them. Finish."

My mother didn't cry. Her voice was urgent, but careful, as if she spoke to Tretite about damaged lace. "You wear dress from Céphaline now. I make a dress for Phrodite, and her mother tell her about the hair. About Bambara. Maybe mark her someday." She put a coffee bean in her mouth. "But maybe you don't believe Bambara words if I tell you.

You believe medicine words. You tell me all your words. But I can't tell you anything."

She lifted her head. "Maybe I finish with lessons."

"I know what happens," I began, but she wrapped the indigo cake again and sat in her chair. She pointed to the floor, which meant I was to sit for my hair.

She rubbed almond oil on my scalp and moved the skin against my skull. She said, "Li travaille—your work is besoin. What they need. Whoever come. The doctor. Maybe Céphaline husband. You have four lips. Three passages. You lie down and be still, they say. You move, they say. What they say."

I whispered back, angry. "No."

"Céphaline become beautiful again, like when she is a child. Then she marry. And you will go with her. But not far. Just to the river. Ecoute. Listen! Tretite tell me the place names. So if you go, I know where." Her voice was calm. "Here Azure. The blue. Là-bas, on the river down, Bois Belle. Constance. Maison Blanche. La Pinière. And Auzenne place, Coeur Fort."

Land named for daughters or trees or wives or love.

"North on the river up is Orange Grove. Les Palmiers." She closed the shutter and whispered, "Besoin. What they need. You do your work, and they take you not far. Feet can get there."

I did know how it happened. The baby. It wasn't difficult to imagine as science. The passages of our body. The womb.

But I refused to imagine it happening to me. Céphaline lay in her bed with my mother's clouds on the mosquito barre over her head. I lay on my narrow mattress, with my moss under me. My tignon was hot. I imagined my hair curling against the madras cloth and the moss curling against the mattress ticking and growing through the threads where the animal fat and wood ashes made soap to clean themselves from each other and my hair met the moss and curled together to make me sleep forever.

Did Mamère still sleep in the chair? What did she wait for?

No one would come for me there, in our room. No one would send a man here, where Céphaline breathed so hard and called for water, water.

I stared at the picture on the wall. Céphaline painted as a baby. Her hand fat and pink as a starfish in her ocean book. Her face fat and rosy as a nectarine in her garden book.

"The books of my childhood," she said when I looked at them, as the days passed. "The only ones I can have now, with pictures. Hardly any words."

"Your eyes," Madame said. "It is not healthy."

"My brain," Céphaline said. "Put it in his jar."

Doctor Tom placed the leech on her temple every day. Large and pulsing black. The ants of her words she wrote smaller and smaller. Madame took away the paper. The whorls of hair in the brush.

He gave her tablets: "Blue mass—mercury to balance the blood."

What was the name of her blood now?

I sewed a tear in Céphaline's sleeve, trying to make my stitches like eyelashes. Fine as my mother's. Céphaline stared at my needle. Her face did not move.

The plaster made her curse. Doctor Tom laid it along her neck, where it raised blood to her skin, and then the leech drank that poisoned blood.

"Cheval blanc," Céphaline said softly. "The more I look up at your face, the more it reminds me of your horse."

Doctor Tom winced. "The blood flows through the veins in the neck to the head—to the face," he said to Madame. "This is what the surgeons in New Orleans say to try, before the injections. The blood carries waste and impurities to the skin, where they collect."

"Boutons," Madame murmured. She was ashamed of the word. Of the face. Her own skin so smooth and white as a bowl, but the three lines on her forehead like threads now.

I held Céphaline's mirror while she slept. Inside my eyes were the colors at the riverbank edge. Brown and black and gold silt.

My mother's new prayer. Not far. Not far.

Down the hall, Grandmère's thumping cane called Félonise to her again. The round glass showed my skin light as damp sand high on the riverbank. Not wet mud, not dry loam. My eyebrows were feathers of black. Who cared about our eyelashes and eyebrows? Did the men have to stare at our skin and eyelashes while they labored through the hair under our dresses?

Céphaline's cheeks were pocked now as if a hummingbird had attacked her face. Hera's scars were raised and shining, Céphaline's dug deeper by her own nails. Her knives.

The Auzennes came to help move Mademoiselle Lorcey to their place, because Céphaline couldn't study during the treatments. The smooth curves of Auzenne neck and cheek, placid foreheads and closed lips, excused the eyes dull as black leather or murky olives. A man wouldn't hesitate to put his lips on those cheeks or that brow, and the eyelids would be closed anyway.

The Auzennes did not come upstairs.

That night the clock sounded like a ghost tapping a tiny heel, the hallway murmuring when someone came to check her.

It was Msieu. The boots were smaller than Doctor Tom's.

He sat next to her bed, his breath moving the mosquito barre. The barre pooled in milky folds beside his foot. I could open one eye and see.

"How could we have known?" he murmured, the smell of his silvery liquored breath floating to my corner. "As enfant you were perfect."

He shifted his boots, and I heard clots of mud grinding underneath the heels. "But your face. Whose face is that? Your breeding from France—the goddamn English doctor knows nothing of France."

He stood up but one boot slipped. Stumbling. He crossed the floor, and I kept my breathing steady as sleep. The mud on his soles crumbled near my face—horse manure and river silt.

He stopped at the altar. "I prayed. The Virgin didn't worry about her looks. She received the child without them. I wouldn't care if we stopped the damn medicine now." He snorted the air twice, fast, and his heel twisted grit into the wood when he turned.

I would see the sand in the morning, would sweep it from the grooved floorboards. He stood over me.

"And this one with a good face and hair, but only to move the tail aside. Like the mare. Goddamn."

He went to the door, turned and said, "Dors bien, petite." Céphaline's breath rasped like the nutmeg on a grater.

The black shadows of his boots crossed the slice of light when he closed the door, and then he blew out his candle.

I waited a long time. Then I felt my collarbone of clavicle, my kneecaps of patella. My nose of cartilage, my hair of something I didn't understand. My spine, and the hard knot above my buttocks. Muscles and fat, like the pig. Under our cloth.

"You can't fix me," Céphaline told her mother, who only left the chair beside the bed now when she slept.

"Oui, petite, we can."

"I am not broken."

"No. You are perfect. Just the—"

"I am not a plate dropped on the floor."

"No."

"I am stained like a damn tablecloth." She laughed.

"No. Simple to erase them. We will erase them."

In the threads, the bluing turns red—blood or wine or berry juice—to white. But in the body? The indigo went inside the skin and breath of my grandmère. How did it penetrate? The liquid of coffee went inside the blood of my mother, made her stay awake night after night in her own chair, waiting for me.

Doctor Tom's bottles lined her dresser. My mother's bottles lined our chest. The wash on the line like people flying. The mosquito barre she had mended, clouds hidden in the folds. The medicine from Paris in a small jar. Doctor Tom said, "This is the particular order sent by Valréas, in Paris. We met in London last year, and he told me this was the newest medication for the skin. A powder that can be mixed not only for application on the face but for injection."

Céphaline said nothing. Her own face, her portrait as a child, watched her from the wall.

He pushed the needle into her arm. I applied the paste to her cheeks, forehead, chin. Madame held her fingers. Grandmère called from her bedroom, and I was sent to tell her that now the medicine was inside and outside.

Msieu came in with sugar smoke on his clothes. When he left, I smelled the sweeter breath rising from Céphaline's bed. Her mouth was open like a new moon, her teeth dry as the moon's chalky glow.

Then Madame went to her room, after midnight. Céphaline's feet moved under her coverlet. White fish swimming side to side.

Madame had told Doctor Tom that morning, "We have only a short time to ready her for the season. My husband will be angry if the treatment continues to fail. You haven't seen his true anger. He wants her to be happy, in an arrangement."

Msieu rode at Petit Clair all night, because frost had descended in halos over the fields and the cane cutters had to work through dark. Doctor Tom sat in the hallway, in case Céphaline called. The pages of his journal stopped rubbing against one another, so he must have slept.

I lay on my pallet, listening. I took my sewing needle now and pricked my forehead. Blood. I waited for it to harden and tasted the small button. Salt and copper. The same as always. But blood couldn't flow into my hair. Céphaline's medicine, in her blood, flowed into the boutons and would erase them.

Her feet rustled again, swimming on the sheet. Then there was no sound. I tasted the salt in my throat. My own blood. I was afraid to get up and look at Céphaline. She had not spoken for hours.

No sound. Was she was not breathing?

Did she hate us all now? Did she hate me for walking freely, for my face without a single mark except for a white scar like a grain of rice at my chin, where Christophe had once shoved me onto a rock?

Did she hate her mother for not having a son? "You say every day you love me, you love me. But you didn't make the right mammal, and now you are sorry. Drown me and begin again."

Was she breathing? She hated Doctor Tom. She would not call him if she were hurting. She would not call me. She would call no one. I couldn't move, because if I stood over her, they would think I had touched her. I might have helped her stop breathing. But if I lay here when they found her in the morning, it could be my fault. Like Nonnie. Tretite said someone must always be blamed.

She was not breathing. If air was not moving in her lungs, was her blood not moving either? Her heart. The muscle. Was it too tired? What if the medicine had stopped her heart?

But I was the only one here.

Pretend to sleep. Nothing on my hands but my own blood, and I removed that with my tongue. Mamère—tell me the word. Sweat on my forehead. Salt. No tears. No.

Dry. Mattress cover dry. I rubbed my face with my sleeve so no one would see tears and know that I knew she was dead. I knew nothing. But what of her spirit? The old people believed in spirits. What if her spirit was hovering here, waiting for help?

"Cheval blanc," I called, high and hard like her.

He would know it was her voice. How could that be me? I would never say those words on pain of the lash.

My face to the wall, my mouth buried in my moss. Dead black spirals. Threads of hair.

The door opened. "Mademoiselle?" English voice rolling harsh on his tongue. Tongue not in a jar.

Sleep. Don't move. Breathe.

Don't hear.

The lamp moved. His air so hissing pulled against his big teeth. The eyes in the jar. Mine are not open.

Don't see.

His own breathing was light and hissing as water thrown on a fire. Then the blankets rustled. He was touching her arms, for the pulse, like he always did, then her heart, like he always did.

He kept body parts in the jars. Was he touching her face now? How could he keep boutons in a dish? I'd brushed a bouton when I pulled back her hair that day—a hard little crust of powder fell off the red bump, and I saw it like a ruby and realized it glowed bright as her mother's ring.

I thought about rubies to keep myself from screaming. Because how could anyone be sleeping with this noise? His hissing breath. He had killed her. They had killed her.

He went out to the hallway. Would he get on his horse? Where could he go? He didn't know the bayous, and if he rode for New Orleans, someone would see him. If he rode south, he would end up in the sea, where the boats entered the mouth of the river. Where everyone came—from France or Africa.

He knocked on Madame's door.

She came into Céphaline's room and began to scream, short and hard twists of sound until he put his hand over her mouth and said, "You'll wake the slave here and all the others. The medicine is unknown. The dosage—"

She pushed him away and said, "Go get my husband."

She covered Céphaline with her whole body when she sobbed. "Petite. Petite. My baby."

I breathed as if sleeping, as if small clouds went inside my mouth and outside my mouth. Grandmère shouted from her room, her bulk falling from her bed onto the floor, the lamp trembling with the vibration. She was trying to get to the screams.

If I ran, I was guilty. If I was not here, I wasn't watching. But I was sleeping. How would I be blamed?

Doctor Tom pushed my body with his boot. "Moinette. Wake up. Run to the stables and get the groom. Tell him to find Monsieur Bordelon in the sugarhouse." I rose and rubbed my eyes. Grandmère was moving down the hallway now, her hand scraping the wall. She was crawling.

I pressed myself against the wall, waiting until Grandmère twisted through the door and over to the bed, so she wouldn't see me slip away.

Tretite's shutters were dark. The moon was fuller now, lopsided and staring over the barn.

"Nonc Pierre," I whispered, at the door of his room off the stables. "Nonc. Wake up."

He opened the top half, his fog of hair crushed on one side from sleep.

"Madame says go get Msieu from Petit Clair. Céphaline's sick."

He bit his lips so hard they disappeared below his scars.

I couldn't say it. She's dead. What if someone asked him whether I knew? I could only tell Mamère, and I couldn't go there because they would look for me.

When he'd ridden away, I ran into the cane.

The fields were mostly stubble, ice and sharp fibers cutting my feet like razors. I ran toward the path my mother had taken me down. There was nowhere to go. Just like the doctor. The river would drown me, and in the swamp, the dogs would find me.

One day. No one would remember me for a day. Then Tretite could tell me what words were said.

On the headland road near Msieu Lemoyne's place, the last of the canestalks whipped the side of my neck, cutting like fingernails. I jumped down into the irrigation ditch and pushed through the frost-stiff weeds the way Mamère had taken me.

The path into the ciprière was still marked by our footprints and no one else's. I ran, my back stinging with sweat, like stars pricked my spine. At the indigo vats, an animal moved in the brush. I climbed over the brick walls and dropped inside the lower vat.

I sat in the corner with my dress over my knees. My kneebones under my cheek. Nothing in our faces where our cheeks were. No cartilage, no real muscle.

The sternum protects the heart.

Was her mother still lying on top of her, to protect her from—from what? Herself? Would her mother die now, too, to be with Céphaline—where? Would les blancs go to the same place we would?

Mamère. Did she hear shouting now? Was she preparing herself to go where I went: là-bas or into the ciprière or—

Where would I go? The air settled more frost onto my head, my shoulders, the bricks. All the women here in the vat, dresses tucked up at their waists like rolls of extra skin. Their faces, when they tried not to breathe. I tried not to breathe.

My grandmère. Four scars on each cheek, her teeth showing when she drew air through her mouth, trying to escape the stench that rose from the water.

How could she have escaped from the very air? And how would I run through the water?

Then I heard horses. Faint snorting and rattling, hooves ringing on the trail through the trees. LeBrun from Bontemps—dogs for nègres—was he out looking for me already?

No dogs. Only men, talking low. Not calling me, or anyone else.

No one had taken this trail for months, my mother had said. Did she know where I'd come? Did they have her on a horse, holding her up to make her look for me?

I climbed out of the vat, slipping once so brick took the skin from my wrist, and fell in the clearing.

Msieu's voice cut through the woods like cane slivers. "Did you lash him tight? He's slipping."

A fox den—I remembered the smell from when my mother brought me here. I pushed through the vines toward the musky scent, praying the fox was out hunting now, or gone forever. The scent was strongest in a heap of branches and leaves. I slid into the fox den, my shoulders and head still outside, and laid my cheek flat on the crackling cold leaves.

Only flashes of movement showed through the tree trunks, and I prayed no one could see me, my black dress and dark tignon like burned wood, my right cheek turned up to the moon like a stone.

"Get him off the horse. He's not dead yet, but he won't wake up. I hit him too hard. Get the horse in there, too."

Nonc Pierre's voice. "Msieu, pardon, but no horse go in there."

"Then you take the horse to the river. No knife or bullet. Hit the damn horse in the head and throw him in so when he washes up south, it looks like the doctor drowned."

The leaves warmed to my cheek, or my cheek cooled to the earth. Msieu had killed Doctor Tom. Would he remember I had been there, too?

Michel spoke now. "Msieu—we have to cover the man up?"

Nonc Pierre said, "Horse didn't hurt nobody."

Msieu said nothing. Something was dropped, in a heap, and then a gunshot, so loud it was as if the bullet went through my own ears into my skull. My brain.

But when the ringing ceased, only silence. No one else would have heard, not across all the cane.

The horses snorted, reared up, and thundered hooves on the earth. Dampness on my skirt, and on my cheek. My heart hit the long, flat bone that protected it like a door.

"Cover him up. I will bring lime. Make certain it is permanent." Msieu turned his horse; the creaking of leather. Then he rode through the brush.

The men were silent until Nonc Pierre rode the white horse away. Then they began to dig.

"All this dirt don't look strange, someone come?" Christophe said. "Best get the dirt from the woods, not right here."

My tears slipped into my right ear, and the ringing shovels were underwater. Now they would find me, and Christophe would make me lift my dress before Msieu killed me, too.

No one would look for me except Mamère. And she would look forever.

I turned my head slowly, so that my silver cheek wouldn't show, but my mud-covered one. Dark like the night, the leaves, the soil.

Michel said, "Nobody come down here. I never hunt here. Have to find something heavy for him, so nothing dig him up. Wrong to leave him like this." His voice broke. He was nearly as afraid as I was.

The mud was colder and colder on my cheek. My legs were asleep. The men didn't speak.

Msieu's horse came back through the woods. He said, "Wait."

Glass shattered on the floor of the vat, against the bricks, again and again. The doctor's jars. Then pages fluttering, books landing.

"Michel—start on the bricks. You got that hammer."

When the horse had left again, Christophe said, "That a eye down there?"

Michel said, "Quiet."

Christophe said, "Damn. All them clothes. Bury now."

"I said quiet."

They dug, and the rhythm of the shovels was my breath.

Then they began to throw in everything they could find—scrap wood, fallen branches—what if they needed the very pile I lay under? But they knocked bricks from the walls and collapsed the second pool.

The warmth of my eyelids was like tiny blankets.

When the thudding stopped, Christophe finally said, "Say a prayer?"

Michel said, "Say a prayer no one ask question and you cutting cane tomorrow."

Then they walked back through the woods, and when I finally opened my eyes, the moon had fallen from the edge of the earth.

Nowhere to run. No one knew what I had seen, but if I didn't get home to my mother and clean myself, someone might guess. And if Msieu knew the slave sent for Nonc Pierre had never come back, he would think me guilty of something.

I pulled myself from the hollow and lay on the ground moving my legs and arms to awaken them. An insect. A helpless, foolish beetle. No brain. The brain was buried under rubble. The second vat was destroyed, a few bricks like jagged teeth all that remained, the four pipes like spindly fingers caressing the spine of the uprooted sapling that lay on top.

"Mamère," I whispered at the shutter. "Mamère." My voice broke, my throat coated with ice and musk.

She opened the door, and I fell inside at her feet. "Mamère. Mamère. Mamère."

She put me in the washtub with cold water, so we didn't make smoke, and my body shook so hard my collarbone felt cracked. She put my soiled dress in the fireplace and pulled hot ashes over it. I told her Céphaline had died, I had been sent to get Nonc Pierre, and then I hid in the cane.

She said nothing. Not a single word. When I was dry and wearing her only other dress, she lay beside me in the bed, warm and solid. She stared at the smoke-darkened ceiling above us, her lips moving only from the inside where she chewed at them softly with her teeth.

We washed nothing. My dress burned with morning's breakfast, the musky fox smell gathered in our bricks. Outside, we lit fires under the pots and began to make soap, with the tallow and fat collected from Tretite. No one came onto the gallery. Not Msieu's hat or Madame's hand over her eyes.

Mamère said nothing. She laid out the wooden soap forms and held a coffee bean inside her mouth. Sometimes her right eyebrow twitched and leaped when the sounds of crying drifted in the wind.

In the afternoon, horses and carriages pulled into the shell road. Nonc Pierre came to the clearing. "Tretite say she need you."

I dried my hands and walked slowly beside him. "Did you find Msieu last night?" I asked.

Nonc Pierre nodded. A bruise darkened his arm, maybe from a horse's kick. He said, "You stay last night here?"

I nodded, too.

He said, "Céphaline die. You know that?"

I shook my head and put my apron over my chin.

"Man come from New Orleans on the boat tomorrow. He make a painting of her. That's what Tretite say."

I waited for Tretite in the pantry. The parlor was crowded with Auzennes and strangers. Félonise took my hand. "She die easy?" she whispered. Her gray eyes moved over my face.

"I don't know."

"Was you there?"

"I went to get Msieu."

She sighed. "Madame stay in her room."

I waited for Msieu to burst into the house and see me, to remember who slept near Céphaline, but he didn't come inside.

After the visitors left, the house quiet except for the crying that tore through the upstairs, I stood on the stairs. Madame stayed in her room, Félonise sleeping in the hall outside her door. Was I meant to sleep outside Céphaline's? Did she still lie in her own bed, or was she in her mother's bed, covered with her mother's skin?

In Tretite's room off the kitchen, we watched the back door of the house. "How she die?" she asked finally.

"I don't know."

"You know them bone and piece," she said. "I hear you talk. What stop working first? The head or the heart?"

"I don't know."

"He put the death mask on her face. How they do. They make the face with plaster. Then he make the painting. How they did Msieu's grandmère, in France. The one over the fireplace."

Céphaline's face, covered with white paste again, her eyes still blue under her eyelids. No. When someone died, did the color fade? What about the eye in the broken jar, black with dirt now in the woods?

Tretite said, "Go home. She wait. She afraid for you."

"Hair," she began. "You believe now. It is not dead."

Céphaline's hair hadn't killed her. But something inside her brain had made her heart stop working. Her blood.

She went across the room to the chest, and I was surprised when she brought out the piece of blue cloth and the bracelet of my hair. Those were hers, hidden. Privé.

But she held them on her palms. "My mother's hair."

The black braided circlet. She always placed it by the candles and prayed for me, so I always thought it was mine.

"Hair hold the *ni*. The inside of—" She stopped, looking out the window. "The inside of you. When the France people talk about Dieu, say the soul."

My braid felt heavy down my back. I was afraid of the glittering in her eyes, the way she held the cloth and the circlet so still. I was afraid of every human animal on Azure.

"I wash your hair, I be careful for your *ni,*" my mother said. "I braid, I hold gentle on your *ni*. My mother tell me on the boat. They leave us one bucket salt water. She say in my ear about the hair. Say if she die, on the boat, who tell me the words?"

My mother got up and sat beside me. The rush back of her chair whispered as it pulled her shape into itself.

Her eyes swam with tiny red veins, as if she hadn't slept since I had. "Say the water around the boat was *faro*. *Faro* is the soul of water. *Faro* give the rain and *ni* of the corn. *Faro* give shells so people have money."

She put the circlet of hair in my hand. "On the boat, the wood scream. Loud like birds. Scream, scream in the waves. One room for us. So dark and listen to the sounds. She whisper like this."

She touched my ear. Cold coursed through my neck. "My mother say *faro* make the wind spirit, Teliko. But *faro* tell the people wear copper rings on the ear, to hear Teliko words, and the French take my mother's copper."

She pressed my lobe gently. "She have four holes in each ear. Cry and cry. Say no one can hear now, say what if I don't remember. But I remember the words. Then we get here, and nothing is the same."

The hair was woven so tightly, it could have been thread.

"She in the indigo all day. At night, I come from the old woman, and my mother wash my hair."

She had oiled the bracelet—almond sweet smell.

Her eyes were night black on me. Did she look like her mother, telling me now? She wasn't sick, she wasn't going to die, but I had left her. Only a long pathway to the house, but I was gone, and she spoke fast, as if I would leave her just now, run away from the story.

"Two years, she can't breathe. Then she can't eat. The old woman say when my mother die, I have to keep her *ni* safe. In the house." She nodded at the things in my fingers. "Some hair and some water. Say the other part is *dya,* shadow of you inside. *Faro* keep the *dya* in the water, keep it clean. Then, next baby born take them both. *Ni* and *dya* go to the baby. The baby of your blood."

The hair in my hand didn't look like mine at all.

They buried Céphaline in the family cemetery. The stone was carved in New Orleans, brought down on the boat. Céphaline Eugénie Bordelon, 1796–1811. The artist took her dress and her death mask back to New Orleans, where he would paint.

Madame never left her room after that day. Félonise carried her food inside and closed the door. I walked up to Tretite's at dawn, after my mother had given me milk and coffee and whispered to me, "Quiet. Don't talk unless someone say. Nobody there now. Doctor gone. Governess. So nobody eat dinner. You stay by Tretite."

I did. Tretite made the food, and I carried the platters to Félonise in the pantry but not to the dining room. I stayed in the pantry by the bags of pecans. I didn't want Msieu to see me. He was gone all day counting hogsheads of sugar to be taken to New Orleans.

After he was gone, I polished the furniture in the office, with the ledger book. How much was I worth now? I never touched the book. In the guest room, the artist had left white plaster dust on the floor. The plaster was absorbed instantly into my damp cloth. How small were the grains?

How small were the pieces of bone? What happened to the hair?

Félonise told me not to go upstairs. Tretite's eyes met hers over my head. Gray and brown. She didn't want Msieu to see me either. She told me if horses arrived, to stay in Tretite's kitchen.

I slept there, on the floor by the fire.

Every morning, my mother came to get the clothes. She asked me almost formally, "Who come to the house?"

"No one."

"Who you serve?"

"No one."

We ate meat Tretite left for us. Roasted chicken, which Grandmère Bordelon ate in her bed. Msieu came back very late, and he only drank brandy. Madame stayed in her room.

Now Madame was as sad and afraid as my mother was all the time. Now Mamère sat beside me in Tretite's small dark room off the kitchen. She didn't pray. She didn't light the candles. We sat in the dark, the moon gone to a fingernail, the shutter closed tight.

The cart wheels creaked up and down the shell road in the morning, sugar hauled to the boat. I gathered Msieu's clothes from the floor of his empty bedroom. Tretite said, "Start the dessert now. Them sugar buyer come tonight, five of them. I can't cook the big dinner alone. Mo toute seule."

I am all alone. She didn't mean only for tonight.

Tretite's headache made her eyes small with pain. The new pecans were soft and pale, and I roasted them in the pan until they browned sweet. We plucked the tiny feathers from the squabs, crowded them in the pan with wine and brandy, put them at the edge of the fire to roast.

Ten small birds on the platter, arranged around a bed of rice, and when I bent low next to Msieu, he glanced up at me.

"Bring us three more—" he began, and then he stared at my face, my eyes, my tignon. I slanted the plate gently onto the table.

But he finished. "Three more bottles of wine." Then he dismissed me with a wave.

Dismissed. Like my mother's upturned chin.

"Azure," one of the men said loudly. "And you named it?"

"My mother did," Msieu replied. "For the color of the indigo."

"Now you got all this sugar, you change it to something white?"

"Sugar isn't white until it gets to the refinery. Brown, oui?"

They all laughed. He didn't. Msieu said quietly, "Now the name means something else to me. The eyes of my daughter."

"May she rest in peace," one man said, and they crossed themselves.

My back was pressed against the cool plaster wall. Was she peaceful now? Là-bas? Where was her là-bas?

I heard her voice then. Patella. Hybrid. Classification. She was my governess. I was her pupil. I closed my eyes. Clavicle. The heat of the tongs bending the hair. The ink on her wrist.

The men moved into the parlor. The cigar smoke rolled to the ceiling, and when I carried dirty dishes past the open door, it was as if moss wreathed their shoulders.

Tretite and I washed the platters last. It was close to midnight. "They maybe want more pecan tart. Take these to the armoire."

Preserve dishes and dahlia plates. Madame's favorites. "If Madame never comes out of her room again," I said, "who will run the house? Grandmère can't get downstairs."

Tretite nodded. "Put them in the armoire case she do."

Inside the dining room, I hesitated at the armoire. Madame's footsteps whispered along the floor above my head. Grandmère's heaviness made four posters grind into the wood planks when she turned her body.

I laid the preserve dishes in a row on the second shelf, as always, and placed the platters on their sides. Pheasants and roses. Dahlias—why was that Madame's favorite flower?

Msieu's voice rang out from the doorway. "Did you count Lemoyne's last shipment? Let me get the ledger."

Then he came into the hallway, tendrils of smoke before him. Again, he looked into my face, and he tilted his head to one side. I bent over the dishes. Then he went into his office.

Tretite's fire was banked for morning, the bowls laid out for biscuit dough, the pan laid out for roasting coffee beans. She was tying her hair up with string. Tretite's hair was long and thick, and when she let it down and put on her white dress, she looked like a young girl from the back. Until she turned around and you saw her face, her lips folding in on each other, her eyes surrounded by lines like cross-stitching, from years of squinting into the smoke.

"They finish?" she whispered.

I nodded. "Where's Félonise?"

"That hallway bed." Tretite glanced into her kitchen one more time. "Go quiet and ask her how many for breakfast. She say one them leaving tonight."

I ducked into the hallway again. The parlor was quiet now; some of the men must have gone to sleep in the guest rooms. But no one ever opened Céphaline's door.

I would never see her again. I would never hear her words.

I touched one dish, not wanting to pass the parlor door and the men. The dahlia had fifty-two petals. I turned toward the stairs, and Msieu stood there. He said, "You will go with the man in the black suit."

He took my arm and turned me out the front door with the wooden sun bursting above it. I tried to free my arm from his fingers, but he pulled me around the gallery and toward the river.

"Msieu, I am going—"

"You will go on the boat."

I tried to stop my feet, but he held my elbow, his thumb digging into the soft part inside. He had seen my face. Did he know I knew? No. He remembered only that I was alive, and Céphaline was not.

Mamère. Mamère. Maybe she could stop him. Talk to him.

"Msieu, I have nothing to take with me. I need to go back and get my things. Please."

We were on the path to the landing, trampled hard by all the barrels of sugar. "My things, Msieu," I said, and tried to wrench away my elbow.

"You have what you need," he said. A small man waited at the landing, on the short dock. The boat lifted and sank with the water, and Msieu pushed me onto the ramp, over the brown riverbank.

Three PASSAGE

She said that boat was dark and the wood screamed. She was inside, held between her mother's legs.

I was in the cargo hold with hogsheads of sugar, which trembled like a thousand drums around me.

She said her mother cried but silent so no one would hear, and the tears dripped into her hair when she sat on her mother's lap, hot when they fell on top of her head and then cold when they slid down her neck. Water on her skull. But Mamère didn't know skull. Skull like Céphaline's, like Doctor Tom's. Under the dirt.

Knowing the word *skull* wouldn't help me now.

I put my arms around my knees. The wood shook under my dress.

She had her mother, on that boat. Her mother had her.

The cargo room was full of burned-sweet smell rising from the sugar and molasses. Tiny drops of brown shook around my feet. Dark like Céphaline's boutons when she scratched them; like a coffee bean held between Mamère's lips.

I cried silently so the small Msieu wouldn't come back.

She had her mother. Her mother had her. I had no one.

The wood of this boat croaked like an angry raven. What had screamed in the wood of my mother's boat?

This boat moved slowly against the current. North. Not skimming fast down the river with cloth and nails and Céphaline's medicine from Paris.

He sold me because every time he saw my face, he was reminded of hers.

I pushed my face into the sleeves of my dress to smell my own hair, and my mother's soap. Back at Azure, my mother's tears dripped onto herself. Not onto me. Her mother had had her, even as the boat wailed and moved and took them away.

My mother said if I was gone, she would join me. Là-bas. But I wasn't dead. How would she find me?

When we pulled away from the landing at Azure, he pushed me ahead to the deck, where some of the hogsheads of sugar had been loaded, but then he'd paused.

The small Msieu looked at my face then for the first time. I could barely keep my footing and put out my hand to the railing. We were headed north to New Orleans. The wind pushed the sails, but the current tried to take the boat back. The lights of Azure were gone.

The batture along the river's edge full of deadwood. The moon lit only the tunnel of trees along the river, and after a time, we passed the heap of charred black that had been Petit Clair. The river water rushed below, marked with the circle of light from the lantern.

"She going to jump?" another man said. He'd been at the dinner table, too, his moustache with tips so thin and drooping, I thought of Céphaline's commas, curling from her pen. He was Msieu Bordelon's factor, the man who sold the sugar during grinding and came south with goods from New Orleans—coffee and cloth and iron hoops for the hogsheads.

"You—are you planning to jump?" the small Msieu said. I was afraid to look into his face. He was only a few inches taller than me. His voice was French, but the hairs on his wrist were pale brown.

If I said "No," that would be a lie, because I was thinking that I could still float now, at this moment, down the river toward home.

If I said "Yes," he might beat me. He might beat me anyway. He might lift up my dress right here. He might laugh. He might burn me, like Eveline said someone had done once to her. I had seen the round gray scars at the soft edge of her breast when she took off a dirty chemise for me to wash.

If I said the truth, which was that I didn't know, he might be angrier than with either of the other answers, because Msieus didn't want anything complicated. They didn't want to hear the word *I*. Never. There was no I.

My teeth held my tongue.

Then palm trees appeared like chimney brushes against the outline of night sky. Maybe Les Palmiers, a place Madame often mentioned. North on the river, closer to New Orleans. But a name Mamère knew.

The other man said, "You bought her just now? She mute?"

The small Msieu said, "I thought she was speaking when she was brought to the boat."

He stared at me for another moment, and the boat shuddered on against the current. Don't look down. He'll think you'll jump. You might jump. If you jump, you can find a branch to float you down.

But Christophe said the river never helps when someone runs. The brown water hides brown skin until it takes the color from the arms and legs, and the bodies wash up white.

If I jumped, how would I see Azure, with the levee banks tangled high with river trash and driftwood?

The full moon wakes in the east and sleeps in the west, my mother said. This moon was on its downward arc. White as a soap cake, but missing two days' worth of a sliver, as if my mother had shaved off a portion for washing.

The boat was slowing for the next stop. This house had an allée of trees covered with oranges, nearly glowing behind the lanterns someone held at the landing.

The water churned—but water would hold my soul. *Faro?* The water spirit? Would I would drift down to her, even if I died? Then she could join me là-bas.

"Orange Grove," someone shouted.

The small Msieu said sharply, "Put her with the cargo. We'll only be here a few hours. If we bring her ashore, she might run."

I could see nothing, not even the outline of all the hogsheads in the hold with me. The eye focused when it was given enough time to adjust, Céphaline used to say.

Your eyes were purple when you were born, Mamère used to say.

Then when you grew, they turned brown and followed me around, every moment of the day until I had to leave you at the end of the canerow.

What did I look at until you came back?

Sais pas. Don't know. Maybe the sky. Maybe nothing.

I cried until my dress was wet as if we'd washed it. No one else was on the boat now. I tried to make my brain work, but my head felt swollen as Eveline's baby who died.

Her baby gone. Madame's baby gone. My mother's baby gone.

Think. Your brain is the same size as theirs. The small Msieu had eaten with Msieu Bordelon. They knew each other somehow. All the sugar was loaded for New Orleans, where everything was sold.

Under my dress was worth money.

The other lips. That night Hera sat with Mamère while she sewed, and they talked about the marks. Two on each side. The four lips. The ones on your face. The ones between your legs.

In New Orleans, someone would lift my dress and stick his hand there and then buy me.

"They put their finger there," Eveline said once, shrugging.

I could mark my face. Hera said she didn't mark Phrodite's face because it wasn't good. If my face was scarred, no one would want me.

I moved my wrists against the iron bracelet, which was attached to the ring in the wall. My apron. I still wore my apron from serving. Maybe there was something in the pocket with which to cut myself. Numb fingers into my apron pocket. Small round objects, smooth long ones.

Coffee beans and clothespins. My palms felt only their shapes, my hands were so cold.

I threw back my head against the wood, banging the bone covering my brain. Nothing to scar me. And if I did scar my face, then what would I be sold for?

What if the small Msieu shot me, like a lame horse, for my ruined face?

Then I would be là-bas. And Mamère would find me there. In the other world.

But what if Mamère waited for me to come back to her? Not là-bas but in our bed, lying there but not sleeping? Sitting, just like me, waiting.

Iron scraped in the lock. My eyes were dry and swollen as if sand filled the holes. I saw the eye in the indigo vat, imagined Doctor Tom's eyes now, and Céphaline's inside the earth.

What was my mother looking at? What did she want me to do?

A brown-skinned man in a white jacket studied me. He put down a plate with cornbread and a small, limp pile of bacon, and left a tin mug of water and a bucket. I wouldn't drink the water. I wouldn't use the bucket. I wouldn't lift my dress. They might be listening.

We left Orange Grove. People shouted, "North!" The iron bracelet left red ridges in my right wrist. My eyes filled with water again. Where did it come from? Maybe all the water in my body would leave through my eyes and I would never have to use the bucket.

My legs were stiff. A rush bloomed inside my back when I tried to move too far, my spine bending wrong. Vertebrae.

Knowing the word didn't matter. I was staked down like Marie-Claire, whorls of pink flesh decorating her cheeks. It didn't matter that Céphaline had taught me all those words, merely by saying them. I needed other words, if I was going to live.

I had to use the bucket. I said words to myself, words Céphaline had used when her mother was angry. Only excretions. Sweat. Urine. Tears. Where in the folds of the brain did our words form?

Nothing on my tongue would help me now. When the small Msieu opened the door and seemed surprised to see me amid the sugar, I waited for the right words to come from a secret branch of the softness inside my bones. But somewhere between my eyes, which saw the key's teeth move into the lock at my hand, and my throat, which filled with fear when they took me out onto the deck where the river reached wide and brown to the levees, where rooftops were visible now, no sentences formed themselves for me.

"He sold you with no defect," the small Msieu said, studying my face at the railing.

Foolish or intelligent? Which would hurt me, or help me? I looked at his buttons. Obedient.

"Oui, msieu," I said.

"Did you try to run from Azure?"

"Non, msieu."

"Why were you not needed?"

He must know about Céphaline. He must not know I had been there that night. I said, "His daughter is gone now."

His eyes were the silvered gray of a new cane knife. My eyes moved down. My feet on the shaking wood. Screaming wood.

"You," he said, and the brown-skinned man came again. Coffee stain on his jacket sleeve. "Stay here while I prepare for the landing. She is not to move."

On the riverbank, two heads were mounted on poles at the bend, where the boat slowed.

The eyes were gone. The skin was dried like hide. Purple brown. The hair was coated with dust from the river road. The curls left were pale as gold.

"Saint John the Baptist." The steward spoke softly. "They try to rise up. Heads above the city and below."

The pikes had gone into their brains then. And how did they find a man willing to mount them there? Lifting them and then . . .

They were not faces. I closed my eyes until the boat stopped moving when we docked at New Orleans.

The other man, the factor, tied a small rope around my raw wrist. I pulled my shoulders in, like a cape. The men were everywhere—their eyes went to my face, my dressfront.

On the wharf, the Msieu and the factor bought coffee, breaking open bags and chewing a few beans. The smell—the bean tucked into my mother's cheek—my eyes filled with water again. It should be dry inside me now.

My mother had had her mother, when they brought her here to the slave market. Or did she come to Azure straight from the boat with sails, sold at the landing? She had her mother's hand.

"I never stay here longer than necessary," the small Msieu said to the factor, who pulled me along the dock.

"With all the balls and dinners?" the factor said.

"People make money at home, and they lose it in the city." The small Msieu studied sacks of coffee, iron hoops, and heaps of cloth.

He gestured to the boat. "Engage dock nègres to move the sugar." Then he looked at the men on the wharf. "I have forty arpents of new land," he said, his voice lower now. "I need five men to clear it. Africans, but it's unlikely I'll find any here. Since the damned Americans have changed the law, I'll have to take a boat down to Barataria Bay. Jean Lafitte always has Africans for sale."

The factor nodded. "When I met you at Auzenne's place, he mentioned it. Did you enjoy the sight of the daughters?" He stopped abruptly, the rope bristles burning my wrist. I was an animal—larger than a dog, smaller than a horse. A mule. Petite mulâtresse.

The Auzenne girls. Their fair cheeks and perfect curls. He might have to come back for one of them soon, and I might come back, too.

But the small Msieu flicked away their names with his fingers. "Too far south. And my son remains in Paris. I want to leave tomorrow for the Barataria."

The factor whispered, "You would truly buy from Lafitte and the privateers? With the Americans patrolling?"

You couldn't watch them or let your eyes meet theirs. A shoe paused nearby; a white toe poked from its hole like a pale grub.

The small Msieu shrugged. "This one can't clear the land. Bordelon said she wasn't needed." He shaded his eyes to look at the levee. "She can be needed somewhere else, he said, and I agreed."

The factor's voice seemed distant. "Bright girl is worth good money in the city. Or trade with Lafitte for some men."

Hera's voice—Bright hardship. My mother—Take but one candle light a room.

While we walked to the hotel, two men stopped us. "You sell that one, oui?" Fingers on my sleeve. A hand with sparse black hairs, a jacket with a grease stain like a map, a knee round as a saucer when a man bent a leg up onto a block and studied me.

If one bought me, what did it matter if he hit me with that hand or covered my face with that jacket or pushed that wide knee between my legs?

I would let all my blood out of my body as soon as I could, and it would clot and dry like sugar boiled in the last pan, and then someone could grind up the solid blood into powder. Drink my body in coffee.

Finally we went into a door below a sign on a large house. The factor handed the rope to a woman with cheeks red from a cooking fire.

She opened the door of the storeroom, and I sat on the cloth coffee sacks piled near the olive oil jars. "You break something, I make him pay," she said, and locked the door.

The bricks were warm and not trembling. I took off my tignon and made my hair into a pillow at the back of my head.

Lie down make me too rested, my mother said. Lie down mean I can't watch.

Watch me. Watch me.

Who do I pray to? *Ni? Faro?* No water here. My blood would turn to powder, and someone could thicken soup with my body. A red soup. Beef meat and sang mêlé.

Mixed blood. From a sugar broker's blood. A tall blond man, eating a soup of beef meat and laughing upstairs now with the small Msieu, who was not the laughing kind. In the morning, we would go farther away from Azure. From Mamère. The sugar broker would ride for another plantation, where he would taste the sugar and talk about money and look for a woman. The one for that night, for that week.

No. He was dead. Tretite had said long ago to Mamère, very quietly when I was in the bed, lying down: "That one, the one Madame call le gros blond avec les yeux rouges? Big blond man, with red eyes? Mort. Dead. Msieu say he don't come back for next crop because he gamble on a boat and they kill him."

I leaned my head against the big jar of olive oil. Lie down mean you can't watch, Mamère always said. So I rest like this.

In the morning, the woman spoke to someone in the kitchen, and the door opened quickly. She screamed.

"Aiee! I forget this little nègre! Like a ghost with la barbe d'Espagnol hanging in her face!"

I tied my tignon tightly. She pushed me out to the kitchen, handed me two biscuits, and reached behind her for the rope.

On the street, the small Msieu and the factor listed goods. Fabric, coffee, white sugar in cones, iron hoops for the hogsheads.

The molasses on my dress was dried at the hem, collecting dust. The water would run brown when I washed it.

The small Msieu said impatiently, "I need two boats—one for all the goods, one for new slaves."

"But then you're trusting *two* Canadians," the factor said. "Hire Chalan. He's named for his boat. Take everything you buy together." He turned away then. "I have to collect the payments for Bordelon's crop and take his goods down to Azure."

His black coat disappeared into the crowd, hundreds of backs and hats and boxes. He was going back.

But the rope pulled me toward the boats and the river, so wide and brown that trees on the other side looked like puffs of smoke.

I wouldn't cry in front of this man. I sent the welling tears back into the hollows in my skull. The salt water burned like lye. My mother could dip a turkey feather into the pools below my eyes, and the quill could come away stripped bitter like a white needle.

The small Msieu engaged the boatman named Chalan. "Lafitte always have cloth and spice. Wine. What else you need?" The Canadian's beard was thick and brown as a rabbit pelt along his cheeks.

"How many slaves will fit?" The Msieu looked at the big boat, the boxes.

"This voiture hold enough. See how many he have when we there."

"How long will it take?"

"My job is to get us there. Your job is to pay."

The small Msieu pulled me to the center of the boat, where boxes were covered by a tarpaulin, and he looked at me for the first time that day.

"If I chain you here and the boat capsizes, you'll drown. You understand that, oui?"

"Oui." I knew what he was asking. But I refused to say it. I will not jump. Not now. Not yet.

I sat on a box. The clothespins in my apron pocket nestled against my leg. He did not chain me. I was not in a box. Fancy piece. Good for one thing. Christophe was right.

The captain said, "When they jump, like a bag of piastres thrown in the river. Bag of black hide, the Africans. Sang mêlé aren't wild most of the time."

The small Msieu said nothing. He hadn't decided whether I was fit or wild or not.

Four slave oarsmen filed onto the boat ahead of another white man. They didn't look at me. They sat in the benches and rowed us away from the dock while the second white man called out to them from his seat just behind. The air was cold on my face, the salt water inside my cheekbones, the words I wouldn't speak collecting in my chest.

The shoulder blades of the rowing men moved up and down, like hatchets under their shirts. Not angel wings.

A white ègret burst into the air when we turned into a narrower bayou, his wings spread like sewn-together fans and his black feet dangling over me.

Christophe used to boast about running away to see a girl below LeBrun's. He said that if he got lost, he would find the egret nesting place in cypress swamps to the south, then walk the right way.

But we had gone north, and now the sun was hidden, and I had no idea which way we floated. Two more egrets flapped away, in a different direction.

Bayou Coquille. Bayou des Familles. Bayou des Rigolets. The men threw the names back and forth. "To lose the Americans, when they look for Lafitte, we have so many ways we can't count," the captain said to the small Msieu. "The Americans are slow. They eat too much beef."

The small Msieu laughed and leaned against the pole holding the tarpaulin. "And you?"

"Me? I live on tafia," the Canadian said. "Cane rum."

Back on the night they sewed together, Hera told my mother about some Africans she'd heard tell never killed their cows. They let blood run every day into a gourd and let milk run into another gourd. The people drank and grew tall, and the cows lived.

Only when someone marry or die, they kill a cow and eat the meat, she said.

Mamère was quiet, and then she said, On the boat I drank blood.

Eh! Hera frowned.

My blood, my mother said. That boat, the men shout and the wood scream. We were so hungry. My mother tell me eat a piece of your finger. I chew around the nail, but no more skin there. Then I taste my blood. Make a cut. Hold the blood in my mouth a long time.

The boat wake moved branches. Steam flew from the rowers' mouths. A nail was loose on a box beside me, and I barely moved my wrist, punctured the ridges left by the iron bracelet.

I made four holes in my wrist. That seemed like a good number. When the fourth sting turned warm, I felt it was enough. The air dried the blood, and I brought my skin to my teeth to nudge the black buttons into my mouth.

"Lake Salvador," the captain said. A black mirror, with the clouds above. Céphaline would have liked it. A looking glass where you could see nothing.

The boat stayed at the edge of the water until a whistle sounded in the trees. "Lookout says safe from Americans," the captain said, and spat into the dark water. "They call this place the Temple because the Indians killed here. Prayed when they killed."

The steep ridge of land was a chênière, where shell mounds were piled high and trees now grew. Michel always said the chênières behind Azure were good places to hunt because the animals fled there in high water. But this island had scattered buildings.

And the captain took me off the boat and put me in a small cage, like an animal. He paused in front of a low brick building and said, "Keep her here. You don't want Lafitte and his men to see a sang mêlé pretty like that. Unless you want to sell her now."

Another man opened the lock at the iron bars of the doorway. Someone breathed inside. Even if the door were open, there was nowhere to run here. Only into the water to drown. Would the spirit be ruined then? Did a hide bag of piastres lose a spirit?

The small Msieu put his finger in my shoulder. "You. Is your father there? On Azure?"

He wanted to know if my father was Msieu Bordelon or the overseer Franz. "Non."

"Do you know who he is?"

"Non."

Small brown hairs on his wrists and even on the fingers, between his knuckles. What had Céphaline said about knuckles? Why did they look so foolish?

He was thinking of selling me here. To Jean Lafitte.

"Can you cook?"

"A bit."

"What can you do?"

His eyes were small—raisins in a biscuit, glossy from risen sugar when they baked. If I said the words—*wash, clean, iron*—would he keep me or sell me? I could—sew. That word made needles move in my throat. I couldn't sew yet. My clumsy, crooked stitches weren't ready. She wasn't done with me. All the lessons . . .

"Only field work. They put me in the house just sometimes for dinners."

The small Msieu shrugged. "No field here."

The captain said, "Inside."

The key twisted like Tretite's knife on the sharpening stone.

Three brick walls and the door of bars. Three women inside. They knew one another, because one brushed a fly from another's shoulder. Two of them talked low, words I had never heard, and the third vomited over and over into the pit dug in the corner.

I sat on the sand in the other corner. They stared at me. I watched the water until darkness rose from under it to fill the sky.

A woman with a lantern opened the door. Her skin was red brown, like old brick, her eyes green blue as shallow water. She said, "Quatre!" and shook her head. Four of us. She put down three wooden plates full of sagamite. The boiled chunks of corn glistened in the lantern's flame.

She came back with one more plate. When I finished eating, she took my hand to examine my nails. "Dirty," she murmured, at my fingers, but she pulled out curls from my tignon. "Lafitte see you?" she asked.

Stealer of slaves. I didn't move my lips or eyes.

"You quarteron? Or mulâtresse, eh? Not Indian like me. I redbone like my father."

I said, "Am I sold to Lafitte?"

She stood suddenly and shrugged, and her dress turned the corner of the doorway after she did.

In the night, the wind blew off the lake, and sand flew against the walls, spattered against the wood and my skull. I was so cold I couldn't sleep sitting up, like Mamère. Purple night erased the bars, and the three women's shapes curled against one another.

Tomorrow they might be sold south on the river. Sold to Azure or Petit Clair. They could walk in the canefields near my mother's house, smell coffee, and knock on her door to whisper when they learned French. "Just get here. You trade?"

I woke to fingers, in the stripes of gray light through the bars. Two of the women squatted next to me, pulling at my tignon. When it fell, I thought they would take it. But they touched my hair, loosened from the braid.

They said nothing. My hair rustled between their fingers when they lifted curls and rubbed them. Then I moved and they pulled back. I picked up my tignon and turned away from their faces, dark as Mamère and Hera, but with tiny raised scars in two rows along their hairlines.

Not Singalee. Not Bambara. A people I had never seen. Their faces didn't show the four lips, but something only they knew.

The ocean-eyed woman came again with sagamite. She left without speaking or looking at me. Molasses sank quickly into the corn.

Mamère melted sugar on her tongue right now, in pearl dawn. It didn't matter whether he sold me to Lafitte or traded me for other slaves. The sick woman sank down against the wall and moaned.

Like Hera had slid against Mamère's wall that night, when she wanted the dress. Now her daughter had the dress. In the cloth we had dyed would be threads of her mother's love and worry and all the words she had collected. The indigo plant torn from the ground was a child of the plants that killed my grandmother. The blue was in her blood.

I had nothing but clothespins and coffee beans now. I waited for whoever would come, holding the carved wood in my apron pocket. I had no wisdom. Just the oils of my mother's fingertips, moving to mine.

The sand under me didn't rock like the boat. But I put my teeth to the black scabs on my wrist until fresh blood welled. Did I taste rust? Maybe rust from the nail would seep into my veins and infect my blood. Céphaline said rust was a compound. Mamère said rust was the most difficult to bleach from the white shirts.

"Sang mêlé," a voice shouted through the bars.

A white man with a beard, hands webbed with dirt. He put an iron collar around my neck and pulled me to the door. When I stopped in the sunlight, he pinched the tip of my breast with his free hand and pulled me farther that way.

It hurt like ants attached to me there. He laughed and said, "My favorite way to make them walk. Pain or plaisir, make the nipple hard and then you just hold on."

The collar was heavy on my neck. I held my head still and followed my breast.

"There he is," the man said. I realized he was the captain's mate. He dropped his hand quickly, and my breast burned and throbbed. The small Msieu turned from the boat deck.

"The iron collar is not necessary," he said. "Ne pas sauvage."

"Maybe she is wild," the man said when he unlocked it. He kept his back to the small Msieu. "But I like to put it on," he whispered to me. "I like to walk them that way."

My breast felt as if the ants were still chewing at the flesh. I stood near a dock. I smelled cinnamon. Then five men walked toward us, chained together, matched step to step like horses. They didn't look at me or at the small Msieu. They stared at the water.

No marks on their cheeks. What did they believe was in the water?

More boxes were brought. I stood still. A patient animal. Small mule. My breast burned faintly.

From the barge moored nearby, moans rose like vapor from the water. A doctor, with black coat and bag, squatted on the deck where men lay on pallets in the shade of a tarpaulin covering. The doctor smeared something on the gums of each man, and one man kept his lips stretched wide, sound winding from his throat, rising and falling.

"Scurvy," said the mate, swinging the iron collar, to the small Msieu. "Africans have scurvy and pestilence when they get here. Doctor buys them cheap and tries to fix them. Sells them in the city."

The white paste on their gums, the greenish paste on their arms and legs and shoulders—their eyes closed except for the sighing man, whose eyes stared at the tarpaulin over him. He couldn't even see the sky, if he was dying. Was he a sky person? A water tribe?

The five new Africans were chained by the ankles into the rowers' benches. The captain made gestures to the Africans, and his own rowers tried to speak to them, but the Africans didn't answer or acknowledge. When they rowed, though, they tried to keep pace with the others.

When the boat moved away from the dock, the wind was cold against my face, and I closed my eyes for a long time. It no longer mattered if I remembered where we went. I would never find my way back.

When I opened them, we were in another bayou surrounded by black willows. Nothing but winter branches and dangling bare vinestems.

The backs of the men were twisting. Each had a brand on the right shoulder, raised shiny as if thick worms had been inserted under the skin. *A*. They couldn't all be from the same people, so that must have been the name of the ship or the captain.

The letters moved when the rowers pulled, scars floating on the skin stretched over their shoulder blades. Not angel wings. No one could fly.

And Mamère—she had been a child on the boat. I had never seen her bare back—she always washed in the dark. Did she have a brand? Would they have branded a child? Quickly I bit at the scabs on my wrist to keep the splinter of fear from my ribs. I wasn't a child. When I got to the small Msieu's place, would he brand me?

The mate's whip was small, compared to the overseer's whip on Azure, but the tip cut easily into the skin. He split a thin gash into the shoulder of one man, and a red smile opened whenever the man leaned forward to pull the oars.

Bile rose in my throat. That was what Doctor Tom called it, the fluid that ate our food for us. And then, seeing his eyes and the jar, lying next to him in the indigo vat, and Céphaline's black boutons and her red eyes, and the skin of the man closest to me now covered with skeins of white salt from his drying sweat, I threw up the sagamite and molasses over the side of the boat.

The captain laughed. "Feeding the fish," he said. "Atchafalaya fish like corn."

At dusk, when the wind came up and the boat rocked and pitched, they found a place to moor. They lashed the barge tight to the trees, and we walked onto a floating mat of driftwood and moss and earth, trembling when we passed over the water. The iron-collar man took the African men into the trees. They came back with wood and built a fire on top of black sand and ashes where others had cooked before.

The Africans were chained to a tree at the clearing's edge, but I was not. The small Msieu said, "Can you cook cornmeal and hardtack?" I shook my head. The captain said, "That's not why you buy her, oui?"

The iron-collar mate cooked the dinner. He served their food onto three wooden plates, then held the pot before me and I scooped a handful. The Africans ate from the pot after me. They held the warm corn in their palms and chewed, looking at the water.

When the trees and moss turned black, the fire was the only light, and only the three white men close to it were visible, their faces and beards and hats. They drank tafia, the molasses turned liquor.

The men's chains clinked near the trees, like crickets.

The small Msieu and the captain went back onto the barge, their footsteps on the sucking raft of wood. The captain called, "Keep watch until four and wake me."

The mate called out, "Don't you chain the sang mêlé?"

"Oui."

He locked the ankle bracelet onto me.

I curled into myself. My hair itched, and my legs were cold with air entering my tucked-under skirt.

The third night since I had left her. Was my mother praying, right now, with her coffee beans and piastre? Had she added something to her church? My peacock plate? My other tignon? Something to bring me back?

I rubbed my fingers gently on one coffee bean in my pocket and then left my fingers over my mouth, so that I could smell her.

I woke to the iron-collar mate's fingers in my mouth. He held down my tongue and said close to my ear, "If you scream, I will choke you and claim a savage did it. Indians everywhere in the woods."

The sounds of night had changed. It was nearly morning.

His fingers put the taste of ash and tafia in my mouth. Then he moved those fingers under my dress and pushed one inside the other lips. A different burning from ants. His finger clenched me inside and I wouldn't cry out. I listened to the sand under my skull. His elbow hit me again and again in the breast. He was moving his hand on himself.

When he breathed slowly again, he pulled away his fingers. The air was cold on my legs. My dress was wet. He pushed his mouth near my ear again, tongue sour-hot. "I had you and didn't pay for you."

Then I heard nothing. No snoring from the boat. No clinking of the chains. Nothing but the water lapping against the banks.

If I got loose from the chain, if I slid into the water, this bayou would take me back to the lake, and Lafitte. The only reason to put my body inside the brown water would be to disappear. To go là-bas and wait.

But if Tretite had heard the small Msieu mention his home, and she told my mother, and Mamère made her way to wherever the small Msieu was taking me, I would be là-bas alone.

I put my hands into the pot of cornmush when he brought it. I smelled him. Céphaline said we receive the formation of babies inside our wombs. Babies were inside the liquid. My dress was dry and stiff. The babies were dead. I ate the corn with my eyes closed.

How much had Msieu Bordelon sold me for? Had he written the name and address of the small Msieu? If Félonise polished his desk—

But no one could read any words except me.

The small Msieu unlocked the chain, and I leaned against the tree, burning between my legs. I took the empty pot from near the fire, cleaned it at the bayou's edge with wet sand, filled it again with the silty water, and went into the woods to wash myself.

Bayou Cocodrie. Bayou Boeuf. Bayou Courtableau was the longest. Deeper, blacker than the others. At the landing, the goods were loaded onto a wagon and the small Msieu paid a man to whip the two mules across their rumps to make them move.

We had legs. We were not loaded onto wagons. The Africans and I walked behind.

This bayou was black as lead, shining like Céphaline's pupils. There was no use to jump. This water would never reach the Mississippi River, only the gulf and then the ocean. The current moved so slowly that a leaf and I took a long time to pass each other when we left the landing, and the dust from all our hooves stayed in a brown cloud on the still water.

Four ROSIÈRE

Even as he spoke, not looking at us but at his own hand moving over the paper as he wrote, I didn't listen.

I don't belong to you. I didn't belong to Msieu Bordelon, and not to God yet. I belong to her. I am hers. Until I die and find her. Là-bas.

"What is your name?"

We stood in the yard between the kitchen and the house. The wind had grown colder as we came farther north. The trees here were bare of leaves, their branches dark as though burned. This house was much larger than Azure, newer, with eight white columns along the front and a front door with stained glass over the top. The brick path where we waited smelled of new clay. The brick kitchen building was larger than Tretite's, and two women stood in the kitchen doorway staring at us.

"Water, Léonide," the small Msieu said. The one who nodded was the cook. She held a spoon as if she never put it down. She was short and fat, even her earlobes plump as licorice drops under her tignon.

"Can you speak any French?" the small Msieu called out.

None of the Africans answered. They were still in chains. The neck of the man closest to me, the one with the cut on his back, was so coated with sweat and dust that trails had formed behind his ears.

"Amanthe," the cook said to the other woman, who wore a white apron. She was about twenty-five. House people. She held out a gourd of water to me. Her eyes tilted upward, and her cheekbones were high ledges of stone flushed with red under brown skin.

I didn't want to know any new people.

But the cook looked at me, and in her eyes I saw fingers. What she thought she knew about me, and cadeau-filles. Gift girl. Bright. "New

Orleans," the cook murmured, low in her throat as if the words were shameful.

The small Msieu sat down at a wooden table. He took papers from his coat and spread them out. His fingers were still dirty, too. They held down the paper in the winter moving air.

All the fingers. Dangling on the man nearest me. The small Msieu's finger pointed again at the first African.

"Athénaïse is your name," he said, toward the first African. He waited a moment in silence. "Sometimes they learn words on the ship. Not this group. So expensive. I even had to buy the chains from Lafitte," he said, turning toward a driver on a horse, a Frenchman with tangled yellow teeth and red-cold hands resting on his pommel. "Let them sleep today. Start tomorrow on the new land across the bayou."

The small Msieu named all the men.

"Athénaïse." The finger stabbed the air before the first African. "Athénaïse." Then the finger moved sideways, to direct the African to shuffle slightly nearer the driver.

"Gervaise. Apollonaise. Hélaise. Livaudaise." Each time, his finger stabbed toward a face, then tore sideways through the air.

A white woman stepped outside now and stood at his shoulder, studying the paper. Her dress was calico, fine figures not faded by too much washing. Not as fancy as Madame Bordelon.

"You were missed."

"Your cousin sends greetings." He stopped writing. I could hear the absence of scratching. I kept my eyes on the sweet olive bush near the kitchen. "I am nearly finished. Then we may eat?"

She nodded. She swung her head slowly around to each figure in the yard, peered toward the backs of the leaving men. "I needed a man for the garden." Her voice was directed at me. "Not a girl."

Her eyes were blue. Not like Céphaline's, with the fierce glow of flame. Milky blue like china bowls. She didn't sound as if she hated me already.

"You'll have a man for the garden as soon as the new land is cleared," the small Msieu said.

"How many men do we have now?" She squinted at the ledger. "Twenty-seven? Twenty-eight? And no one to spare?"

"No one." He pointed at me. "I don't like African names. But certainly you are not African."

He wrote words again. I didn't want him to know I could read. I glanced quickly at the papers when he put the pen in the ink. He wrote next to the men's names: Congo, Congo, Congo, Ki, Ki. African tribes.

I was half Bambara. He knew nothing. If I told them my real name, and they didn't like it, and they changed it, then only Mamère would have my name. I could keep it inside my mouth. For myself. Until I saw her again.

But how would she find me, if I had a different name?

"She seems slow," the Msieu said. "All the way here. Very slow. Bordelon said she was good at dressing hair. But she was not needed."

The Madame said, "Someone besides Amanthe to dress my hair is not needed here either." She didn't sound angry. She sounded as if she were choosing cloth. "How old are you?"

The way her eyes moved over my outline, vague and slow, I realized she couldn't see me well. That was why she didn't hate me. Her hair was pinned in a chignon. Dull and brown as acorns. Her knuckles were big, like pink roses. She wanted a man for the garden. Not a gift.

"Fourteen, madame," I said. The small Msieu's pen scratched again. He could see me.

"Do you only dress hair?" she asked. Then she turned to her husband. "I can't imagine why you bought her."

"Guillaume Bordelon needed a favor, and she was inexpensive."

"What else can you do?" she asked, her eyes fixed somewhere to the left of my face.

If I said washing and ironing, I would stand every day in this yard, next to a woman who already did laundry. I would smell someone else's soap, hear someone else's words at my ear, and I would never be able to learn the boundaries of this place, to be able to run from the closeness of this yard.

"The field," I said.

He had already written Creole mulâtresse, 14.

His finger drew the same slanting line toward the driver. Then he paused and frowned. "Name?"

"Moinette," I said.

A blanket, a bowl and spoon made from gourd, and a cape. That was what the woman named Sophia handed me. She said, “You from south? Past New Orleans? Get cold here. You near Washington. Cold and ice.” She showed me how the hood lifted up, for when wind scoured the fields.

Hers was the second house on the street that ran down le quartier. I couldn’t see the big white Rosière house, only the barn and stable. Then the drivers’ house—Mirande and Baillo, fox-haired brothers from France. “One sleep, one ride all night keep a eye on us,” Sophia said.

Twelve houses, and trees down the center of the street.

Two doors on this house. Inside one door sat an old man and an old woman. The woman’s fingers were so thin and dry, they looked covered in burned paper. She sewed the hem of a child’s garment. When she looked up, the whites of her eyes were filigreed with brown.

Inside Sophia’s door was a front room: a fireplace, a table, and three chairs. In the back room were six wooden sleeping shelves, two on each wall.

Sophia studied me, almost like the Madame but her eyes moved faster. Then she put her hands up to her face and rubbed, her fingers disappeared in the hair at her forehead. “Why they put you here with me? So tired. I don’t have time for someone else.”

I didn’t belong to her, either, so I didn’t answer.

Sophia handed me an extra dress. Coarse cottonade, dyed yellow brown, with stains of black at the hem, like mud painted on. She didn’t speak to me but to the table. “Give her to me and don’t give no clothes. Madame forget everything. Sunday I have to say to her, No clothes. Because I have only one girl, I get other girls nobody want.”

I held my tignon in my lap, my fingers on my mother’s stitches. When my mother’s mother arrived at Azure, she had a small girl. She must have had nothing else.

Two girls entered, picking splinters from their skirts.

I wouldn’t look at their faces, only at the weave of their skirts.

“All that wood we carried,” the smaller one said.

"Sang mêlé," the older one said, looking at me.

"You mixed blood, too," Sophia murmured. "Congo mix with foolish. Your mama told me. Wash up." Then the younger girl held out her hands, and Sophia said, "This Fronie. She ten. She mine."

"Fantine," the older girl said. "I my own. My mother have three more boys. No room for me, so I stay here."

"Bring in more wood," Sophia said, frowning near the fireplace.

She heated water and poured it into the washtub. "You wash, Moinette. Don't want bugs in here."

"I don't have bugs."

"You got something."

I had my bundle—my apron tied around the coffee beans and clothespins, the apron strings wrapped tight. I hid it inside the cape on my shelf. I didn't know yet who stole here. When I took off my dress, sand fell like sugar around my feet. Sophia took my dress outside to shake it.

"Sang mêlé," Fronie said. "What color your blood?" The girls stared at me, and I knelt in the hot water.

I bit at the raw thumb until the red dripped to my palm and held it out so they could see. Then I felt the water reaching inside me, to the passage.

In the dark, on my shelf, I held my clothespins and the coffee beans. One bean had already splintered, into three of Céphaline's black commas. Céphaline bent over her paper, murmuring that one comma changed an entire sentence, and one letter changed an entire word.

I missed her voice. Her words like embroidery in the air. She didn't love me. But I had heard her voice all my life.

Three pieces of bean, and water flooded my mouth when I brought them to my nose. The water was bitter as if it sprang like lye from my cheeks.

Mamère holding the coffee bean in her tongue all morning, to help her through the hours. I couldn't put this bean in my mouth. It would wear out in my teeth and I would swallow the brown liquid and then it would leave me. Through one of the passages.

I don't belong to God yet. I belong to her.

Three coffee beans. Two clothespins. Where could I keep them safe tomorrow? Who came inside this room when we were in the fields?

Sophia's voice came from near the fire. "Li mère?"

"My mother is on the other place. Azure."

Then she was quiet. The fire made a shimmering sound in the dark. Glistening. Like Mamère's. All the fires, in all the houses, all next to the rivers and bayous. All the mothers. I breathed the coffee. What did she want me to do? To ask?

Sophia said, "No trouble for you. If you quiet. Want quiet all the time. Nobody argue. Everything quiet. Every day, every night. Winter, put the fire out when they ring that bell. Summer, keep the shutters open, and they come every hour to see you sleep. Everybody in the bed. Don't sleep in a chair or get your name in the book. Name in there two time for the week, no meat. None. Just corn."

Doors clapped shut on houses down the street, and pots clinked on the old woman's hearth, the other side of our chimney. Fantine and Fronie were already asleep.

The fire shifted and Sophia said, "So. Enough."

A horse moved slowly down the street, lingering outside each door. The bare wood was hard on my shoulder blades. Did anyone here know the bones? My cape was under my body, my tignon under my head.

If my things were wrapped in my tignon, someone might steal the cloth. And my hair had to be hidden.

My hair. I tore a piece from the ragged hem of the dress just given to me and wrapped the pins and beans tightly. In the morning, I would tuck them inside my braids.

On the second day, Fantine waited until I had lifted my arms to braid my hair, and she struck at my lap quickly as a snake. My bundle was undone in her fingers, and then she laughed at the clothespins. The coffee beans were shrinking, splintering all the time, and they fell onto the floor without her notice.

"Thought you had money," she said. "Jewelry. You have nothing."

Standing slowly, so she would think I was ashamed, I held out my hand for the clothespins. When she dropped them into my left palm, I brought my right wrist up to her chin, as Christophe had done once to me. The bone of her chin was sharp as a small stone, and I pushed harder, upward. "Don't ever touch my things again," I whispered. "You can't hurt me. But I can hurt you."

Her nostrils flew wider. "You have nothing. All you have is hair like la barbe d'Espagnol. A man beard hanging down your back."

When she went outside, I gathered the coffee beans. Three shards of one, the other two still whole but smaller, drier.

My hair. Moss. Spanish beard. A fat man—a man who would tie me to a tree with my hair, who would jerk my head like a horse, who would choke me with my braids. My hair—how did something dead mean anything? How could there be a *ni* inside, a spirit, if my mother, who believed in that god, never touched my hair again?

My hair, heavy and dirty down my back because I had never washed it myself. My mother washed it. My mother's tightly coiled black curls, the sugar broker's blond hair—like useless chaff that flew off hay? How did bloods combine? In the passage? In the fist of womb?

Outside, I was the one afraid. Fantine would tell her mother, who shouted at her boys now, who had a hard face with lines like antennae that sprang between her eyes.

But her mother nodded and brushed past me at the well. Fronie and Fantine studied me that night near the fire, as if I were a rabbit with five legs. Lying awake for a long time, to see if Fantine was still angry, I heard only the hooves outside, ringing sharper where the ground had frozen.

Every night, I looked at the wall near my face, wood chinked with bousillage, mud laced with horsehair, moss, straw. Had my mother run by now, to find me? Would she wait, as one did when lost?

I couldn't run. Every tree was bare, every bayou low and dank. Every morning for weeks, the sun came through the shutter cracks like silvery ice. I couldn't measure the distance—two days on the river north from

Azure to New Orleans, two days from there to Lafitte's place, and four days north on the Atchafalaya and bayous to Rosière.

How many days by foot?

In the breathing dark, Sophia stirred, but I always started the fire. I wanted it to be mine.

But no matter how early I rose, the old woman next door was already at her hearth. The scraping of pot on brick came through the air swirling in the chimney we shared. Her name was Philippine, and her husband was Firmin. She spoke to him in a low, unceasing trickle while he carved spoons and bowls from gourd. His face was collapsed into his bones, his cheeks ribboned with odd scars.

At dawn, the bell rang in the tower, and hooves moved up and down the street.

No coffee. Only cornmeal to boil into cush-cush. Sometimes milk. No sugar.

The scabs on my wrist had dried and fallen off now. I chewed at the corner of my thumb until I had a piece of meat between my teeth, until I tasted the warmth of blood.

The people measured me. I said nothing except in answer. When anyone spoke to me, I had to decide how intelligent to sound.

We are all animals, Céphaline said. We eat and excrete and breed.

You listen and be careful, Mamère said.

The two drivers, Mirande and Baillo, didn't look at me except to say I held the hoe wrong. When I saw them the first days in the field, brothers with ocher eyes and moustaches red and sparse as ants on their faces, I was afraid. But Sophia said they never touched the women. They were waiting for wives from France to join them when they had land of their own, and Sundays they rode to a church in another town.

Every morning we walked behind the cart that carried hoes and noon meals and water. Mirande rode his horse above the men, the new Africans chained at the back of the line—cutting the cypress and draining the new swampland.

Baillo rode above the women—clearing for next year's cane. The fields were all stubble, littered with burned stalks and dried leaves. When I wiped at my face, Sophia said to me, "This ain't even cane. This January. Pas même. Not the same. Cane is October when we cutting, yes."

My hoe blade chopped at clots of dirt. The earth was frozen until the weak sun appeared. The frost dissolved into water. The water entered the earth, and we moved the dirt from place to place. Furrows and rows. Every day.

We gathered the cane trash from last harvest into piles. Mirande lit the fires. The smoke burned hard into the gray sky, and I imagined the clouds crystaled with sugar, moving south, the rain falling on my mother's tongue.

Where did she wait? Here on earth? Or là-bas?

Bayou Rosière cut through the land, too narrow for large boats, only pirogues loaded with moss or skins or solitary hunters who passed the fields. I watched the path to the ciprière where the men disappeared with axes and chains.

I measured east and west by the sun. I measured the fields by the ditches and bayous. Five fields. Boats passed on Bayou Courtableau.

I couldn't run yet. Every morning, frost covered the steps to the porch gallery, gathering like white fur in the splinters. The branches of even the lowest bushes were bare, nothing to hide me in the woods at the edges of the fields we cleared. Roofs were white as if the ice contained bluing. I wrapped my cape tighter around my shoulders, pulled the hood over my tignon. A circle of cold air hung before my face when we followed the cart to the fields. We hardly ever had ice like this at Azure. I saw Mamère sitting by her fire, sewing, holding her lips still. Waiting.

The dark came before dinner, and one of us girls stood in line to grind corn in the two hand mills, with light only from the torches. Then Sophia baked corn cakes or boiled mush.

The street was a tangle of voices, but I didn't want to sort the people, to know them, because I wouldn't be here long. But they spoke to me. The women tried to ask me questions, their eyes shining like coins in the light. The men grinned and nodded, their teeth floating in the dark.

Sophia said, "You better speak. Be polite. Who grind corn for them Africans? You come here with them."

I shook my head. "I don't know them." The one with the grin-scar on his back, Athénaïse, always glared at me with his eyes narrowed to fierce crescents. He spoke a word to the others. I knew the word was African for me—mulâtresse, light skin, white blood—anger at how the mate on the river spoke to me, at what my very existence meant.

I looked back at him, imagining my mother and her own mother, and spit on the ground. I said out loud, "Saliva is all the same."

Sophia said, "Africans think they better. But how they gon eat?"

Fantine's mother sent her three boys down to the house occupied by the Africans, at the end of the street. The boys reported that the Africans had made their own mortar and pestle with a cypress trunk and trapped a bird, which was roasting in their coals.

Sophia said, "Big bird or little one?" She was thinking of meat.

Every day, I kept my eyes on the cart ahead of me, then on the trees at the fields' edge. At night, I kept my eyes on the porch steps. The edges of women's brooms. The men sat in doorways waiting for dinner. I saw their shoes.

I listened to Baillo's shouted orders in the field and to Fantine's soft, high voice while we ate. She was in love.

"When you sixteen, you get a man," she said to me. "Madame marry you with the Bible."

"So you can make her some money."

"No. So you can be happy."

She walked with a boy near the slave cemetery.

Breeding, I wanted to say to her. Curling myself near the fire, I thought of Hera. "Where your man?" my mother had asked, and Hera had replied, "We sold three times, me and mine. I'm gon be warm at night, all a man is."

At night, Sophia was happy not to talk to me, and I was happy not to listen. She hit my arm with her piece of kindling to move me to my bed. She didn't want the hooves to stop outside our door. She wanted her meat on Sunday.

Sunday mornings we walked up the long road to the big yard behind the house for prayers. Madame spoke from the Bible, and I understood some of the words. Céphaline used to read Latin aloud. *Deus* was God. *Corpus* was body. Doctor Tom said corpse was a dead body. I told my mother the word *Deus*. Her voice was low and harsh in her throat at night, when she prayed over her altar, her piece of cloth from her own mother. When she prayed to keep me alive.

I was alive. Msieu would hand me dried corn without looking up, keeping his eyes on his papers with their scratchy black lines of ink. I was not a corpse. I was alive. She wanted me to be safe. She didn't know if I was alive or safe or a corpse.

Mamère prayed to find out the name, the place. She prayed to the same gods. She was patient. She had to be patient.

Sophia stared at the pile of meat and the knife.

When Madame's voice had finished, silence hung in the air until we moved our feet.

If your name wasn't in the book—for not finishing your work, for talking out of turn, for sleeping in your chair or by the fire when Baillo heard snoring from the wrong room when he passed by on his horse and he poked open your shutters with his long stick to see where you were—you got a piece of meat. Salt pork in square chunks, sometimes bacon, sometimes strange pieces of a pig's body. Corpse.

Dried corn. Molasses in a wooden bucket.

Sophia ate all her meat on the first afternoon, while we washed our clothes. She boiled it with dried peppers she kept in a bag or fried it until the fat spit. Every time we hung up a dress, she took another bite of her meat until it was gone. Her eyes were focused far away while she chewed, and when she handed small pieces of the meat to Fronie, she looked at the trees.

I remembered my mother slipping pieces of dried meat into her mouth while we washed, remembered the splinters of flesh she worked with her teeth. She gave me the fresh and she ate the dried.

Fronie said one Sunday, "I don't like the fat."

Sophia glared at her. "Fat good for you. So you don't be cold."

Fronie glared back defiantly and said, "Warming up now. The sun staying into night. I'm not cold."

Sophia whispered like wire cutting through wood. "When you a baby, I chew meat and put it in your mouth. So you grow. You eat this piece even if I want it. You don't be kind. Kind don't work."

She saw me watching and said, "Look at Moinette. Used to eat plenty meat where she come from. Meat from the msieu. Your father, no? Plenty meat. Your mother, she chew meat for you, no?"

I stared into Sophia's eyes, flat and black like iron nailheads pounded into her forehead.

She folded her arms, her elbows pointed sharp at me. I had felt them so many nights to move me from the fire. "You sang mêlé. No other sang mêlé here. You miss your place where your father treat you good. You très jolie."

I said nothing. She accused me of beauty. Mamère would keep her words on her teeth, with the coffee beans.

"Make a new place here or keep a old place in your head. Only two choice," she said now, her voice softer.

One night, when Sophia was outside, Fronie said that they used to live on another place, and her father had died, and all she remembered was her mother breaking dishes to cover the grave. "She break em special," Fronie had whispered. "Not wooden dish. China dish, with red trim. Two of em. Crack crack. I remember. I was scared."

The Africans passed by carrying wood. They kept their place in their heads, they hadn't made a place here, because twice the one named Gervaise had refused to understand orders in French, and he was put in stocks. No food, no water, no clothes. He whispered to himself all night in African. We could hear him through the shutters.

Msieu didn't whip. Baillo locked the people naked in stocks in the center of the street, under the bell tower, and they had to sleep and pee where they knelt.

One night, I came back late from the privy, and Athénaïse knelt beside Gervaise. Athénaïse spoke that word that meant me, and he spit in the dirt near the stocks. I said, "I don't speak African."

Gervaise—head floating in the dark before the pale wood. The heads on the pikes. I could say my mother's words—*ni* and *faro* and *dya*. But these men were Congo, Sophia said. They didn't believe in the same spirits.

On Sundays, the men moved the privies and shoveled dirt and lime over the pits, and our smell went inside Msieu's earth to move with the rain into his fields.

The skin on my palms was raised with calluses. I could see all the tiny lines on the calluses, like pillows with fancy stitching. Around my fingernails, the skin was hard and dry, torn from the cane and the hoe. It was easy to find a loose piece, to worry it.

Loose thread—pull it and ruin the shirt. Pull it and naked the man, Tretite said one night, when Mamère was sewing for her.

I caught the tag of skin between my front teeth—like a rat—and pulled gently until blood welled. It didn't hurt, not along the nail where the skin was tough, but when the strip tugged into the corner, the skin resisted. I cut the base of the shred with my teeth.

I chewed on the meat for a long time. I took it from my tongue and examined it—the dull skin had been dry and hard but now was translucent from my saliva. Saliva. Why do we have that? Céphaline used to ask Doctor Tom. All that liquid. Tears and perspiration and saliva and—excretions. I couldn't remember his answer.

My skin—a splinter of hardtack, like the men had eaten on the boat that delivered me here. My skin was gold on my body, but now this sliver was white as bone. How did saliva take away the color? How did the river turn drowned bodies of slaves white, as Christophe had said, but all our washing did not?

I swallowed the softened meat. Now it entered my stomach, my blood, and some of it went back to nourish my fingers.

Our excretions were inside this cane. We pulled the long pieces from the matelas, the cane piled last year for seed, and then the men cut them into joints. We dropped the green bones into the furrows, so that we could eat the molasses we would make and drop our own leavings in another hole.

Each field had a place for our leavings—one tree inside the edge of the woods, marked with a whitewash stripe. But I knew not to run from the fields. There would only be the ciprière, swamp and animals, and then more land, roads on which people would pass. I could never walk all the way to Azure. I would have to go by water. Find a boat and push my body down the bayou. South. Back to Barataria and trade my body for passage. I leaned against the tree. Just as it was at Azure—drop cane into the furrows, cover it over, wait for rain. Rain would fill up the bayous again, make them passable. Water from the sky to grow the grass. Then we would cut out the bad grass with the hoe, let the good grass grow. Grass from India. Grass from India, people from Africa, dishes from France. They came by ship, over the ocean and river and bayou. Anything that came one way could go back.

I kept my hands down. I used my eyes and never my mouth unless someone asked me a question, and all my words—from Mamère and Céphaline, from Doctor Tom, from Tretite and Eveline, and the words I heard that night in the indigo woods—all those words—*besoin, lime, dahlia, bagasse, scapula, womb, iris, octoroon* and *sacatra, ni* and *faro*—stayed behind my breastbone. My heart was a small muscle. All the words swam around it inside my blood, but I knew my heart was only meat for another animal.

One night, Sophia stayed awake long after she had sent me to the other room. The hooves passed. The door opened quickly, and feet slid along the wood floor. A bag dropped onto the table. No rattle—something soft inside the bag. A sharp intake of breath. The breath drawn inward the way someone does before blowing out onto the fire to redden the coals. But no breath huffing out.

I slid around the wall to the doorway. Sophia's feet were small and bare, wide from each other, her knees like little faces just below her uplifted skirts. The man hid the rest of her from sight, moving against her, against the wall. But I recognized his back. Gervaise. His back, with bones like hatchets under the skin when he rowed the boat. The hatchets moved now when he steadied himself against Sophia and the wall, pushing, pushing.

In the morning, when I made the fire, four small birds were roasted in the coals. Sophia came quickly, her eyes hard. She said, "Wait for I portion that. Don't you touch."

I didn't. She woke everyone and gave us each a small bird leg, then Fronie a breast. "Where you get these?" Fronie asked.

Sophia looked outside at the still-dark sky. She knew people could smell meat in the smoke. "A man got traps, in the trees."

"What you give him?" Fantine smiled.

Sophia didn't smile. "Got plenty for trade. Bowl, spoon, sew his shirt." She put the wing bones on the hearth. I held the leg, the meat like a black pearl on the little bone. I knew she thought of the place in her head every day and every night. The place from before, wherever it was, even though she wouldn't name it.

Moving up and down the canerows, Fronie followed her mother, waiting for her to turn, to touch her sometime during the day.

I wanted to tell her that when I stood near my mother at the washpots and the ironing board, the smell of bluing and fig leaves rising around us from black crepe, sometimes I clapped my hand over my eye and told her a cinder had blown inside.

Then my mother would bring my face close to hers, frame my temples with her damp fingers, pull the skin softly around my eyes to look for the cinder, her breath soft on my forehead, her shining black eyes so close to mine, I could see my face swimming in her tears. The tears we always have. The ones that don't fall, just hold our eyes in place.

But I couldn't say anything to Fronie. A hard knot blocked my throat. Like a pecan lodged there, where the words should come out. My eyes stayed on the end of my row, where the trees began and the bayou ran silent.

Two pirogues had floated past us, with bearded men poling the small boats loaded with skins. Flattened animals with their flesh removed. They must be trapping somewhere farther up the bayou and taking the skins to the landing to sell.

A boat would tie up here someday. And I would take it or trade for it. If I had to sell my skin to get back to my mother, I would.

Athénaïse ran. He disappeared from the ciprière where they'd been cutting trees in waist-deep water. The other men said it was as if he swam underwater to a place where no one could see him anymore. They had to cut his wood by torchlight, long into the night, and they wouldn't have meat for a month.

Fantine told the other women when we stood in line to grind corn. "He disappear. Like a spirit. Msieu get them dogs from over to Opelousas. They run him down, when they find him."

Their elbows were a line of wings, the way they waited and held their corn. Their voices moved past one another's shoulders.

Where was Athénaïse going? What was his real name? Was he running back to Lafitte's place, for one of the women with scars that matched his own—the wreath of dashes along his forehead?

He was running to the swamp where we heard runaways made maroon camps. Maybe he was running just to be somewhere else.

"Them dogs," another woman said.

Wherever we were, someone would always have dogs. Animals like we were animals, always eager to find something. Searching for a smell.

When I ran, I would have a plan. I would go by water, as my mother wanted me to. Water would leave no tracks, no scent. Water gods would protect me.

After we'd eaten, Fantine kept looking out into the purple evening. "Who tell you Msieu get the dogs?" Sophia asked.

"Basile."

"Where you see Basile?"

Fantine lifted her hands, as if she didn't remember.

"You fifteen. You got a year. Madame rules."

"I know."

Fantine smiled toward the door. Sophia argued with her all the time—she wasn't allowed to marry until sixteen. Madame's rules were about the church, but Msieu's rules were in his book, about the place. Too young to breed, and he would lose money and time from dead babies. Sixteen, marry, get a fireplace and bed.

Fantine said, "Love don't care about the time."

Fireplace and bed meant baby. The only purpose of marriage. Céphaline and the Auzennes wore silk dresses and stockings and corsets laced tightly. Fantine wore the same brown dress I did. The Auzennes danced and played the piano. Fantine put her forefinger up to Basile's cheek and brushed away a cinder, and let the finger trail down his jaw.

A baby was only stock. Fifty dollars. Five sets of dishes.

Athénaïse had been a baby. Who said his real name now? His mother. Every day, wherever she was, she said his name, the real name, and prayed.

Or she was dead. And he was dead.

Mamère held my name inside her mouth every day with the coffee bean. I knew it. I had been gone for many weeks, but she said my name only to Tretite. Maybe to Hera. Maybe Phrodite was in her own room, if now, with a man, her indigo dress in the corner. A baby.

Why have a baby when someone would sell it? Or it died? Madame Bordelon slept in her room all day and night waiting to die and see Céphaline again.

I slept on Mamère's tongue, in the little cradle of the back teeth where she cracked things.

When Athénaïse had been gone three weeks, and the dogs had not found him, and Baillo stopped following people to the tree where they relieved themselves, looking away but hearing the stream against the bark, I began to collect corn.

Fantine led the way to the fields. My breath streamed like smoke past my cheeks. Was Athénaïse swimming down the bayou, without a boat, all the way to Barataria and the ocean? Did he think he would swim to Africa? Or kill someone for a boat?

I waited for a boat.

If I saw him on the bayou, would he kill me? Or help me? Someday a boat would be left unattended at the tiny landing on the bayou. Trappers stopped here to sell skins, or rum they made in the woods, and a wandering trader came in a small boat to see if Madame wanted needles, candles, or spoons.

Every day, I took ten kernels of dried corn before we ground it for dinner and put them in a bag made from my old apron, pulling the drawstring tight, touching the grease stains that had altered the threads.

In the beginning, I hid the bag inside my dress, because I had nothing. No tin box or wooden barrel, no washpot or lamp.

Fantine collected small things Basile brought her—feathers woven into a strange brooch, carved wood combs, even two nails heated and formed into a cross for a necklace. Sophia gathered her pots and salt Amanthe brought her from the house. Tiny crystals of coarse salt she kept in a metal can.

Collecting something meant I planned to stay here.

I needed something for water. I stayed at the edge of the people one Sunday, while Madame read from the Bible. The kitchen was down the brick path. They had built an arbor to shelter the path from the rain, so the cook could bring the food hot inside the dining room, Amanthe said.

Léonide, the cook, was listening to the verses. I waited until the food was collected in front, and the people were lining up, and slipped down the path to the kitchen.

A jar of something red on the table. It slid easily into my coat before my feet turned back toward the yard.

In the evening, we helped Philippine, who lived in the room beside us. We sewed summer shifts for the women. Her daughter Amanthe, the housemaid, brought chicken legs she'd hidden in a bag. A feast for April, given by Madame for her friends from Opelousas and Washington.

"L'Africain en la ciprière," Philippine said.

"He ain't close by," Sophia said, biting off thread. "Them Attakapas Indian wouldn't help an African."

Attakapas—the name of the Indians meant Flesh-Eater, everyone whispered. They liked to char their captives, chewing on the thighs.

But the old man Firmin shook his head and said something low. Philippine smiled. "Say his mother Attakapas. Say she never ate him. Only birds."

Amanthe said, "Msieu de la Rosière told about the runaway at dinner, and someone said runaway is a crime against God."

Firmin spat into the fire. While we sewed, he wove baskets from split rush. But tonight his hands, knuckles swollen and black as burned almonds on his thin fingers, were still.

"C'est crime à Dieu, to die," he said. He didn't look at us. He stared into the fire.

But he didn't speak again. Philippine spoke for him. "His father Bambara. Mother Attakapas. Her people sell her when her mother die. Sell her to the French. They work near the fort, for the soldier. Every day his mother leave him with an old woman. Tie him to a chair so can't follow. Every day he stay in the chair, look out the door to see his father and mother work."

The needle made a deep line in my fingertips when I pushed it through the cloth. Firmin spat again into the fire. Flames turned orange where his saliva hissed.

"Soldiers drunk all the time. They fight with the Indians, and one day Attakapas man kill his mother, cut her in front of the soldier. His father cry and cry. He hang in his cabin that night."

Sophia said, "By his hand?"

Firmin nodded.

Philippine said, "Soldier take the father body to the fort. To the judge. Judge say kill yourself crime against God, must be punish. Tie him to a cart and drag him through the street. His face down. They pass the open door where Firmin tie to the chair. Waiting for them."

I tasted salt in my throat. His waist tied, but his hands free, to reach for the air in the doorway?

"Take the body back to the fort and hang him again. Two days. They bring Firmin to see. Then they throw the body in the river."

Firmin stood up, paused in the doorway. "Say then Dieu satisfy." He went outside.

Philippine's hands had never stopped moving, but her stitches were very slow. She said, "He tell me that story before. When someone say life too hard, time to dead himself. That African—Athénaïse?—he don't dead himself. Too mean. He still run."

I ate the jar of stewed tomatoes, the soft, salty flesh sliding down my throat while I stood in the privy. A splinter of silver from the moon, on the wooden floor. I washed the jar quickly with water from the gourd outside, smearing my shoe over the smell that lingered in the ground. Sophia would smell it. Food. Anything.

In the night, I pushed the jar of dried corn into the nest of my cape and laid my arm over the lump.

A crime against God, to run, to die. Where was she, my mother? She believed in her own gods.

I saw her face, her lips folded upon themselves, her brows glistening with sweat like tiny jewels where the moisture caught in the small hairs. I laid the green bones of seed cane in the rows, all day. A thousand thighbones. I pushed the earth over them with the hoe and followed the cart back to the matelas for more cane. The square pile of seed cane was like a raft, floating in the first field, where the men had piled it during the harvest last year.

The cane in my hands was so hard, like a femur, that I couldn't imagine how it would grow. But each joint was already swollen, where the new stalk would sprout. Grass. Sugar. Blood. Bones. I was dizzy when I bent and moved down the row. The sun stayed out longer and longer, and we planted more in the extra daylight. But it rained now, too, and when we walked back from the fields in the rain, our dresses slapping our legs, the bayou rose black and swift.

They said it flowed backward sometimes, depending on storms, tides, or magic. But now that the water moved, now that leaves covered the trees and the cane grew already knee-high, I was nearly ready.

An Indian brought Athénaïse back to Rosière. We saw the back of Athénaïse's head first, as if his face had been erased in the woods. His elbows were bound together by a length of leather while he walked backward into le quartier.

Msieu de la Rosière did not come down to the street. Athénaïse was tied to the oak tree near the bell tower. Baillo and Mirande branded him on the left shoulder with the fleur-de-lis. The law, they shouted loud so we could hear. First time you run, fleur-de-lis on the left shoulder. Second time, hamstring, and fleur-de-lis on the right shoulder. Third time, die. Crime against God.

Ham. String. Doctor Tom had told me it meant the tendon was cut, to hobble someone. Maybe a pig. But this was a man.

What was the name for our meat? Did we have hams?

We stood in front of our doors, as we were told. We looked at the catalpa trees. We could smell the burning meat. Athénaïse said nothing. He stayed at the tree all night, and in the morning, when I looked through the crack in the shutters, he was curled on his side, sleeping, like a child.

When his scar was a shining worm on his skin, he ran again.

This time, he didn't come back. No Indian found him, no dogs.

The small Msieu shouted as we lined up on Sunday that Athénaïse should be a lesson, that he'd been eaten by alligators and garfish for certain, his body reduced to chunks of meat.

"God watches," he said. "God punishes."

I lay awake listening to the hooves, but I could hear the wind. In Céphaline's Bible, she had loved only one line. The wind does what it wants, comes from nowhere, and brings the news over the mountains.

The messenger wind.

My mother heard it, too. It moved from south to north, rustling all the leaves, making scudding sounds across the road.

She wouldn't have given up.

I had a jar full of dried corn and a gourd for my water. I prayed that no rats chewed through the cloth to find the food.

Maybe Sophia didn't love Fronie the same way my mother loved me, but her finger didn't hesitate to push the best piece of meat into Fronie's mouth.

Madame Bordelon would die in her bedroom, waiting for her time again with Céphaline. In their là-bas. What if she killed herself? I thought suddenly. Was that a crime against God? Would her body be hung for punishment? Or because she belonged to herself, was she allowed to choose her time to die?

I knew Mamère had not chosen her time. I had been gone five

months. I knew south and north from the sun and the moving water. Athénaïse had run on foot. I would take a boat.

Twice when we had come back from the far field past the bayou and bridge, I saw footprints in the mud near the bank, where a boat had been moored. The litter of discarded feathers meant someone had brought geese.

Every day, ashes trembled black near my hoe. We moved them into the earth once they were still and cool. When it rained, our dresses were spattered with mud and ash. We took off the cloth and sat near the fire in our blankets, and when the mud dried, we scraped it off in clots onto the floor. We pushed it outside, where the rainwater melted it into a pool under the house, and I imagined the earth rising higher and higher until the wooden floor oozed mud between the cracks.

The rainwater collected in barrels under our eaves. The water moved inside my brain. The water left me. I rinsed the earth from our clothes. The particles left the threads.

The wash water held the earth from our feet and hems, and we threw it outside, where it dried and joined us again in the morning.

The bayou rose and fell when it rained, when the sun shone, when we passed it on the way to the fields. Where were the water gods? *Faro*? Only in the ocean? Which god watched me, with these buckets and dippers and iron tubs holding mud?

I kept plans in my brain, stored somewhere along those wrinkles I remembered from Doctor Tom's jar. But the day I saw the moss boats, the gray tangles piled high, a stab of pain went behind my eyes. The empty sockets of my skull. My mother's hands and mine in the moss when it lay in soft piles.

We walked back to the house. Philippine had cooked her own corn early. I could smell the wild onion she'd put in the meal. Her daughter Amanthe was visiting le quartier. She told us, "Two men argue with Msieu up there, bring all that moss to sell, but Msieu tell them cure it first and bring it back—my people too busy for moss."

It was my turn to grind our corn, and I didn't even think. Sophia and the others stayed outside. I took my other dress off the peg, rolled it with my clothespins into a bundle, and tied it to me with my apron strings. I wrapped the jar of corn and the empty gourd into my cape, turning away from Fantine's shelf of small things—broken gourd with shiny insides, pretty pieces of bark, stones.

Her brothers were racing in the street, and people cheered them on. I walked behind the privies, to the narrow ditch where they were perched. The ditch ran to the little bayou in Msieu's woods.

The smell of our leavings was strong in the ditch. The rain washed our dirt all the way to this water.

At the bayou, a smaller pirogue trailed behind the larger chalan boat, which held high piles of moss. I took large handfuls of moss and dropped them into the pirogue, and then I got in, untied the rope, hunched myself into the moss up to my waist. It was high enough to hide me if someone saw the boat. The sun was hot red in the trees. I picked up the paddle. The pirogue slid fast down the narrow bayou.

If someone shot me, in my skull, or in my heart hitting the bone in front of it so hard, then my body would float down the water anyway. What did it matter now, how I got there? Là-bas?

The moss was blooming. The first time I saw the tiny lavender flowers at the end of a curl—three tongues of bloom, small as a clothespin doll's would be—I was six. The flowers went under the boiling water in Mamère's washpot, and her wooden paddle held them under for a long time.

Bayou Rosière entered Bayou Courtableau near Washington, the town with the large boat landing. Amanthe often talked about what traders could bring up from Washington and what they had to take by cart instead, like an armoire.

If another boat passed me, it would be a trader, an Indian, or someone looking for slaves. But not yet for me. Not yet. They thought I was grinding corn—or in the privy—or in the woods.

The boat moved in dark water, paddle turning the ripples silver. I prayed that no one else was bringing moss, prayed that I would hear anyone approaching. Branches dangled in the current. I needed a story. If the boat made it past the plantations that lined Bayou Courtableau, with the sun now red as embers between the tree trunks, I would try to pass the same way the men had brought me. Then the Atchafalaya? The swamp.

Someone would see me, before then. Someone would have to take me through the swamp. I would have to pay with my skin to get back to New Orleans, before the bayous went south to the Barataria and the camps run by Lafitte. Lafitte's privateers would sell me or keep me there, like the ocean-eyed woman who had brought me the food.

The trees were lit from behind as if on fire. All the msieus. Tall and fat and small and deadly. Fingers and red eyes and boats.

I kept to the left bank of the bayou. No one would be looking for me yet. The moss-sellers were having coffee with Msieu and Madame now. They would argue about price and then go down to the boat and see the pirogue gone.

Sophia would lose her meat, for losing me. Losing my body. And suddenly I knew I would miss Fantine, her soft voice and her huge cheeks, her touch on my shoulders when we were in line.

I slowed the pirogue too much, and the boat shuddered sideways in the current. Water splashed onto the moss at my knees. A new current was pulling toward the left, a bend of wider water. Bayou Courtableau. Heading south.

The water pulled me of its own strength. The darkness was indigo now, the color of Mamère's piece of cloth. The mosquitoes were thick around my eyes. I pulled the pirogue to the bank near a root and held on while I slid mud thick and slimy like mucus over my face and arms, the way men did when hunting at night.

The mud dried into a mask over my cheeks and around my lips. My mouth pressed tight like Mamère's. My face the color of hers.

The only light was directly ahead of me, a faint blue stripe painted on the black water as if on a snake's back. The new moon had risen above the trees. It was very thin, a rim of white plate peering from dirty dishwater sky. The banks and trees beside me were silent, until men's laughter echoed far behind me. Like barking.

I paddled closer to the side, looking for anywhere to hide, any break in the trees. There were pauses in the laughter, places where the bayou bent and the sound was muffled. Then an eddy pulled at the nose of the boat, leading past a caved-in place in the bank.

A frayed rope. I tied the boat to the huge root dangling from the cave-in. Please don't let the bank fall on me now, I prayed, looking up. Là-bas. Please. I have nothing to show you. Nothing.

The water was black. *Faro.* The gods of water. Please. Here is my hair. My hair. I slid off my tignon and felt the mosquitoes settle on my forehead. I pulled hairs from the nape of my neck, felt the skin holding and then the prickle of hurt. Baby hairs, Tretite used to call them. They dropped from my fingers into the water. Here. Please.

Sell myself. Ask for money or offer diversion on their journey south. But when they were finished, they might kill me anyway. So they wouldn't have to feed me.

They were closer now. Creaking of wood. A big boat or raft. Several voices. From de la Rosière?

I lay flat and covered myself with the moss. My neck a collar of dried mud, my face stiff, my hair full of mosquitoes.

"Somebody leave a boat."

"No, somebody hunting."

"Right there?"

"Picking moss. Look." The men spoke the rough French of Acadian trappers and hunters.

"We can use another boat. And whatever he got in it."

"I can't use no buckshot in my face. Maybe one them Attakapas. With a knife."

"We got this load of skins now. Can't use that small boat."

"Maybe he got skins in there."

"Maybe Attakapas, and he skin you. Eat you at midnight."

But their voices were past now, drifting, muffled, through the hair covering my ears.

I had wet myself, and the liquid mixed with the water in the boat to smell sour and sharp. The mud on my fingers cracked. The nape of my neck stung.

My heart. It wasn't a small burned muscle. It bloomed and then shrank. The pain breathed inside my chest. The heart inside Doctor

Tom's office, so long ago. Mine had burst. The blood warmed that channel behind the long bone. I would lie here and drown in my own blood and waste and the bayou water soaking into my skirt. The water gods had chosen liquid for me.

The moon moved.

I closed my eyes. My heart.

When my teeth tore at my fingers, the skin renewed itself. Meat. Each time something happened, my heart hurt so badly that there must be a tear, a gash. Did the heart repair itself? Were the scars raised and shiny like those on our skins?

They could kill me like a fox and strip my skin and sell it to someone who would lie on the flatness and force himself inside it. Or hang me on the door and my skin would lean against it like Sophia while they pushed at me.

I still couldn't move. Rustlings in the woods, movement in the water, and night birds in the branches. Finally my stomach beat hard with hunger, not my heart, and I reached for the jar of dried corn.

Holding three kernels in my mouth for a long time, I tried to cook them with my saliva. Hot liquid. My teeth worked the dried corn. I was an animal now.

Some of the mud fell from my lip into my mouth and settled onto my tongue, under the corn. The corn rested on my tongue—the stove of my mouth. I couldn't see the moon at all.

A rope. A rope was looped around my neck. Loose and then tightened.

Crime against God. I tried to sit up. They would kill me and then punish my body.

The rope scratched my throat, pulled from behind. I tried to hold the sides of the pirogue. The sky was purple now. The trees were not a wall. Whoever was behind me pulled steadily.

The water was black and smooth. No one would punish my body. It wasn't theirs. It belonged to my mother. Then God. Là-bas. I rolled over the side of the boat into the bayou.

The rope went slack. I worked my fingers between it and my skin.

But the water pulled me, too. My eyes opened. Particles floated past me. I breathed the water through my nose. The water in my hair, like floating in Mamère's washtub when I was small. I had never floated since then. My mouth opened. The water entered all my passages. I would see Mamère. Mamère?

Wood hit me on the back. Then my hair was pulled hard. My arm wrenched as I was pulled up into a boat.

One hand held my hair, one hand hit me in the chest and belly. Pushed hard. The water came from my nose and mouth.

An Indian man studied me, holding my hair and the rope. His fingers twisted my hair to turn me back onto my stomach, and he put one foot on my back as he paddled.

We bumped into my pirogue, and he reached over. My corn. My bundle. My clothespins and dress and tignon.

He put them down and tied my hands behind my back, then pulled me over with my hair. My forehead burned. My mouth was full of iron.

His eyes were black as pot bottoms. He was the same man who had brought back Athénaïse. He tied my feet to a ring set in the bottom of the boat and put his rifle over his legs and began to paddle again.

I couldn't move. Only my head. The last of the water fell from my mouth onto my chest.

We floated down the bayou for a long time. No houses. No town. No other people in the light when the forest turned green. A great heron lifted when we passed a bend in the water. Forever I would be propelled down roads of water while birds flew away with annoyance in the snap of their wings.

Barataria. Back to Azure. Just take my skin. Take my hair and sell it to France. Céphaline said they needed hair in Paris for wigs. I will grow it again, and you can cut it and sell it. Over and over. I can be a crop.

I couldn't turn to see him. I wasn't a crop. The minute he untied me, I would take his gun. Or make him shoot me. I would shoot myself if I could get the gun.

We entered smaller bayous, wound through water oaks and then cypress until faint hammering echoed through the trees.

The pirogue stopped at a raft of cypress trunks. Beyond them was a clearing, where a white man in a boat pointed a long rifle toward the sky but stared at eight black men up to their waists in murky water, swinging axes in the cypress trees.

The Indian whistled.

The rifle dropped, and the man swung around to point it at us. Reddish beard and blackened teeth when he grinned. A crushed hat, a smear of mud around his eyes like a raccoon, but the fingers holding the gun were white.

"A favorable expedition, I see," he shouted, and motioned for the Indian to bring me in.

I had never heard a voice like his. Rolling and slurring. He spoke English, but not like Doctor Tom.

The Indian man never spoke.

The white man said, "Where did you run from, dear?"

I sat on the ground in front of a low shed with four doors. An Indian woman came from a palmetto-thatched house nearby. She said something in another language to the Indian man. She held a rifle of her own and nodded toward the black men in the swamp. The sounds of axes had lessened.

The white man said, "I don't want to hear those guttural Attakapas words, Sally." He pointed and she got into the pirogue with the gun.

"Not all day, dear," he said to me, and slapped me across the face.

"I didn't run. I belong to Msieu de la Rosière," I said, trying to remember all the English words. I hadn't spoken English in a long time. "He sent me to gather moss."

"With corn." He held up my bundle.

"I like to eat corn."

"You hadn't gathered much, then, dear?"

"I fell asleep."

The Indian man sat nearby with his own gun, watching.

"Rosière is north by five miles or so," the man said. "Surely there are plenty of trees close to there for moss. You see, Joseph finds people when they run. Not when they gather moss for a few hours."

I didn't know if he would hit me again. Blood coated my teeth. Either he would use me or kill me. It didn't matter.

"How long have you been gone?"

"A few hours."

He slanted his head to study my dress, my hands. Bayou mud clung to my face and neck. "You've been working in the fields, dear. What else can you do?"

I didn't answer. I waited for him to hit me or tear my dress. Hera said when Msieu Bordelon bought her, the trader made her strip, and Msieu looked away and said, "How many children?" She said the trader told Msieu, "Pinch the milk parts and guess."

This man slapped me harder and said, "This is your job?"

More blood trickled onto my teeth. It tasted just as it did when I tore my own skin.

"To act as though you are above speaking to a man? Do they then fuck you with a vengeance, dear?"

The bayou water still inside me rose and flew from my mouth, landing on his boots.

"Tie her up, then, Joseph," he said to the Indian man. "Strip her and throw some water on her, for she stinks. If she just ran last night, they won't have been looking long. How long's the other Rosière nigger been here?"

He must mean Athénaïse. I tried to look at the men cutting in the ciprière, but the Indian man jerked me toward the long, low shed.

They left me chained to a ring in the first room, the wooden door propped open. My clothes were in a pile beside me, and the water dried on my skin. I curled into a baby-circle with my back to the door and heard voices pass and fade, heard the axes ringing and men shouting and cursing, heard the white man laughing. I never heard the Indian woman, though she left a dish of sagamite near me, as if for a dog.

My skin. The splintered boards of the wall were pocked with termite holes. Céphaline's skin had betrayed her. Killed her. Her skin hung on the wall of her mother's bedroom, or in the downstairs parlor, perfect and white in her portrait.

After a time, voices rose in a clamor. Men were in the yard. I smelled meat. Maybe Joseph had killed the white man and roasted his thick thighs.

I sat up and tied my tignon around my chest. Gooseflesh. Like plucked birds. My dress was wrinkled and dirty as cleaning rags. Chains on my wrist and ankle. I could only tie the sleeves around my waist, so that my dress was an apron to cover part of me.

My neck bent when I tried to look out the open door. Doctor Tom said the animals whose necks didn't bend had a hard time in life. My fingers. My teeth chewed there until I had a piece of myself to hold in my mouth.

Eight men sat around the cooking fire. The tallest—his back with grin-scar on one shoulder, fleur-de-lis on his other. Athénaïse. He'd left twice, and the Indian hunter found him twice.

The Indian woman came in to take my dish. She had a small pistol in her waistband. Her hair was straight, to her shoulders, and a faint line was tattooed from each corner of her mouth to her jaw, like a strange dripping of blue. Her eyes were blacker than the water.

She unlocked the chains, left the one on my wrist, and led me to the trees behind the shed. When I was finished, she brought me back toward the fire and chained me to a post. The trees turned dark.

The men spoke in low voices, French and African and English. The Indian man was gone. Athénaïse kept his eyes on the last light hanging silver in the sky, the only man not staring at me.

"Have you decided what it is you're good for, dear?" The white man threw animal bones into the fire.

When I didn't speak, he said, "Let me help you decide. I left Ireland with nothing, dear, just as you ran with nothing yesterday. But now I own this little enterprise. Sally, though, isn't the best of cooks. And as she's my wife, I can't really let her sell her other useful wares, dear, but you, on the other hand, could make yourself comfortable here, cooking and washing. All these men are working for money, to buy themselves freedom. We take them to New Orleans when they've earned it. Work for a year, and you'll be free to go. And if you want to provide other services, the men can pay you. I'll deduct it from their wages, dear."

The Indian woman spat into the fire.

The sagamite rose in my throat. The white man's boots were black with mud, like a second skin over the leather. The black men were barefoot. He drank from a flask, again and again, before lighting his pipe. Some of the other men had cigars or pipes as well, and two of them drank from a gourd.

I had to gamble. It would be safer to tell him a story away from the other men.

"I can tell you inside," I said softly, and he rose and motioned to the Indian woman. She unchained me again and led me back into his room. He shut the door and chained me to the rings.

"Don't think to try anything brilliant," he said.

The smell of alcohol wafted from his skin, and the burned meat on his fingers.

"Msieu de la Rosière bought me in New Orleans, just a while ago," I said. "I'm a—" What was the English word?

"You're a high yellow bitch," he said softly.

"Cadeau," I said. "Gift. A gift for his son, when he returns from Paris. I am—untouched. Msieu de la Rosière will pay you."

"You can't be free from your master." His voice was soft and reasonable. "But if you work hard, you can be free here."

Behind him, the Indian woman shook her head slightly, twice.

I said, "Take me back, and he will pay you. I wasn't running, just gathering moss and got lost. I left my jewelry and my good dresses at Rosière. I am not to wear them until I am given as the gift."

He swallowed again from the flask and pulled the tignon down with his walking stick. He moved my breasts with the tip of the stick. "How does he know you're untouched?"

My eyes focused on the wall behind him, making him a blur before me. "Msieu checks me. With his fingers."

"Goddamn it. If Joseph takes you back, and you tell about that other nigger, and they come for him, he'll hang. You tell about me, I'll offer de la Rosière so much money he'll have to sell you. And I'll make you wish you had hung." He drank again and stared at my breasts. "You'd be better off here. The men will pay you. They won't argue."

He dropped the empty flask and said loudly, far too loudly for our conversation, "I'm first. And then everyone else can pay."

He wanted the other men to hear.

He put his head down to study the opening to his trousers, and the Indian woman named Sally came up behind him and pulled a sash around his neck. She tightened it quickly, and he fell to the floor.

I put my arms around my chest. She lifted her chin, and I understood that she meant for me to wait. She pulled him to the bed, laid him on his side, and his mouth sagged open like dead fish. She slid the sash from under his throat, and he drew in a huge shuddering breath and remained unconscious.

But she backed herself into the wall near the bed and knocked against it, several times, grunting and moving against the wood, and I thought she had gone mad. Her face was as blank as if she were grinding corn. She screamed.

Then one man laughed outside, and one spoke in a murmur low and long, and I knew what she was doing. The men thought they heard his pleasure. They thought their turn would come tomorrow.

I hid my face in my arms until she unlocked the chain, careful not to clink the metal, and put my clothes before me. When I was dressed, she opened the door, holding the rifle, and motioned to the men at the dying fire. They breathed heavily, and one said, "Not time for sleep yet," but she pointed the rifle at him, and the men filed into the other room. She followed them and then fastened the huge padlocks on the door.

One man cursed inside, and another whispered like boiling water.

Then she handed me my bundle. When we had walked silently, far into the ciprière on a narrow path, she took a candle from her pocket and lit it. Her eyes were so black that the small flame danced in her pupils when she leaned toward me. After what he'd said about her, maybe she would kill me herself now.

Her throat worked and she spoke awkwardly in French, not English. "No one is free," she said. We stood near pools of black water and huge cypress stumps, some so old their centers had collapsed into hollows like washpots. No one had been back here for a long time—the brush caught at my skirts, and she slashed at vines with her rifle.

"Jamais," she said. Never. "They are never free." She pointed to the ground, and then held up eight fingers.

In the trembling circle of candlelight, the earth was rucked up in places. Footsteps of a giant who'd traveled in the woods. A water god.

I bent closer and saw an edge of cloth.

Graves.

The Irishman pretended to take the men to New Orleans when they'd worked long enough, but he killed them here. She saw my face and nodded. Her voice was flat and harsh. "Two years of work. Then he cuts with the knife." She ran her fingernail across my throat. "No shot. The other men can't hear. My brother hunts for new ones."

The Indian man stepped out of the trees, and I screamed. She moved forward so quickly that the candle caught the edges of my hair, and she clapped her hand over my mouth.

The smell of burned hair made me choke and pull against her. Now they would kill me and burn my muscles for meat.

"No, no sounds," she whispered. "No screams." Her brother came closer to me, his mouth held tight as a sickle blade.

She took her hand away. "You can't stay here. No other women. I know how to work him." She put her finger on her own chest.

I spat the burned-hair taste from my mouth. "Why do you stay?"

She leaned close to me, breath of clear water, somehow sweet. "He is my husband. He has papers. Wife. My uncle sold my brother for a slave, but he sold me for a wife. We cannot go. Our names, the papers—we were in jail."

She said something in her language to her brother, and he came forward, holding a piece of cloth and a rope.

To me, she said, "He takes you back for gold. And I say to my husband that you ran." She pulled my wrist up. "I want money. Gold money. For me. For New Orleans."

He was tying my hands again, and I turned to her, the rope burning my skin. "I can—"

"No," she said again, and sliced the cloth into my open mouth, tying it tight behind my head, my hair wound into the knot until tears stung my eyes. "Don't run again. Money is you."

Her brother tied another piece of cloth around my eyes. The current of the bayou pushed gently under the boat. He took me back the way I had come. The water gods far underneath me were silent, curled at the bottom, only watching the wood slip past above them.

The drivers, Mirande and Baillo, left both pieces of cloth tied. It was just daylight, because the sun was barely warm on my head and my shoulders where my dress was down.

I couldn't see the doorways but heard people gathering. No one was cooking yet. The single fire I smelled was the one the drivers had built for me, behind us in the street.

"The old man says she's valuable because of the looks, but what of her brain? He said she's been slow in the head since the day he bought her," Baillo said behind me. I heard the ringing ache of iron in the coals. I made myself see Mamère's fireplace.

"They do the face elsewhere. Like the old man. Look at his face."

"That's foolish, for financial reasons, and inhumane, for religious reasons," Mirande said. "The old man said lightly. Don't hold it hard as for the African. Didn't teach him anything."

I heard it only as a falling away of ash. A sparkle.

Then I tasted black, saw black, felt the sear on my shoulder. Blacksmith. Molten. Red in my throat.

I lay in the dirt. A tiny sharp stone was embedded in my cheek. My dress was put up over my shoulders. I heard breathing in all the doorways. My blood was moving to my shoulder, to the burn, the blood surging forward and then pulled away, gathered again there, beating hard. Pulse. Pulse. Trying to find the problem.

The blood tries to clean the wound, Doctor Tom said.

Sophia's sharp fingers took my wrist.

"If she runs again, you are responsible," Baillo said, and she pulled me inside.

"You run again, I find you and kill you, me," she hissed, pouring cold water on the burn, then tying a piece of salt pork there with the cloth from my mouth. She studied the material for a moment. Red trade cloth. "Where this from?"

My whole body felt hot now. How did the burn travel through my blood? Is that what blood did, take heat everywhere to disperse it?

"Where?" she spat, wrapping the cloth under my arm, over my shoulder, around the meat.

"The Indian found me. Same one found Athénaïse. Hunter."

"That was my meat," she whispered in my ear. "On your shoulder now. Time to work. You run, I kill you."

In the field, my hoe took the small grass. Unwanted grass. No money grass. The hoe moved the earth in rows around the other grass. The India grass. The sugar grass. The money grass.

The sweat dripped in my eyes. Salt. Seawater. My tears. My blood. Salt inside. Salt meat melting on my skin. Meat tied to meat.

Flesh. Sophia wants flesh. The Indian didn't want my flesh. Wanted money. Gold flesh. Doctor Tom said the wound from a duel rotted in a man's leg once, and he cut it off. What did you do with the leg? Céphaline asked. They were in the parlor. She was supposed to play the piano. But she asked him about legs, skulls, eyes.

His family took it, Doctor Tom said. I don't know what they did with it. Strange to bury somebody piece by piece, eh? His leg could hold the spot until the rest of him was ready.

My shoulder cooked. The passages. We eat the meat, sugar juice, dried corn. We move the earth around the good grass. We cut down the tree. We catch the chicken and burn the flesh.

Someone had cut off the heads of the men I'd seen along the river when the boat took me from Azure. What did they do after they mounted the heads on poles? Why waste the body? The body was gold. Why not dry strips of leg and arm in the sun, with salt? Hardtack. Humantack.

Pickle.

The sun beat down on the rows. Salt. Water. Falling on the grass that waved chest-high, would grow over our heads until we cut it down, burned the leaves, and rolled the bones in the grinders.

Fantine walked home beside me. She led me to the tub, untied the salt pork from my back, and threw it into the fire, where it hissed.

She helped me step into the washtub. The water felt as if it etched ice on my burn. A flower. A flower of—of what?

Fantine poured water onto my head and rubbed soap, then a few drops of sweet oil into my hair. She began to untangle the snarls with her fingers and a wooden comb.

"Only way is get somebody love you," she said softly.

Outside, Sophia said loudly, "He give me a chain to lock up at night. So she don't run. She like a wild animal and who knew?"

Fantine said, "The men look. But you won't look back." She stretched a section of hair into a black web on my arm.

"Get them love you, you get things. A place. Some oil for your hair. A dress."

I looked up at her. "I don't want love."

"Sophia don't want love. But she get what she want."

The little bones lay on the table. "I want to go home. If you love, you get a baby. I don't want a baby."

"She stand up when he love her," Fantine whispered. "I stand up."

Fantine's mouth curved. Her cheeks rose dark and full like velvet pillows when she smiled.

Basile kissed those cheeks until Fantine's head fell back. So he could have her neck. But no man had ever looked at me that way. I meant something different to them—Christophe, the men in New Orleans, the fingers, the boat, the white man in the shed while he flicked my breast with his stick. They wanted to clench their fists in my hair and pull my head back themselves.

"You bright. You get anything you want."

Take but one candle to light a room, Mamère had said to Hera. I closed my eyes.

I could wash my dress and start over and pray.

Sophia came inside. "Get out there and finish."

Fantine said, "She look pretty now." A new edge shone hard in her voice. She wanted me to use my brightness.

"She look pretty at night when she chain up. She run again, Msieu blame me." Sophia made her voice thin and low as roots along the floor. "You girls only here cause nobody want you. Nobody have room. I only feed you. You are little animals, and I lock the gate."

A bruise. A contusion, Doctor Tom had told Céphaline the name. The blood rushes to the site of injury, he said, then collects there and the ill humor of the place turns the blood black.

Under the skin, she said.

The skin merely holds the liquids inside and protects the organs.

How would you know, she said, if someone black—like Marie-Thérèse—had a bruise?

Doctor Tom shrugged. You could touch the skin, feel for swelling.

But Moinette—you could see under her skin.

Ah, yes. Half white. Maybe she would have half a contusion. Then he placed the leech on her temple, just at the hairline. Be still, my love. We bleed to restore the balance. Your poor blood is rushing to help your head, but there is too much. Your poor head aches. I know.

My shoulder. I lay on my shelf, on my side with the branded part in the air, and blood rushed to the burn and then rushed away. Blood was hot. That wouldn't help. You can't have cool blood. Cool blood is a hard shell over a cut. Then I could chew it. Cool blood bread on my teeth.

So hot. Dead skin. Burned like Mamère's from the fires and lye. Fire made a raised scar. Lye made a pink hole.

A steam burn on Mamère's forearm, from a kettle—then, after a week, the whole piece of dried skin lifted off, thin and crackling.

Leather.

My body shivered around my burn, which took all the heat of my blood for a time, then gave it back.

Underneath the burn, Mamère's skin had been pink as a puppy tongue, smooth as glass. I seized her arm each day to look at it. She let me. She said nothing. Every day, more etching appeared, the wrinkles of dryness, new skin tinted with smoke and dirt—with the very air—until that large oval was only a bit lighter than the rest of Mamère.

I didn't know what my skin did, at the burn. I couldn't see it. Sophia dressed it with lard and cloth. Under my shift, it dried and the skin fell off, the fleur-de-lis crumpled into flakes of my body that disappeared into the canerows and yard dirt and washed into the cracks of the wooden floor.

At night, Sophia locked the cuff around my ankle and bolted the chain to the ring Gervaise had put in the wall beside my shelf. He knew metal-work. He brought Sophia a new spider pot to hang over the coals. Tiny bones—wings and legs—floated on the broth.

She unlocked me in the morning. I ate the boiled corn, remembering the hot liquid of my saliva working the stone kernel.

I hoed the grass. I heard Fantine and Basile in the trees. I heard Sophia and Gervaise at the wall. The rain dripped into the chimney, and I heard Philippine next door speak to her husband, Firmin.

His cheeks were scarred with *V.* Voleur. Thief. And the same flower that had healed to a scar my fingers could trace.

By the fall, Gervaise was making cane knives with a small curving hook. And he forged the new brand Msieu de la Rosière instructed him to fashion—a rosebud shaped like a diamond, with a curving stem and two slanted lines for leaves. It would brand slaves, if necessary.

Gervaise showed it to Sophia. She said the brand was my fault.

Amanthe came from the house to tell us what Msieu told his wife about the brand. "Say he lost one and almost lost Moinette. Say he see run in people eyes. Say you show the horse the whip, sometime you don't have to beat him."

Sophia shouted at me, "Msieu say if one more run, he brand us all. Round up like cattle." She caught my arm. "If Fronie get burn because of you, I hurt you worse than fire."

I jerked my arm from her. "There is nowhere to run," I said. It was true. At the edges of the canefields, I imagined I saw the Indian, in the sudden wash of water at the bayou's edge or in a shiver of branches in the forest.

I pulled each stalk toward me and hit the base with the knife. We cut it blade by blade, like cutting someone's beard by pulling each hair separate and clipping it. The horses pulled their grass from the ground near their stable, their teeth sharp as our knives.

And it was clear to me, then, that every free person I met—Indian, white, African—would only sell me or use me as an animal. My skin. Hide. Pounds of money—my fat and fingers and breasts.

Mamère was wrong.

I belonged to anyone who could catch me or buy me.

The cane stalks stripped of leaves, their joints like knuckles when we loaded them onto carts. All around me—the knocking cut, then the whisper-slash of trimming, the rough swipe of the sharpening stone. At the end of the row, glints of water beyond the piled-high banks.

No one would ever love me but her. She wasn't wrong. I would be caught, sold, traded. I would never belong to anyone. I would never love anyone. Her fierce prayers rose each night and drifted into the water, the rivers and bayous and the rain, and stayed damp in my hair.

No one ran. We were too tired to walk. We woke when the bell sounded in the dark, ate cold cornmush from the night before, and walked behind the cart. The cane blocked all the moonlight, rustling over our heads.

The wall of grass was alive, moving in the wind as the sun rose. We lined ourselves before it, each with an entire row to cut.

Again. Again. Again. Like a puppet Céphaline had made with her governess once. The legs moving at the knee, the arms lifting and falling, the strings of ropy muscle.

Every day. Even Sunday. We stopped working at three on Sunday and went to the house for our food, with our clothes furred by dust clinging to cane juice, splinters in our hair.

Madame couldn't see us anyway. She said a prayer over our bowed heads. "Let the harvest continue safely and prosperously for all."

At night, when the December wind blew cold, Philippine sat by our fire and said, "She don't pray for us next year."

Sophia frowned. "She going?"

Philippine nodded. "Amanthe say she go to Paris for her eyes. In spring. She stay with the son. The Msieu sister come to run his house now. She order new furniture, new curtains. She can see. Amanthe washing all that dust Madame never see. At New Year, have a party. Show all them people in Opelousas and Washington the house."

In the morning, I stayed in the woods to relieve my stomach. The barrel water was sour. The sky was bitterly cold, as it had been when I first arrived. The air hung like glass in the branches above me.

At the path, Baillo was waiting on his horse, his yellow eyes rimmed with red, his face unshaven. "I haven't forgotten you. Slow in the mind, but fast when you try to run."

I was silent, as always. The words that I kept in my throat and chest swirled now like silt on the bottom of the bayou when I'd walked there for a moment, before the Indian pulled me up.

Baillo stared at me. "My father was a soldier when France came here. Seventeen sixty-nine. They never fed soldiers. He left one day to trap birds in the forest. When he came back, they said he had run. They tied him to a board and cut him in four pieces. The law."

He nudged me forward with his canestalk, pushing at my hip, pointing me back to the field.

My words wouldn't stay inside. "What did they do with him?"

"They threw the pieces of him in the river." He sighed and rested the canestalk on my shoulder, without pushing me. "But you—you are safe in the field. And you are fed."

I hoed the grass and heard the birds above me.

When we walked back, over the bridge, the water was black as oil around the cypress stumps. There were no gods in the water here. Only in Africa. In the bayou and Barataria and the cypress swamps and the Mississippi, which raced brown and wide past Azure, there were only pieces of flesh and the animals that ate us. The fish and alligators and even the tiny shrimp that crawled along the silt and mudbanks. They chewed our flesh, and it went into their own black sandy veins, and then they let the liquid left of us back into the current, which carried us away.

Five JARDIN BLANC

Madame Pélagie was her name. That first week, she called for me all night, every night. I lifted myself from the pallet of two blankets Amanthe had made for me in the hallway outside Madame Pélagie's room. She was propped on three pillows, her thick red-brown hair wrapped into curling rags by my nervous fingers, her eyes fastened on the window or the wall. She couldn't sleep. Her sewing lay on the coverlet beside her, even though it was after midnight.

She wanted scissors. A biscuit because it had been so long since dinner. A new candle. A book she had seen on Msieu's shelf.

Water. It was so hot here, she said, even in January. An hour later, she called me to empty the pot. I can't sleep with the smell, she said.

By the seventh day, I wanted to put the pot over her head. My eyes ached as if they rolled in sand. But the cuts on my hands, from the cane, were healed already. She slept all morning, and the cook, Léonide, roused me at dawn for my chores.

New candles for the dining room and parlor. Breakfast for Msieu, who would ride the fields or travel to town. Then begin the midday meal, Madame de la Rosière's favorite. Pinch the heads and shells from the shrimp—hold the clear, curved case in my palm. Try to think of the word Céphaline had used. *Carapace.*

Don't think about the water now. Not in the hallway, the planks of shining wood stretched under me where I lay on the blanket, hearing Madame Pélagie call high and light like singing.

Her clothes were hung carefully in the armoire. I had arranged them from light color to dark, from finery to ordinary.

I had a new dress, too, a plain blue from Amanthe taken in at the waist and shoulder for me.

"I want a bright one," Madame Pélagie had said when she'd seen us all lined up for the New Year, seen us all receiving our cloak and one set of clothing. "That one."

"But that one doesn't know the house." Madame de la Rosière squinted toward me.

"She will know me. I will train her myself."

My old brown dress hung in the room next to the kitchen, where Amanthe and Léonide slept.

"They don't sleep inside with us," Madame said.

"C'est de la folie! What if I need something in the night?"

"We are finished with the day at ten. Then Amanthe and Léonide go to the kitchen for the evening."

"My brother has no valet?"

Madame shook her head, and Pélagie said, "This one sleeps in the hallway near my door until I become accustomed."

Our carapaces. Our coverings. Pélagie measured coverings and hair and shoes and vases and carriages. Like the Auzennes, but not like them. I remembered Céphaline when she watched the Auzennes arrive in their carriage. Madame Pélagie was twenty-five years old, but her voice didn't have the sly, mean threads of those girls.

She was afraid. I lay near the glint of candlelight under her door. She moved restlessly on the chair, her bare feet brushing the floor while she sewed. She was here from France, to stay with her older half brother, Msieu. From the way she watched doors and paced at night, she was afraid of the dark hallways, like me.

On the seventh night, I filled the pitcher downstairs. The full moon rose over the roof. I missed Fantine's bubbling-water laugh. Was Sophia awake now, too, waiting for Gervaise to return with a small animal she could tear to pieces with her teeth?

The rainwater from the barrel smelled black and mossy. My mother was in her chair, the moon in her open window.

I closed Madame Pélagie's door and sat up against the hallway wall. The moonlight was a silver knife down the canal of wood that Amanthe and I had polished that morning.

I imagined myself Mamère. Watching over myself, not sleeping, planning a way to keep myself safe.

I had been gone one year. Did she still stay awake, waiting for me? The smell of burned cane hung in the eaves here at Rosière, just as it had every year at Azure. The sugar had been packed into hogsheads and sent on the cart to the boat landing at Washington. Molasses dripped from the barrels, made glistening buttons on the dirt. I bent to touch a drop—already covered with dust. The smell of molasses would forever make me remember the cargo hold, and the darkness.

On New Year's Day, we lined up for Msieu, who wrote down name, age, and health. When he came to me, standing after Sophia and Fronie, he hesitated. "You have been here a year now," he said.

"Oui, msieu."

"You are not going to run again."

"Non, msieu."

"When I bought you, I was told that you dressed hair. You will come here in the morning." His finger cut the air.

My ankle had a band of darkened shining skin, smooth as leather when I rubbed there. Tanned.

I would not run. I walked to the house. I saw a rabbit shivering under a bush, waiting for me to pass. When had my mother talked about rabbits? I passed the bell, the house of Mirande and Baillo, their two cows, the hog pens.

"Because my mother die and I was like a little rabbit out there," Mamère had said one night. "Seven or eight. I move with Ama. Ama breathe that smell and die, too. Then we all, Ama children and me, we sleep in one room with the old woman. We call her Tante. So old her eyes like watermelon seed. But she watch us."

That first day, when I reached the edge of the yard, the chinaberry trees were bare, branches like walking sticks reaching for the sky. I stood beside the sweet olive bush. Madame de la Rosière couldn't see well at all now, Amanthe said, but she still knew the keys. The piano music was like white clothes hanging in the trees, billowing. Céphaline's chemises.

Moving like people against my hands as if they were friends, in our clearing, coming to tell me secrets.

No one knew me here, near this porch, in this big house. No one in le quartier. The piano notes went dark and soft. Quavering.

Mo tout seul. Mo tout seul. Christophe used to say that to me, fiercely, in the cane. You can't hurt me. I'm all alone. All alone.

"Look at this," someone said from the porch. A man whose voice I had never heard. "From New Orleans? A daughter of joy."

"Monsieur Antoine!" a woman's voice rose, light and calculated, strange to my ears. "She doesn't look very joyous."

"The joy was in her past. In her creation."

"Monsieur Antoine," a darker, disapproving voice said. Madame de la Rosière. The piano had stopped. "Is that the little mulâtresse? That is not joy. That is licentiousness. And it is not her fault."

"Not her fault, but her bestowal," the man said gently, then went inside, closing a door.

"Come, child," Madame de la Rosière said, her face turned toward the trees.

She wore a new dress, a fine silk with a sheen like oiled skin. Beside her was a younger woman, very beautiful, with red-brown hair lit as if from inside, and skin white and perfect as Céphaline's could never have been, even with the paste.

"Where did you learn to dress hair?" the younger woman said, her eyes moving over my clothes, my hands. "New Orleans?"

"No," I said, and I saw her breast rise with words she would say to send me back to the field. I wanted to be inside the house, to find another route toward New Orleans, toward Azure. "But I was trained by a woman from New Orleans. She learned in Paris."

The beautiful woman nodded.

My skin is a sheath, I thought, laying out Madame Pélagie's clothes from her trunk while she ate in the dining room. Silk, wool, cotton—I tried to remember the receipts for cleaning lotions. The wool coat smelled of animal.

Animals have fur or hide. Mesdames have layers of corset, petticoat, linen chemise, and silk. I stopped at the mirror. My forearms were scarred with the finest white lines from the sharp blades of grass that had whipped around me when I cut down the stalks.

My face was nearly the same as when I left Céphaline's room, but my cheekbones held hollows underneath them. My skull. Cats have cheeks, to hold their whiskers. Mice hold corn there. What are we meant to store? Only smiles? I moved my lips and the bones rose, while the hollows moved.

We store nothing when we are not smiling, I thought.

"Laurent is gone for how long?" Pélagie asked. They sat in the parlor with their embroidery.

Laurent. The name of Msieu de la Rosière.

"Perhaps a month," Madame answered.

I sewed flowers onto new napkins in the hallway just outside the door. It was my place now, my black-painted chair straddling the river of light down the wooden floor. Mamère was right—I tried very hard to make my stitches smaller than an eyelash. Had my eyelashes grown? Did they grow like our hair? I put down the linen square.

Mamère. She had sewn by her fireplace while she waited for me to come back from serving the dinner. I never came back. Was I taller, or were my arms only darker and thinner and marked by cane? My fingers and wrists marked by teeth?

My shoulder marked by fire.

"He is buying cloth in New Orleans?" Pélagie asked. Madame held her linen square close to her fading eyes, as if she were sneezing into a handkerchief.

"Cloth and flour, sugar and oil. Coffee. Slaves. Last year, I asked for a garden man, but Laurent needed to clear the new land."

"A garden man?" Pélagie's voice was soft.

"I cannot plant the garden and move the earth, but I want to be outside. I can still see something there. If you weren't here to distinguish these threads for me, I would burn this in the fire."

"What can you see outside?"

Madame was quiet for a time. "I can see the leaves moving, somehow. The arrangement of the trees. Pale things."

"How many men will he buy? No women?"

"The Americans have made buying slaves nearly impossible. No ships are to arrive from Africa. Laurent and the others go to the Barataria. It is illegal, but the only way. There will be mostly men, he says. The only female he bought last year was Moinette, and not for the house. He doesn't understand why you insist on her here as well as Amanthe. Amanthe has taken care of me for years. Since she was sixteen."

A silence. In it, I heard that Pélagie didn't think Madame was taken care of. Her hair. Her clothes.

"I want one who looks good. Because she is seen with me. And I like the bright one. She's the only bright one you have."

"Laurent says she ran last year."

"But she sleeps fine here," Pélagie whispered.

"The mixed-blood children are proof of wrong," Madame whispered back. "I don't like to see them."

"I am proof of wrong, apparently, because my mother died at my birth. That is what the old women in Lyon told me." Pélagie laughed, high and sweet as cold water. "They said none of the first three girl babies had killed her, and they had all been bald, just like my father. He was sixty-seven when they married. They said when I came, I had a pate of red fur and must have been a child of the devil."

"Pélagie," Madame said. "That's not true."

"What is true is that I never think of Lyon, only of Paris. I will never return to Lyon. I remember a jardin blanc in Paris. A white garden we can make here."

Barataria. In the dark, in the narrow bayou with white-plastered walls and my own hair for a pillow, I remembered the sparkling sand thrown against the cage bars, the scars of the women, the endless roiling of the water.

In Barataria, I had believed I could swim to my mother.

All those nights in Sophia's house, fingering the corn kernels—they would have floated. Dried corn rose in boiling water—the kernels had gone farther down Bayou Rosière than I had.

Madame Pélagie's footsteps whispered. One choice remained: make her happy so she would take me to New Orleans. If I curled each section of her hair into a perfect spiral, if I stitched the rose pattern on the napkins, if I washed her linens to whiteness, she would need me in New Orleans.

Amanthe was accompanying Madame de la Rosière to Paris in June. I would accompany Pélagie, when she went back to Paris. We would dock at New Orleans, and then the boat to Paris would sail south, down the Mississippi. We would pass the places with familiar names. Orange Grove. Les Palmiers. Petit Clair.

At Petit Clair, when I leaped, the current would carry me, and the batture would give me a piece of wood to pull myself to shore amid the swirls of yellow water where eddies circled over a shallow snag, the riverbank where I'd spent hours as a child, watching the boats.

In the pond of light from a candle, I made my stitches smaller.

I wondered why Pélagie was nervous in the house at night with only Madame and me, and the groom, Manuel, who kept watch in the yard. She slept only a few hours. She must have sent a message to the town of Washington and asked for Msieu Antoine, the lawyer who took care of her money when her husband died in Paris.

He had called me a daughter of joy. He inclined his head at me now and said, "I'll be staying in the garçonnière." That was the place for unmarried men and visitors.

Amanthe said, "Take him coffee and prepare the room." She put her hand on my arm. "Do what he asks."

Cadeau. Gift for an afternoon. A lifetime.

The garçonnière and pigeonnière were new and separate buildings on either side of the house. Eight sides on each tower—I tried to remember what Céphaline called eight sides. Octagonal. And diagonal—the brick paths that led to the towers. I had sat folding, and she had spoken around me. Triangular. Parallel. Our lives not parallel. She would not have been a gift. A sale, she said. A trade.

He sat at the ebony-wood desk. He did not look up. I put the tray with coffee and sugar and milk on the desk. Upstairs, where the air was damp over the wooden floor, I made up the three beds, dusted the wash-basin and chamber pot.

"You are from New Orleans?" he asked when I came downstairs. The brick floor was tinged with green. "A mulâtresse such as yourself?"

"No, msieu. Farther south." My hands were crossed over my apron, my eyes on the floor. That was how we were meant to wait.

"Near the Balize, the mouth of the Mississippi? Where all commerce enters the river from the sea?" His lips drew in coffee with a hiss, as if he needed it badly. "Merci." He sounded as if he smiled. "Look up, please."

He was older than Madame Pélagie, younger than Msieu. His eyes were gray with flecks of green—tiny pieces of torn leaf. His beard was narrow, black sleeves reaching down his cheeks to cradle his chin.

If he touched me, I could only comply.

If he made me go upstairs because he thought I was a daughter of joy, if he were from New Orleans, he might take me back there if I was pleasant. I could not care how I left this place.

But he turned to the desk, his back bent so sharply over his writing that the spine showed through his shirt as I left. Dashes of bone.

At dinner, Msieu Antoine said that he had decided to open an office in Opelousas. He asked who ran Rosière when Msieu was gone, asked about Mirande and Baillo, but he never rode his horse down the street to the fields or le quartier.

Night after night, I stayed awake, gliding my hand along the wax of the floor, listening for her footsteps and for his. But he never came at night to seek me, or anyone else. He was not in love with Pélagie. I had read his letters.

It was difficult. It took me some time. I knew many words from Céphaline and Doctor Tom, but at first, it wasn't clear how the words were strung together, the stitching of the smaller words to connect them. Madame Pélagie wrote no letters, only lists of household tasks or things she wished to buy: *Polish moldings and table legs. Launder tablecloths again. Squab, tartes aux fruits.*

But Msieu Antoine covered pages and pages with his ink. I could read only scattered words on those long documents. Arpents of land. Beloved son. Division of estate.

To love. To divide.

How did the words stay inside the skull, in those arrangements? How many words could the brain hold? I did not smile at him while I hung his clean clothes and saw his fingers stained black, moving across the page. Céphaline's brain had been so full of sentences and numbers that her skull pushed out her hair, and her skin pushed out boutons.

Mamère could measure with her eyes bullock's gall and cabbage juice for her recipes. Léonide could judge the fire below the pot with only a glance and tell me to add exactly two pieces of wood.

I had to measure the whites now, their words and eyes and hands.

After dinner, he played cards with Pélagie. He was not in love with her, and he still did not touch me. He studied me, but with nothing in his face except curiosity, as if he studied a species of dog. Alone in the garçonnière, I looked at his letters, in which he complained to his aunt about his love.

Tante Justine: The Americans here in Louisiana have disgusted the Creole French, and the French-born, with their greed and low habits. I know this, and am sorry that the object of my affection was born in Philadephia, but I wish you could overlook citizenship for character.

Companion. A friend. An American.

But the next letter was more than friendship, and he left it unsigned.

It is difficult to pass another month without your company. Your sly asides at the table, your assessments of character flaw. I cannot express how much I miss your fingers in mine.

He loved someone far away. At night, in the hallway, I wrote my own letters, in my head. It was difficult to read without anyone knowing, but to find paper and ink and a place to practice writing?

I think of you every minute. I remember every lesson. I measure things in my head, so no one sees. I will find a way back.

In the mornings, Pélagie stirred much later than anyone else, and the first words she spoke were always the same. "My hair," she said without moving, and I put down the cup of coffee with no sugar or milk on the vanity. Every day the same. She sat in the chair before the mirror. The fourteen curls piled high on her head came down gently into my palm. Scars from the curling tongs of her past. Like silver wood lice on her neck and even two on her ear.

After her hair was finished, and she had powdered her face and I had helped her into a dress, she drank another cup of coffee and went to meet Madame in the dining room.

"How can you not have had a trained laundress?" she began one day, while they sewed for the Paris trip. "Did you see how Moinette has taken care to brighten your chemises?"

Madame nodded. "They smell like rosemary."

"I brought it from Paris. When I heard about your sight."

Then they were silent, and we sewed.

Léonide said, "I don't touch les blancs, me. Hair like spiderweb."

But mine is moss, I thought. Yours is wool. Touching her hair is my task.

We moved about the pantry, in the cool brick-paved area under the house, counting the huge jars of olive oil from France. It was Sunday, and Amanthe had secreted away bits of the roasted chicken from dinner, the splinters of white meat she picked from the breastbone, and spongy pieces of dark meat from behind the back. Madame, Pélagie, and Msieu Antoine had eaten. Amanthe carried the meat wrapped in paper, in her apron pocket.

When we walked to le quartier, I chanted to myself the receipt for cleaning white clothes, because Philippine and Firmin would be glad to see Amanthe, but no one would care whether I had come or not.

Fronie and Fantine were elsewhere with their friends. And Sophia was asleep on her shelf. When I went inside, to touch the place where my coffee beans had been ground into the cracks of the floor, she heard me. Her back was curved like a turtleshell, and she turned her head, opened one eye at me, and then covered her face again with her tignon.

"Opelousas?" Madame said at breakfast. "You and Monsieur Antoine need the carriage for Opelousas? But that is half a day's journey, and it's very rough in places."

"He says I must see the French dressmaker in Opelousas. For Mardi Gras. For the dinners and dances."

"But everything you have is new to the people in Washington and Arnaudville. And to Opelousas."

"A lovely dress from her would show I want to be part of here. This place." Pélagie moved her curls carefully from her ear. "I want to see her display."

"Your clothes are from Paris."

"The women will know that soon enough."

"Clothes. Always clothes."

"I had only one dress when I was young. One dress. You will never know how it feels."

"No."

"One dress, and when it's being washed, you sit inside in your chemise, with the shutters closed. All day in winter. Like a foolish, helpless cat with no fur."

"Your eyes did look like a cat's. When you were small. Slanted like that."

"You can't know. And I'm sorry that you're going. But I will take good care of Etienne when he comes. My nephew, and he is only five years younger than me! So handsome now. I saw him twice in Paris."

"Yes."

"He doesn't want to return to Louisiana?"

"I don't know. I will know when I see him in Paris. Oh—what if I cannot see him? What if the treatments are too late for my eyes?"

"No. No. Paris has the best doctors in the world." She turned to me. "Moinette, Monsieur Antoine's shoes need that bootblack you made. He says he's never seen them shine so."

I had my own bottles now. Every day, when I saw them lined up on the kitchen shelf, my heart turned like a small animal curled in sleep, hunching tighter.

The bottles were marked with thread I had braided at night. Bootblack: Eight ounces of best ivory black, rubbed fine, with three ounces of molasses, one ounce each sugar candy and sweet oil. Gum arabic dissolved in sour beer. Shake well and cork four days.

The threads were miniatures of my braids, tied around the bottlenecks. I rubbed the bootblack in small circles.

Madame said, "I don't understand you, Pélagie."

"You don't have to. I told Laurent when I first saw you, when I was five and you were being married, that your eyes were like the ocean and I knew you would leave France."

"Now my eyes are gray and black."

"No, darling, they are still full of ocean. But the doctors in Paris will cure you. Paris has the best of everything in the world."

Behind the house, between two chinaberry trees, I had made my laundry. I washed out Pélagie's cloths, from her monthly blood. All the blood that left us, and how did we make new blood, exactly the same? When a leech gorged itself on the human liquid, how did the body make it anew? Was it always the same, the mix of mother and father?

When the African was brought to Louisiana, how did his blood not change inside him?

Msieu had bought four Africans. Two perhaps my age, and two older. Léonide said the Africans had gone straight to le quartier because it was night.

The blood smell was coppery in the rinse. All I knew of Africa: the sentences Mamère told me and the sentence Céphaline had recited for her tutor: Africa is a vast continent of savagery and war, containing many of the great rivers of the world.

My blood. Mamère had left with her own mother, to go on the ship where men and women died and leaped overboard to swim back up their rivers. Their *faro* guided them. Had her mother's sisters and brothers remained, to make the marks on the faces of their own children? And had those children been captured and sent down the river? To enter Barataria Bay?

But when the new Africans came to the yard for their clothes, they did not have marks like my grandmother and like Hera. They had no marks at all.

From the trunk in the pantry, I took out trousers and capes. Like my cape. The wool so heavy on my neck, that first week in the fields.

Msieu had his ledger on the table. February 4, 1812—Esclaves: Augustin—Mina. Philomen—Mina. Célestin—Ki. Berquin—Ki.

Not Senegalese or Congo. They fixed their eyes on the trees beyond the house and shivered. Three backs bore brands from the ship.

Like Mamère's?

That night, when the women had gone into the parlor to wait for Msieu, I stood before Pélagie's mirror.

You belong to me.

The scar around my ankle was smooth and dark, purple on cold days, brown on warm ones.

You belong to me.

I uncovered the blade of my shoulder and looked at the fleur-de-lis. Etched brown, flat, not shiny. The petal sharp as sword.

I don't belong to you.

The curling tongs were hot over the candleflame. On my forearm, not my wrist scarred with lavender rosettes from the boat nails, but higher, where I could see it anytime I pushed up my sleeve, I burned small images with the ends of the tongs. Sharp, like a pen nib. Three coffee beans, little circles of white pain. *M*—for Marie-Thérèse: four lines, with the tongs laid flat.

Tears ruined my vision, blood raced to the burns, and I dropped the tongs.

Her name was not Marie-Thérèse. That was given to her. What was her real name, from her own mother? How could I not know?

I smelled wax and picked up the tongs, but not before a small black mark had seared into the wooden floor by the vanity's legs.

When Madame Pélagie came up from dinner, she smelled burned wood. She could smell a single rose petal. "Why have you heated the curling tongs? Take that cloth from your hair. If you have touched them to—" She frowned at the braid that fell from my tignon. She had never seen my hair.

My arm was covered by my sleeve. She couldn't smell the scorched flesh. I had rubbed ashes into the burns to make them darker.

She bent to touch the mark on the floor. "Burned wood cannot be restored without sanding."

Burned skin—sanding would never help.

"I will not beat you," she said, cutting off each word in Paris French, not like Louisiana French. "I have never had a slave. Only a maid. I will not touch you. But if you begin to touch my things, I will recommend to my brother that you be sent back to the cane and ask him to purchase someone who will not be careless. Comprends?"

I nodded. "Oui, madame."

Two of the new Africans were dead within a week. Baillo rode for the doctor in Washington, and Madame had me take her down to le quartier.

The Africans were in a newly built house at the end of the street. Two wore leg chains attached to the wall. The youngest kept his back to us. His hair sat on his skull like a hundred black pebbles. Two were outside, their faces covered with blankets.

"The disease of the gums," the doctor said, his lip rising. "They tell you the men are healthy, and they shine them up with oil. But half the time, they've been in the barracoon for months waiting for the ship, and then eating rotten meal on the water."

Madame sighed. "They weren't baptized. There was no time."

Msieu said, "They must be buried at night, then, in the field."

"Laurent," Madame said, but he lifted his hand, palm out.

"The code."

They turned to the house, and we waited for the coffins.

A carpenter brought them on his cart, pine boxes so newly made that they bled golden sap. The men carried the coffins into the woods and dug the holes amid the weeds near the bayou. The new graves filled with water. When the coffins were lowered, mirrors of black broke and then stilled again around the wood.

The carpenter stopped me with one finger. "You have some water, mamselle?"

He said his name—Hervé Richard. His forehead shone like syrup, even though the air was cold. His skin was a bit darker than mine; he had French blood. Was he free? Was I allowed to look at his face? I glanced up at his hair—black waves combed down from a part. His scalp was paler than his forehead.

He said, "You don't mind I ask—you not free?"

"Me?"

He shrugged, leaning against the well. "So light, like some mulâtresse in New Orleans. When I bring furniture, sign the name and FWC. Tell me that is free woman of color."

"This is not New Orleans." The knot in his throat rose and fell when he drank. "And you? Free?"

His smile worked deep only on one side of his face, making a second grin in his cheek. "Msieu Lescelles buy me last year from New Orleans. Sign his name FMC. He run a carpenter shop near Opelousas."

His horse blew air through its nostrils. "Free to come and go with wood. Maybe your people buy armoire or chair. Maybe I come back." He checked the axle on his cart. His sleeves were rolled up and his forearms light as gold, but marked with cuts and nicks. A splinter was lodged like an exclamation point in the webbing between his finger and thumb. "Come back when I don't make something so sad."

I walked alone toward the house. But ahead of me, Sophia slipped into the blacksmith shed. At the half-open door, I peered inside. Loud pounding, mixed with strangled noises coming from Gervaise, lunging sounds forced from his throat.

He held a cane knife in the fire. It shimmered red and softened, and he pounded it with the iron mallet. He shouted, "Bring men here all that way and they die. Bury tout seul because nobody put water on the head. Nobody need water from les blancs. Water inside them."

"Gervaise," Sophia said.

"Alcindor."

"No. You leave that name. Not your name now."

"Hashim. Azor. Accara. Aguedo. They say names to me. Nothing else. They Mina and no comprend. Not the names on the paper." He hammered the knife until it broke, sharp as a bird scream in the night.

In Pélagie's room, clothes had arrived in a trunk. She would meet a husband, go to Paris to choose clothes and furniture for her new house. I would make my way off that boat, floating like a corn kernel atop the water. I took off my tignon. Did Gervaise believe what my mother did—that in my hot, damp hair were spirits named *ni,* traces of my other life? Our other lives?

"Some women will look up, at the paintings and mirrors," Pélagie said. "Those must be dusted every day. And women will look down, at the floor and table legs. Those must be swept and oiled every day."

"You cannot have another woman for the house," Msieu said impatiently. "We are planting cane. We cannot buy new furniture and clothes without sugar."

"I know women. If you want to marry your son next year to someone from Opelousas or New Iberia, you will let me begin work on the house now. The mothers of the girls will have eyes. And despite what you think, women have some power in the family. For marriage."

Amanthe and I worked into the night, and when once our palms slid cloth in the same circles over a table, I remembered Félonise's hand sealed to mine with the sheen of our work. Amanthe's hand was broad and dark, her arm quivering with extra fat above the elbow, but she fit her shoulder companionably to mine when we left a room. "I am glad you came," she whispered once.

I nodded. "I am glad you gave me your dress."

We worked dust and grit from the floorboards with small brushes.

The women began to come, when Pélagie saw them at Mass in Opelousas and invited them for dinner. They looked at Madame—her hair in a chignon but with a golden fillet wrapped around the forehead—and Pélagie with a rosy satin ribbon worked around her forehead, anchoring the curls at her ears.

"Your hair!" they said, and Pélagie slanted her head proudly. "My girl was trained in New Orleans."

I made them believe that. She would take me to New Orleans someday. The carpenter, Hervé Richard, had mentioned free women of color who lived there. They had somehow bought themselves. They could sign their own names. They could dress hair for money.

The women studied the garden, where Pélagie had Manuel the groom planting white-flowered crepe myrtle trees in an allée from the road to the house, and five orange trees in a circle, not for their fruit but for the white blossoms, and in the pathways white roses.

"When my sister-in-law returns from Paris next spring, her eyes will be clear, and she will see an angel garden. All white, in the moonlight."

Madame said she could see only what was inside a small circle directly in front of her. When she spoke to us, she turned her head and brought it forward toward our faces, like a turtle coming out of a shell, and powder fell from her cheeks.

"Moinette. Bring us coffee. Léonide has made a fresh pot."

Msieu Antoine was writing a long document, and Pélagie was poised over the paper. "Why does Laurent want this notarized?"

"Because we are leaving for Paris soon, and Laurent is worried about supervision and succession," Madame said.

"Etienne is the successor," Pélagie said. "I have my own little money."

"Yes, sweet, but explain it to me now. Laurent won't ask you."

Pélagie pleated the muslin of her dressing gown over and over on her thigh, her fingers moving as if she played an instrument. "I was married at sixteen to Micael Vincent, as you know, and went to Bordeaux with my husband, but he died three years later. I remained with his family until last year, when I decided to go to Paris."

"And he left you community property?"

Pélagie looked out the window, a tiny pulse moving in her cheek. "The Bordeaux property is owned by his father and brother. I signed it over to them after he died. I didn't want to stay in Bordeaux. I took some settlement money and went to Paris."

Madame de la Rosière nodded. She said softly, "Pélagie, I cannot see your clothes or jewels. Laurent said your mother gave you jewels and some cash for your dowry, when you married, and that your husband's family thought there would be more."

"They did." Her cheek pulsed again.

"You are happier here, no?"

"Yes."

"Laurent wants to name you owner of a large portion of the new land along the bayou, the parcel he bought last year. Monsieur Antoine will make certain the transaction is legal, and then you will be able to bring something to your new arrangement, whomever you meet here." Pélagie began to speak, but Madame said, "We have a long voyage to Paris, and crossings are always dangerous. You and Etienne are to take care, if something happens to us. My uncle Phanor will come from New Orleans to supervise this season. And Laurent says you are not to overspend while we are gone."

Pélagie was silent; how did Madame de la Rosière know she had agreed? I poured the coffee. Pélagie's fingers were pressed so hard on the small table that her nails were white.

"Pélagie. What is your middle name?"

"I won't say it."

"What! Won't say it? I'm sorry I never knew. After Laurent's mother died, when your father married again, Laurent was fifteen. He was sent to school and never saw you until you were already five."

"It means death. Three times."

"I don't understand."

"You don't have to.

"Pélagie Ernestine. Three times my mother was pregnant, and three times my father hoped for a son, and three times she had a girl she named for him. Ernestine. And three times they died. Then when she had me, she died. In childbed. So he named me Pélagie, after her. Ernestine for the son he didn't have. And sent me to my aunt in Lyon."

There was a long silence, and then Pélagie raised her voice. "Moinette! Will you hurry? I have ink on my sleeve now."

Everything Pélagie said was prepared. She felt nothing. She had calculated ahead of time answers for any questions, responses for any admiration—and if someone said something unexpected, a quickness in her face let her reply.

I watched her closely, to learn. Ever since the boat had left Azure, I had only listened. Slow in my mouth and quick in my brain. I needed to plan the right sentences, to say not what I really thought or felt—as Céphaline always had—but what people wanted me to say.

Mamère—she said so little because she couldn't keep her true thoughts from her sentences. When she spoke, she meant every word.

When I returned to Azure, I would tell her about everything—the bags of coffee on the wharf in New Orleans, the African women with wreaths of scarring, the blackened marbles of bird meat on my tongue. The way the water had felt when the gods rose in the silt under my feet and floated away down the bayou toward her.

For now, I listened to Pélagie, fastening her into a new dress just as a carriage arrived.

She said, "Oh, Monsieur Prudhomme, look at your sideburns. Dark hair looks so much more attractive on a man than on a woman. Your coat? Moinette—" She handed me the man's coat and said, "My brother tells me you know everything about horses, and I am ashamed that I never learned to ride. But in Paris—"

One night, she spoke to herself, voice fierce and low as Céphaline's reading from her own pages. Pélagie murmured, "A window. Only a window. I can do the rest."

Did she mean a mirror?

"He will not come. He will not know."

Did she mean Etienne? Was she planning to take Msieu's money, somehow?

Pélagie wrote a letter.

Dearest, Can you not find your way here, to the wilderness of Louisiana? for my heart is sore with the loss of your company. Can Paris not afford to lend you to me for a time?

The wilderness of ciprière swamp and canefields, of this house miles from a small town.

But if a lover came from Paris, who would she love here? Her plans were to find a husband. My plans depended upon that, as well.

They rode in the carriage, Msieu and Madame, Pélagie, and Msieu Antoine, who would escort Pélagie to the dances. We rode atop, with trunks full of clothes and gifts. To my surprise, Amanthe whispered to me that she would see the third man she had loved.

"I can only love him a few times a year. He cannot leave his place, and I cannot leave Rosière." She turned her head to the trees, and cords of muscle stood high in her throat.

I wondered if Hervé Richard, the carpenter, ever came to a dance. But his owner was a free man of color. The French Creoles wouldn't have him in their houses. And there wouldn't be any use to love someone for only a few nights. It would be dangerous to love at all.

Grand Piniére was the name of the first place. The pines made a carpet of needles to quiet our wheels. The house was yellow, with green and red trim. The wind chattered in the pine trees, and women's voices like breaking glass all around us. Pélagie is your sister? But she is lovely! Ah, oui!

I heated the curling tongs in the guest bedroom. Pélagie's marks, my marks, Mamère's marks. I slid the tongs down each section and rolled them up steadily, just tight enough, and counted to eight. Ten curls on each side. She stared in the mirror, not at the other women moving around us. Eight. Move to the next section. Eight. Then five fingers of each glove. I counted the same way as in the field, hoeing weeds from the cane. Move the hoe once, twice, thrice, and then take three steps. Three, three, three, three.

Even a fly breeds before it lays eggs, Céphaline whispered once in front of the mirror, where I dressed her hair for dinner with the Auzennes' cousin. But it doesn't have to look at the other fly.

The last curl dropped onto Pélagie's shoulder. It was so hot that she flinched and let it hang for a moment in the air before her.

While they danced, we stayed outside the kitchen. The sounds from the violin were shards inside my ears. Amanthe waited for the man she would love tonight, but he hadn't arrived.

By the time we slept, in the horse barn, in the long central hallway between the stables, she had heard. She shivered with tears beside me. Manuel, the groom, had just told her the third man she had loved, the valet named Autin, had died of a fever weeks before. She said Autin's lips tasted of mint, because he chewed the leaves before he saw her, and his mouth was soft as baby's cheeks, the only other time she had ever kissed someone.

She put her shawl around her face and lay shaking, while around us voices rose and fell in the straw.

A week later, we rode a long way to a ball outside Perreauville. The house, Cécile, was very large, and when the dancing and dinner were finished, people who lived in town left in their carriages, and the ones staying settled into the garçonnières and guest rooms. The slaves had pallets all along the railings of the gallery, wrapped around the entire house. I lay on my side, my cheek to the cool green-painted boards. The water of this bayou broken up by islands of sleeping people, their shoe-soles brown or foot-soles pink, or their feet tucked into blankets like puckered cocoons. How did some people stay warm, with no coverings, and others shivered each night?

I was awakened by a hand on my shoulder, on the cloth over my scar. Fingers hot. Branding iron again. I twisted away, but a man whispered, "Non, non, mademoiselle. Your madame. She call."

A groom? He smelled of horses—his coat black, his trousers lighter. He walked ahead of me, his head uncovered, a few strands of silver hair twined like wire at his temple when he turned his head.

He pushed me into a storeroom and closed the door. Then his hand clamped over my mouth. Calluses hard as dry beans on my lips when he rubbed his palm over my face. No windows. Coffee beans. My skull's empty spaces filled with tears. I couldn't breathe.

"I know why she call for you. He saw you. I know what you work. And me—I see you, too."

He tore off my tignon and crossed my two braids over my mouth, held them tight with one hand like reins and worked at my dress with the other hand. He knew how to unfasten women's buttons. When I bucked away, he pulled my head back hard.

"I first this time. You scream, no one hear."

He said, "Stand still. You move, I hurt you where he can't see."

He held my braids tight. Strangle. That was what my hair was for. He worked open his trousers and rubbed himself against my thighs. Blind. Rooting. No pain, just wetness as before, with the boat's mate on our passage north. They spent themselves on their idea of me. Not me. Not me.

When he hit my head against the wall, my brain shivered. My skull. Céphaline said it was such thin bone. My thighs are muscles. We eat the muscles of the cow and pig. His saliva dripped onto my shoulder.

His elbow hit me in the side when he used his handkerchief on himself. But wetness remained on my thighs. "Now mine mix with his," he said, low. "I first."

Then he said, "Scream I say I catch you in here thief." He took the braids from my mouth and pulled. My neck bent. Leash. Reins.

"Scream I say you thief this money from Msieu Ebrard." He held a gold coin. His teeth were white.

Slapping games with Fronie—my hand shot out, and I raked the coin with my fingers.

He couldn't hit me. He couldn't leave a mark.

He turned me with my braid, and the hairs at my temple pulled my skin away from the bone.

Madame Pélagie sat at her dressing table, in the guest room. I had thought the groom was lying, but she nodded for him to leave.

I tasted leather from his palm. He was gone.

Pélagie tightened her wrapper. "I know you were sleeping already. There is another task."

She led me down the hallway, much longer than Rosière's, and at the back door, she paused. "Do you want to work in the window?"

What was she speaking about?

"In New York. Dressing the models?"

"Madame, I don't understand."

She glanced outside. "In the garçonnière is Monsieur Ebrard's son. He saw you earlier. They say this is how it is done here in Louisiana." She whispered, "I am sorry, Moinette."

The grass was damp. He was pale in the darkened room. His sideburns were yellow-red tongues licking his cheeks. He said, "You are a vision. Take out your hair. A black cloud. How old are you?"

"Fifteen."

"Vrai? Truly? And what do you know?"

"Rien, msieu."

"Non."

"Nothing, msieu." My hair fell from the braids. I pulled my scalp away from my brain. What was I meant to know? Think quickly about what they wanted. Like Pélagie.

"Première fois, msieu."

"First time? I don't believe you. But you are crying. Why? I don't have to pay you, non. But I will give you this if you stop crying."

A gold coin.

He pushed. Blind, too. Were they all the same except for the smell of leather or pomade, except for whether they were angry or not?

No hand on my mouth. But he was a tall man. He told me to take off all my clothes. He did not remove his clothes. The cravat tied at his throat worked its way onto my face, and then, when he pressed harder and harder, the knot of cloth brushed my teeth, lodged there at my lips. Coat buttons on my ribs. Hands on either side of my head. The pain was rubbed into me again, again, and tears ran hot into my ears but turned cold inside my head.

"Sang mêlé. C'est vrai. True, what they say of your kind."

Calluses on my hands. Would this rubbing, over and over, make a callus inside me? When he lifted himself from me, left wetness on my leg, I saw him look. I saw the blood.

"Première fois," he said.

An ache pulsed like a ring pushed inside me. A circle brand burned.

"And true that money makes a girl cease crying," he said when he turned around.

When I was lying in the hallway at Rosière, on my blankets that smelled of me, the passage still burned.

Première fois, Tretite said to me once when I was very small and refused to pick up mule droppings for her garden. First time you do something you don't like, you do it over and over, you grown.

I hadn't done the task over and over yet. I wasn't grown. What would grow inside me? Breeding. From one time?

The slave groom wanted his seed mixed with his msieu's. I was the gift he could not have.

Cadeau. But I had two gold coins. Which was worse? A gift or a purchase?

I tied the coins in my old tignon, with the clothespins and memory of coffee beans, and hid the bundle in the left sleeve of Madame Pélagie's oldest, plainest dress in the back of the armoire.

Hervé Richard said, Maybe I come back for something not so sad.

He wouldn't want me now.

The twinge of pain behind my ribs was sharp, like fingernails run over my insides. This was the money for my journey to Azure.

But then a dog barked in the distance. Dogs. My plan was a child's idea. Leap from the boat, swim to Azure—and Franz the overseer wouldn't see me? Circle through the ciprière swamp, past the indigo vats where Doctor Tom's bones would be black now? Hide in the cane and surprise my mother in her room? Expect Msieu Bordelon to allow me to stay? Take Mamère with me? Take her where?

I turned over on the pallet. If a baby grew, there would be no journey.

I was ashamed to ask Sophia. For days, I waited to feel illness, as Sophia said she felt with her new baby by Gervaise.

On the night of the last dance before Mardi Gras, before people received ashes on their foreheads from the priest, before they surrendered joy for Lent, we traveled to one more plantation outside Loreauville. I lay in the barn with the others.

If a slave came for me this time, I had a knife. If Madame Pélagie sent me to someone, I wouldn't let him hurt me.

He saw you. It would happen, again and again. He saw you.

The alligator's eyes rested above the water. Our eyes sat inside the holes of our skull, but what moved them farther apart, the way wide-set eyes were beautiful, and what made some lashes longer? He saw you. It's your fault you look like that. Mulâtresse good for dressing the hair. For the gentlemen. She so bright. Take but one candle. What was beautiful? Madame Bordelon said men looked at her ankles and wrists when she was a girl. She told Céphaline that lovely ankles were important. Céphaline said, "And may I cover my face now and leave my ankles out for display?"

Did we all look the same inside? Did we feel the same to the men? Did skin and hair and face mean my passage would be any different?

Fantine told me, "Basile say, I have nothing each day but your face." All day in the cane, he saw her eyes and lips, but at night, he stared at the arrangement of her eyebrows and mouth and then reached to push himself into the passage. What else existed?

Amanthe breathed beside me. She knew no one here, at this plantation. The moths flew into the barn windows. All the roads and bayous leading to all the towns. Small places named for the man who owned the largest house, the land. All the less important people coming to eat his food, drink his wine, smile at his wife. All the people on the roads, and in the hallways that led to the rooms where they ate and danced and studied one another. And only to decide whom they wanted to use—to breed like the animals in the woods. In the cypress swamp with the Indian woman. Gervaise carrying dead birds to Sophia's door. The deer along the pathways, the horses in their pastures. The frogs at the edge of the pond. Ouaouaron. Calling to one another all night.

The flies sped along their own roads in the air, drinking at the lips of those who slept, searching for other flies. We couldn't see their pathways.

All the hallways, and the rooms like honeycombs. The people lying on each other or standing up so they wouldn't have babies, but babies growing. And filling the rooms and hallways and cabins. Then like puppies when the mother nips them sharp with her teeth to say Go. The puppies digging their own holes where they lay and panted and stared until they began to look for one another. The flies on their droppings.

A lunging sound, in the parlor. Breath expelled from the throat again and again, with sobbing force.

Madame de la Rosière held the elbows of a man, her face close to his, inside that small circle of her vision, and her crying was a rhythm like clothes scraping on the washboard.

Her son. "Your face. Your face. The sideburns."

He said, "You'll hurt yourself."

"I didn't think I would see you until I reached Paris, and I worried that the ship would take the rest of my eyes. Too much light on the water. I remembered it. But you knew! You knew what I was thinking! Look at your shoulders."

"I thought I would be better able to withstand the voyage than you, Maman. And I know my father will be angry that I came early."

"I can feel your shoulders." She didn't hear, didn't see, she only touched his coat again and again.

I couldn't watch.

Soldier coat. He was a soldier. Soldier blue.

The silence of Sunday made me curl into the back of Pélagie's closet when they went off to Mass. My gold coins were cold. Indigo. Teeth like pearls in the dish and then they were bone.

On Sunday, I had no one. I hadn't wanted anyone.

Tretite's white dress used to float ahead of me. My mother heard us approaching her house. But her eyes would still peer up from her sewing as if she were shy, and surprised that we had come.

Madame's son had known what she was thinking. Across the ocean.

I walked to le quartier, where no one knew what I was thinking.

Fantine waited for water at the pump. She turned to me and said, "Moinette, look at your blue dress. Mine let out now."

Her belly swung around, and she gave me that smile, deep into her left cheek. "We move into a new place. Side of Gervaise." She touched the fabric of my sleeve. "You sleep with Amanthe, eh?"

"Alone," I said. "Mo toute seule." I couldn't tell her I missed her.

She pulled me to her room at the end of the street. "Sophia stay with Fronie. She glad not to share now."

Fantine had a washtub. I washed her hair, water rushing down the thick shoals and onto her shoulders. She washed mine, and we sat in the weak sun spilled into the doorway.

"Basile say, 'I ain't have to be with you every minute in the day. But every minute in the night.'" She traced her long finger along the hem of my sleeve. "The Madame have lace fall out the sleeve, oui?"

She wanted to hear the details. "Lace, and the little buttons are pearl. The skirt is silk. And everything is trimmed in ribbon. A ribbon right under the bosom, to hold it up like a shelf."

Ribbons are our stripes, I couldn't say. Our markings.

Fantine smiled. "How many dress you have?" She was measuring.

"Three," I said. "From Amanthe. Not Madame."

Fantine pressed her hand onto her belly. "A ribbon under my bosom," she laughed. "Not now. Baby under there."

Nothing under my bosom. No baby. Rien, Mamère used to say to Eveline at night. Rien en coeur pour qui n'est pas sang.

Nothing in the heart for someone who isn't blood.

That was the way the whites lived, and the way we couldn't.

Nothing in my belly. Nothing but soreness that left.

One night, Mamère made tiny braids for Tretite, fingers lingering on her skull until her eyes swam as if she were drunk. Tretite said Félonise had loved her madame and msieu, when she was young. She said nothing about her own love.

My mother cared for them. But she loved me, in her heart.

I had listened to Céphaline, had touched her hair, had loved her words and hated them. I had been afraid of everyone else.

I had never loved anyone either. Only my mother.

Sophia was fierce for Fronie, but she didn't love her. Fantine loved Basile in a foolish and dangerous way, with her brain full only of his smell and skin.

Her curving cheeks held a smile inside even when she wasn't smiling. She hadn't felt the white man in the woods flick her breast. She hadn't tasted her own hair rope. She stood up while she was loved, with her face against Basile's face.

When Pélagie and Msieu spoke alone, especially of their time back in France, their voices floated to me in the hallway, and in the quietness and ease of their words, it was clear that they had cared most for each other. Once, Pélagie said to him, "Our mother's blood is foremost in us, Laurent. We are closer in a sense than any other humans, even to those in our marriages."

He had said, "If Etienne had a brother, he would feel that way. But he has always been solitary. He prefers to hunt over anything else, to be alone in the midst of trees."

But Madame de la Rosière's face, always turned expectantly toward her husband, was somehow vague and sad in love, in the darting blurred eyes and the chin so still while she listened to his impatience.

When Etienne arrived, her whole figure turned into love. Her mouth wasn't set and waiting, but open and expectant, while he entered the room. And her eyes didn't matter, because she touched him every day, his hair, his coat, his knee.

I didn't want to feel that way about anyone else, ever, to have to wait, and die a little while she was gone. I never wanted a baby.

I said to Fantine now, "I will get you some cloth and ribbon, sew you a dress for when you are thin again."

When she threw her arms around me, her belly felt so hard; how could water and blood and baby be hard as a gourd?

Madame Pélagie said nothing to me about that night. My blood came, and hers and Amanthe, all at the same time now. When I washed all the cloths, the smell of the water tipped out near the two chinaberry trees was heavy and thick as freshly killed pig. The trunks should grow tiny fingers or maybe fur.

The white squares of linen hung on the line were like sheets of paper in the early summer sun.

The best dogs had papers. Horses had papers. Msieu examined them before he bought, before he bred. I had papers. I was worth more now, because I could sew and dress hair. Pélagie had papers that Msieu Antoine had written and notarized at the courthouse in Opelousas.

When Fantine had her baby, I went to le quartier to help, cleaning the hot blood and skin, the baby covered with white wax like myrtle.

When we told him, Msieu said, "First infant to arrive since we were sold to the Americans. Louisiana will never be American. She will be named for loyalty."

He wrote in the book: négritte, Francine, 28 de mai 1812.

One more time, all of our blood came together, and disappeared with the water and bluing. Then Msieu and Madame left for Paris, Amanthe riding up in front, Philippine crying, and Firmin watching with his purple-rimmed eyes and collapsed cheeks.

Back at her house, staring into her fire, Philippine said, "Ocean passage never certain. Ocean have storm and wind."

"Msieu said the ships are bigger and faster now," I said. "His son just arrived, oui, with no trouble? They will write to us from Paris. Pélagie will get a letter, and I will come to you."

"You read?" Philippine whispered.

"You cannot tell anyone. Not Sophia. No one."

Philippine said, "No. No one."

Firmin said, "Get a letter, but letter say nothing of Amanthe."

"But she will be inside the paper the same."

I had never written an entire word, only the *M* on my skin. Each time paper or ink was near, I was afraid to try—if the ink made a blot that wouldn't launder clean, how would I explain?

My plans were on the paper inside my head. I had made Pélagie need me, for her beautiful hair and skin. In New Orleans, I would tell her about my mother's laundering skills, her fine seams and decorative stitches far better than mine. Msieu Bordelon would always need money; he would sell my mother, and she would sew lovely clothes and linens for sale in New Orleans, in Paris.

I read over Pélagie's shoulder when she made her lists of material to purchase, glanced at the pages of Msieu's daily journal when dusting his desk—not the ledger book of accounts. Msieu's flowing script slanted like people walking against a wind.

Temperatures dropping. Price for sugar increasing. Two hands sick with putrid throat and one with pleurisy. Apollonaise in stocks again for breaking tools.

In the garçonnière, Etienne wrote no letters. When I brought his coffee, he was writing lists as well. The names of animals:

Four deer in south quadrant near bayou. Raccoon. Raccoon. Nest of snakes in lower canefield. Feral pig sighted near Washington.

He did not glance up at me. I moved behind him. He was taller than his father. His jackets collected dust from his riding. His hair swirled over his forehead like black feathers, and beside his eyes, scrolls of lines curled out like carved decorations from the sun.

Another week, he wrote names and towns:

Livaudais, New Iberia: gelding. DelaHoussaye, Saint Martinville: four bays. Rapides Parish dealer: quarter horse.

He hunted nearly every day or disappeared looking for horses to buy. I swept the dirt from the garçonnière floor, and collected dirty clothing, but rarely saw him.

Before he left, Msieu instructed Uncle Phanor and Etienne that no one could be spared the cane weeding and woodcutting for the sugar mill; with Amanthe gone, only I was in the house.

Pélagie argued with her brother. "During summer season, with few visitors, Moinette will be capable. But in November, Laurent, when you return for the harvest, I will need a new girl as well, to prepare the house for the holidays and spring."

"November is grinding, and all the slaves work the fields."

She smiled. "Bien sûr, Laurent. Fine. I will sell a horse and buy a girl."

Léonide was old and moved so slowly with all the weight gathered around her legs and waist that she refused to leave her hearth. She sat on a chair to cut the vegetables now and moved the chair close to the fire to stir her pots.

Etienne rode the fields only briefly, Uncle Phanor complained. Etienne often returned after dark, carrying dead animals—deer, rabbit, birds. Léonide roasted the meat, and Pélagie studied the bodies on the table, frowning at Etienne.

I heard them in the parlor.

"I was trained to shoot by the men who guarded Marie Antoinette—did you not know that? Have you seen a mob, in Paris? We ride above the crowd. Not above endless fields of cane that don't move."

Uncle Phanor, his white hair dancing in a circle around his pink skull, drank his wine and said impatiently, "First you didn't want to be sent there. Now you don't wish to be here."

"My father chose the military college, and I obeyed," Etienne said. Pélagie motioned me to cover the food with netting. "My father chose my return, and I obeyed."

"He wants you to show some regard for the land."

"I am meant to ride above bent backs now and look into the distance. I prefer the forest, where I roamed as a child."

"You are not a child."

"You are not my father."

He was gone for weeks to horse races. I removed Uncle Phanor's fingernail parings and Léonide's vegetable parings and Pélagie's fabric parings and her blood.

In late summer, rain fell almost every afternoon, and the clean clothes hung dripping and transparent on the lines. I remembered the muscles in Mamère's wrists leaping when she twisted wet shirts.

My fine sewing needle slid easily into the gray spots on my wrist. Old wounds. The boat. The bayou. The blood rose in its usual buttons.

Boutons. Boutons on skin had brought me here. Foolish red bumps on white skin. I dipped my finger into the blood and painted the heads of my new clothespins, the ones Firmin had carved for me.

As a child, before I knew how to work, I had scratched eyes and smiles into the heads, made them moss wigs and leaf skirts. I had danced them near my mother's feet, tickled her with their hair.

The blood wasn't paint. It sank into the wood and turned black and rubbed off.

The letter came in August. They had been a month at sea and then a month for the letter to return to Louisiana. Madame was in Paris, in her aunt's apartment, seeing the best doctors for her eyes and her shortness of breath and her headaches.

In le quartier, I whispered, "When Pélagie read it to the uncle, she didn't say Amanthe is no longer with me or Amanthe is ill."

"Nothing for Amanthe," Philippine said.

"That mean she is fine," Firmin said. "Only talk about the bad, for us. If we die or run. If nothing, we work." He went outside, as he always did when his face couldn't contain what he felt.

We were all waiting for the harvest, and for January, when Madame would return with Amanthe, when Pélagie would find her suitor during the balls and dinners of spring, and we would prepare for our journeys.

River waters rose at the end of September from a storm out at sea, and all the rain of the summer gathered in the yard and fields to meet Bayou Rosière when it spilled over. The earth was covered in brown trembling. Etienne stayed inside, swearing as the water rose to the edge of the porch. "My father will blame me. Somehow I will have brought the rain from France."

The cane in two fields was washed away. Le quartier was flooded, and people waded up to the barn. The water finally receded, leaving behind lines of black dirt on trees, walls, the brick pillars of the house, watery lines like horizons of a ghost world hovering above the earth. Pélagie ordered us to scrub everything.

The waters had washed over the grove where the two Africans were buried, left gaping holes without the rough boxes Hervé Richard had nailed together. The men were gone, into the Atchafalaya, down through Barataria, out to sea, where storm winds had swirled them, maybe all the way across the ocean to Africa.

But their bodies would have been bleached white by the water.

Their souls—did they believe in *dya*? If they believed, maybe their souls would wash onto the African beach where they had been captured, and maybe they could rest there.

Msieu returned for the harvest in November with a young woman: Lise, Pélagie's cousin. Madame was to stay in Paris for treatments.

Pélagie clasped Lise to her, the woman thin and small, with black straight hair done in a braid around her head. "I missed you so, I couldn't bear it. You'll stay all spring season in the wilderness!"

Pélagie's letters had not been for love, then, only loneliness. She and Lise spent hours in Pélagie's room, sewing, whispering, laughing, and I learned to dress Lise's hair in the new Grecian style.

Msieu rode the place with his son. Msieu's face was altered, deep lines grooved around his forehead and down his temples, like a replica of his drooping moustaches pasted above his eyes. In the office, Etienne said angrily, "The rain was incessant, and the cane was rotting before the floods did their damage."

His father said only, "Blow after blow. That is to be expected."

When Etienne came out, he frowned at me, where I was polishing the small table in the hallway and the gilt mirror on the wall. "Nothing is ever to be expected with him," he said, passing me with a rush of smoke and alcohol on his breath.

Because of the floods, the cane harvest was bad. Msieu spent hours in his office with Etienne, with sugar brokers, and Msieu Antoine, the lawyer. "I'm strongly suggesting that you mortgage, Laurent," one broker said. "For security, you have the house, some land, or slaves."

Msieu poured another drink. "I do not mortgage. It is a dangerous practice."

"It is an accepted measure," Msieu Antoine said. "You need money for repairs and planting."

"It means the possibility of loss. It is how French land falls into American hands."

"We have the surety of loss now," the sugar broker said.

I finished oiling the wood in the hallway beside the office door. Mortgage must not mean sell. Lend? Which slaves would they lend?

In the parlor, Pélagie chose new plates for the dinner parties. "It must be fairly lavish, or perceptions will not be met," Pélagie said. "The Prudhommes are making a decision."

I slid the bed warmers under her coverlet. She and Lise pored over a magazine from Paris, and Pélagie said softly, "I want a window."

"A house?"

"No. A window, in a city, with my apartment above. That's all."

"In New Orleans?"

"No! In New Orleans, I am not a Creole. I would never be respected. They love only those born here."

"You plan to return to Paris?"

"No! He will never find me in America."

"But to never see Paris again?"

"In Paris, I am only a foolish young widow from Lyon. But in New York, I am from Paris. I can sell clothing. Parisian style. Perfume, gloves, hats. Madame Delfin—do you remember her? She is waiting to send me the dresses. But I need a place. A window."

"A store."

"A window. A wall with a window and my name over it."

"How much will you need?"

Pélagie whispered, "As much as a plantation will bring."

"What?"

"Look at me. Look at this Attakapas territory. The women here are barbarians. My brother's wife cannot see, so she may be excused. But you have seen the farm wives and drab little women in town?"

"I have seen everyone noticing your beauty."

"My brother has expanded Rosière every year. Some of that land is mine, though I've never even looked at it. The men can exclaim over dirt. Dances and dinner parties. It will be easy."

"But to marry again, after one husband already dead?"

Pélagie closed the magazine. "There is nothing else to be done. And sometimes, when the man is older, and the heart is weak, too much love can be—"

"What?"

"The last thing you enjoy on earth."

"Pélagie!"

"Oui?"

What did the whorls of her brain store? She called for me again and again, in the night. She called me to make certain she was still executing some order or plan. Her husband was dead. Who was trying to find her? How would the window hide her?

Pélagie and Lise planned the meals. "I've hired five slaves from Madame Prévost in Opelousas," Pélagie told her. "For the whole weekend. Three women to serve the food, one extra groom, and one cook. Léonide is beside herself."

"How many people are you expecting?"

Pélagie shrugged. "We will see how successful my work has been. But I hope to see forty or so. Monsieur Prudhomme's family, I know."

"Ah." Lise smiled. "That one."

Then Pélagie called me to her dressing table, where we were trying different accessories. "Moinette. Monsieur Ebrard will attend."

I twisted up a section of hair to pin with the feathered ornament she was considering. His sideburns. His cravat. His groom.

"Monsieur will remember you. He will stay in the garçonnière."

I couldn't ask how old he was, why he didn't want to see her, or Lise. Or maybe he wanted to see them, dance with them, marry them. After a diversion for the evening.

"Yes, madame."

Lise looked through dress patterns holding a swatch of blue silk, pale as summer sky through glass.

I went into the hallway when she asked for the stone to sharpen scissors, but waited until they spoke.

"Pélagie. You are without shame."

"I am without a husband yet, and with an abundance of hospitality required of me. There is no need to be coy, as Americans pretend to be here. She is fifteen, I think. She could have been sold for a high price in New Orleans, but she wasn't. How my brother acquired her I don't know. Ebrard will notice her again."

"And what if she has a child?"

Breed. Like good dogs. I bit at the loose skin on my thumb and tasted almond oil from her hair. "If she has girls, they will be attractive. Do you know what they are called? Daughters of joy."

Lise turned pages, with the cricket sound of paper. "And boys?"

"Someone in New Orleans told me her mother drowned one like a kitten and told the woman it had died at birth. Isn't that horrible? But the men hate to see them. They're useful for nothing, apparently, so often they're sent to school in France."

"But she belongs to Laurent, oui? And so would her children. You wouldn't have to decide."

Pélagie must have moved the dresses in the closet again, because the sachet scent wafted out the doorway. "I will make my own purchases when married. Moinette understands me, and she is indispensable as well as quiet. I will buy her when we leave."

I wouldn't think about joy and kittens, because I only cared about the part where we left.

The women dressed in Madame de la Rosière's room and in Pélagie's room. The silks glowed like butterfly wings, but when I began dressing hair along with the other maids, the smell of burned oil and pomade mixed with clouds of too-sweet powder. As I moved from neck to neck, the scent made me feel ill. Some of the necks were very young, white and smooth and unmarked, and the curls fell fat and lazy to their napes. Some of the necks were darkened by the sun, etched with lines like palm bark. The rats of extra hair were like small animals. My fingers held them onto a skull and pinned the thinning brown or black hair around the pad.

What if I were to offer them mine formed into a rat? Curling black hair on the white scalp, wrapped with blond strands?

The older men dressed in Msieu's room. The younger men dressed in the garçonnière.

Msieu Ebrard had ridden with Etienne and others on horseback, come from a race. He had no carriage, and no groom. I would dress the models in the window. In Paris. My mother would sew. Just a few minutes with Ebrard's voice and the ache.

Only his eyes moved, when I passed. He wore a blue coat. Etienne watched him watch me. Another young man stood with them. A tan coat.

During the dancing, violin and piano music twirled over our heads, and skirts twirled at our feet, while we carried trays of ham and squab. Meat torn with teeth.

The skirts fell away like dead flowers onto the floor when the women retired. I helped Madame Ebrard's servant undress her. The skin hung from her sides, under her arms, in heavy dewlaps. Where did that fat come from? Her angel wings had fallen. I took her dress, which had a spot of oil on the bodice from a dropped piece of meat.

Then I went downstairs to clean crumbs from the tablecloths.

Fat and ashes in the threads.

The older men talked about Americans in the parlor, smoke like moss curling under the door. The younger men played cards in the garçonnière; shouts of "Five! No!" rang out.

"He will ask before the weekend is finished," Lise said to Pélagie, checking dresses for tears. "He cannot be more than an arm's length away from you."

Msieu Prudhomme. Widowed, his eyebrows gray as ash, but black hair combed forward over his forehead, as Msieu Bordelon's had been so long ago. He dressed his hair with blacking, like Céphaline's.

Pélagie said to me, "You will go to the garçonnière, to collect any coats that need repair, yes?"

But I sat in the kitchen with Léonide.

"Have to start breakfast in a while. Roast chicken, ham, tarts with strawberry and lemon. Oysters and shrimp."

"I'll do the shrimp."

"He look for you. The one with the blue coat."

I nodded.

"Bright skin not a blessing." Léonide's hands were still on her knees, a new burn on her wrist covered with a damp cloth, like a veil.

The darkness was purple behind the pecan trees, just a faint breath of morning a few hours away. "My mother told me take but one candle to light her room."

I had never said those words aloud.

Strawberry preserves in jars behind us. Lemon curd. Jars like those in Doctor Tom's office. The eye. The baby's brain. The womb.

If all they needed was the passage, why not cut that from me and keep it in a jar? Preserved. Liquid to keep it soft. Then take it out when it was needed. Lay it on the coverlet or the earth. Sew it into a cloth doll. Close your eyes.

"Open your eyes," Léonide said softly.

Msieu Ebrard wore a white shirt, bobbing up and down on the brick path in the distance. Not clothes on the line. Nowhere to hide.

I wouldn't meet him or walk with him.

Léonide sucked at her teeth. I slipped from the kitchen and then around the house, through the garden of white, I stopped at the pigeonnière where we had pulled the young birds through the holes to roast them. Their feathers were in a sack in the kitchen.

I listened at the oleanders near the garçonnière. Both buildings shaped the same. What if a giant hand pulled out the men by their coattails and plucked off their sideburns?

"Etienne," he said. "Pélagie's slave has been summoned. You are fortunate."

"I don't see it that way."

"Then you are foolish."

"Not foolish, but not interested."

"Then maybe you learned nothing in Paris. Or you learned from the wrong men. The ones—"

"I learned what was necessary in Paris. And it doesn't matter here. Nothing I do matters here."

"Etienne!" The third voice—the tan coat? "You have land. I have five older brothers. There's no land left for me."

Msieu Ebrard said, "Etienne should prove he isn't foolish. Or unnatural. You should prove it, too, Gustave. I have procured the medium of proof, but she is slow. Go find her, Etienne."

My shoulder went first inside the door. My eyes stayed on the desk. No letters. Cards and glasses of wine. I went up the narrow stairs to the beds.

Etienne came first. He closed the door. He said, "Take off your dress," very quietly, lower than the sounds of the bottles clinking and the slap of cards.

He opened his trousers and left his shirt and shoes on. I imagined I was dead. Floating inside brown water. Smoke, sour wine, and then my own soap when his shirt became wet. He was inside a jar, moving. I was in the den with the smell of fox, sleeping.

I didn't open my eyes.

A mule. To carry things. Moving a man down a road. Just moving him. His elbow hitting me in the ribs like a man kicking the animal to make him move faster.

I didn't have to move.

He went down the stairs. Voices rose and fell. The door closed. A body sat on the bed. Something pinched hard, like a crab, on my inner arm, and I opened my eyes.

The tan coat watched my face. He pinched me harder, the soft skin just inside the upper arm, and I cried, "You're hurting me, msieu."

He said nothing. He twisted. He had pinched, and been pinched, many times exactly this way.

He twisted until I cried out. He kicked the bed a few times and then went down the stairs. A performance. Like the Indian woman Sally in the swamp.

A long time later, Msieu Ebrard sat on the bed. He took off his cravat, the material that had pushed like a fist into my mouth the first time he lay on me. "Only one way to tell if they listened," he said. He used his fingers first, as if examining a horse, but his breath lied. Then he took off his shoes.

"You are from New Orleans."

"No."

"You really haven't learned there?"

I didn't answer.

"Les mulâtresses from New Orleans are famous."

I didn't answer.

"There are women who could teach you. Then you wouldn't cry."

I wasn't crying.

Move the white clothes up and down the washboard. Sew the buttons back on. Push the needle into the linen until my fingerpads split.

Lie on the pallet when the tasks were finished, and the work washed from my body, my fingers and muscles shivering and then finally still. Bluing and cane dust gone.

But now, on my pallet while the women breathed behind their doors, inside me the passage burned and fluid trickled out hours later onto my legs. The formation of a baby. My task would never be finished. Breed. Fingers. Saliva dropped onto my clavicle. I couldn't wash it off. I couldn't reach inside myself to wash it off.

He had left the cravat. I found it coiled like a white whirlpool under the bed. In the dark hallway, I lit a candle and cut the cravat into twenty small pieces of fabric, then sewed them back together, with blue thread. For good luck. For indigo breath. A mosaic of cloth that looked like nothing else, like twenty small ponds of water.

Ribbon scraps from Pélagie's basket made a red collar. The back of the blouse was stained napkins, two sewn together, and the sleeves two more. I could not sew like my mother. But I walked down to le quartier and gave the blouse to Fantine.

His cravat, to choke the words down into his throat, held up to Fantine's collarbone like bubbles.

Etienne didn't look at me when I served dinner on Monday, after the last guests had finally gone. He said to Pélagie, "Paul Ebrard wants to buy your maid from my father."

My task was not to speak.

He pinched the skin between his brows and looked down the road. Pélagie only laughed. "But Moinette belongs to me now. In truth, we are expecting Monsieur Prudhomme's offer, and then your father will sign her over to me. At present, she is not for sale."

I reached deep inside the large pot to scour the bottom. The cast iron released its smell, damp and black, into my face.

I would go with Pélagie. New Orleans. New York. One window.

When I dressed her hair, for her trip to Opelousas to see the Prudhommes for the marriage contract, she said, "You are part of my dowry now."

"What is a dowry?"

She closed her mouth while I curled the last two sections. She didn't like to move at all when I held the tongs. Lise was careless, and flung herself about while I dressed her, but Pélagie concentrated on every move.

"A dowry is what the woman brings."

She said nothing else. Why explain? I would never have a dowry. But I heard the negotiations during the engagement. Marriage contracts were complicated. Céphaline would have brought land to her marriage instead of beauty. Pélagie had beauty and social standing, but no property in France. Msieu de la Rosière wanted to write to Bordeaux and Lyon, to their relatives, but she shook her head.

"I will be Louisianan now. I want a wedding party with all our family here. I don't want to be married like a widow. I want to be married like a new bride. Not damaged goods," she said in a low voice to Msieu. "I want you to give me away like my father didn't."

"I forgot his age when you were born."

"Sixty-seven," she hissed. "Monsieur Prudhomme is fifty-nine. Don't write to Bordeaux. I have nothing there. Everything is gone."

She had her jewels, her land here, and me.

I was part of her wedding gift, along with the child forming itself inside me.

Six CODE

Cadeau. And cadeau-mère.

I hated the thing inside me. How did it reach up into my throat to push out my coffee and biscuit? Did it not want food? Did it want to kill me?

When it swelled and began to twitch inside me, I pictured the shriveled white organ inside Doctor Tom's jar. Grapeskin. The womb. What if the womb split, and I died? I hated the gift even more then, because I would never see my own mother again.

Had she hated me unseen, a heaviness that pressed down on her other organs, a burden that made bones shift and ache? How did a baby move my bones? The soft form inside me pushed against my backbone. Vertebrae. Back then, Céphaline chanted the names of the bones and organs as if knowing what we were made of would save us.

In August, the swelling could no longer be hidden by my apron. "You a mother," Léonide said, when I reached for her pots on the wall.

Not a mother. An animal.

Sugarcane grew from joints in the stalk. Seeds grew with a sprout that ruptured the shell. This thing bloated my whole body, my legs and breasts and even my hair, so wild and thick under my tignon that my head hurt.

I ate little, but that didn't stop it from growing, and finally everyone could see what was under my dress. Lise looked embarrassed, but Pélagie only sighed.

Pélagie said, "We have so much sewing and preparation for the wedding, Moinette." When Lise went down the hall, Pélagie studied the pile of napkins we had been embroidering. "Monsieur Ebrard, oui?"

If I said I didn't know? It was proper for her to conduct me to Msieu Ebrard, but to know about other men was not pleasant. And if it was Etienne—

Who would know? Francine was Fantine and Basile's baby, but she didn't truly look like either of them. Sophia's baby, Amadou, had Gervaise for a father but looked like Sophia.

Did I look like my father? Maybe Mamère had never even seen him; maybe she kept her eyes closed, as I had; maybe during that week he was on Azure, he came every night in the dark.

And then he died on a boat.

This baby would have the blood of Mamère and of that blond man. What if this baby had blond hair? The eyes of someone dead and no one alive? How would I know who the father was?

I didn't answer Pélagie. She didn't care about the father. The baby would belong to Pélagie, unless the father bought it.

A girl would grow up to breed, like me. A boy—

No use for a boy.

In the afternoons, during the September heat, Pélagie and Lise slept in their shifts, and I lay on my side on the hallway floor. Once a hand or foot tapped the wood through my skin and made me sit up and hit my head against the wall.

Etienne glanced at me one afternoon while I put clean clothes in the garçonnière, and he looked away quickly, as if someone pulled a string attached to his ear. He hadn't been in the house all summer. He and his father oversaw the repair of irrigation ditches from the flood, and planting the new fields, and the road to Washington had to be cleared again as well.

In November, when the harvest began, I was big enough to have difficulty moving. The pain came during daytime, and when I went down to Philippine's, she and Firmin were among the few people not in the fields. After midnight, when Sophia and Fantine were done in the sugarhouse, the burned-sweet smell clinging to their eyelashes and hair when they bent over me, the pain grew to rings that belted my back and belly. Hot rings. The ring of pain inside the passage, from the men, then moved up to circle my body now.

What would she say to me now? Mamère? Besoin. The need. What did I need? The three passages. Your *ni*. The *dya* who waits for the next life to be born. But whose *dya*? A white man dead—my blood—had no *dya*? Sang mêlé. Whose blood mixed with hers and mine?

All the animals under trees and in caves and bushes, lying on their sides, with infants pushing down the passages.

I cried for my mother, not for the pain. If I died now, as so many women did, as Pélagie's mother had, I would never see her again.

Water and blood poured onto the cloths they had laid under me. How would I live? How did that much liquid leave my body, and what remained to make milk? The blood left me in pulses, lifting me up as if the rags were a raft and we swirled away down my own river.

But then the blood trickled, and the baby made sounds that tore through the smell.

A boy.

He had no bones. He was a shapeless, colorless bundle in my arms. He was a mouth, attached to me so hard it hurt. He was a passage where black excretions left immediately after he drank. I cleaned both passages. He had only two.

But he had no bones. He was curled like a frog, legs soft and useless, his eyes barely open, only a glint of murky purple like dusk.

He was the first baby. The person who chewed the grass and tasted sugar. The person who tasted a wild nut and found it sweet.

We were truly animals now. He had fur on his shoulders that Philippine said would rub away. He was mewling and blind, his fingers soft worms, his fingernails—our claws, our only weapons aside from teeth and brains, and this baby had no teeth, and who knew what was in his skull?—his fingernails like paper.

What if I dropped him? What if the cold December air seeped into his ears and nose and mouth and his insides froze? What if his pale skin wasn't as hardy as Francine's, plump and strong, her hair tied into strings?

He was pale as almond shells, with down sparse and black on the back of his skull, and eyebrows like ant trails across his forehead.

I slept in Philippine's bed, and she sat up all night holding the baby. She said, "My Amanthe find a man when she back from Paris. She wait for that Autin, and he die. She never love someone here. But she find one, and she have a baby, too. A sweet smell. A bundle."

When he cried for me, she said, "He smell you. Can't see. But they smell the mother."

So if we were in the wild, lying in the damp nest of covers, the last of my blood sliding into the rags tied to my hips, he would know me when I came back from hunting?

But my task was to sew and wash and curl and powder.

After four days, I had to return to the house, and I left him with Philippine, the way mothers left their children when they went to the fields. The babies slept on pallets beside her feet, waiting for the times we came to nurse them at dawn, at noon, and at night. Firmin made a wooden box for my son.

The fourth day, Msieu asked me about the baby.

He wrote in his book: Infant, quadroon, b. 29 décembre 1813. Jean-Paul.

Pélagie did not mention the baby. Msieu and Etienne left before dawn for the harvest, one in the fields, one at the sugarhouse, where the grinding went on past midnight now and left the air black with falling sweet ash.

I woke before dawn, too, and walked past the kitchen, where Léonide had already stoked the fire for their coffee. Her doorway was outlined in glow.

Le quartier seemed so far. That first day, I had only reached the barn when his crying echoed from the road. A desperate bird, caught in a branch. My breasts stung, and then my dressfront was wet.

He drank as if it didn't matter how I smelled or whose animal I was. "Look how he know you," Philippine said, trying to reassure me.

Yes, because he's only an animal. Blind. Rooting.

It would have been hard to kill him when he was inside me, without knowing what to drink or do, but watching him mewling and his legs drawn up helplessly to his chest, his eyes unseeing when they tried to focus on my face, I understood what some women did.

Just don't make them live.

My bones were so tired, from the pain that lingered between my legs and in my back.

Every dark morning, I was alone on the road. I had hardly walked alone since Azure, my head thrown up to look at branches and late stars and smudges of dark fur or feathers moving through the brush. The other animals, finding food. Here, it was always assumed I would run again.

Now that this child lay waiting for me, it was assumed that his body would bind me to this path, that my feet would never turn of their own accord toward the bayou or the road.

Past the barn, past the work bell, toward the ragged scarf of smoke from Philippine's chimney—making those clinking sounds at her hearth as when I was first here, when I was still a child.

My child was screaming for me. For my milk. His cries flew with the smoke.

Three times a day, he stared at me while he drank, seeming smaller than when he was born. I couldn't wish for him not to live. By the third week, he cried constantly. He woke everyone on the street. He was desperate, and Fantine shook her head. "Francine never woke anyone?" I asked, angrily.

Fantine said, "She sleep side me, and I wake up and feed her before she know she hungry."

"You don't sleep in a hallway," I said. I didn't want her to feel so superior, even though she had touched my hair and my clothespins and thought she knew about me. Still, no one truly knew.

But Fantine said, "I give him milk from one side if he cry. Till you get here." She put her hand on my shoulder, and I could only lean my cheek down toward her knuckles.

One morning, near the trees before dawn, a cart came toward me, wheels creaking loud. The horse's breath streamed out like smoke, and a man's breath streamed out like steam as they came nearer. Then Hervé Richard said, "Joli fantôme. A beautiful spirit in the woods."

He was delivering a cypress chest carved with delicate filigree, for Pélagie's linens. He said, "You haunt the road so early?"

He kept his eyes on me as though I would run. He got down from the cart and stood close enough that I smelled tobacco. His eyelids quivered. Did he smell milk?

He said, "I wait all this time to see you."

"You don't know me."

"You just like me." His hair glittered with dew. His hair uncovered.

"I am not like you."

He put his hands gently on my wrists, and I pulled away so hard my breasts shook. They hurt. He said, "Don't be afraid. I just want to touch your skin. All this time, I think about you. You waiting to run. You run before. Blacksmith—he tell me."

"I am not running now." Were those faint baby cries? No—only the horse breathing and the first bird calling.

He moved my sleeve up over my forearm again. "But look—you brand with *M*. This Rosière."

"That is not a brand."

Hervé Richard stepped back and lifted his hands. "My mistake." Drops of water fell onto his shoes. "But you walk alone now. Toute seule. You free to come and go."

My breasts pulsed with milk. "I have to see someone in le quartier."

"A man?"

"No." His hand landed again on the bone of my arm, careful as a moth.

"Then you talk to me awhile."

"No." I dropped my arm from under his fingers and walked down the road. Ahead of me, Philippine carried her night jar to the privy, and Jean-Paul whimpered fast and hard. My dressfront was wet in spreading warm circles that turned cold as I ran.

At noon, Hervé Richard sat on a stump near the barn, working a rag over a harness. Pélagie still had not examined the chest; she slept very late. Hervé Richard said only, "Fantôme moves fast in the day, no?" He smiled on the one side again, a dent appearing in one cheek.

Inside Philippine's cabin, we held the babies to our breasts. Fantine said, "That man? He speak to you?"

I nodded. She said, "Skin like cornbread and syrup. Like you could taste it."

"Hush, Fantine," Sophia said, frowning. "Free nègre like that. He sit in the road cause mulatto not good enough for the house and think he too good for the barn."

I put my finger into the corner of Jean-Paul's mouth to pull him away from my breast, and he jerked awake as if burned. "He is not free," I said. "He is like us."

"He's prettier than me," Fantine said. "I see him talk to you before."

"Before?" Sophia said. "When?"

"He brought the coffins last year," I said. In the dim light from the doorway, my son's eyes were purple, blue, black.

"I look at dead men that night. Not no yellow nègre." Sophia stood up and went outside.

Fantine shrugged and said, "Not yellow. Just pretty."

On the road to the house, he was waiting. He began to walk beside me. I glanced sideways—his shoulder was level with my eyes. His shirt was mended clumsily, with wide stitches like a caterpillar crawled up his arm.

He said nothing until we reached the clearing where my laundry hung. Then he turned to me. "If I come back, you meet me somewhere?"

His eyes were very black. Darker even than my mother's. I said, "Meet you in the woods? For what? For you to touch my skin?"

He didn't smile. He said, "To talk."

The shutters were still closed over Pélagie's window. This was not a dance. "Talk about music? Talk about flowers? About painting?"

"Talk about New Orleans."

If anyone heard us, we could be whipped. I moved away quickly and said, "I have work."

I sat outside Pélagie's door, not sewing, waiting for her to awaken, for the sound of her voice, calling my name.

In the morning, he was there in the cart. I spoke first. "I am not a fantôme. My madame will look at the chest today, she says."

He got down off the cart and stood before me. "In New Orleans, so many people no one knows who is owned and who is free."

"I cannot run again."

"You don't run. You ride."

"I cannot ride a horse." The mist hid the trees like rain on a window. Hervé Richard smelled of tobacco smoke; while he waited for me, he added his gray breath to the fog.

"If you meet me in the woods, I will bring an armoire."

"For Madame?"

"For you. Put you in the armoire and lock it. Drive the cart to New Orleans for delivery. No one find us there. Too many slaves."

"Someone would stop you on the road."

He shook his head, and again, drops of water fell from his hair. "I have a pass from a friend."

The horse moved forward and the cart wheels rubbed and creaked. "They say the wheels cannot be greased in New Orleans. So the guard will know if you steal. You would be stealing me. They might—"

I put my hands warm over my ears. Hamstrung. Fleur-de-lis. A crime against God.

"You cannot steal yourself," he said, and as if he had seen inside my skull, "God doesn't believe that is stealing." His forehead was calm. His smile was only a fingernail mark in his left cheek. "I don't care about les blancs," he said. "Every man need a treasure. Gold. Your face is gold. You are the same as me."

"You only know my face. Nothing else." The tips of my breasts began to ache, as if pinched. The milk would flood my dress.

"You know yourself. You know my face. Now you know your chance."

He took the reins of the horse. The shoulder muscles rippled. Not angel wings. A brand. A triangle containing an *L*.

"I will sand wood for the armoire. You think where to meet me."

Pélagie refused the chest. She did not approve of the grain of the wood on one side. She said to Lise, "The carpenter will bring a new one in a month. He will check the pattern on all sides. I won't tolerate Louisiana standards."

Hervé Richard or his owner would come. The woods. Who would know if I met him there? Who besides Pélagie would care if I disappeared? Sophia would still have her meat—it wouldn't be her fault this time.

Only my fault. No one was in charge of me. I was not in charge of Jean-Paul. Would he know? Would he taste my milk different from Fantine's?

But Pélagie would notice my absence if it was more than a minute. She did not mention an armoire or more trunks but talked of the wedding guests, plates, the food, lights in the garden.

Did she remember what she had said about quadroon boys? Drowned like kittens? She never saw my son.

The overseers didn't even look at me on the road so late at night, after Pélagie had gone to sleep. I fed Jean-Paul, cleaned him, and then gave him back to Philippine. After a time, his eyes opened wide. He studied my face as intent and uncomprehending as an old man. He wanted something from me. Milk? The sight of my face? What was his besoin? What did he *need*?

He was no one yet. His cheeks were red when he was born, then so pale it was as if no blood moved through his body.

"The father?" Philippine asked one evening.

I shrugged. "Sais pas."

Gervaise had come to take his son, Amadou, who was already stumble-walking, holding on to knees and chairs and tree stumps.

"Sais pas?" Philippine said. "The eyes. The chin. They don't tell?"

I shrugged again.

"Sometime a mark tell you." Fantine already knew everything, with her smooth, satisfied cheeks.

"Like what?"

"Mark on the face or the body," Fantine said.

Gervaise spoke suddenly, staring at Jean-Paul's hand dangling outside his blanket. "Non—ces enfants, too much mix the blood. Them baby all new people."

He didn't say it with hate. He looked again at Jean-Paul, with interest as he'd give a tree or an unusual stone. He had been here, in Louisiana, for the same time as I'd been here, on Rosière.

This life, on Rosière, was my second life. It was Gervaise's second life, too.

"Look his fingers," Philippine said. "Around the nails."

A rim of gold clung to the skin around his nails, where I used to chew tatters from my own fingers.

He scratched himself near the eye, and blood nestled into the cut. I used my teeth to trim his useless claws, which hurt only himself.

All new people. My mother could believe in *dya,* in the transference of one soul to the next soul born. But if she knew nothing of my father, and I knew not even who this baby's father was—Etienne or Ebrard—how could the right soul, any soul, hover and find the place to enter this child? And enter where—the skull? The open mouth, crying and crying for me while I moved clothes up and down the wooden ripples of washboard?

If Hervé Richard came for me, would he believe my son was the same as him? His people? Would he ever love Jean-Paul? He thought he loved me, but he only knew my face and hair. He imagined me, like the other men imagined me.

If I came late, Jean-Paul's mouth fastened onto me like the pinching of the white man in the boat. But baby fingers held tight to my thumb.

In the mornings, I washed. In the afternoons, I sewed in the hallway, while Pélagie and Lise sewed in the parlor. Dresses and napkins and lace. All so she could marry Msieu Prudhomme, and he could lie on top of her, and she could hope he died. Or maybe she hoped to have a son. But she didn't want to share the window. She wanted me to arrange the dresses and hats and stockings there, and she wanted to present them to the women.

And Jean-Paul? Wherever her window was, he would not fit into her display.

What would Hervé Richard bring? I pricked my finger with the needle so I could taste one drop of my blood. A crying baby, inside an armoire?

A few weeks before the wedding, Etienne read his mother's latest letter to his father while they smoked at the table.

I have decided to return home, for Louisiana is my home now that you are both there. My sight has faded altogether, and the doctors say there is no further treatment. I have received your letters of Pélagie's impending wedding, and I would like to hear and smell and taste what she has undoubtedly worked so hard to prepare. I am bringing company—our cousins Gaston and Amélie Valmy, and a relative of Pélagie's late husband, who I only met recently. His voice was very refined, and his hand soft, and he said, "You must be the sister-in-law of someone I haven't seen in three years." He was quite happy to hear of her successes.

The letter ended with,

Last month, my beloved Amanthe died due to the cold here in Paris, which must have settled in her lungs and become pneumonia. I have engaged a servant here who will travel with us.

Philippine cried silently when I told her. The tears could not run down her cheeks. They were caught in the etchings below her eyes and disappeared.

Firmin went outside, to the edge of the woods. His ragged shirt floated like paper against the trees where he whirled in sorrow.

They didn't speak to anyone for days. At dusk, when I arrived, the babies all cried and stared at me. They weren't wet or hurt. But no one had spoken to them or held them.

Philippine's face was vacant. Just like Madame Bordelon's had been after Céphaline died—a way of mothers holding the skin over the skull so that it matched the unmoving child. Madame had never left her room after Céphaline died. But no one left other babies with her, and her door didn't open onto a dirt lane crowded with laughing, running children whose feet made clouds.

Philippine lay in her bed as if held inside a casket, staring at the ceiling.

No one knew what Madame de la Rosière said to Philippine and Firmin after she called for them. In the bustle of unpacking the trunks, we became sure that she was blind now, Etienne leading her carefully around the house with his four fingers draped over her sleeve. It was from the upstairs window that I saw Philippine and Firmin, their small backs floating in the dust halfway down the road heading back to le quartier.

My forehead rested against the wooden shutters. The Bordelons had once brought a relative's body from France for burial, but of course Amanthe would have been buried in Paris, in a paupers' cemetery. She owned nothing. She was owned.

But no. Slavery was illegal in France. She was free now, her box disintegrating, her bones sliding into the earth.

That night, Firmin met me near the barn, carrying Jean-Paul's box. Fear leaped under my breastbone.

Was the baby dead?

Firmin handed me the box where Jean-Paul slept, his face turned to the side, his fist small as a candle nub. "We don't keep him. Rosières do not keep us. They do not keep our bones. I am not a crime against God."

He was going to run again. I was afraid to say anything; then I could be an accomplice. Carrying Jean-Paul, I rehearsed the words for Pélagie: The baby was sick, so I brought him here.

In the morning, near their cold fireplace with heaped, silent ashes, I let myself cry. They were gone. Philippine's fingers like twigs in my grip when the pains came. Firmin's fingers carving clothespins.

Gervaise said, "They go to the next world. If they don't die, Firmin know to live out there. With cimarrons."

Cimarrons—the maroon runaways who made camps. But in the cipriére somewhere was the logging camp and the Indian hunter and the Irishman—what would he do with two old slaves?

Philippine's grief might kill her in the trees. Firmin's father had taken his life, and his body had been punished. But the de la Rosières had nothing now of Firmin's blood or Philippine's hands.

Pélagie stayed late in the parlor and didn't notice the sleeping baby. Many boxes had arrived for the wedding, with silks and haircombs and glasses, and his box was merely another.

In the morning, I carried him out before anyone awoke and fed him in the kitchen, where Léonide sat staring at the coals she knew like her own heart.

He stared at my face the same way. I moved his fingers, hands, feet. He still had no bones. Those soft, pliable things inside him couldn't be bones. He was only meat. He was not mine. But then I touched his head, to move him to my other breast, and felt the skull. Bone. Shield for the passages and folds of his brain.

He knew me. I didn't want to know him yet.

"They run?" Léonide said finally. When I nodded, she sighed.

The babies had to go to Emilia, a woman who had been hurt in the fields and couldn't work. Her leg, gashed with a cane knife during harvest, was swollen and infected. She sat on a chair with her leg on a box, the babies beside her.

Léonide and I cooked oysters brought by a boat peddler. My fingers were numb from shucking, but the shells inside were patched with pieces of pearl, and I kept the best one, with the most shine, to show Jean-Paul someday when he was a person. Not a baby.

The company from France arrived in the carriage just before dinner, and so when Pélagie came downstairs to the dining room, she made her false greeting smile as she looked around the table.

When she saw the man, with his sharp-waisted Paris coat and his black hair curling over his ears, she dropped her gloves.

She didn't speak first, as she always did. She was not charming. Her face was white as rice powder, with two spots of dull red at her cheeks as though someone had knuckled her hard.

"Madame Vincent!" the man said. "So good to see you after all this time." He turned to the others. "She was married to my brother Micael."

"Your brother!" Madame de la Rosière said. "I knew only that you were a relative. Why, you must have been so sad when he died." She inclined her head toward each exhaled breath, trying hard to listen to who would speak. Her eyes were rimmed with ice now, pools of water clouded and cold.

"It was tragic," the man said. "A fever."

"He was a good husband," Pélagie said carefully.

"Madame says you plan to marry again soon," the man said, tilting his head to the side to study her.

Msieu Laurent didn't like him. He said sharply, "An old Louisiana name, Oscar Prudhomme. He is a widower, and a good match. Often, those who have lost loved ones make a quiet triumph."

I removed his plate. The cousins talked about the sea voyage, but the man watched Pélagie, who ate nothing.

He slept in the garçonnière with Etienne. When I brought their hot water for washing, he said in his precise French, words stinging separate, "Your dressfront is wet."

"Oui, msieu."

"Are you burned by the water?"

"Non, msieu."

He stared at me again. "You have a child."

I nodded.

"And you belong to Madame Vincent?"

"Oui, msieu."

Etienne came inside and frowned at me. "My mother needs you in the house now. Her new servant is incapable."

The new woman was French and twenty-five. She would not speak to me. I showed her silently where the cistern held our water, where the bed warmers were, and where I collected the soiled clothing.

For a week, the brother-in-law smiled and watched, and Pélagie moved about the house like a cautious pheasant, her dress trailing behind her slowly rather than flicking sharply around corners as it usually did. Lise left one morning for New Orleans. Pélagie's face was drawn as if she hadn't slept, the hollows of her cheeks holding nothing. Not even air. Purple dusk collected under her eyes.

Msieu Vincent spoke little when Msieu Prudhomme called on his way to Opelousas. Both men watched each other, like hunters watched everything—branches, grass, vines—waiting for movements.

On Sunday, when the cousins would be taken to Grand Coteau, Pélagie said softly, "Monsieur Vincent and I will remain here. My brother-in-law and I have much to discuss. Please tell the others we will miss their company."

She was afraid, the way she had been when she first came to Rosière. This must be the man Pélagie mentioned, the one she thought wouldn't find her. Did she have something that belonged to him?

"Moinette, do you have that tablecloth?" Pélagie called, voice high. "Bring it to me in the parlor, so I may see the hem."

When I brought it, the afternoon light was like syrup in the windows and on the parlor floor. Two empty wine bottles and remnants of cold meat stood on a platter. Pélagie motioned for me to wait while she looked at the hem, and he began speaking fiercely to her.

"Are you prepared for me to tell them now? To show them the marriage contract?" He sat in Madame de la Rosière's chair, his legs crossed.

"This is not France. That contract—"

"You are now married to me. There is no divorce in France, and you are still a French subject."

He spoke to her as if she were a slave. She raised her eyes to mine and handed me the tablecloth, straightening her back. She said, "When I marry Prudhomme, I will be a citizen of Louisiana."

He walked over to bend close to her. I could smell his pomade. "You will not insult my family further with this transgression. You insulted my brother with your dowry. We had been led to believe it would be substantial, and you brought only that bit of cash and those damned jewels no one could touch or sell."

"My aunt controlled the rest. You know that."

"You refused to speak to her."

"My aunt told me every single day that I killed my mother with my birth. How could my words force her to sign the Lyon property to me? And I was only sixteen when your brother married me."

"When he died, you were twenty. You had used his money, eaten his food, and provided him with no issue."

Pélagie didn't cry. She tightened her hands on the arms of her chair until her knuckles were white stars. "He provided for himself. He provided elsewhere and brought the disease to me."

He leaned forward and put his finger in the space between her collarbones. What was the hollow called, where his finger went deep? "And you gave it to me."

"You provided yourself as well," she whispered harshly, pinned to her chair. "You forced yourself onto me. Do you hear that, Moinette? He came into my bedroom and—"

"Why tell her? She is not present here."

"Yes, she is."

"You. Go get coffee and cakes."

Pélagie breathed hard when he removed his finger, a red moon dug by his nail in her throat.

I told Léonide that the man inside was frightening Madame Pélagie, and Léonide shrugged. "Blankitte business. Belong to the whites. Not yours."

From the kitchen door, I could see the road toward le quartier, where Jean-Paul sucked on his sugar-rag and stared at the ceiling or the sky, at the face that hovered over him now and then.

If this man made Pélagie go back to France with him, I would be taken as well. Or more likely, he would sell Jean-Paul and me.

I was so angry, I spilled some of the coffee on my hand, and the splashing heat somehow made the scar on my back sting. Fire traveling along my skin. The smell of the coffee. My three coffee beans washed from Sophia's floor to the earth outside.

I wished I had poison for his cup. Slave women poisoned men, the whites always whispered. Maybe he would make me taste it first.

I cut the sugar with the tongs. The pot of coffee and two cups, along with a seed cake, on the tray. Léonide was asleep now in her chair, her huge shoulders rising and falling with her breath.

His mouth was so close to Pélagie's hair that his words moved the curls.

"Your aunts saw me inside you, in your bed, and your legs open wide. There was no choice but to marry me. And you have been useless to me ever since, except that now you own something. Your brother's wife told me in Paris that you own land, and slaves. Both are mine as well, by the laws of community property, and you are depriving me of that income."

I put the tray on the table between their chairs. She met my eyes. Her pupils were huge and black as jet beads.

"I have nothing to give you."

"I want the land. A fresh start, to move here and begin anew. I am tired of Paris."

"You are tired of owing money in Paris." She glanced at the darkened window. She saw herself. "My brother says that I was legally right to leave you."

"But by French law, you were not permitted to leave the country without my permission. And I gave you none."

"You were living in Paris with a woman!"

He shrugged and smiled. "Which is not illegal. I may leave, as long as I provide for you, which I did."

"You were starving me. There was no heat. You tied me to a chair."

He turned palms to the ceiling. "You do remember what the judge said in his ruling. There was no sufficient reason to justify your absence from the conjugal domicile."

"The judge did not live in that house. The judge was an old man."

"The judge said you would be subject to arrest if you left. You have been charged with criminal desertion, which allows me to take control of all your assets. Have you slept with this man you thought you would marry? A criminal liaison will add to your prison sentence." He touched a shred of meat on his teeth with his tongue.

"I will not return to France."

"You will return speaking or not speaking."

"What are you saying?"

He pinched her lips closed, and she tore her face from his fingers. We were alone. Everyone else was in Grand Coteau.

Msieu Vincent reached for my arm now, and I saw the gun. "Pour the coffee. Madame Vincent is going to kill herself in despair over her fraud. Her shame." He put the gun into my dressfront. "If you scream, I will shoot you like a dog."

One of Msieu's pistols, with his initials engraved in the silver.

"Madame Vincent, your slave is obedient. She is mine now. Everything you own is mine. When your brother returns, your brother whom you talk about as if he were a deity, I will show him the notarized marriage papers. No one in this parish will speak to you again."

Her eyes moved to the window again; I saw us both in the glass. She twisted her necklace around her finger. "I owe you nothing."

"Then your only choice is to remove yourself from this world."

Pélagie stood up, and he pointed the gun at her. "Madame Vincent, you are going to die in a few moments. One thing you may choose, as a woman, is how you die. Your slave belongs to me now, and I will kill her afterward if she does not cooperate."

I felt the space of the room around me, the room I swept and dusted and straightened, the brocade fabric and wooden table legs.

"There are two stories. Your slave found this gun in the desk and shot you because I promised to bring her to Paris and you refused. She became angry."

"Moinette! You will not forget a word when you tell them!"

The gun's mouth—a perfect circle of black.

"Unfortunately, madame, you have not read the Code Noir. Your own slave code in Louisiana. I have read it. Article Twenty-four forbids slaves from giving testimony unless it praises whites and forbids their serving witness against their master."

"She may tell my brother!"

He smiled. "She may tell him whatever she wishes, if she lives. But no one is required to listen. She is not a viable presence here. She is nothing. You are nothing."

Pélagie circled the room, the gun following her, and he said, "Sit down and think about this for a moment. Drink your last cup of coffee. If you try to take the gun, the wild shot will only prove that you knew I would reveal your fraud to your lover, and when you missed, I had no choice but to shoot you in defense."

She didn't back away until he raised the pistol to her face.

"Drink your coffee. Eat your cake."

He sat in the chair again, his hand steady with the metal circle directly across from her forehead. The black iron was exactly the size of the seven curls on each side of her face, the curls I had formed that morning.

She glanced up at me, near the coffee service on the small table. The cherrywood table, with grains inside the wood.

"Moinette," she said, and I poured more coffee. Her hand shook so hard she removed the saucer.

She leaned forward and threw the hot coffee into his face. The gun went off so close to me I felt the air move. Pélagie's chest flew back into her chair, and blood filled her dressfront.

But she stood, groping for something in the air. He wiped at his eyes, saying, "I will push this gun up your barren, diseased—"

I swung the silver pot and hit him in the head, and he fired the gun into the ceiling. A cloud of plaster swirled down like a white veil, hanging in the air with smoke.

The clawed foot of the pot caught him in the eye, and he screamed. Pélagie kicked him twice where he had fallen from the chair, and then she collapsed. The gun skittered along the floor.

I was afraid to touch it. I ran down the hallway and out into the yard. Léonide? Testify. We could not testify.

A horse's hooves clattered into the yard.

Msieu Vincent would come outside and shoot me, or Msieu de la Rosière would have me hanged for striking a white man. I was dead.

"Moinette!" Etienne shouted. "You are covered in blood!"

He got down from the horse, carrying five dead birds on a brace in one hand and his hunting rifle in the other.

"He is killing her inside," I said.

The coffee had stained the wall in brown flames. He was trying to fit the gun into her hand, on his knees, blood trickling from one eye. "Monsieur!" Etienne shouted. "Leave her!"

"She has shot herself in despair," he said thickly. "I was trying to revive her."

I whispered. Testify. He owned me now. You don't belong to anyone. You belong to God.

"He shot her. I hit him to stop it."

Msieu Vincent's cuffs had rested in her blood. The red liquid crept up his wrists. He said, "She sold your son to me for a hundred dollars while you were in the kitchen. You would lie for her?"

Her face was hidden. Her skull was a white line where I had parted her hair, over and over. "He shot her for no reason, Msieu Etienne, he came here to kill her. Please, msieu. Look."

Msieu Vincent pried the gun from her fingers and raised it toward me, and Etienne shot him with the hunting rifle.

Her body. I bathed her. So much blood—the smell of it when my wet rag turned the ceramic clotting into liquid again. My maid dresses hair. Dress the body. The bullet hole like an insect's home in her chest.

The midnight blue silk dress. Not black crepe. She was not in mourning. She would never display dresses and hats in the window. She died with no issue. Issue forth from the body.

I dressed her hair. It was not dead. Her arms and legs were stiff now, her lips purple and slack, but her hair curled around my fingers. What did the French believe in? Where was her soul? If the French believed in heaven, and souls were with their god, then they had only one life. One chance. But if Bambara people were right, the soul slipped into the next infant and the *dya* had the chance to live again. To try again.

Pélagie's mother died giving birth to her, and so her soul hadn't had far to travel. I went to le quartier to feed Jean-Paul. I smelled of blood, even though I washed. I touched his scant hair. Did I have my mother's mother's *dya*? The woman named Amina, from Senegal? Then why did I not love my son yet? I fed him, I cleaned him, but he was still a mysterious animal.

Dress the baby. Dress the table. Dress the meat. Dress the body. Dress the table again. Again. Again.

I did not dress Msieu Vincent's body. Manuel, the groom, washed off the blood inside the barn.

In the front room, while Msieu Prudhomme wept, Etienne told him, "My father will not have his body in the house. He will be buried in the farthest section from my aunt."

"How could she not have told me?" Msieu Prudhomme said, his whiskers trembling on his loose cheeks. "And how could you not have saved her?"

Etienne rubbed the skin beside his eyes again and again. "I came a few minutes too late. Her slave tried to save her."

"And you saved the slave." Msieu Prudhomme shook his head. "I will bid my adieus now. I cannot return for the burial. I cannot."

I kept away from her bedroom, where he closed the door. He stayed only for a moment.

Msieu de la Rosière said, "The coffins are here from Opelousas."

But Msieu Prudhomme said, "I cannot bear it."

The drive was full of carriages. The cousins from France who had arrived with Madame were leaving for New Orleans. They didn't wish to be associated with the deaths. Msieu Prudhomme's carriage waited as well, the black horses moving impatiently.

Hervé Richard got down from his cart and untied the ropes. Then he and Manuel carried the first coffin into the parlor. Pélagie's initials were carved on the side. I opened the door for them, and the smell of gunpowder and blood breathed from the heavy curtains. I had cleaned and cleaned the floor, but it was as if blood flourished in the grooves of the wood.

Manuel went outside to help Msieu Prudhomme into his carriage. Hervé Richard held my wrist at the parlor doorway and said quietly, "I will come tomorrow. Meet me before dawn in the woods near the road. Just past the Rosière gate, where lightning scarred the oak."

"How will I breathe?" I closed my eyes, imagined the darkness inside the armoire. I couldn't tell him about Jean-Paul. Not yet.

"A wedge of paper in the door where your face would be. Let a crack of air in. Bring your coat to make it softer for you inside."

He went back out to the cart and lowered the other coffin with Manuel. When they returned from the barn, Manuel said, "Get him some water from the kitchen."

Hervé Richard followed me there. The fire was low, and Léonide had covered her dishes. Her breathing was loud next door, where she napped in her chair.

When I gave him the cup of water, Hervé Richard set it on the table. He put his fingers on my temples and pulled my face to his. He said, "I would never stop you from breathing."

The table's edge was at my back. His eyes and mine, his mouth and mine, his chest and mine, his hips and mine. The width of paper between us. A wedge of paper for me to breathe. The paper with my name. He said, "I want to love you."

I pulled away to look at him. His hair was curlier than mine, brushed down in two wedges from a part, which shone nearly white. His eyebrows were thick and black. I wouldn't look into his eyes yet. His throat worked when he swallowed his own saliva. He hadn't touched the water. His collarbones were like branches through the damp fabric of his shirt. He wanted only to be kind to me.

Léonide's breathing stopped, and her feet shifted on the floor.

"Why?" I whispered.

"You don't know what they say? You just see the one and you know? That's the one for you."

He leaned so that only his shoulders bent down to touch mine, and Léonide got up so heavily, her chair thumped against the other wall.

Stand up and don't get a baby, Fantine had said. Another baby. He wanted to join himself to me and make another baby. He moved away. Air rushed between us.

Outside, where he was untying the horse, I said softly, in case Manuel heard, "What if someone tries to rob you of your armoire, on the road?"

Hervé Richard fixed his black eyes on me, and now I looked into the pupils. I could see myself, frozen. He said, "I won't let nobody stop me moving. I get what I want."

Etienne spoke to me in the empty house of Firmin and Philippine, where I slept now.

"The burials are tomorrow."

I sat in the chair worn smooth by Philippine's movements. Carved wood. Jean-Paul barely fit in his box now.

"My father wishes me to interview you."

"Oui, msieu."

"He has asked me to record exactly what happened before I arrived."

"Oui, msieu."

Jean-Paul murmured under his blanket, and my breath caught in my chest. Etienne did not look at the baby. He did not look at me. He looked at the paper before him, on Philippine's table, and I saw the webbing of red in his eyes. He had wept. His aunt, the only smile here, was gone; his mother was blind, and his father angry.

"My father has asked, repeatedly, exactly when you struck Msieu Vincent."

Le Code Noir—the penalty for striking a master in the face was death. But he became my master only when she was dead.

"When he shot Madame Pélagie, msieu."

"Did your action make the ball hit her?"

"No, msieu."

"You cannot testify in court."

My hand was at the back of Jean-Paul's skull.

"You are telling me, *only* me," he said sharply.

"Oui, msieu. I struck him with the coffeepot when he was going to shoot her again. She was standing. She was still alive." I fixed my eyes on the door. "She was still my mistress."

No one came that night to visit with Msieu or eat with Madame. No one came that night to stay at Rosière for the burials in the morning. When Céphaline had died, Azure was full of guests. But the shame of Pélagie kept this house empty.

The servant from France slept on a pallet inside Madame's room.

The doors down the hallway were all closed. The floor shone silver as when I had first arrived. I did not sleep outside Pélagie's door. Her body lay downstairs inside the wooden box. Her husband's body lay in the barn.

I lay in Philippine and Firmin's old bed, with Jean-Paul beside me. He lay on his stomach with his arms and legs curled under him like a large beetle. But his mouth was open. His breaths dampened my arm.

It is dangerous to be so rested. My mother's voice came to me. The window shutters were closed tight. I would have to leave before dawn. If Mirande or Baillo saw me on the road to the house, I would say Léonide needed help early for the funeral.

I would have Jean-Paul tucked inside my cape.

But Jean-Paul fussed when the before-dawn air hit his face, as the door closed, and I pushed him inside my dress, where he latched onto my breast. The houses of le quartier were all dark. Someone snored in Sophia's room. No one cried.

He drank while I walked, and the feel of my feet moving while his mouth pulled at the milk made me dizzy. Sideways and forward. Slowing my steps. The stocks. The bell. He slept inside my dressfront. Milk leaked from his mouth and ran down my ribs.

Just past the bell, I shifted without thinking to the narrow footpath beside the road. The road was marred with deep ruts from cart wheels, full of water. A small reddish bayou alongside the foot trail I walked every day and night. When I stopped to listen for a cart, deep in the woods, Jean-Paul stirred, and each time my movements stopped, he made the bird sounds that would escalate into cries if his lips hadn't found my breast.

There was no sound. No animals. The sky was the deep black of no moon or sun or promise of anything. Not day and not night.

This was an animal trail. My animal trail, from Pélagie's room to Léonide's kitchen to le quartier. Every day. If I stayed, my feet would wear down wood floors and brick walkway and earthen road until my shoulders were swallowed by banks along my way. I would walk the same circles until I died, until Jean-Paul walked taller than me.

I heard nothing. No owls. No rustling. Only my son's throat working, though no milk came now, though he swallowed his own saliva and thought it sustenance.

A baby would never last inside an armoire. We would be found. Hervé and Jean-Paul could be killed. I saw my child dashed against a tree. Tucked into a basket and sold. Drowned like a kitten. Useful for nothing. I saw myself lying under men in the trees. The trees were a wall beside me. I couldn't take Jean-Paul into the trees. Hervé Richard thought he loved me.

He loved what he thought of me.

I didn't know Hervé Richard. Only that he wanted me. He didn't know I had a son. Pélagie had been the property of the man who'd shot her. Her shame—that she had run from him, even as he'd tied her to chairs and starved her—her shame, not his, now kept everyone Creole and French away from her body. Her body was dressed in fine silk, but she belonged to those men.

She wanted a window.

You belong to no one. Not Msieu. Not God. You belong to me.

My mother. My son. What if Hervé Richard made me leave him here, on the soft bed of oak leaves near my feet? What if Hervé Richard took me in the armoire to New Orleans and then tied me to a chair? He wanted my face. What if he didn't want my brain or my measurements or the issue of my body?

No issue.

I could take Jean-Paul back right now to Fantine. She would feed him. She would love him. He might love her. I could come back for him someday. When I was free.

His lips pulled hard again when I turned to hurry back. My arm hurt from bending. My left arm. The arm that did less work except to hold him.

I wrapped my cape around me more tightly and ducked past the low branches along the trail. If he stayed with Fantine, he would live.

The hooves approached from the street. Jean-Paul slept now, from my walking. Baillo leaned down from his horse and said, "You forget something?"

I said, "Léonide wants to start cooking early, for the funeral, so I have to leave my son now."

He waited outside Fantine's door. I laid Jean-Paul next to her, and she turned away from Basile's back. The cabin smelled of sweat and milk and salt, warm cloth and almond oil. Jean-Paul jerked his head against her. Fantine said sleepily, "Ain't time yet."

I whispered into my son's ear, "Adieu."

My nipple was sore and cold. I buttoned my dressfront outside under my cape. Baillo slumped on his horse. I walked quickly up the road, and the sky began to turn purple in the trees. The hunting path through the woods was past the allée of crape myrtle trees. The hooves followed me at a distance all the way to the kitchen, where Léonide's fire sent smoke in black smudges across the dawn.

The second time he spoke to me, Etienne said, "Your baby stayed here with the old couple who ran. You never heard them plan to escape?"

"Non, msieu."

"You were here but never heard them speak of where they would go?"

Did he not know that Amanthe was their daughter and that his own mother had taken her away forever? Did he not even know their names?

"Non, msieu."

"Two more ran last night. For anyone who knew of these plans, or where the slaves are hiding, the penalty will be death."

"Oui, msieu." I tucked my lips between my teeth to keep them from shaking. Hervé Richard had come and gone. A week had passed. Pélagie lay under the earth. Jean-Paul lay sleeping on the bed. At night, he twitched and moved against my ribs, as hot as bread.

Etienne rubbed his middle finger hard between his brows. "My father doesn't want you to serve in the house again. He is not certain that you had no part in his sister's death."

Was I allowed to say: I tried to save her, I touched her more than I have ever touched another human animal, every day I washed her and curled her hair and pulled the stays on her corset until her shoulder blades, not angel wings but shoulder blades, rose and a deep hollow formed between them and she couldn't reach the sweat so I wiped it from her skin there?

I said nothing. These words were not allowed.

"My father is unmoving in his opinions once they are formed." Then he put his elbows on his knees and curled his shoulders toward the fire as if the heat were a cape.

But when Msieu Laurent went to New Orleans, Léonide insisted I help her with the meat. A hard freeze had set in, the cane couldn't be planted because the furrows were solid as stone, and the cold meant pigs should be killed for the smokehouse.

At the long wooden table we waited for the sound of iron crushing bone. Pig skulls were long and slanted compared to ours. Their brains would be made into jelly.

We were covered in blood, after we had cut the ribs into curving shelves. The ax severed the spine. The wind blew tiny splinters of iced blood from the table. The entrails, for sausage casings, were transparent as wet muslin in my fingers. I breathed in the salty, coppery blood—why did blood scent not enter my lungs, as the indigo smell had spread its poison in my grandmother's body?

When I went to feed Jean-Paul, his whole face drew back like a frightened turtle from the smell of my stained dressfront. In the lines of my knuckles, the dried blood was black.

His fingers were still curled soft as shrimp—easy to bite off if the wrong animal found him. His arms and legs tender. His skull pulsing under the useless thin fur in the cold room.

When the meat was ground into sausage and cooked into jellies and the hams submerged in their salt baths and then hung in the smokehouse, I went back to the canefield.

The silver air turned gold, and the frost melted into the earth. We pulled the seed cane from the matelas pile, where it was stacked in the field against frost. At night, my nostrils were coated with rings of white frost—no, rings of dried salt. I tasted the salt. All the excretions of our bodies contained salt—tears, urine, sweat. Saliva?

Like the taste of my own blood. Salty and rich.

Sophia craved salt, and a few times I had brought her small pinches of salt from the house.

Now, nursing Jean-Paul with my hands still cold and my legs aching from the canefield, I understood how much they needed salt, and meat. Mamère and her coffee, warm under her fingers in the morning.

I understood how desperate they were for the feathery pink ham, salty and solid in their back teeth. I bit off a callus from my palm. Hardtack. No salt in my skin. Where did the salt go?

Gervaise ran that night and took his baby with him. Sophia didn't scream or cry in the morning. She simply said, "He say Msieu could sell his son. He say you was sold to Madame Pélagie but who know about your son? Say nobody take his son or he die."

"But how will he feed Amadou?"

"Amadou make a year last week. He eat cush-cush. I don't know what Gervaise feed him, but he live."

Fronie came outside, her braids mussed from sleep, and Sophia smoothed the hairs. "Didn't say, What she do I take her son? Nothing. Say in his mind, She got Fronie."

Was Gervaise in a camp of cimarrons with Philippine and Firmin? Or had they all been caught and taken to the cypress camp? Would Athénaïse see them? What if he had killed the white man, and he ran the camp himself now? Or the Indians? What would the brother and sister do with a baby like Amadou?

Days later, Gervaise slipped into le quartier and left Sophia a curl of Amadou's hair inside a map he had drawn. But she burned the map, saying she couldn't understand what he had tried to show her. She tucked the curl into her pocket and turned away from the fire.

Msieu Antoine came while Msieu de la Rosière was still in New Orleans. The Frenchwoman had been sent away as she was incompetent, and I was called to the house. Madame de la Rosière looked at the walls with her cloud eyes. She did not play the piano. She asked Msieu Antoine to read to her in the parlor.

When I brought breakfast to Etienne in the garçonnière, he glanced up from his maps. He asked me nothing. He began to speak.

"The Prudhommes will never visit this house again."

My fingers arranged sugar on the tray. White, sparkling shards.

"I was trained to kill for the protection of royalty, not to save a slave. All people will remember is that two French citizens are dead. And you live."

His boots needed blacking.

"All my mother ever wanted was to see me again, and my father refused my return until now. Now she touches me but cannot see me."

Am I meant to feel pity for you? All I ever wanted was to touch my own mother again.

He lifted his chin at the fields. "Reading Latin wasn't necessary for me to grow sugarcane. And unless I'm going to kill everyone here, with a massive plan, the military was useless as well."

But he'd killed someone to save me. My eyes stayed on the bootheels. "How old were you when you were sent away?"

"Twelve," he said. "I was always in the woods. The Indians lived on the back of this place, by the ciprière, and one old man taught me to hunt. He called me a voyageur. Coureur-de-bois. A woodsman. We went for miles into the forest, hunting deer, even bear. We skinned the bear and took the grease down the bayou to sell." He moved his fingers on his hand-drawn map—preparing to hunt Philippine and Firmin? To see where the slaves could be hiding? He had inked in forests and bayous and slices of land along the water like crowded long teeth. "Now there are plantations everywhere. The Indian hunters are drunk in Opelousas."

Etienne didn't know about the logging camp, the red trade cloth in my mouth. The clearwater breath of the Indian woman, the smoky smell of her brother's hair.

"Son." He moved his boots on the wooden floor, and some of the drying mud fell into the cracks. "I will be the only son forever."

Until your father is gone.

"My mother will stay blind here, until she dies."

But you'll know. My toes pushed the clots of mud I would add to my land outside this door. You'll know when she dies. She will call to you. My mother will pray, holding the bracelet of hair, saying the African words I will never hear again unless someone sends me to Azure and she hasn't been sold. I will never know.

His eyes—darker than his mother's milky irises. Not the fierce flame blue of Céphaline's or the gray blue flecked with gold of Pélagie's. Etienne had eyes dark and muddy like indigo cloth. Soldier blue.

Taking the key from Madame's table, I told Léonide we needed ham. Madame had ordered a large dinner for Msieu Antoine and Etienne. She could see nothing. The men were in Opelousas until night. The dinner would be very late.

I cut two large slices of ham and wrapped the meat in rags. Léonide slept in her chair by the fire. I ate the slivers that fell on the cutting table, my fingers slippery with the greased skin.

In le quartier, I put half the meat in Sophia's room, on my old sleeping shelf. She had fed me pieces of small bird. She hadn't had to. I left the other meat in Fantine's. My palms smelled of fat, as when I'd measured tallow for Mamère.

Shreds of flesh on our teeth, ground to satisfy us. My milk bluish white in drops on Jean-Paul's cheek when he let go. The salt would float inside him and enter his blood.

The third time Etienne questioned me, he said, "Who is the father?"

I stood before his desk, where he was surrounded by books, maps, lead balls in a dish.

The metal toys lodged in Pélagie's heart.

"I don't know, msieu."

"Ebrard or Léonce?"

Léonce must have been the boy who pinched me. I had never seen him since. Etienne didn't include his own name. Did he pretend he had never been with me? Or did he want me to say the words—c'est vous? But I didn't know, truly. Did he want me to name Léonce because none of us would see him again? That would be convenient.

Did he want to sell Jean-Paul?

"I don't know."

He looked at me furiously, his cheeks white under the sideburns, which always looked like pelt decorations men had sewn to their skin. "How can you not know?"

My eyes dropped to the floor. Dust, tiny bits of paper like eggshells, and mud in the shape of small flowers where he had stepped on it. I was afraid to say anything now. If I said, How could you have taken me upstairs? I was insolent. I had no idea what he would tolerate. His father tolerated no eyes or words.

"Who does it look like?" he asked finally, writing quickly. He wrote numbers. Prices for Jean-Paul? For others?

"It looks like a baby." My words were careful. "When they are only infants, they don't look like anyone sometimes."

"What kind of hair does it have?"

"Not much hair has grown yet." Jean-Paul's head still looked naked under his sparse black hair, veins pulsing when he cried.

Bluish purple blood. Sang mêlé. Quadroon. But a girl. Not a boy. What made a boy useful?

Then Msieu de la Rosière walked inside, and my brain felt filled with blood. Père. Père et fils. He said, "Are you finished with the calculations yet? We have to pay a blacksmith from Washington, now that mine has run." Then he pointed at me. "Every slave must be branded. Even her child."

Saliva rose bitter in my throat. Jean-Paul's small, limp arm, the thinness of his skin there.

"These Africans keep running, and I will not tolerate the assistance they find." He leaned out the window and spat. His earth. His liquids. "In Africa, they live in huts and burn cattle dung. They starve and kill one another."

But he didn't know Firmin was born in Louisiana, from an Attakapas mother. Firmin's blood was that of people who'd lived in the woods.

Etienne said, "The old man was already branded, no?"

"Firmin? Two fleur-de-lis. He will not return."

They would hang Firmin. Three times running meant death.

Etienne wrote quickly. "Even brand the house slaves?"

"Everyone. Everyone except this one. She is sold."

Seven OPELOUSAS

I left him lifting his head. He lay on his stomach in the box, while I folded little shirts made with scraps of linen from the wedding tablecloths. Heaps of cloth still in Pélagie's room. Madame couldn't see them, and Msieu wouldn't look at them. Only two days to prepare after he told me I was sold, and I sewed all night.

On the last day, a sound woke me in the chair where I'd slept. My neck was bent, and moving my head sent pain coursing down through my muscles. My left hand held the shirt. Snuffling—Jean-Paul was pushing himself up on his chest, raising his eyes to the top of the box, his forehead like a new moon rising over the edge.

I left him that morning, his head bobbing as if he were underwater. I carried his box to Emilia's room. She faced her open door, Francine crawling on a blanket beside her. Emilia's leg was up on a crate, and the skin of her calf was purple and swollen around the dressing over the cut. When I turned, Jean-Paul had raised his head to stare at her toes.

Everything was a lie. Céphaline had believed in words. Pélagie had believed in cloth and beauty. Amanthe had believed in waiting.

My mother had believed in her prayers. Or had she?

I now had nothing in my head or heart or hands. No words. Cranium. *Faro.* Dress the baby. Dress the table. Dress the body.

His footsteps made trails in the ceiling above me, where I lay on the pantry floor. Msieu Antoine's shoes. Then his feet. Washstand. Armoire. He knelt at the small altar. The knocking of knees.

When would he come? After he had prayed for himself?

Everyone believed in something. My mother and Hera. Each madame and her Catholic god. Marie-Claire, back on Azure, had believed in her own excretions entering the earth.

Philippine and Firmin had believed in Amanthe.

Hervé Richard had believed in me. He had believed I would wait for him in the woods and take his hand to step inside the armoire.

Jean-Paul was a baby. He was too small to believe in. And my mother? She couldn't still believe in her lessons, of *ni* and *dya.*

I believed in nothing now. I lay in the storeroom seeing my son's eyes. All new people, Gervaise had said. New people who could believe nothing.

Eyes tell. But Etienne's were blue, and I had never looked at Msieu Ebrard's eyes. We were not meant to look into white eyes.

Jean-Paul's eyes were purple. A raincloud at evening. No one's eyes.

I hated Msieu Antoine.

I had not hated the Bordelons, even Grandmère. I'd been afraid of them, except for Céphaline. But I had not loved her.

I had not hated the de la Rosières. Even Etienne, when he lay on me—he was the rider, I the animal. The animal did not hate as much as it was tired and bitter and pained.

I had not loved Pélagie, but I wanted to spend my life with her.

I hated the man who slept in the room above me now. We were alone in his brick house in Opelousas. His footsteps moved over me.

Knives waited in the kitchen. Dress the meat. If I killed him, my name would be in the newspapers as far as New Orleans. Slaves who killed masters were always famous. Everyone knew their names. The heads on the pikes at the river road had names.

Then my mother would know where I had gone. My own son would not wonder why I left him to search and smell and cry. I left him lifting his head. I had not hated him, but I had not loved him yet. I hadn't had time.

"You can be useful to me," Msieu Antoine had said this evening at the table. "More useful than you may understand. In fact, no one else in the world could accomplish for me what you can."

He ran his fingers over the table's gritty surface. Thin black hairs like insect antennae danced on each knuckle. His lips twisted like he held in a laugh, and I hated him with a burn that seared my throat. He went upstairs. He would come to the storeroom and ride me like an animal. I would kill him.

My eyes stayed on the floor. The bright pool of light from a candle would slide under the door before the feet arrived.

He did not come to the door. Before dawn, the milk knew what it was meant to do, and it coursed again into the dried, crusted-hard cloth over my breasts as if a ghost suckled there.

"You may begin with coffee."

The morning light streamed onto the floor around my blankets.

The knife would slide between his ribs. Cut off the long white fingers like ègret feathers. The bones at the edge of each wrist like tiny eggs. His coatsleeves moving when he reached for the cup.

"Who taught you to make such dark coffee?"

I wouldn't tell him. The dented pot. The working throat at dawn, eyes studying the slice of sky through the shutters.

"It is wonderful. I need coffee more than air. Thank you." He smiled vaguely, as if I were his wife, and went into his office, where he closed the door.

I was not a mother. Not a daughter. Not a sister. Not a wife.

I swept the brick floor of the kitchen.

Every time I tried to become some semblance of those words, a shadowy replica like a mimic butterfly, someone took away the necessary person. The person who defined me.

Your eyes could never meet theirs. Your pupils, the black dots of your vision, could not be reflected in the colored orbs Céphaline called mere decorations of iris. You were to know what they wanted by their voices and hands and whips and words.

He said only, "You will make this a fine house."

He needed sheets, curtains, wood for the stove, eggs, and plates for the eggs. He needed the hands to set plates on the table. But if this was a fine house for a bride, there was no bride.

On the top floor were four bedrooms. Three were bare. On the bottom floor, a kitchen with a dirty hearth, the pantry where I slept, a dining room with a scarred table, and a parlor Msieu Antoine had made into his office.

That room was comfortable, with a large desk and chair, with shelves to hold papers and books, with a couch and chair for clients, and a beautiful small table with curved legs to hold the coffee tray.

I made a second pot long before noon. "The coffee served at Madame Delacroix's boardinghouse is a poor imitation of this," he said, standing in the kitchen doorway while more beans roasted in a shallow pan. "I have eaten there for a year."

This was a statement. There was no answer.

"You didn't say who taught you to make coffee? Your mother?"

"Oui, msieu."

"In New Orleans?"

"Non, msieu. South of there. Azure."

"But you resemble a daughter of joy," he said thoughtfully, and returned to his office.

This was not a question. Resemble. I resembled things I was not. Was I a replacement for someone who had brought him joy and then left? Was he waiting until I ceased resembling a mother? I had wrapped my breasts with flannel rags, so tightly that the milk seemed to move hot into my shoulders when I turned the grinder handle.

A large silver coffee urn had been delivered, a few pots, and simple white plates and cups. Spoons.

Boiling water onto the ground coffee. The smell filled the kitchen like burning earth, like night erased by a different dark. Sun filled the shutters on the street windows with gold splinters.

I brought the coffee to his desk. He blew at the edge, took a sip and said, "Perfect." Then he studied his ink and motioned me to open the shutters. The silver salt liquid leaped from my heart to my throat to my eyes.

In the kitchen, the bitterness of coffee swam over my teeth and burned my tongue before the heat dropped into my ribs. I was my mother, but I was not. She had felt this rush of warmth and then a movement in her brain as if a tongue had licked at her skull. She had begun each day looking at me. But Jean-Paul drank Fantine's milk; he saw Emilia's face. His brain was small. He learned lessons when his stomach was empty, and he tasted molasses soaked into the weave of rag Emilia put into his mouth.

I wiped the tears with my sleeve before they reached my own mouth. A cricket moved uncertainly from the broom's edge. Cricket babies grew antennae far longer than their bodies. Their mothers taught them nothing about watching and waiting. My eyelashes were long. Fantine's and Pélagie's lashes would probably measure the same, if they were ever compared. Jean-Paul's lashes would grow in my absence.

Msieu Antoine wrote all day. Men knocked on the front door. I looked at their shoes, heard their words, brought coffee to the office. An Acadian man wearing blue homespun appeared at the back door holding a dead chicken by the feet.

Beyond the dining room window was the street crowded with carriages and horses and men arguing. Bills of sale. Settle the estate. The suit claims wrongdoing. The words flew inside his office and in the dining room. In the kitchen, I thrust the black skewering iron through the body of the chicken and heard it tear the flesh.

The men examined me for joy. They said low and approving, "Very fancy piece." "But this one cooks, too, eh? In addition."

Msieu Antoine replied, "She is already invaluable in many ways."

When the rooms grew dark, I was only afraid of the fingers. It sounds strange to say I hated the fingers more than the other, because the other seemed like a separate animal, a blind, foolish animal itself, and the fingers were attached to the man, his eyes watching.

"I would like to see your hair," he said, near midnight when the front door was locked. I had sat for hours near the low kitchen fire. I pulled the tignon from my head and unpinned my two braids. My hair was dirty and the curls matted down, so that the six sections of undone braid hung about me like ropes.

But if he wanted to ride me as a horse—a mule—ropes would be fine. My eyes focused on the embers.

He did not move. He said, "Was your mother's hair as long?"

"No, msieu."

"What color was your father's hair?"

"Sais pas, msieu."

"In Paris, they say each generation of New Orleans courtesans is more beautiful. But Pélagie told me you are a hairdresser."

This also was not a question. His hair was not in need of my attention. I was tired of not having antennae. My hair hung limp and heavy on my shoulders.

"Didn't you run once from Rosière?"

He sat at the scarred kitchen table. He looked into an empty coffee cup. His cuffs were blackened as if burned by the ink. An answer was required. "Oui, msieu."

"Tomorrow I am to go to court. The courthouse is the large building directly across the square. I will be inside, not watching this house. If you run from here, with your looks, you will most likely be attacked at the edge of Opelousas or sold immediately to a bordello. You are intelligent enough to understand that."

"Oui, msieu." He was not trying to frighten me. His voice was like that of Mademoiselle Lorcey, the governess, when she gave a lesson in which she was very interested.

"You are extremely valuable. If you run, your circumstances would undoubtedly worsen. Are you branded?"

"Oui, msieu." How did the words send heat to the scar? "With the fleur-de-lis."

"Then you would be identifiable only as a former runaway but as no one's property. It is dangerous to belong to no one."

This was not a question. The embers shifted into a thousand rubies. Madame Pélagie had a ruby necklace. The crystals were rectangular as burning wood.

"Can you calculate?"

"Oui, msieu."

"I know that you made household goods for Pélagie. I will have cloth delivered and furniture. Three more beds upstairs and three more armoires."

Armoires. If Hervé Richard delivered them, he would never meet my eyes again. I had refused him. He could have been killed.

"I wish to have the rooms upstairs readied for boarders. Opelousas is in need of accommodations."

Accommodate. Was I to accommodate the boarders as well? Was that why he bought me? Or was he waiting for Msieu Ebrard or another man to see me here and offer more money than he had paid?

Accommodate. Acclimate. Accompany.

Accompany. I was to have accompanied Pélagie to New Orleans, to New York. If her husband had shot me, I would have been with her là-bas rather than my mother.

I couldn't remember this kind of silence. When he left, and the shutters were closed against the heavy rain that fell after daybreak, the house was like a mudswallow's nest attached to the eaves of God's house. Dark and hissing outside; dark and quiet inside. My mother's voice near the glistening fire. The women whispering in the barracoon and the men's laughter like barking dogs on the boat. Philippine's pots. Pélagie's incessant calling. Jean-Paul's cries rising to the trees even while I approached.

When Céphaline's spirit left her body, I had lain in the corner. Was that alone? In the indigo vat, waiting, and then the fox den, I had been alone, but the men labored near me.

The rain fell heavier, all afternoon, and no one delivered anything in the storm. I put my cape over my head and sat before the smoldering fire. No candlelight. Take but one candle. Like the cargo hold of the boat that took me away. Alone. Dark and shuddering and pounding all about me.

He spent all his time in his office. He gave no more instructions. He was a man. Women ran a house, telling you what you could not touch or eat or open. He said nothing.

At night, in my pantry room, on the new rope bed, I tried to think, but the pain inside my head was sharp. My brain was scarred now, scarred like my wrists and fingers, scarred so that the thoughts would not pass through the wrinkles. What could Mamère do but wait? Even if someone had told her I was sold to Rosière, I was no longer there. What could Jean-Paul do but drink his milk from Fantine's breast, look into her face, and know her as his mother?

It would be better if I died.

The milk collected in my breasts and washed back toward my brain. Thick sweet blue inside my eyes. If I opened my veins with a knife and waited here in my room until everything went black, Jean-Paul would not know. He was still a small animal. What was in the gray meat of his brain? The pulsing skull? He stared at me or the branches or Emilia's toes with the same concentration just now.

He was most excited, arms trembling and head bobbing furiously, when he saw Francine's face near his own.

If I died, Fantine would be his mother, Francine his sister, and they would love him. No one would have left him. He would leave, someday, if he were sold, but he wouldn't leave me, as I had disappeared from Mamère without a last touch.

His mouth had fastened onto my bare shoulder that last day as he butted his head against me. His gums were hard and hot.

With a needle, I opened the scars on my wrist. The blood pooled as fast as before, on the boat. Scars didn't hinder the blood. I made a hole in one of the burn marks from Pélagie's curling tongs. Dark as a coffee bean. My mother wouldn't have killed herself, after my birth. My mother was not of the tribe who drank blood, but once the liquid no longer trembled, once it turned darker in preparation to become blood no more, I took it in my mouth.

No tribe.

In the morning, in the narrow backyard in Opelousas, I built a fire under the black washpot. My washline stretched between two chinaberry trees. The dawn showed hundreds of chinaberries dangling like tiny suns from the black branches. I hung Msieu Antoine's white shirts with their purplish cuffs.

The milk dried on my dressfront, like all liquids from our bodies, and then turned to dust on my skin and flew into the air, to be washed into the earth behind this house.

"How old is she?"

"Seventeen."

"My God."

"Oui."

"Worth every dollar."

The pause let me know he smiled. "Oui."

I would believe in money. The only thing there was.

Céphaline had known. Pélagie had known. My mother was wrong. The only reason to breed was to transfer money from body to body. The transfer pattern on the cloth let the dye bleed into the threads.

He would breed with me and sell my daughters.

But another day passed, and still he didn't touch me.

Only with the words that floated toward me in the kitchen from the men who sat in the office or dining room or stood at the front door.

"A virgin?"

"He says no."

The silence was a shrug.

"I heard in New Orleans you can get them young or pretend."

"Pretend?"

"Remove the hair. All of it."

I could own nothing. Not even hair. If Msieu Antoine chose, he could remove every hair. If he chose, he could decorate my skin with burns and brands and ink. Every morning, he refilled the inkstand. His cuffs were blotted with ink.

"Msieu Antoine."

He looked up, surprised that I had spoken first. "I will make a special cleanser for your cuffs if you give me the money for the dry goods store."

If he thought I would run, he would never hand me coins or let me walk to the store.

He laid coins on the desk without looking up. His fingers did not touch mine.

The buildings were taller than high cane, and the alleys wider than the rows.

I found Bayou Carron, where one of the peddlers said he sold moss. I was free. At the muddy track along the low water, shacks on stilts leaned over the ditch. A man urinated into the stream from his porch. A trapper. He stared at me as the yellow drops flew into the air.

All these days waiting to leave the house and find water, but that was another child's dream. This water couldn't carry my body, or my prayers.

A child would throw herself into the water, into any water, and pretend that walking along the bottom, with the spirits her mother had told her about, would carry her back to that mother. A mother would never be so selfish.

But my son was with Fantine. I was alone. I spit into the water and watched the map of my saliva float.

My marks, on my body—the tattooed *M*, the coffee beans. My fingers pressed the scars. Mamère had not raised me to live as a coward. I left the idea of death, or running, in the liquid that was all of ours.

The coin was in my fist, inside my apron pocket. I walked toward the dry goods store.

It was easier to believe in the money than anything else. I could hold it and count it and hide it and move it. The money would not help Jean-Paul. A slave could not buy a slave. But in my hands, the coins were not Msieu Antoine's any longer. The money—bits and wedges of silver tied into my tignon and hidden in a new place every day, in the dirty laundry, in the tin box of coffee beans, in the yard under a flat stone where the bluing and wash water made the earth rank and soft—the money would help me learn how to get my son.

The silver reales and Mexican pesos and gold coins kept me alive.

Each day when I stepped onto the wooden sidewalk, something moved in me that took days to define. The words Céphaline blurted with her hands held up in the air after she had put together a long string of numbers. "Not elation," she told her governess. "Satisfaction mixed with calculation."

Past storefronts and cottages, my feet moved in a pattern of my own calculation. Somewhere outside Opelousas, Hervé Richard fashioned armoires and chairs. But I had not seen him.

My task was to buy necessities.

Msieu Antoine burned candles most of the night, writing letters. He drank coffee all day. He ate bread. He liked salt.

The patterns of my feet were only interrupted by the men who spoke from doorways, from the road, from horses. The French kept their voices quiet; the Americans did not.

"Have you been trained to use your mouth?" "Who is your master?" "Do you work for Jeanne Heureuse?" "I don't have to pay if I catch you somewhere in the dark, sweet." "Tell Heureuse I want you next time. Damn you, don't walk away. Goddamn French slaves need to understand Americans don't tolerate it. I'll catch her and teach her to listen."

French clerks, Irish ditch diggers, German farmers—but the worst were the Americans. New planters, lawyers, speculators, boat captains.

My glances were careful and sideways at the women, never their faces so they wouldn't demand that I be whipped. Creole wives of planters, their dresses preceding them from the carriage, their curls gathered like fat black worms at their cheeks. The back of a neck white as flour, but downy black hair like a fairy spine. Acadian women in bonnets and homespun, lips thin as wires, hands browner than mine when they sold fruits and vegetables from baskets.

But the men were everywhere, touching my cheek if no one looked, sliding their hands under my sleeve, shouting at me on the street.

I made my ears underwater.

"Jeanne Heureuse!" a man yelled once, and tore at my sleeve to turn me around. Then he laughed and said, "You must be her daughter. Look just like her. But I'd have to see you naked to know for sure."

She owned three women, the men in Msieu's office said, their cigar smoke tendrils like white vines. She was a mulâtresse who lived outside town in her own house, who had become free and made her name "Happiness" because that was the service she provided. Each of her girls had a task.

Were their mouths full of cloth or fingers or their own hair?

The three women were draft animals, with papers. Not cows; if they had babies, that milk couldn't be sold. Maybe Heureuse wanted more babies, lighter and lighter, but only girls.

Not boys. Quadroon boys weren't useful for anything. Animals of inconvenience. Their passages were not useful to anyone, and their faces only remembrances of something no one wanted to see.

Even though the milk had somehow disappeared into my body, strange twitches still moved in the looser skin of my belly. Where Jean-Paul had lain curled. I didn't know what my brain felt.

On Sunday, Msieu Antoine went to Mass, and I went also to ask God about my son.

I walked behind Msieu Antoine. We passed the courthouse, the building where he went daily, where all lives were decided on paper, and the spire of the church where we headed, where all lives were decided by the sprinkling of water and rush of smoke.

We passed the dressmaker's—a piece of glass, a sign over a doorway. Mode de Paris. A silk gown, draped and ruched, hung there. Ostrich feathers sprang from a hat.

Glass was made from sand, Céphaline had said. Sand burned and melted by fire. Pélagie had wanted glass. Msieu Lemoyne's house had burned to the ground and made ashes, and Mamère cooked ashes down to lye for soap.

The glass was cold. My finger made a mark on the window.

From the back pew reserved for slaves, the smoke of the incense was faint. Madame de la Rosière had babies baptized, with water on their heads, and grown men from Africa. Jean-Paul, Francine, and two other new babies had been daubed with the holy water by the priest when Pélagie had lain in the parlor, her hands on her chest, over the wounds covered by silk.

Amadou was baptized by Gervaise in the ciprière, with the black water where they lived. Sophia might never see him again.

I had not felt God since I lay in the dark watching my mother pray.

That night, holding my clothespins, I prayed. I had nothing of Jean-Paul. His hair was not long enough to cut. I had bitten off his fingernails and spat them into the dirt.

I didn't feel one God but prayed to the gods of all the water, the bayous and Barataria and the Mississippi, the water in my mother's washpot, the saliva and tears in our skulls. I imagined God inside everything that shone and trembled.

Should I love my son? And my mother? Would Msieu Antoine—who seemed alone in this world with no wife, brothers, or parents of his own—ever go to New Orleans? Would he let me see my mother?

The embers crumbled. I wanted to see Jean-Paul, before he could speak and call someone else's name.

I knew now what my presence accomplished, what no other presence could.

I was in the imagination of all the men who came to this office, to this building, even those who never entered the door.

They saw me there, my body working even after the cooking and sewing and cleaning were finished. My body under Msieu Antoine's, my mouth open in pleasure or pain or fear, my hair tangled in his elbows. And my mouth closed in the morning.

An elderly man named Msieu Césaire stayed in the office one day while Msieu Antoine went across to the courthouse. For days, they had been meeting about the sale of an entire estate in Arnaudville. I heard his name constantly: "What does Césaire think? He's still the wealthiest Creole in Opelousas. Césaire's grandmother came here with a land grant from the king."

Msieu Césaire told me to stand before him. Then he lifted my dress hem with his cane, until the fabric edge was near my own eyes.

He examined me for some time. My linen pantaloons, discarded by Pélagie long ago, were attached to my thighs with sweat.

He dropped my hem and said, "You are wearing underclothes. That is foolish. An impediment. You should be prepared to lift your dress at any time, if that is your purpose." He dismissed me by moving the cane across my spine and pushing me toward the door.

The next day, Msieu Antoine said, "You are not a daughter of joy, but your very existence makes men think of particular joys."

Was I meant to acknowledge this, while gathering discarded ink-stained pages from the floor?

"It is assumed that your status is concubine." His mouth was not the kind that smiled upward; when he was amused, his lips drew back and made two hollows in his cheeks, above his moustaches.

I had to learn how much was allowed. "I do not know that word."

He drew his lips back again. "The origin—maybe Chinese. Another term for mistress. The woman who performs the duties of marriage but without the official legal sanction. With no papers."

When he said the word *performs,* drawing it out to make it not true, he sounded almost like Msieu Vincent before he drew the gun.

"Everyone has papers." The words fell from my mouth.

Msieu Antoine was not angry. He was amused again. "Every human and horse, it is said."

"Dogs."

"Yes."

I put the silver coffee urn on its small brazier, the same kind that heated the curling tongs every morning in Pélagie's room. "Madame Pélagie was killed because of papers." Was I allowed to speak of actual events or only amusing generalities?

He finished his coffee and said, "Come this way into the office."

He showed me the pages, the ink, the seals, the letters and contracts. "Do you see all these transactions?" He bent his face under mine until I had to see his eyes. His eyelashes were like small paintbrushes. I didn't allow myself to flinch but looked into the black spots of his vision.

"Yes," I said.

Finally he nodded. "Madame Pélagie was killed because of money and paper and desire."

He was a man. He didn't understand. Not desire. Desire was too sentimental. Besoin. The mere need for the passage.

"The assumptions will be convenient for both of us. It is clear to me that you were not trained in the arts of physical love. I see no avarice or desire in your bearing."

Did he see besoin? I wanted my mother and my son.

"Do you understand? I want you to be accommodating if you are asked about your duties. Domestic pleasures of all kinds. Right now, my satisfaction lies completely in the smooth running of this house."

He looked down to end the conversation. I moved around the desk, collecting blotter paper and bits of sealing wax. He did not know I could read.

The pages were covered with ink spiders crawling across in Msieu Antoine's curling, slanted hand. He wrote down events to make them official. Marriages, births, deaths, transfers of property. Sales.

Estate of the Widow du Plantier. Lartigue—Creole nègre, 45—850 piastres. Charité—Creole négresse, 20—450 piastres.

If he did not write them down, they did not exist.

My name was written on three pieces of paper now. Azure, Rosière, and here, in this room somewhere. My mother's name had only been written once. My son's name remained in Msieu de la Rosière's office.

Msieu Antoine moved his pen over the paper. I looked into his face again. He was writing. His mouth burrowed into his cheek on one side as if he chewed on that part. His hair was black, and his left fingers lined up on the paper as his right hand wrote.

Long ago, he had written letters to someone he missed. I had seen them in the garçonnière. He missed the woman's fingers in his. He had loved someone else. Was he waiting for that woman?

I still looked at fingers.

He wrote, "The owner testifies that—"

I could not testify. My words would not be written down. I would have testified for Pélagie, lying on the floor with her collarbone coated in blood. Her husband had lied. She had not sold my son.

Jean-Paul, quadroon, infant. No price.

Madame Lescelles had her name painted on the window of the new dry goods store two blocks from the courthouse. She looked up from her ledger when I came in to order cloth and coffee. She never spoke to me. She only lifted her chin, as Mamère had, to let me know she had noticed my presence.

The name—Hervé Richard's owner was a Lescelles, a free man of color. But could a slave ask about another slave?

I studied her when she was not watching, when she was counting the money placed into her hand by a customer. She was somewhat darker than me, with skin the reddish copper of new pots used only a few times in the fire. She always wore a tied-high tignon of blue, royal blue, and her eyes were a strange green. Verdigris. The color that collected on the statue outside the courthouse.

A statue at her counter, only her eyes moving when people touched her provisions. Flour, coffee, sugar, candles, myrtle wax.

Today I said, "Candles, please, and coffee. One pound of lead."

She narrowed her eyes and spoke. "Why do you buy the alum and the lead and beets? Who eats so many white beets?"

I was startled into my chance. "They are for soap, for ink stains. And bootblack for Msieu Antoine. I could make extra, if you wanted to sell them here."

She said nothing.

I said, "Does your husband own a carpentry shop outside town?"

Her eyes narrowed again, to a tiny horizon on her cheeks. "My nephew." Then she rolled the candles into a bundle and tied it with twine. An American appeared in the doorway and shouted in English, "You! Get your master out here to take a look at these deerskins."

Madame Lescelles's fingers didn't shake as she tucked the twine under tightly. "I have never had a master," she said, slowly, blandly, her eyes lingering at the man's knees, cupped with bowls of mud. "I am born free and remain so until I die."

He was a trapper, one of the men who came in winter to sell their skins, to buy liquor and women, to fight in the bars until the trees were ready to receive them and their weapons again. They lay drunk in alleys, beards flecked with food and blood.

This trapper had skin red and mottled as boiled shrimp shells; he was missing two bottom teeth, the dents fresh and purple in his gums.

"You could die right now, mongrel. Yellow as babyshit. Worth as much. Where's the owner?"

"I am the owner. I do not buy deerskins."

He spat onto the floor. "Maybe I'll take you and your daughter here in the woods and fuck you both until you ain't free. Skin you and sell you in New Orleans. Sell anything there. Even free niggers."

We had moved our eyes. We looked at each other's shoulders. Hers were plump as hams under the printed cotton of her dress.

"No master to complain if I steal you."

Her eyes remained on my own shoulder.

He spat tobacco again. When he left, she still moved only her eyes and fingers. It was as if her feet were part of the wooden floor behind her counter, and I wondered how swollen they were by the end of the evening.

The foamy circles of saliva trembled like gelatin on the planks. She said nothing to me when I paused in the doorway where his smell lingered. Not "Adieu, not my daughter." Not "Don't be afraid, petite." Not "Bring your bottles tomorrow." Nothing except, "The price of candles will increase next week."

Hervé Richard might have already run. Madame Lescelles had said she was born free. But if her father was French and her mother African, how had her mother gotten free? Had she bought herself?

Her nephew had bought Hervé Richard in New Orleans. Washing the front steps and windows, I watched for his cart.

A few weeks later, in her store, she said, "Bring the articles. I will examine them."

The presentation. I stayed awake most of the night, my throat thumping with nerves. My mother's ribbons. The beauty of the ordinary. I braided black thread for the bottleneck of the bootblack, white to tie around the paper wrapping the soap cakes.

Madame Lescelles said, "You did not label them?"

I shook my head.

"You cannot write." She sighed.

She gave me two silver reales, which I tied into a cloth and pushed deep into my hair.

The next day, the items were arranged on her counter, priced at twice what she gave me. That was what a window did. That was why Pélagie wanted a window.

I found a tobacco tin for my earnings, but left my old tignon wrapped around the coins to muffle the sound of money.

One day, I put down the coffee, which Msieu Antoine needed so very badly. I was not afraid of him now, but this would not be a lesson he had begun. He was silent.

I asked, "Why did you not purchase my son?"

He took some of the coffee between his teeth, as he did when it was very hot. "Monsieur de la Rosière agreed to sell you for a very high price. Nine hundred piastres. I paid him five hundred piastres, and I will owe him the balance until exactly a year. April 1815. He holds a mortgage on you until the sale is final."

"Mortgage?"

"Security. If I do not pay by that date, he may take you back. But I am only waiting for payment from the settlement of an estate and will pay him the balance on that date."

"And my son?"

He sighed. "I did not feel I could inquire about your son. De la Rosière mentioned that he never sells male slaves, as they are always needed for the fields. And having your son here would have called too many aspects of our relationship into question."

I had no answer for that, and no more questions.

But what if he couldn't pay for me? Then I would be returned to Rosière, to Jean-Paul. Msieu de la Rosière might sell me again, and farther away. What if Jean-Paul's silvery face reminded Etienne or his father of me—of Madame Pélagie's death? Did Jean-Paul crawl now, over the floor toward the fire, while Fantine bent her head toward her own baby? Did he reach for a piece of meat? Was he that kind of child—greedy, grasping? Or did he lie still and stare?

What did they tell him about me?

One morning in December, when the smoke from the burning cane had reached into Opelousas, when in a few days my son would be one year old, I opened the front door and Etienne stared at me with no expression. His forehead was brown, as if he'd ridden the fields all summer. My eyes dropped to his boots.

"Monsieur Antoine is expecting me."

He brushed past me and went into the office.

Animals couple in the trees or the barn or the water, and when the babies are born, the mother feeds them until their bellies shrink from comical to lean. Then they are killed for food or money, or they scour the woods looking for their own food. The adults cannot recognize each other or the offspring in the cypress or the river.

Only if they are tame. Enclosed. Owned. Hunting dogs. Horses. Mules.

The front door closed when he left.

In the kitchen, my fingers tore the skin of the chicken from the boiled meat, and I returned the muscles to the pot.

The trees were cut and shaped into walls. We walked through the forest of town seeking food carried by other animals in baskets or held behind counters. The men hunted money and sex. The women were hunted and captured, even the white women, and they demanded money for cloth and plates. The store owners wrote down what people bought and what they owed. In the courthouse, words were the only truth.

Each day, Msieu Antoine's hand moved across the pages. When he left for the courthouse, I read what he left on his desk. I wanted to know the truth of this house.

He did not write to the woman whose letters had been so tender when I read them in the garçonnière back on Rosière. He wrote letters of business, but nearly every night he wrote to Mr. Jonah Greene, of Philadelphia. While cleaning the shutters, I read words: *favorable climate, expanding populace, methods of transport.* He tried to convince Mr. Jonah Greene to come to Opelousas as his business partner.

It was necessary to see everything the way the whites did. Money and business. To ask him to buy my son was business. Perhaps he'd purchased me for Mr. Greene, since he did not touch me himself.

But I never saw my name.

When he slept, I took paper, ink, quills from his office and hid them in my basket of sewing. He noticed nothing. The French hadn't cared much if a few slaves read and wrote, but the Americans had made it against the law. They whipped slaves to death for writing. I had to teach myself now, before Mr. Jonah Greene arrived.

At night, when the streets were quiet, I put down my sewing and held the quill, dipped it into the ink moved to a tiny empty salve jar.

When the quill touched the paper, blotches of thundercloud spread like storms. I burned the paper and smelled blue. India ink. Indigo on the quill, so like the ones my mother had pulled from her pot of boiling lyewater.

It was harder to form the letters with my fingers than to see them with my eyes. And spilled ink would stain my fingers or sleeves, to give me away. I began with *M*. M M M M M. It took several nights, the curls like tiny hairs, the slant as if they were running off the page.

I began by writing their names over and over. Jean-Paul. Marie-Thérèse. And maybe the whites were right about that—seeing the names come from my own fingers, on the tiny piece of paper folded in my apron pocket, did make me feel as if I owned something. Someone. Their names, if nothing else.

Msieu Antoine sold words. But how did he know they were true? Did the words become truth only because he wrote them, and he had the title of notary, and the seal? Were words clearly false made true when he wrote them?

What if Msieu Vincent had lived, and I had died there on the floor next to Pélagie, and when our blood was cleared from the wood and fabric, Msieu Antoine had written that Msieu Vincent said I had shot her because she wouldn't take me to Paris? Years later, those words would have been truth to Jean-Paul if he ever asked what happened to his mother. "Who was she, Fantine? Why did she kill her madame?"

How did the truth turn into words? How did Céphaline read all those words and know the person who wrote them and then bound the pages knew the truth? Not words like *horse* and *mule,* and *hybrid,* and the names of the birds I remembered from all those afternoons with her—*egret* and *crane* and *gull* and *sparrow* and *wood duck* and *canary*—but words like a man said to Msieu Antoine: "I, the undersigned, on November 20, 1813, do bequeath my property as follows: to my son Pierre, my sword; to my son Adolphe, my gold watch and chain; to my daughter Marguerite, all household goods, furniture, four slaves, and the residence at Bayou Grégoire, with 1,217 acres of land, because of the care and pain with which the said Marguerite took care of her father for many years after the death of her mother."

The man was small, his hands clawed like chicken feet on the blanket over his knees, and his daughter so plump and watchful when she took coffee from the table where I had placed it. How did Msieu Antoine know that she had not hurt her father, that she had not starved him until he said those words?

But once they were written, in Msieu Antoine's ink, and signed, and the papers taken to the courthouse across the street, the words were true. Toujours. Always.

Numbers were always true. They did not alter themselves. I wrote his birthday. December 29, 1813. I had been gone for eight months from Jean-Paul, nearly the time he'd been carried inside me.

I had been gone for nearly three years from my mother.

But my mother remembered everything—my face and voice and fingers and heart. She would remember the words she hated—*patella, clavicle, iris.*

My son, if I didn't see him, would remember nothing.

I knew Msieu Antoine would refuse, if gently, but I asked him. Jean-Paul's birthday was a Sunday. He would be moving himself across a floor, gripping skirts with anxious fingers. Would someone make him a toy? Would they remember the date? It was written in Msieu de la Rosière's ledger, and maybe in someone else's memory but mine.

Preparing for Mass, I said, "Msieu, you said the first boarders arrive in January. Could I travel to Rosière to see my son?"

"You cannot travel to Rosière alone." He frowned, not angrily, more as if he studied a puzzle. "It is more than twelve miles."

"You will never have a chance to visit Rosière? Was there business brought last week?"

"No. That was Etienne's first outing to Opelousas in some time. The family has been isolated." He waited for the shirt I was ironing.

I'd overheard men speak of Etienne: "The son seeks a wife in New Orleans this winter. I wouldn't marry my Amélie to him—he killed a man from Bordeaux last year. You don't recall? To protect a slave, it was said. A groom who'd had a dispute."

"Something about a duel."

"So far out in the country, hard to say what went on. But people talk. They talk about a Frenchman's blood spilled for a slave. No honor in that."

The iron was heavy. "I could walk to Rosière," I said, pressing the cuffs, clean stiffness at the wrists that meant he was who he was.

He addressed an envelope at the dining room table. "You cannot walk. It is too dangerous. And I cannot hire you a carriage. It is against the law. The Americans have revised the code, to make it much more harsh for slaves and free people of color. Les mesdames in New Orleans have become angry about women who look like you. You may not ride in a carriage. You may not wear jewels in public."

I didn't want to wear jewels. The iron moved over his sleeves. They were not lavender from ink stains now. They were white.

I could not ride behind him on a horse or across from him in a carriage. It was acceptable that men in Opelousas thought Msieu lay on top of me, so that they could imagine us joined, my hair uncovered for his pleasure. But it was not acceptable for me to ride with him in public, my legs covered with cloth, near his.

Msieu Antoine did what he did when he was tired. His fingers raked through his sideburns and then rested there, white bones in fur.

"You are an investment," he said. "You cannot walk. Even with a pass, some men in this district may harm you. You will have to wait until we have reason to visit Rosière."

I had reason every day but could say nothing. To hire a cart would mean I had money, and my coins truly belonged to Msieu Antoine. I could not even own a visit.

When he took the shirt, my tears fell as fast as the water from a window.

His palms pulled the skin at the corners of his eyes, making them slanted and small as melon seeds. "Moinette," he said. "You will have to wear a black veil in the carriage, so that people think you are a widow. A client who lost her husband, who has inquiries at Rosière."

"Thank you, msieu," I said. In the kitchen, and when my eyes had cooled from the heat of tears, I made a fresh pot of coffee and a roasted chicken, sprinkling herbs on the skin, as Tretite taught me so long ago to do.

The livery driver said nothing to me. He was old, hair like white wire along his black cheeks. My face and shoulders were covered with a black veil.

Twelve miles. Dust sifted onto the carriage like dirty flour. Msieu Antoine's papers, quills, ink, and brandy were in a leather satchel at his feet. I had nothing. Not even milk.

The garden was not white now. The crepe myrtle trees were bare, their seedpods black. Msieu Antoine nodded toward me and went inside. I hurried down the road to le quartier. Permission to walk here, my answer would be if questioned. I was someone else's animal.

The road was shrouded in dust. The fences and pigs' backs and catalpa trees and then, the bell that had called us every morning. But the voices calling and laughing and scolding were clean.

I couldn't run. They all stared at me, and then Fantine, with her cheeks even broader and fuller, rising to hide her eyes, ran toward me with her arms out. Sophia and the others smiled and lifted their chins to recognize me, and Fantine took me inside.

Our cheeks hold nothing. Mamère's a dark ledge of bone under her eyes. Madame de la Rosière's broad and soft as slabs of pork fat. Céphaline's stitched with red holes. Firmin's shriveled into caves that held burned birdwings.

Jean-Paul's cheeks, against my lips, were fat and silver. My face was only another in the circle of faces above his, as he was passed from smile to smile, from shoulder to shoulder.

Whose *dya* did he have? He was the color of water, his eyes twilight. He looked nothing like me or anyone else. He couldn't speak yet, only made the sounds of babies—bird squawks, cat sputters, and the sneeze of everyone.

I lifted his hands, and saw the scar on his forearm. The brand. A diamond for a rosebud, one stem and two thorns.

Smaller than the flower on my shoulder. I touched the burn, which had healed to a smooth lavender scar on his tiny arm.

Fantine said, "After you sold. Mark everyone, so they can find who run."

She held out her arm. The same place. The flower raised pink satin. Like Mamère's sequins of pink, from the spitting fire.

Jean-Paul pulled his arm away and reached for her wooden spoon. Fantine said, "One scar don't matter. Look. He is perfect." Then she twirled around. "And look at me! Scars, oui, but now my shape back, and I wear your blouse."

While she put it on, I lifted Jean-Paul's arm and touched my tongue to the scar. Flat. Not raised. How did the African blood thin to French, to sunken scars rather than tribal marks?

We sat near the fire. Fantine wore the blouse I'd sewn for her, the circles of white cloth that had been a cravat torn to puddles.

She pulled off my tignon. "Show him your hair. Let him feel."

Jean-Paul pulled at one braid. He put the end into his mouth with a sudden ferocity, and everyone laughed. Everything in the mouth.

He pulled out the wet hair and stared at it.

"Your msieu—you not—" Her own hands went to her belly.

I shook my head.

Sophia said, "Safer in the cane. Do your work, nobody look. Dangerous in the house."

I would rather be in the cane all day, too, and then come here at night for Jean-Paul. His brand so big on his tiny arm. All Msieu's pages, descriptions of slaves bought and sold: missing left eye, guaranteed against drink, branded on left cheek *V*—voleur, thief. Infant nègre. Infant quadroon.

Francine moved pecan shells on the floor, and Jean-Paul threw himself from my arms, toward the shells. Francine hid them in her chubby fists. "He always want what she have," Sophia said.

"Babies always want babies. Children always want children. They want someone the same size to be with," I said. Then I added, "We are all the same size now, too."

Fantine smiled. But she didn't know the words. All those pages from court. Slaves sold with the horses and tables and knives. Dahlia plates and peacock plates.

This msieu don't sell, Mamère said to Hera, so long ago, that first night she came to our house on Azure. But who knew when Msieu de la

Rosière would see Jean-Paul and decide he knew who he was? He didn't have Ebrard's pink fatness or his sparse brows. Jean-Paul had tiny points of hair beside his ears already, and I brushed them sideways. His eyes were the same soldier blue as Etienne's, but washed over with smoke. I knew whose son he was. No one saw him, now. Because Emilia could not walk, she kept the babies even while Fantine and the others received their provisions Sunday. Only someone who went into le quartier would see this pale silver child. Madame was blind, and Etienne had no wife.

No one would notice Jean-Paul until he began to work, when he was about five or six, and would be set to gathering cane trash and carrying milk.

By then, he had to be mine. His name had to be written on a paper with numbers and moved into my hand, so he belonged to me.

Eight CONVEYANCE

I saw him two more times in two years.

In March of 1815, when Msieu Antoine was invited to a Mardi Gras dinner and dance, where everyone would meet the young woman from New Orleans who was meant to marry Etienne.

I rode on top of the carriage with the livery driver. My task was to assist with laundry and cooking.

The dinner was elaborate, the plates new, but under the tablecloth was the same pale water-stain on the wood, like a halo around the moon. The young woman's arms were dappled with tiny brown spots, her hair blond and worked into a knot at the top of her head, with spirals of thin curls hanging before her ears and on her forehead. Etienne did not appear until the guests arrived.

I cleaned Msieu Antoine's coat and shoes and laid them out on one of the beds in the garçonnière. The damp bricks smelled the same as that night. I pulled down the coverlet and spat into the mattress cover. My fluids mixed with theirs.

In the kitchen, Léonide's huge arms trembled while we sliced the vegetables. Near dawn, the breakfast food laid out, Léonide finally pulled me close to her woodsmoke-smelling chest and then told me to go.

Jean-Paul was asleep. Fantine glanced at me and then turned over.

I lay beside him in a nest of blankets. His breath was loud and rhythmic as a tiny bellows applied to a fire at my throat. He pushed his finger into my nostril. The sun was up. Jean-Paul slanted his head and studied me.

He slid his feet cautiously along the floor, holding on to my skirt, clutching fierce rosettes of cloth with damp hands. I picked him up, and he struggled to get down, but he touched my sleeves then. My dress was figured calico I'd sewn last week. The fabric was softer than Fantine's and Emilia's clothes. He patted the cloth and then lifted two handfuls as if he held reins.

Sophia said, "Tout a travaille. He do his travaille like them."

So he could grow and cut cane and eat and grow and cut cane and eat and grow. He sat abruptly on the floor.

"You do your job?"

They thought Msieu Antoine slept with me, so I could grow babies to sell or train.

"Wash and cook and clean. My only job."

"For now."

Chicken bones lay like bleached twigs on her plate. Wings, legs. Sophia against the door, Amadou in the ciprière with his father, hunting birds, throwing the feathers into the trees.

Jean-Paul inched away from me, holding on to the wall.

The next day, Hervé Richard was unloading wooden bins for Madame Lescelles at the store. His shirt was darkened with sweat in butterfly wings. When he saw me, his chest grew larger and the veins stood out on his neck.

He said nothing. I nodded and went inside the store. My throat shook with words: *coffee, sugar, flour.*

When I stepped outside with my packages, he spoke quickly. "I was in New Orleans for months. He sent me there to make furniture for one house." He picked up another box. "I waited for you. That morning. You never came."

My eyes stayed on his knuckles. "I was ill. I thought you ran."

"I thought you ran." He glanced into the doorway. "You were sold?"

"To Msieu Antoine. On Court Street."

He dipped his head to the side as if he'd been struck. "Then you are with child?"

Cold air hurt my teeth. He had seen my packages under my shawl. "I am not now with child. No."

He said quickly, "Are you free to come and go?"

"In town."

"Meet me tomorrow at Bayou Carron."

I lay in my room that night, thinking of his voice when he said the word. *Child.* He did not want someone else's child. A white man's child. But he would have to steal Jean-Paul as well as me.

Msieu Antoine did not mistreat me. But he did not even own me yet. I was mortgaged. I could be lost, like a horse. A mule.

A mule screamed at me near Bayou Carron. The first two boarders, both men from New Orleans, had gone to the courthouse with Msieu Antoine. I'd left carrying my market basket.

Two Indian men slept on a blanket under a tree, and a trapper's American voice banged from the door of a shack.

Hervé Richard said, "If I touch you—"

He put his fingers on both sides of my neck and his mouth on mine. The click of our teeth sounded deep inside my skull. The taste of smoke. Cigar leaves.

It was only a taste. His mouth was only something attached to his face. But he still wanted me. I was gold. If we made it to New Orleans, I could find my way to my mother.

Jean-Paul.

He put a finger on my collarbone. "Coffin has to be nail shut. The cook write me a pass."

"Nailed?"

He nodded. "Someone stop us on the road, nails make them think before they pry it open. But if they do, I take care of them."

The water of Bayou Carron shifted; fish rolled underneath. "You would hurt someone, just to get away?"

Hervé said, "Tired of Lescelles. He treat mulatto worse than African." Then he noticed the trapper. The same one who'd been at the store—his nose was scabbed and red as chicken wattles, and his beard flecked with food. His eyes were nearly as blue as Céphaline's, but blurred from drink.

The trapper walked toward us, and the Indians stirred. Hervé began to walk his horse, pulling me along toward the street. "I ride past Court Street when it's time. Leave something small by the door. Clothespin.

Then you meet me here that night." He whispered, "You don't like this, but somebody think you Heureuse girl, and they don't wonder you here. Think you look for trade."

Voices shouted behind us as I pulled away and walked quickly home.

Licking my lips that night, I only tasted the smoke. Hervé loved my face. When he left the clothespin, I would tell him about Jean-Paul.

I waited for days and days.

Two weeks later, Msieu Antoine rode to Rosière to pay for me in full.

He didn't tell me he'd gone until after the transaction was complete. He said, "You wished to visit, but I didn't want complications."

I went to my room and did not cry. I had twenty-one piastres. Not even enough for an infant. Five piastres for someone old, like Marie-Claire. Ten for dahlia dishes.

I had smelled Jean-Paul. He had smelled me.

Mamère had smelled of coffee and soap and damp mossy water.

I must have smelled bitter like fig leaves, from cleaning Msieu Antoine's good black coat, and sweet, from the sugar always kept in my apron pocket for Jean-Paul.

The cart wheels stopped. A man bent down as if to examine them in front of the house.

I took a damp rag and went outside to clean the panels of the front door, where dust collected every day.

Two clothespins lay on the step.

"I have a son." My whisper was one breath.

"What?" He turned the spiral of his ear toward me. His fingers were busy at the axle. Lashed to his cart was a shelf with wooden drawers, the kind Madame Lescelles used for spices.

"On Rosière. He is one."

Hervé said, "One. One year old. You didn't come to the woods that morning on Rosière. You had that baby."

"I would get him tonight."

Hervé Richard didn't stop moving his hands at the axle. He said, facing the wheel, "A white baby."

"My baby."

"He would cry. We wouldn't get past Washington." He stood and made as if to put his tools in the cart.

"I would nurse him."

"Not for all them days." Hervé Richard wiped his forehead with a cloth that turned translucent. His liquids. "We can't steal a baby from Rosière. Too dangerous." He leaned forward. "You would have another baby. In New Orleans. Your own child. My child."

Then he pulled himself up into the seat and touched the leather to the horse's shoulder.

My body was paid for.

A seventeen-year-old virgin when he bought me, the men believed. Now he came into my room off the kitchen, the way he did a few nights every week when the new boarders were upstairs. He sat in the chair, and I sat on the bed. He said sentences enough for the time expected to bed me.

"Pélagie taught you about cloth and arrangement. But someone taught you about color—the way blue dishes look with yellow cloth.

"Monsieur McAdam wishes you would cook dishes less spicy. He is Irish and American.

"Was it better to see your son? Or worse?"

When I didn't answer but continued sewing, he said, "If he could be brought here . . . But he cannot."

He sat with his shoes splayed on the floor like two crows who hated each other. I was sewing a new dress, to make myself appear more of a mistress.

When he went upstairs, I wrapped myself in my blanket. Hervé Richard would be leaving now from Bayou Carron. Or maybe he would stay here in Opelousas and wait, for me or for someone else. Someone who was better at being treasure.

But I did not see him again. Two days later, while measuring coffee beans, Madame Lescelles said to someone, "My nephew's slave ran off and left all his orders. You can order a chair if you wish, but . . ."

When Msieu Antoine sat beside my bed, his fingers laced around his knees, I watched the half-moons at his fingernails.

I couldn't speak at all for days. He understood that my throat was painful.

I had no one. Not Hervé Richard. Not Jean-Paul. If my son were here, why could he not hide in this room? Where your secrets seem quite safe? How much to buy Jean-Paul's body? You would not have tasks for him. Instead, Jean-Paul would ruin my work.

Do you need the illusion of me because you cannot lie with a woman and reproduce? Are you damaged? How are you so skilled at flirting with Madame Delacroix and all the widows and wives of your clients? How do you know what to say to them about their sleeves and their children and their husbands?

If you found my money, if you knew that I would have disappeared inside a coffin, what could you do to me? Sell me or kill me? Who would provide the illusion and the food and the comfort?

"It was better to see my son," I replied one night. "To not see something doesn't mean it doesn't exist."

He pulled his shoes together and stood up. The leather was spotless from my bootblack. "I will remember that."

When he left for Baton Rouge, Msieu Antoine said, "I will return after midday tomorrow. As the house is empty for tonight, keep the heavy bar over the front door."

My fingers did not shake, because I had practiced every night and burned the pages.

My slave Moinette has my permission to visit the plantation Rosière on Sunday, May 14, 1815. Julien Antoine.

My hair and some of my face was covered with the black veil. Passing riders would see a widow walking, maybe an Acadian widow with a basket of cloth.

The thick tangle of woods and vines along the road from Opelousas to Washington hummed with insects and movement. Clouds of dust approached and retreated. On the side of the road now, as on my little paths back at Azure, my paths of field and house at Rosière—I was a mule. It was true. I could calculate and write, but I was confined to the tracks of the other animals like me.

But after a few miles, my forehead ached with the freedom and the fear. I could go anywhere. Find anyone with a carriage, like I had always dreamed at Rosière. How far would someone take me for eight piastres? But the carriages riding past me could be filled with people who might tell Msieu Antoine his slave had been out walking.

When a cart with heavy wheels approached, I kept my face turned to the trees, so the dust wouldn't enter my nostrils. My mule nostrils. One hoof down. Then the other.

The bridge was ahead. The narrow road to Rosière was marked by two ancient red rosebushes, their blooms black and untrimmed. At the garden, the crepe myrtles were in blossom, thousands of white halos suspended in the air.

No one was in the yard, and Léonide's kitchen door was closed tight. At the back door, a white servant came outside and frowned at me. "I have a pass to visit in the quarter," I said, holding up my paper, but she looked behind her and then shook her head. Her cap was stiff with starch, and her voice was French.

"No one is to visit. There is sickness in the house and in the slave quarter. The doctor will arrive soon." She raised her finger back toward the road.

Under the crepe myrtles, where the path led to le quartier, my feet turned that way. Was I allowed to ask what kind of illness? Fever? Pox? Jean-Paul's skin covered with sores? The door had closed firmly. No one was on the path.

It was near dark when I reached Opelousas. I kept the veil tight over my cheeks and cried much of the way, like a new widow. Look at my bereavement, I would have said. The bones of my feet rang inside my shoes.

The wooden bar locked the door. The golden dust rinsed from my skirt into black water. You cannot walk. He cannot know me. Is it better or worse? Voices dwindled outside after midnight. I was too afraid to sleep. You cannot steal yourself. Was I afraid of myself? Take but one candle to light a room. Jean-Paul could die from the illness, and who would tell me? Mamère could be sitting now staring at her stub of candle exactly as I was, thinking exactly my thoughts. My one candle burned until it was only a red whisker in the dark.

My son knew nothing. He had no one to leave behind.

It was months until I saw him.

Etienne came to the office in November of 1815. He was bigger somehow, as if riding the canefields had made him fill the black coat. I filled his cup with coffee, but he said nothing to me. His eyes were still soldier blue, his sideburns neatly trimmed to a swordspoint at his cheek. He told Msieu Antoine that his wedding would not occur for at least a year because his mother was dead, and Msieu Antoine was needed at Rosière.

Madame lay in the parlor. Frost sparkled on the iron bands of the empty hogsheads, waiting for sugar. The tops of the cane were turning brown.

Jean-Paul didn't move when I came to the door of Emilia's house. He had not been ill. He sat on the floor, arranging bits of stone inside the termite trails of a piece of wood. Making pebbly veins.

He froze like a rabbit. How do baby rabbits know to be wary, when a pale stranger appears? Silent? Watchful? I knelt to let him study me. How do baby foxes know to kill?

He had never seen himself in a mirror, I knew, because his suspicious glances at my face, my hands, told me he trusted only those around him with dark skin. He saw pale skin, Mirande and Baillo and anyone else, as dangerous. But he had to have seen his own hands and arms lighter than mine.

He knew the word. *Maman.* He didn't call maman to Emilia or Fantine. He called them tante. Aunt. I cried, from gratitude to them, and said my name over and over to him. Maman. Maman. Here. Maman.

It was only a word. Like Lolo, the horse, whom he called as well.

On the darkening road back up to the house, my tongue gathered sweat from my lip. Salt. I'd forgotten to pray to the tiny gods in that salty water. I could work harder, make enough money.

Madame had never seen the white roses Pélagie had planted—blossoms nearly blue when the moon rose.

I would never see a coffin or an armoire without wondering what the wood would have smelled like if I lay inside, the cart moving under me, my lips tasting of Hervé Richard's smoke. The pads of his fingers like stones on my neck.

I would never taste mint leaves without thinking of Amanthe, her mouth shared with her lover. I would never see white flowers without thinking of Madame de la Rosière, her unseeing eyes closed. I would never see a mosquito barre without thinking of Tretite's white wedding dress floating down the road. Every word my fingers wrote made me remember Céphaline's voice. Every window glass belonged to Pélagie.

Coffee. Meat. Sugar. Every day—Mamère.

And now I was eighteen and had already collected memory people.

Is that how the balance shifted for the rest of life, as Tretite had once tried to explain to me? She said you grew older and lived inside your memory, the things you saw and tasted and smelled in the past.

My son hadn't remembered me at all this time. Not until I said my name.

Nine NEW ORLEANS

Every morning, I woke as my mother had. After four years, if someone had asked me whether or not I still thought about her, whether or not I still ached behind my breastbone remembering her face or hands or the smell of sugar on her breath, I wouldn't have answered him. He couldn't have lost a mother.

I woke in the dark, just as she had. I always wondered how she knew it was the dark just before morning and not the dark of midnight. What if she got up and blew gently on the embers to light the fire, drew water from the rainbarrel under our eaves, and started to make coffee only to find it was two in the morning?

But now, I knew. Waking from a noise, maybe a horse in the road or a boat whistle far away, one of the men upstairs turning in his sleep, I knew from the way the dark sounded that it was near morning.

Like my mother had awakened.

The four rooms upstairs were full. Msieu Antoine, Mr. Isaiah McAdam the writer, Msieu Estevez the sugar broker, and Doctor Vidrine's nephew, Jacques, who had stayed for a month now while working for his uncle. In two months, Mr. Jonah Greene would arrive in New Orleans from Philadelphia.

I started the water for breakfast, took down the dry clothes. Every night, I laundered their shirts and linens, and now, while the water heated, ironed their shirts to be hung on their doors. I ground the coffee beans, putting one each day into my apron pocket, and boiled the water. I made biscuits and ham and cush-cush.

The plates went on the long wooden table covered with a finely patterned tablecloth. Dahlias. When Msieu Antoine asked about the price, I replied, "Madame Pélagie would have chosen it."

The extra four piastres went into in my apron pocket.

Every day, I put flowers in a vase in the hallway, and an arrangement of lemons and blossoms on the fireplace mantel. The boarders might not have noticed, but they came back every time they had business at the courthouse. Their clothes were clean, their beds were clean, their food was good, and I didn't talk too much, as did Madame Eibsen or Madame Delacroix, who owned the other two boardinghouses.

When the men left, discusssing their defendants or who had died and left an estate worth fighting over, I cleaned the dishes and began to wash the bed linens and shaving towels. Then, when the brick house was calm around me, the sounds of the street filtered through the red dust and cement, my willow basket was filled with laundry. If I were a white woman, my husband would have just left for his work, and my son would be playing nearby, and perhaps my mother would come down from her room in a moment to lecture me about my housekeeping.

But I was not a wife.

Outside, in the long, narrow piece of land from the back door to the wooden fence, I moved the sheets on the washboard, and my throat filled with my mother. I hung them up with new wooden clothespins. The sheets shifted in the breeze, so big and filled with light like clouds in the yard, as when I was a child, and my whole chest ached for Jean-Paul.

I had coins and paper. Spanish money and French and American. Fifty-seven piastres locked in the metal tobacco tin with my first two pieces of gold and my tattooed clothespins, in a space under the floorboards in my room.

The white sleeves reached for me.

Was Fantine taking good care of him? Had he caught a cold this winter, or was he sitting by a fire at night? Did he eat a piece of meat with his cush-cush in the morning?

Did he believe I was coming back for him, or did my face slip from his mind now, a smudged gold forehead that he used to kiss, only a blur in his memory? A kind woman. Her lips. Who was she, Fantine?

But he was safe for now.

If I took the pain of not seeing him, and multiplied it by a hundred, for all the days longer that my mother had known and loved me, if I thought about how little I had held Jean-Paul and touched him and then added the years that my mother had believed my life was hers, I could not say that my mother was safe. Either every muscle of her heart still ached for me, or she had been sold to someone else and told to make a new life to believe in. And how would she believe in anything now?

What I had of my mother, four years after I last saw her, was the touch of a stranger's gnarled white fingers.

An old corbateur, a trader, walked down the wooden banquette. He was trying to sell plates and jars to women washing front windows. I brushed the dust from the shutters and watched him. We used to see the traders on Azure, when they slid through the bayous behind plantations, with goods to trade with the slaves, always at a secret place. But here in town, this corbateur didn't have to hide.

His hair stood up in a white shock, and his left cheek was marked with a red map of his own country. He'd told me that when I was small. My mother had gotten my peacock plate from him. His country was Hungary.

He laid out plates and two silver spoons and a rice pot on my table. I gave him coffee and pralines, asked him if he remembered a woman on Azure, south of New Orleans.

"Oui," he said, looking at the ceiling as if reading his route. "English Turn. Then Orange Grove. Magnolia. Petit Clair before it burn. Azure." He frowned. "Azure—they say Madame never appear after the daughter die. The only child." He shook his head and crossed himself. "I remember many women."

"She was Singalee. Marks on her cheeks. She made soaps and dye."

"Oui." He lifted his chin, but I could see that he knew many women like that. "I stay north now. Better business here."

I bought a small plate. Pheasants at the edge. Indigo blue. When my fingers touched his, I thought, his fingers touched hers. His were leathery and pink, hard as wood at the tips. He took my coins.

Mamère. Every morning, when my aching feet slid onto the floor, I drank the black coffee sweet with sugar, felt the surge in my veins, heated the blackened iron, and looked at my son's blue plate. The plate said he was better than anyone believed he was. I would take it from the mantel every morning when I would give him his breakfast.

"McAdam has said that he misses the food of Boston. Potatoes."

Today's dinner was simmering. Stew of chicken, tomatoes, herbs, peppers, and celery. "Perhaps we should hire a cook for certain days," I said to Msieu Antoine. I had waited for weeks to suggest this. "With the boarders, there's so much extra laundry. There is a wonderful cook on my old place. Near New Orleans."

Msieu Antoine was reading mail. "McAdam will be with us for at least another month while he finishes his book. He will interview early families of the region. Perhaps when my partner arrives, I can think about acquiring a cook, though the purchase price would be high."

He left a bottle on the table. "Here is the sour beer you asked for. The barkeep was amused."

When he left, I mixed fine blacking and sweet oil in a bowl, a midnight sludge. I dissolved the gum arabic in the bitter beer, corked the bottles. Small-shouldered soldiers on a shelf. Jean-Paul was safe. No one would sell a child that small, useless yet. But Mamère. She had waited for a long time.

I had to sell more soaps and bootblack.

Mr. Isaiah McAdam sold books. Collections of lies or half-truths.

"Some Observations on the Development of the Colony of Louisiana and Its Present Statehood," he said to Msieu Antoine one morning.

"You decide the title before you are finished?"

"Well, I do. A publisher in France is interested."

"But the book is critical of the former crown, no?"

Mr. McAdam shrugged. He was the son of an Irish father and American mother, and spoke English and French. He said, "It is critical of laziness, critical of inaccurate spending to hasten development of the colony. Especially here in Attakapas Territory."

At dinner, he read sections to Msieu Antoine.

The Opelousas tribe once occupied the area, and one may see some remnants of the savage people who have civilized themselves enough to find work selling skins or navigating the numerous bayous. But formerly they, along with the cannibalistic Attakapas, were barbaric and savage enough to attack both settlers and shipments.

His writing slanted as if in heavy wind. The Attakapas would be known in France as men who ate men. To whoever read them, the words would be true.

The Africans recently purchased from that savage continent are best suited for the malarial, fever-ridden climate of the swamps in Louisiana. Baptism and religious instruction were encouraged by France, which made them law, but America sees little benefit to allowing Africans access to God.

When he wrote of mulattoes and sang mêlé women, he would write his truth. Best suited for the climate of bedrooms.

Once he asked Msieu Antoine. I came inside the kitchen with a basket of eggs, and in the dining room, the Irishman said, "She doesn't breed for you?"

Msieu Antoine said, "She has a child who lives at the plantation of her former master. But she has not borne another."

"Those yellow girls are likely, yes? But they don't breed as well as the Africans, one of the planters told me."

"I didn't buy her for breeding," Msieu Antoine said carefully.

"But she's useful for pleasure."

"She is useful in every way."

Two of the eggs were streaked with blood. What was the word Doctor Tom used? A mirage. Not a dream, not a ghost.

My mother had said to me one night, "Rêve. A dream. Les autres—the others tell a nice story to their girls. Dream of a man. Or they tell nothing. They say, Go with that man and find out. Learn yourself. Touseule. But me—I tell you everything. All of the maybe stories."

I washed the cuffs of the white shirts and the sleeves of the black and green coats; the soap cakes foamed and pulled the ink into their bubbles. Something inside the bubbles made its own miniature wind, which held the ink. Leeches pulled the blood from the body. Our mouths pulled the coffee from the rim of the cup. The heavy iron blade at Madame Lescelles's cut the silver real into eight bits, and she picked up six bits for the paper. I put the change—two sharp wedges of metal—into my pocket.

I read everything. Paper and money were all that mattered. Paper moved people from place to place, moved goods to where we could eat or use them.

Bills of lading, at the dry goods store: mosquito netting; linen for napkins, which I embroidered with *A*; sacks of coffee beans and flour and rice; bolts of cloth. Salt meat. Pork. Eggs. Adult chickens. Babies unborn. Tongues in a jar. Feet swimming in pickled water.

Hands. When someone died, and the estate was partitioned, every item was detailed in Msieu Antoine's office, down to each plate and glass. The children fought over hands. Field hands. House slaves. Griffone. Mulâtresse. Congo. Senegal.

Msieu Antoine's letters were addressed to his tante Justine in Paris and to Mr. Jonah Greene in Philadelphia.

Mr. McAdam wrote letters to no one, had no friends, and wrote nothing except his book.

> *Brute Africans, commonly called bozals, might appear stronger than the Creole-born negroes, but the newly arrived slaves tend to fare poorly in the miasmas that rise from the swamps during the summer months, when yellow fever removes profits from nearly every planter in Louisiana. Creole slaves seem to have an inbred resistance to certain plagues and are able to work in all seasons.*

I read the pages in his room while putting away his clothes. Many times he crossed out words and began again, heavy lines like rope drawn through sentences that he disliked.

I didn't hear him in the doorway.

"You can read."

I had found these pages on the floor. "No, msieu. No. These were discarded, and I wondered whether to burn them for you."

"What do the words say?"

"I do not know, msieu. The ink blot on this page looks like—like a country."

"A country? On a map? You have read maps?"

"No. But they are colorful shapes." I put the pages on the desk and turned to pick up the bundle of dirty linens.

His eyes were hard on me. I didn't need to see the eyes. They were faded glass green.

Msieu Césaire refused his request for an interview. Msieu Césaire's cousin refused to see him. Mr. McAdam asked to speak with Msieu de la Rosière, but he sent his son.

"My father does not have the time to speak with you at length. We are planting cane," Etienne said in the office.

Mr. McAdam said, "Of course, one afternoon of annual planting is more important than a permanent record of the history of the area."

Msieu Antoine lowered his chin and signaled Etienne with his brows. Mr. McAdam's lips were thin as wire while he readied his papers. When I put down the platter of cold meats and bread and coffee, Etienne said, "You have an open wound, Moinette."

I froze. While chopping an onion earlier, I had sliced my thumb, and it was bleeding again. "Merci, msieu."

"You are acquainted with this slave?" Mr. McAdam asked, frowning.

Msieu Antoine said, "I purchased her from the de la Rosières."

"Ah, yes," Mr. McAdam said. "An intelligent purchase."

"I believe you wished to discuss the geography of the area and the distribution of Indians in former years," Etienne said. "I am pressed for time."

They were silent until I left.

His new liveried driver came to the door the following week. "Msieu de la Rosière wishes to know if Msieu Antoine is present."

I shook my head. Etienne came inside then, listening at the front room as if he were hunting rabbits, waiting for a rustle. I kept my head down, my hands crossed before me.

"Did you tell that writer you bore a child by me?" he said angrily. When he bit the insides of his cheeks, hollows formed in his face. "He mentions a planter near Washington who has a child with a mulatto slave."

"No, msieu. I told him nothing."

"He has written of the abomination of race-mixing between Creole men and African women. He has no right to make conclusions about anyone."

His boots had countries of mud splattered on their sides.

"I have not spoken to him."

"He thinks he has deduced some truth. But your child is not mine. It is obviously the son of Gustave Léonce, who left Louisiana for the territories of California." He frowned at me.

Léonce. Pinching and waiting and angry. Like a child himself. If he were thought of as the father, no one would care. There was no other answer but "Oui, msieu."

He turned, but then his jaw swung back around to my sight. "You were brave to try to protect my aunt. Your child is well and healthy, from my glimpses of him with the other boys when they bring water."

Jean-Paul rode on the back of the mule-cart with the other small boys. I could see him with my eyes closed. Their legs dangled into the raised dust. They held on to the buckets, and when they reached the fields, the hoes paused while the smallest hands brought water gourds to the end of the rows.

That picture was meant to comfort me. Sometimes it did.

I wrote his name at night. I wrote the truth on labels made from scrap paper: Formula to Restore Whiteness. Formula to Remove Oil Stains. I attached the labels to empty bottles of brandy, the smallest ones. Mr. McAdam drank more and more each night. His book was nearly finished, but he could not write what he wanted to. He said to Msieu Antoine, "The parochial nature of these people infuriates me.

They have no interest in the wider world except for fashion and wine from France." He took another glass of brandy. "You have been to New York and Philadelphia. Do you not find Opelousas intolerable?"

"I find it my opportunity."

"I find it finished for me. I will move on to New Iberia."

"Then you may settle your account with me in the morning," Msieu Antoine said angrily, and went upstairs.

My plates were clean in the cupboard. The men were sleeping, so I took off my tignon, which needed washing. The white shirts hung before the fire, as the evening was so damp and foggy that the yard was invisible outside the window. We were underwater.

Mr. McAdam's feet. Larger than Msieu Antoine's. He put his glass on the table. "Get me something to eat that doesn't have peppers or onions in it."

"We have only the stew, and bread, msieu."

"Sir!"

"Sir."

"You are insolent. Cut me bread. I would pay ten dollars for someone to make a dish of potatoes and cabbage."

I put the bread on a plate. He wavered in the doorway, steadying himself with his palms on the frame.

"You are not French."

"No, msieu. Sir."

"Don't belittle me." He shoved me aside and leaned hard on the table, grasping the bread.

"You are drunk, msieu."

"I am not a monsieur. I am an American. I am Sir. Say Sir."

"You are drunk, sir."

"You are impertinent. You are not to tell me my condition."

"Oui. Yes, sir."

"You are an abomination. An insult to American women."

"Msieu Antoine—" I looked into the hallway.

"—Doesn't know that you can read, that you are dishonest. There are diseased French whores everywhere, but he doesn't touch you. Why not a French cook?"

"I am not an abomination. I am an animal. Like you."

He threw the bread into the fire and steadied himself against the table again. Then he spat onto the floor. "I am an American. You are nothing. Not French. Not American. Nothing."

My clean floor. His saliva moved. I dropped a napkin over it so as not to see his liquids. While I was crouched there, Mr. McAdam stood over me, so close the knee of his breeches touched my forehead. Then he shoved me out of his way so roughly I fell backward against the hearth.

"Get up. You appear nearly feral with all that hair. Get up. No one wants to lie with you."

His boots slid along the wooden floor and out of the kitchen.

I had landed on my back against the bricks. The pain was in my spine—no, between my buttocks. I tried to lift myself, but the pain sent black rags over my eyes.

Msieu Antoine's room was directly above the kitchen. His chair scraped over the wood floor.

I couldn't move. As a child, I had shouted once at a riverboat passing by, and the faces turned toward me like those of the turtles on the banks.

My scream hurt my chest. Not my lungs. My legs wouldn't move at all. My scream hurt the muscles in my throat.

We do not have tails. But we must have in the past. If we descended from God, who took off our tails and left us with only a bone?

Femur. Tibia. Spine? I did not know the name for the bone between my buttocks, which was broken.

Doctor Vidrine smiled and shook his head. "Monsieur Antoine, your slave must stay in bed for at least a month. Otherwise, she could do permanent damage and be unable to—"

Msieu Antoine frowned. "To work?"

Doctor Vidrine turned his head and spoke softly. "To bear children. The pain would be too intense to even—"

"I understand. She cannot perform any of her normal duties."

Doctor Vidrine nodded. "For pain, you may give her a tincture with laudanum. You will have to hire someone to run the house."

They had carried me to my room. When my legs moved against the sheets, pain felt like a knife inserted up my spine. Msieu Antoine said, "The first task is to wake the American, who is drunk and still sleeping upstairs. He will pay for this damage."

Doctor Vidrine was mixing a tincture when Mr. McAdam burst in, smelling of the sour used alcohol seeping from his skin. He shouted, "I have done nothing! This mulatto bitch tried to seduce me, and she was pushed away! She is fabricating an injury."

Doctor Vidrine said, "Are you calling my medical opinion a lie?"

"Where is the injury? The blood?"

Doctor Vidrine said, "Her tailbone is broken or severely bruised. She fell as if someone pushed her down to—" He shrugged.

Mr. McAdam laughed. "Tailbone! Her African blood gave her a tail too long for a human!"

Doctor Vidrine said, "Monsieur, I have seen two men with exaggerated tailbones, protrusions you could see clearly at the base of the spine. One could actually make that bone move. Neither were African. Both were Jews."

Msieu Antoine said, "She told me you harmed her for no reason."

"I didn't touch her! She lies. She can write! Somewhere in this room, she has written plots against you. There is poison here. I've seen her taking bottles."

I looked up at Msieu Antoine. He kept his face very still, even when I made my pupils match his. I said, "Inside my trunk you will find words on the labels for cleaning solutions, to keep them separate for the laundry."

Mr. McAdam threw open the lid to my trunk. He dumped the clothing on the floor and held up the bottles. "Formula to restore whiteness," he shouted. "Perhaps she meant to drink it to make herself human."

Msieu Antoine took the bottles from him. He said, "If you never touched her, how did this come to be attached to your cuff?"

He held up the writer's hand. From the button dangled a black curling hair that reached halfway to the floor.

In court, he said, "The slave Moinette is valuable property, and the American, Isaiah McAdam, attacked her and damaged her. She has been unable to work for several weeks. I have had to hire Charité, the slave of Madame Lescelles. This civil suit asks for one hundred fifty dollars to cover the costs of Doctor Vidrine's attentions and for hiring a replacement servant. Compensation should be forthcoming immediately, considering the fact that Monsieur McAdam has tried to leave Opelousas."

Msieu Antoine had written what he would say on paper. June 12, 1816: Proceedings of civil suit. He had asked me questions. Slaves could not testify. But he spoke for me. He touched my hand and said, "Your words are represented."

I looked across the table at his eyes, the flecks of green. "Your words are appreciated."

Mr. McAdam insisted the proceedings be in English and French, which took longer. Mr. McAdam said that I had uncovered my hair in a public place, as a means to try to seduce his attentions, and that was illegal according to the Code Noir.

Msieu Antoine said that the fireplace was not a public place. The dining room was a public place. The kitchen was private, his slave was his private property, and Mr. McAdam had lied about touching me.

The jury, twelve landowners from the parish, including Msieu Césaire and Msieu Laurent de la Rosière, found Mr. McAdam guilty of property damage and awarded Msieu Antoine $120.

Msieu Antoine sat beside my bed and said, "You are aware that the jury thought his intentions amoral."

I met his pupils with mine. "But intentions are my task."

He stroked the sides of his chin as if it were a small pet. "You have performed all your tasks to perfection." He looked at my trunk. "You sell the soaps and cleansers?"

"And bootblack. To Madame Lescelles at the dry goods store." There could be no lying to him. He had spoken for me, and if he did not trust me, he would not buy my mother and my son. "Every coin in this house is yours. I would have given the money to you when enough was saved for—"

Msieu Antoine held up his hand. "Your son."

He buried his fingers in his sideburns again. "I believe you. In my accounts, twenty dollars of the award Monsieur McAdam was compelled to pay is marked for you. For clothing or material or even jewelry."

"It is illegal for me to wear jewelry in public. Even in front of your fire," I said, and he raised his brows. With each cough, somehow the bone moved, just as it did when a cat or dog coughed. And when I tightened my muscles there in fear, when Mr. McAdam shouted horrible accusations about me, the tailbone drew itself under.

But Msieu Antoine had sat in this chair close to my bed telling me what was said. My name had appeared in the books of the courthouse. I had lain here sewing and thinking while Charité sang in the kitchen. I had learned to speak. "My son cannot live here. I know that. I have fifty-seven piastres to add to that sum. When you go to New Orleans, I would like you to buy my mother."

I did lie again, telling him about the dishes she could cook: roasted squab, tartes with apricot and peach, ham bathed in clove-scented glaze. Pralines and rice balls.

In February of 1817, Msieu Antoine planned to go to New Orleans to meet Mr. Jonah Greene, who would arrive to take up residence in Louisiana. Mr. Greene was a lawyer, too, and they would be partners.

"The trip could take three weeks. The weather makes ships' arrival uncertain, and then we will need to make purchases in New Orleans. I have not been to the city in some time."

I had waited for those words—New Orleans—all these years, and yet there was no real reason for me to accompany him. Pélagie would have needed me for her hair, her clothes, but he could find someone to launder his shirts in New Orleans. He might even meet a woman there. Whatever had happened to the woman of his letters long ago, he still flirted with the planters' wives: "Your hair gleams in the sun—amazing how much light can be given off by such darkness."

Possibly he would be gone a month, would return with Mr. Jonah Greene and a woman, and they would have me sent away. Or I could be sold to Mr. Greene, an American—he might hate me as much as Mr. McAdam did, or he might use me every night.

But Msieu Antoine had sat next to me, had defended me. I had to trust him.

I wrote what I felt, as my mouth could not say it while he sat at the long table with Doctor Vidrine and the nephew, while they laughed about New Orleans and the gambling. I left the note on his bed and sat beside the fire.

I am afraid to stay here alone. I am afraid of the men. I want to accompany you. My mother is at Azure. South of New Orleans. Please. We need her here.

At the new steamboat landing in Washington, I sat on the cargo deck with other slaves. Bayou Courtableau churned below, black and clear turning to dirty beige foam. The steam dissolved in the air. Water. I had come this way, on that first boat, and then floated on the pirogue on this water, this water in a branch on another bayou. I had walked on the bottom.

We traveled all night, the steamboat stopping to buy wood from an Indian man who sat with his back against the huge pile he had cut. His signal fire pulsed in the blackness when the boat pulled away from the bank.

Msieu Antoine stayed in the stateroom playing cards. At dawn, the waters of the Atchafalaya River slid past us like silver.

Backward. I was going backward. I was a daughter.

The second night, an American planter, with a soft brown hat and white moustaches, said in English, "That's a likely gal. How much you want for her?"

Msieu Antoine's fingers were long and white on his coffee cup, the tiny black hairs moving in the wind. "She is not for sale."

"But you can name a price for a fancy piece like that."

"Merci, monsieur, but she is necessary."

On my pallet in the passageway, I heard the men snoring in the stateroom where cots had been set up for them.

My mother had to be necessary. What if Msieu Antoine bought her to be—a concubine? What if Msieu Greene took her? Would my mother hate me? This man had never touched me. But he was nearly forty. Maybe he wanted someone else.

Would my mother sleep with him to be close to me?

I would sleep with anyone to be close to her, and to Jean-Paul. I would not breathe. I would touch what I had to touch. I would finish the task.

When he had read my note days before, he said softly, "You are still your mother's child. My mother lives in Paris. She will never see me again, by her own choice." He sighed. "I will consider it."

What if Msieu Bordelon only laughed, or asked so much money Msieu Antoine said no?

What number was written next to her name?

My name was crossed out.

Marie-Thérèse. Dahlia plates. Quadroon infant.

What if my mother had another child now? What if she were happy there on Azure, with another child, and she smiled tenderly at me with her head slanted, stroked my hair, and then turned away to her room where the child she loved now slept?

I prayed, holding nothing but my own braid.

The steamboat left us on the wharf, which was crowded with boats vying for space. Men shouted and rolled hogsheads from the boats, and girls held baskets on their heads and screamed what they sold: pralines, cakes, flowers, cloth.

Hervé Richard was somewhere in New Orleans. He was right—no one could keep track of all these slaves; runaways hid in plain sight, selling or working on the docks, holding false work papers.

Leaving the hotel's slave quarters for the market, I looked for his face. But I could never kiss him again. His lips might form words, but I could not listen. My faith was now in Msieu Antoine, not in treasure or what might have been love.

Msieu Antoine was gone most of the day and night, pursuing his business, waiting for Mr. Jonah Greene's ship to arrive. He wrote list after list, and letters as if his fingers could not stop, as if he were a gambler moving cards across a table.

On the second morning, I asked, "Is he older than you?"

Msieu Antoine glanced up sharply, taking his shoes from my hand. "By five years."

Was Mr. Greene wealthier? Msieu Antoine was so anxious to please him.

I gathered his clothes from the floor. "The cook spoke of a house south of here. Orange Grove. It is very near Azure. The owner has died, and the contents of the house are being sold. People used to talk of the furniture from Paris in that house. You could purchase a desk, perhaps, and we could then go to Azure, to see about your new cook." I smoothed my lips with my fingers and waited.

He nodded. "Tomorrow."

His clothes were clean, and the hotel cook made meals here. The narrow slave quarters behind the hotel were crowded, and the coachmen gambled and argued constantly. I remembered the pantry where coffee sacks were my bed, the smell that clung to my hair. Coralie, the hotel maid, was required to sew one shirt a day for her mistress, for extra money. I sewed with her, making my stitches small.

The cook bought onions, peppers, and nutmeg from peddlers with baskets riding on their heads. African faces, with tribal marks on the cheeks. What if my mother had run years ago and hid here to wait for me? What would she sell?

Money clinked and folded and passed hand to hand, tucked into pockets and dressfronts. Every brick, every coffee bean, every hand holding out an egg or a madras tignon.

Each stitch small as an eyelash. Jean-Paul's eyelash. My eyelash, when she held me as a child.

I said the right words over and over in my head, but Msieu Antoine had to speak for me. If Msieu Bordelon refused, at least my mother would know where I was. With no one else looking, I would write down for her my name, and Jean-Paul, on a scrap of paper she could tuck into her pocket with her coffee bean and her pinches of sugar.

The river surged past the batture, the tangle of driftwood and cane trash. English Turn, where the river bent. Then the allée of blooming trees at Orange Grove. I had seen it only from the boat, that night, the trees lit by lantern. Now I followed Msieu Antoine through the orange trees to the plantation house, which was cold and empty, the fireplace clean, the furniture marked for sale, the walls dirty around white places where portraits had hung.

My heart. It pushed the blood hard against the bones in my chest, against the bones in my wrists, even somehow in my forehead. Did my mother feel me coming?

Once, standing behind her where she ironed, I had yawned silently, and she'd yawned, too. We were so tired, folding clothes late at night, the fire drying the last of the linens. I yawned again, and I heard her mouth open so wide something rustled in her jaw.

Msieu Antoine bought two chairs at Orange Grove. The light moved past the ghost squares on the wall. In late afternoon, a boat stopped for us, then took us the ten miles to Azure.

"The end of the world, eh?" Msieu Antoine said, looking down the river. "The beginning of the sea. I'm waiting for a boat from Philadelphia coming north, and we could be passing it now."

"Thank you." I could say nothing else.

The old landing at Azure trembled under my feet. We passed under the front oaks that belonged to Madame Bordelon. The moss for decoration. For her eyes. Could she see me? Was she still in her room?

We walked toward the house. Could my mother see me? Was she in the kitchen with Tretite? Tablecloths and napkins. Wine stains.

Christophe. He came around the side of the house, leading a horse, and stopped when he saw Msieu Antoine.

"Msieu?" he said, indifferently. Then he looked at my dress first, my face, and his eyes narrowed to gashes of black under his brows. "Madame?" But in his brain, he said, Cadeau. Gift girl. I was not a girl now.

I said, "Christophe. You are well. Msieu Antoine would like to speak to Msieu Bordelon."

He said nothing, but led us around to the kitchen.

Tretite was not there. A huge mulatto woman threw shelled corn to chickens in a pen behind the kitchen. She said, "What you want?" to me. Then Msieu Antoine rounded the corner, and she curtsied.

Christophe rode to find Msieu Bordelon. I stood outside the kitchen. The path, my path, to the clearing was wet and muddy. My hand shaded my eyes from the low sun, my fingers a shelf as Madame Bordelon's had been all those years ago.

I couldn't run down the path. My feet wore shoes, and my body did not belong to my mother.

I touched his cuff.

I had never touched his body. Only his clothes. "I will walk down to le quartier, if you permit."

He nodded.

The huge cook had on a white apron. She was waiting for me to say who I was. All my life in this yard, when strangers saw me, my mother had explained my existence however she chose.

"I am Moinette," I said in French. The cook only nodded. "Where is Tretite?"

Now her face had a guarded look. She nodded toward the street. "Là-bas."

My blood moved faster. "And Marie-Thérèse?"

The name. The name. The feel of my tongue against my teeth, my lips against each other.

She frowned and shrugged, shoulders lifting like flour sacks.

I walked quickly to the clearing. Only a thread of smoke, wisp of moss curling upward into the sky. I ran the last few yards, and in our doorway sat Tretite, holding a pipe to her mouth.

"Cher bébé, bébé," she said, holding out her arms.

"Last year. Cinq année, she say to me one night. Five year I wait. One night we don't see her, and we look everywhere. She gone."

I didn't know what my face would do. But nothing collected in the hollows of my cheeks. Eveline, Hera, and Phrodite crowded into the room. Tretite sat in the corner with her pipe.

I said, "Where was she going to look for me? The city?" She could have been walking past the hotel every morning before I'd finished cleaning Msieu Antoine's boots.

Eveline covered her mouth with her fingers. "Moinette. She wait so long, and she so tired." She went to her trunk, rough cypress planks with a lock. A cloth bag with braided hair, coffee beans, and three shards of broken plate. Feathered tail and purple wing.

"She go down Bayou Les Palmiers. Where the traders come. Say that water go into another bayou and down to Barataria. Slave stealer used to come up that way. She tell me, I go now. She leave this by her door. Christophe—he say he saw her in a pirogue on the bayou. By where the white birds live."

She couldn't have made it all the way to Barataria. I saw her night-water eyes, her thick wrists covered with scars. Mamère. She was going to New Orleans.

She wouldn't have known I went to Barataria. She would find something to sell in New Orleans. We could go back and look for her.

The fire was burning high. All those eyes on me—Eveline was crying, Hera's tears smeared over the scars on her cheeks. Phrodite—I had hardly known her. She was pregnant, hands on her belly.

Christophe stood outside the door and said, "Msieu Bordelon back from the field."

He waited outside. Tretite said, "Madame look out her window one day, see me wear that white dress, and say never come to the house again. Say do the wash and leave it on the back step. No bride here."

"Tretite," I breathed, and held her close. She felt full of air, soft and collapsed. "If she comes back, tell her I am in Opelousas. North. Opelousas. Court Street."

Christophe waited near the ashes heaped under the pecan trees. "You married Phrodite," I said.

He nodded and we began walking.

"Your mother don't get in no pirogue," he said suddenly when we reached the back gallery. "I say that for Eveline and Tretite. For they feel better. I don't think you come back. Never."

"Was she sold?" My fingernails buried in my palms. Red moons.

"She walk in the bayou and go under."

His teeth didn't show, and he didn't raise his chin as he had when we were children; no anger in his eyes, no desire to push me onto a rock and pull up my dress.

"It's not true," I said. "Pas vrai."

"I see her go out past Petit Clair, and I follow."

"You hate me, and I will never see you again."

Then he shook his head. "I don't hate you. Never think of you." He was wide in the shoulders now and dressed in groom's clothing, with tall boots splashed by mud. "I follow her down by my traps. Maybe she have a boat hide there. But when she get in the bayou, she roll over on her back. Like she swim before. Roll over on her back and look up in the trees, and float down the water."

On her back. Resting. It is frightening to be so rested. You might never get up. Like flying.

I put my knuckles in my mouth. Maybe she was truly gone. Maybe he was lying. Msieu Bordelon's voice rose high. "Where's the damn scraper?"

"Christophe," I whispered. "If you're telling the truth, go get Tretite. Please. Bring her to the house. Tell her to only walk and not think. Not talk."

He began to walk, and I began to cry.

At the back gallery where Madame had stood all those times with her hand shading her eyes, the door where my palm measured Msieu's head, I wiped the tears from my eyes, pulled at the skin beside them. This would never work if I cried.

Msieu Bordelon knocked the mud from his boots onto the gallery. I had to say it to him now, before he went inside. He did not own me. I belonged to Mamère. But if she was là-bas, and she belonged to God, then I belonged to God now, too.

"Do you remember me, msieu?"

He turned. His lips were even thinner, only an edge of skin over his long teeth, and his eyes were still fierce. Céphaline's eyes. "No. I do not."

"Moinette. Your daughter's servant." I was afraid to say her name.

He ran the scraper under his boot. "I sold you."

"Oui, msieu. Msieu Antoine owns me now. He would like to buy my mother."

He put down the scraper. "Your mother ran away."

My brain was filling with blood, the wrinkles running red inside my skull. He was a coat. A black wool coat, hanging on the line, the sleeves moving gently. "Msieu Antoine wishes to buy Tretite. She can be called my mother. She isn't useful to you now. You can strike me for disrespect, but I know there is a man buried in the woods. I saw it. It is written on paper in Opelousas."

He frowned and inclined his head, as if listening even after I was quiet. Then he said, "You cannot write."

He could whip me for admitting it—no, I was not his property now but Msieu Antoine's, and yet he could demand that Msieu Antoine whip me. My back trembled under my dress. "Mademoiselle Céphaline taught me to read and write," I said, turning sideways. "She taught me things while we made her beautiful."

"Do not say her name," he shouted behind me.

Msieu Antoine sat in the parlor, drinking coffee and looking at the paintings over the fireplace. "Msieu," I said, calmly as possible. My mother. Her hands trailing in the water. The water cold.

"Did you find her?"

"Oui. She is coming."

Msieu Bordelon stood looking down on Msieu Antoine. "You are a lawyer? I don't like lawyers or speculators."

Msieu Antoine stood and smiled. "Then it is fortunate that I am not a speculator. I am a clerk of the court in Opelousas." He lifted his hand to the portrait. Céphaline. Her eyes open, her cheeks flushed. Not dead. "That is the most beautiful woman I have ever seen painted. Your wife?"

Msieu Bordelon's chest rose high and fell. "My wife has not left her bedroom for five years. Since the day her daughter died. What is the reason for your visit?"

"Not for speculation but for sentiment—I came to buy my housekeeper's mother."

"Her mother?"

The red moons on my palms stung. I said, "Christophe is bringing her. My mother is coming."

Msieu Bordelon disappeared into his office, and he came out with the ledger I had dusted so many times but been afraid to open.

"Moinette. Creole mulâtresse. Born September 19, 1797, Azure."

Tretite came silently inside and stood with her small mashed-in face turned to the floor. I said, "My mother used to be the cook. She has been replaced, no?" My eyes stayed on Msieu Bordelon's fingers. Short and strong, with webs of thick skin where he held his reins.

He waited for a long time. I waited for him to say my mother's name, to say my lie out loud. But he read, "Jeannette. Nègre. Born 1765, St. Domingue."

"How much would you ask?" Msieu Antoine said, frowning at Tretite's wrinkles, her shoulders slumped like dove wings flat to her sides. "For the mother?"

Msieu Bordelon didn't look at me. "Her breeding days are certainly past now. But that doesn't mean she has turned into a bargain."

Christophe put out the flag to signal a steamboat. Tretite held my hand as she stepped onto the cargo deck, and she trembled with fear when the engines groaned. "Jamais en bateau," she whispered. Never on a boat.

"Don't move," I said. "Don't look at the foam."

Back at the hotel, we learned Mr. Jonah Greene's ship had docked.

He was olive-skinned and tall, with wells of darkness around his eyes. He asked me to make tea. He handed me a tin filled with curled black leaves, and Msieu Antoine said carefully, "In a city famous for coffee, you bring an English drink."

He waited for Mr. Jonah Greene to smile and again shake his hand.

Tretite slept in the slave quarters. I walked back to the kitchen. All the years I'd waited, and now I stood beside a hearth waiting for water to boil. As every day. No ladder to heaven. To là-bas. No pirogue to the gods of water. Only leaves in a cup.

All the heat inside my face, stored in my cheeks and behind my eyes and even under my tignon—I squatted near the fire and covered my skull with my hands and cried until my face felt as if it had melted into wax.

Ten | COURT

"She is not your mother."

"No." I lay beside him. My back was curled against his chest. "I would not lie to you. She is not my blood."

Msieu Antoine let his breath out as if it were a small, silent laugh against the back of my hair. "But you have chosen her so. And you did wait to admit it until now, when we're on the boat home. So she is to be your mother in Opelousas."

"Yes. Msieu."

The steamboat labored against the current. North. Nothing was meant to go back up the river. Only to float down and end at the sea.

Msieu Antoine's breath moved the hairs at the back of my neck. "I thought something was strange by the way you spoke and moved near her, but perhaps it was that you had not seen her in years." He sighed. "Did your mother run?"

"I will not run."

"I didn't ask you that."

"She may have run."

The engine made his shoes tremble on the floor, as if they were walking of their own accord. I could smell the secretions on his body behind me. I didn't know their name. All the fluids that Céphaline had named—saliva, blood, sweat, tears, but no one ever named the fluids of sex, or the organs. Not even Doctor Tom would have been foolish enough to name that for her.

"Which man frightened you?" Msieu Antoine asked.

"The steward."

"Where is—the woman you may consider your mother?"

"Her name is Tretite. She is asleep on the deck with the other slaves." The engines shuddered so hard that the skin of my cheeks shook against my teeth. "She has always been able to sleep. And I can never sleep when I am afraid."

"Did you sleep at all when I first brought you to Opelousas?"

"No." Just his shoulders touched the backs of mine, through his shirt and my dress. "I thought you would hurt me."

"You were hurt before."

"Oui."

But he did not ask who. That was another set of words no one wanted to name.

And now we were not to talk about Mr. Jonah Greene.

He was a different animal. He would not even taste the coffee. He drank tea. He instructed me to measure out the dried, curled black leaves from the tin and tie them into a muslin square.

He was a few inches taller than Msieu Antoine, with olive skin. His throat was long and it looked as if a stone was lodged above his collar. He did not kiss the men who greeted him in the hotel or on the boat, as the French greeted one another; he grasped the men's hands and patted them on the coat with the free hand, like some dance he had rehearsed and they had not.

I was afraid of him. He studied me when he thought I was not looking. He spoke English with a strange step inside the words. He didn't know I understood him. When Tretite sat in the hotel kitchen with her hands so still in her lap, I applied blacking to his shoes.

"They make me uneasy. It's different with an Irish housemaid. They want their pay for the least amount of work."

"This isn't Philadelphia," Msieu Antoine had said. "You must learn to live French. French Louisiana."

"It is American now."

"No—it is still French, even if Americans do not believe so."

"They are like odd pets. Angry, watchful pets. They stare without staring."

"She wants to know what you want."

Then there was a long silence, and Mr. Jonah Greene's voice changed. "She cannot know," he said. "No one can know."

The cabin was dark and close as the cargo hold years ago. But I was not chained. Msieu Antoine's arms were twined with mine. He only lay behind me, in the small bed. His hips did not touch mine.

I had gone back to his table after midnight, when most of the passengers were asleep and only a few men drank and played cards. He had seen me wipe my face. Sweat and tears.

Mr. Jonah Greene had just left the table for his own cabin. "Sadly enough, gambling is not my favorite pastime," he said in English, and the other three men frowned until Msieu Antoine translated into French.

Msieu Antoine had signaled me with his hand then. He said, "You may wait for me in the cabin."

He said it quietly, but several of the men around him laughed, and one said, "The rhythm of the boat, oui?"

"You appeared agitated," he said now, his mouth behind my neck.

Première fois you do something you don't like, Tretite had said. First time. Then you do it over and over and you grown.

Première fois to speak to him like I was grown.

"Sometimes the men don't even touch me. They stand near me and pleasure themselves. They get close in the kitchen or the store and they rub against me. Then they rub themselves." I took a breath. "The steward has touched me twice already."

"Touched you? Though he knew you belonged to me?"

"He accidentally caught his finger in my tignon and knocked it from my head. Then he stood close behind me when I was preparing your tray, so close I could feel—"

"Ah. Yes."

I didn't feel that now. His body lay behind mine as my mother's had lain curled to me, a stripe of air like cotton batting between us.

There was only softness behind me because Msieu Antoine was spent. He had been to Mr. Jonah Greene's cabin next door. He thought

I had not heard the sound caught in a throat. Kept there. The way Gervaise used to keep his longing in his throat, while he leaned Sophia against the door. That same sound.

When Msieu Antoine came into his cabin, he'd said, "I needed air. Moinette, you cannot sit in the chair all night. It is not your fault you are frightened. Lie down. No one will hurt you here."

Lying at the edge of the narrow mattress, I knew that smell—acid and biting, salt and snail. The fluid that men left on my dress, on my legs.

The engine shuddered harder. We were going home. He said, "You are nineteen now. How old were you when you left your mother?"

I bit my top lip the way she always had. "Fourteen."

"That is the way," he said. His fingers rested on my shoulder for a moment. "Whether your true mother ran or is lost to you in another way, as is my own mother, I am sorry."

Then he tucked his hand along his side again. Past the thin wall near our faces, Mr. Jonah Greene lay on his bed. We could hear him murmuring to himself—was he praying? Was he angry? From the way Msieu Antoine drew in a breath so deep that his shirt moved against me, I knew he was not sleeping either.

He was listening.

"He is not the father."

"No."

"He doesn't look at you," Tretite said. "Not like that." She smoothed a wooden spoon. "Where your son?"

"He is on the place I left. He is three."

"Who the father?"

This was the woman who'd slid already-chewed meat into my mouth when I was a baby. But now she looked bewildered, moving around my kitchen, touching pots, trying to feel the heat of the cooking fire and how those embers compared to her own hearth on Azure.

"I don't know," I said, and she slid her eyes toward me without moving her head.

She ran her fingers over the rice, picking out tiny pebbles. I sewed the buttons back onto a cleaned coat.

"All these men upstairs?"

"No."

Every morning, she looked puzzled by the men's boots and feet and voices from the floors above us. Sometimes she watched the ceiling. When she went to sleep in our room, where I had given her the rope bed, her round, plump back was turned toward me, trembling as though she were cold, even though it was nearly April.

She missed the women on Azure. I lay on the pallet beside her and heard her held-in sobs. We had no doorway here, no clearing, no Eveline or Hera.

In the morning, I said to her, "Charité brings vegetables and fruits every day. People bring chickens or fish or squab."

"To the door?" Tretite frowned at the open back door. "I don't cook but for me. Madame say, No wedding dress. But Céphaline never die from my food."

"I know," I said.

She studied the bowl of pecans. "He like praline?"

"Msieu Antoine?"

"Your son."

I had no idea, but nodded. We would pretend. Tretite said, "Li mère, she look for you. She don't give up."

She knew nothing of Christophe. I bent my head to the brass button and said, "I haven't given up either."

My tobacco tin was empty. The first few coins dropped in like rain on a tin roof.

At night, when Tretite had fallen asleep, and I stayed in the kitchen to watch the fire, to live with the memory people, even Jean-Paul, whom I had not seen now for two years, the bare footsteps moved quietly above me. Long after the boots and shoes had dropped onto the floorboards and the boarders had turned and settled in their beds, someone walked cautiously from one room to another.

Msieu Antoine had been patient as well. He had waited a long time. He went to the room of Mr. Jonah Greene, whom he loved.

Every morning, I poured water through his leaves. He didn't look at me. He ate bread with his tea. He ate butter. He did not eat bacon or ham. He tried to speak French to the clients, and when they teased him, he tried to laugh, but he didn't laugh very often.

He took a bath every night in the tub we moved to his room and filled with hot water. When he was finished, we emptied the cool gray water pitcher by pitcher into the backyard. In this way, he entered the earth, though he hated Louisiana.

Msieu Antoine's hand rested near his whenever no one else was near them.

Though they had to be cautious, I saw the way his fingers settled on Mr. Greene's wrist, in the morning, if no other boarders were present when I poured the coffee. The footsteps above my head, the soft movement of feet to the other's room, only happened when the house was empty, but when there was a big trial, and the rooms were full for days, Msieu Antoine found a way. I had heard them once in the parlor, long after midnight. Only a breath. A sharp intake of breath, twice, three times. The wanting of all other functions to cease for a moment.

Two men. Their lips on each other's? Did one pull back the other's head, fingers in his hair? I crouched near the fire, my face hot, trying not to imagine someone's throat exposed to another's kisses. Did they kiss? But they had to, for Msieu Antoine to make that sound in his throat, that breath of shock at the strength of his feelings.

That breath had hovered over me, but it was not love.

The fingers of Msieu Antoine, on the other's wrist, judged the texture of skin, plush and clean from the morning washing.

I stood in the hallway, hearing that gasp, and inside my hip bones, where Jean-Paul had lain, something twisted. They were wrapped tightly around each other. Fantine's head thrown back. Msieu Antoine? His head thrown back?

They used other passages.

Did white men want to feel whether the insides of African women were different? Or only free? Pélagie's husband and his brother had lain with diseased women. The passages. The movement between them. They accomplished love. I could hear them moving against the wall.

I had lain near Msieu Antoine as a child, as a friend, and he had touched me with tenderness. I would never love anyone with that tenderness except my mother and my son, and those aches were different—a stiletto of fear that moved inside my belly or behind my lungs.

At night, when I thought of Hervé Richard and the way his mouth had tasted, sometimes I felt that twisting between my hip bones, but I would never see him again. No one would ever love me that way. Even he had only known my face. He had asked me to choose him over my child. I was not to love. I stood against the wall and listened until someone whispered a word again and again.

"Please. Please."

Then I moved down the hallway and back to the fire.

Tretite sang the same song every day, the song she had sung when I was a child. "Moinette, Moinette, les zozos dans les arbres, les poulets dans les herbes, doucette, doucette."

The birds in the trees. The chickens in the herbs. Sweet, sweet.

Loneliness rushed into the useless space behind my collarbone. What did we keep there? Jean-Paul's palm would be fatter now, his cheeks lifting so high his eyes would disappear when Francine made him laugh. Or perhaps he didn't laugh. He stared solemnly at everyone. He asked nothing.

Every day since Tretite began to sing, I dreamed of my mother's shape in her chair while the fire burned low, her needle glinting like the smallest lightning, of Fantine's fingers parting my hair to braid it, during that time when we returned from the cane and washed each other's hair, that time Jean-Paul slept beside me.

Tretite's voice was low and burbling like boiling water, but I still missed my mother's murmured prayers. Jean-Paul was twelve miles away. Not in a pot or branches—someone else sang him a song. He sat in his own doorway, making pecan shells into boats for a puddle, plaiting strips of bleached palmetto for a hat. I had been hungry there, on Rosière. He was hungry. I had bought a mother, and now there was no money. But the longer I waited, the more that floor would be his place, and he might not ever love mine.

I saw him again in April of 1817. Msieu Antoine and Mr. Greene rented a carriage. Their law business had brought them new American clients, but the old Creoles were hesitant to trust Mr. Greene, an American from Philadelphia, with their estates and their marriage contracts. Msieu Antoine said they would call on the de la Rosières.

Jean-Paul was braiding palmetto with Emilia, who had lost her leg and was housebound. He was touching the diamonds of paler green inside the band of the hat they were making.

He was three. He called me Maman, but that was only my name.

He was pleased to see me. *Genial,* that word applied to certain men who liked everyone, but no one more than another. He leaped into my arms, he kissed me and spoke to me, and lay beside me, but I felt that he would have done the same for Emilia, for Fantine, for the next woman who would pet him and feed him and wash his cheeks.

I wanted there to be no one else who did that. I wanted him to love me the way I loved my mother, with that binding strong as spiderwebs woven into a rope. The silk threads individual, gossamer, floating across a bush, but when Firmin used to pull the cradles of web from the corners of the room, and roll the threads between his fingers, he made a dirty string no one could break.

I wanted my son to love me like that, soil and crumbs and hair and kisses and words all particles of gray in the thread of each day.

"I have never owned a human before."

"You do not own her now, so why are you concerned?" Msieu Antoine was amused.

"Wouldn't it be more useful if she were pregnant? For—"

I paused in the hallway. For the illusion that a mulâtresse was Msieu Antoine's lover and not him.

Msieu Antoine laughed. Five low sternum-barks. "Though I own her, I do not wish to mandate her reproduction, Jonah. That has happened to her in the past."

"She has a child."

"Yes."

"But then why not bring the child here, so others will think—"

I put my hand against the cool plaster to steady myself. My bare feet. The wood floor hot from summer.

"I have tried to purchase the boy. But the owner insists he will not sell him until he is ten, in order to abide by the slave code."

"Code Noir. Black code. An outdated and insulting list that began with the illegality of my presence. The first article stated that all Jews be expelled from the colony."

"Jonah. We agreed that there was good money to be made here and that we would find another place eventually. Moinette will be patient. As are we. Trust me."

But one day, when the house was empty except for me and Tretite, Charité delivered beets and came inside to drink coffee. She pointed to the pheasant plate over the mantel and said, "Very fancy. But so small, who ever eat from that?"

The taste of coffee. My peacock plate. My son not here. My mother dead.

She was dead.

I lay in my room until Tretite came. The truth. "Christophe said my mother drowned herself in the bayou. Not looking for me. Giving up."

Tretite shook her head. "She never give up. Christophe don't know."

"He saw her."

"He saw her leave." Tretite sat on the bed and said, "My hair hurt my head. Please?"

I unwrapped the strings from her hair, grayer now like faint white salt circles on her temples. She said, "You are nineteen now? You can know the truth."

"He told me the truth."

Tretite shook her head so violently her soft jaw quavered. "No. Only Ibo people kill the self, so they can fly back to Africa. To their people."

"She was Bambara." I had read the word now, beside the names of so many slaves, in Msieu Antoine's papers. "From Senegal. That's what Senegalese means."

Tretite shrugged. "Singalee people not like Ibo. When we live in Santo Domingo, I see Ibo people. They come on the ship, and the first week, they hang from the tree. I go outside in the morning, and twenty of them hang from the tree. Fig tree. Tie around the neck with rope from the barn. Together."

I combed out the thick gray coils of hair until she fell asleep in the chair. Feet dangling from the branches. But I still saw my mother lying on her back in the bayou that led toward Barataria, her eyes closed to the branches above her.

The next night, she said, "Marie-Thérèse—not Ibo. One day, we will look outside that door and see her face."

She cooked in her new white dress. I sewed it of fine linen. Not scraps. Absently, she rubbed the skirt between her fingers. While we sat beside the kitchen fire, after the men had moved to the office with their cigars, she watched me mend Mr. Jonah Greene's black coat, where a loose nail had torn a flap in the sleeve.

"People rise up and kill the masters on Santo Domingo. Madame Bordelon people come to Louisiana to start over. Bring Marie-Claire and me. They start in Pointe Coupee. Seventeen ninety-two. And no Ibo people. They don't buy Ibo. Only Mina or Singalee. But I see a man on the next place, and he tell his msieu he will marry me. I twenty-two then."

Tretite's glossy chin trembled. The grooves beside her mouth were deep now, as if her chinbone was wooden, attached to her face by threads.

"Where did you meet him?"

"In the woods. He is hunter for his place. But his msieu say no, he doesn't marry. Ramon. Ramon say his msieu cannot tell who love. The next day, he shoot his msieu with the musket. Three balls. He come to me that night and leave a bird. Pheasant. With the long tail. I pluck the feathers and make a hat, but Ramon never come back. The army come and bring me in chains to Ramon place. His msieu dead in the house. Ramon hanging in his room. Ibo."

She held her hands before her. "Inside the pheasant—two balls. Inside the msieu—three. They take all the slaves to Ramon room. The belt around his neck. Say, 'Who kill your master, he hang there. Who prove the love of the master will not be punish. You prove the love—cut off the murderer head.' "

I bent forward and covered my face, but the coat smelled of bitter tea leaves and smoke, and I dropped it on the floor.

"Hippolyte the driver cut off the head. Manchac the gardener cut off the right hand. Gustave cut off the left. Hang the pieces over Ramon door for one month. Let them be warn." She pleated the white fabric over her legs. "Bury his body in the street. Say now he never leave. Say Ibo foolish to think they fly back to Africa when they die. Say he never buy Ibo slaves again."

She put the pot on the stand over the low flame and sat down. After some time, she said, "Marie-Thérèse not Ibo. She run to find you. One day, you open that door and she stand there."

But even if my mother had run, she would never know the words we had left on Azure, with Christophe and Eveline and Hera. Msieu Antoine. Court Street, Opelousas.

Christophe had told me the truth. He didn't hate me now. He meant to save me the years of turning my head sharply at every knock, of my heart making that small leap like a fish searching for a fly, when the muscle would only knock against the flat bone that covered it.

"Aside from the absence of intelligent or original thought?"

"Jonah. There is more money to be made here. Louisiana planters have more assets than half of the eastern states."

"And apparently that excuses them from the necessity to use logic and reason."

"Can you not be patient?"

"Can you not be impatient?"

They both laughed at the dining room table, and then the long silence and turning of pages that meant they both read.

In September of 1817, the newspaper reported that hundreds were dying of yellow fever in New Orleans. We were far north, but someone must have brought the fever miasma to Opelousas, as a cloud that clung to his hair or coat or hands.

Miasma. What had Céphaline said of miasma? An air that contained something? How was that possible? I served dinner to Mr. Greene and a client from Baton Rouge, and the house was quiet. The night before, we'd been kept awake by men shouting in the streets about fever. Msieu Antoine had gone to New Iberia on business.

When I went upstairs in the morning, to bring the hot water for their pitchers and shaving, Mr. Greene was moaning. It sounded like the noises men made when they lay on top of women. I put my cheek against the door.

But he said, "Help me, please."

His barre was torn, his bedclothes wet as if lifted from the washpot. He called again and again: "Julien. Julien." Msieu Antoine's first name.

I took his clothes from him, and Tretite brought new sheets. His head was thrown back, and he panted. Water stood out on his skin. Salt and the smell of disease. I bathed him again and again with cool water, as Tretite told me. She had seen fever before. She said, "Doctor bleed him and give him bad medicine. Kill him. Like Céphaline. Don't get doctors. I make the beef broth and keep the windows open. Cold. Cold for hot blood. Not take the blood away."

I prayed and prayed. If he died, we would be held responsible. Msieu Antoine would—what would he do? The sweat ran from the skin, and his eyes turned yellow as old wax. I prayed that the fever was inside his blood but that the blood released it from the skin. But that night, when he was unconscious, writhing and turning like a wind inside his white sheets, I told Tretite I would find Doctor Vidrine.

Near the alley gate, I stepped on a hand. An Indian man, sprawled near the shed, his blanket open and his chest bare. His mouth was open as if to receive rain. He didn't move, but air went in and out past his teeth. Was that miasma?

I covered my mouth and nose with a rag and ran toward Madame

Delacroix's boardinghouse and tavern. Three men walked down the street, American drunk voices, and I ducked into another alley.

And at the back of the boardinghouse, I heard moaning again. What if someone here had the fever? I peered into the yard. A man leaned against a tree near the cistern, and a woman knelt before him, her face pressed to the front of his pants. His white hands in her black hair, clenched into fists.

I turned my face and went to the back door. "Doctor Vidrine," I breathed to the maid who answered. "Please. Please."

He finished his bourbon and picked up his bag.

In three days, Mr. Greene was weak, but alive. He drank beef broth and said that he had lived because he never touched alcohol. Doctor Vidrine laughed and said that bourbon in the blood, or African immunity, refused entrance to the fever. "You don't have that, eh? But you are a Jew."

Mr. Greene was quiet.

"I have seen the—the indications when the servant washed your body." He laughed. "Perhaps the Jews have different blood, as well, that protected you from the fever. Two slave brokers from Virginia died this morning."

I went upstairs to take away the last soiled bedding. The liquids from his body—blood and sweat and vomit and excrement. I boiled the linens with vinegar and alum.

"Do you know what a Jew is?" Mr. Jonah Greene looked at me from his bed. He drank leaves instead of beans. He didn't like sugar. He did not attend Mass. He loved Msieu Antoine. He was an American.

I shook my head.

"I am not certain I know anymore, myself." He turned his head to the window then, and I went down the stairs.

When Msieu Antoine returned, he asked me to sit in his office.

Inside the courthouse, he said, ledgers recorded every transaction in the parish. Marriages, deaths, births, divorces, sales of property, suits brought against parties who had injured or wronged someone, such as the one against Mr. McAdam when he had hurt me.

He wrote for some time, the ink smooth as trails of excrement from an insect. I hadn't written anything except the labels for my bottles since we returned from Azure. I had nothing to record.

"This says that you will be freed on your twenty-first birthday, in consideration of services rendered by you in the saving of your master's life."

I stared at my name. Moinette. But Mr. Greene was not my master.

Msieu Antoine looked at me as if he knew. "In saving his life, you have saved mine."

I had no words.

"The code states that slaves cannot be manumitted until they are twenty-one. You were twenty this week, no? But this paper promises that you will be free on that very day you become twenty-one. Then you will continue to live here, but I will pay you for your services." He put his fingers into his sideburns and rested his chin on his hands. "Doctor Vidrine asked if you serviced both of us."

I nodded. Understood the indications—the bare purple bulb. The piece of flesh I washed for Mr. Greene, like nothing I had ever seen. Not like Msieu Ebrard and his groom. A hood of skin. A cape.

An absent piece of skin meant he was a Jew?

I touched the paper's edge. It was acceptable that two men, three at a time, lay with me. But it was not acceptable that one man loved another. Or that one would marry me.

"Moinette." He lowered his forehead to look at me.

I knew him better than he knew me. That was what Mamère and Tretite had always said. Never trust blankittes. You are property. You are not people. They will sell you or kill you as they please. You know them. They don't know you.

But he was trying to give me my life. His name on a piece of paper said I was free. "Where will you keep it? What if it burns?"

He smiled then. "No thanks, no tears. Always practical. This is a brick building. Our important documents are in a metal box. But these papers will be filed in the courthouse tomorrow." He waited. "And next you will ask me when you can buy your son."

The fifth time I saw Jean-Paul was March of 1818. Etienne had delayed his marriage, had chosen a different bride. Msieu Antoine prepared the marriage contract, specifying the dowry and obligations for both families.

We stayed two days. Jean-Paul was somber and quiet when he sat beside me while I sewed. He was four years old. A pale, small, beautiful boy with silvery skin and black hair in waves that I combed down close to his skull. Eyes dark as indigo. He was the son of Etienne.

He had the same way of watching, seeing every small detail, hunting for what he wanted, but inside the house, the yard. He touched my skirts, my boots. He knew people were judged by the cloth and the hat and the boots, leather or hide. He trailed the colored threads through his fingers, and when I pricked my finger with the needle, sitting in Emilia's doorway, and I licked at the blood, he took my hand to examine the small hole.

I could see that he loved no one. He had not allowed himself to truly love. He held himself aloof from us, classifying everything in the folds of his brain. My brain and Mamère's and Etienne's, which meant Msieu Laurent's as well. He was me, measuring everyone.

He would be sent to the fields when he turned seven. If I did not buy him before then, he would lose fingers or legs or the intensity in his eyes. He would float in the green cane and the smoke and be lost to me forever.

I had fifty-two piastres.

That night, the men left the dining room for the office, for bourbon and cigars. Msieu de la Rosière, Etienne, another man I didn't know, and Msieu Antoine. Black coats, dark green, one gray. Only bones and skin inside the wool. Floating in the window, pale faces and black fur.

I couldn't hesitate. They were animals carrying paper. I was an animal carrying coins wrapped in cloth. I caught Msieu Antoine's glance before he entered the office.

"Please. If you sign a mortgage note, and use me as security—"

He knew. "I have made discreet inquiries already, pointing out that the Code Noir specifies the slave child shall not be sold from the mother before ten years, and that there is no mother here. But he specified no mortgages. He has been ill-used from those transactions in the past. He wants one hundred fifty dollars in cash or the trade of another slave."

I could not trade myself.

I did not own myself yet. I did not own Tretite.

I owned only coins—from washing laundry for Madame Delacroix's boardinghouse, from selling bootblack and soap to Madame Lescelles.

Near her store one day, I spent twenty of my sixty-three piastres. At home, I left my purchase in the kitchen.

I waited for both men at the dinner table. The meat was arranged on the platter. They argued upstairs. Mr. Jonah Greene hated Opelousas. His clients were the Americans, traders who stank of tobacco and rum, who wanted papers drawn up to sell horses and carts, or rawboned farmers who'd come down from Illinois and fought with their French neighbors about cattle and fencelines. Though he was learning French tolerably well, most of the Creoles barely acknowledged him.

Msieu Antoine loved him. He did not love me.

He admired me. He was comfortable with me. He depended upon me. But I was not his wife, daughter, or sister. And even if Msieu Antoine purchased my son, a small disaster, such as bad business, or a large disaster, such as yellow fever or death, could mean that Jean-Paul, Tretite, and I would belong to someone else. There were no heirs—we might belong to Mr. Greene. We could end up in Philadelphia.

They ate the muscles of a chicken, the way Tretite had cut them and poured sauce along their skin. Then I sat down.

I had never sat down where white people ate.

Msieu Antoine raised his eyebrows. I said, "I could say that I am twenty-one tomorrow. There is no paper record of my birth here."

Msieu Antoine said carefully, "This is true."

"If I am free tomorrow, I can own my own slave the next day."

Mr. Greene said, "You would participate in that which torments you? Slavery exists in the Christian Bible, in the children of Ham, in Moses leading his people. But it is only about money." He held his napkin tightly. "I have a million nightingales on the branches of my heart singing freedom," he said softly. "My grandmother knew someone who sang that. So always someone is not free."

"But Moinette, you can't have saved up so much money so quickly." Msieu Antoine lifted his chin. "The rent paid by—"

"I have not touched your money." My palms moved across the tablecloth. Pale yellow linen. I had embroidered ferny indigo branches along the edges and blue dahlias. Imaginary flowers. Darkest blue. But they could be mistaken for ink blots if someone weren't careful.

"Madame Pélagie used to talk about the French court. About how a beautiful woman could appear there and cause a stir. This is Court Street. Everything is recorded in the courthouse."

Mr. Jonah Greene wiped his mouth. "The American court is not full of beautiful women. It is fat Madame Richard appearing every week to file suit against her cousins for imagined offenses."

But Msieu Antoine said, "Here you have the court of law. The laws of France gave way to Spain, and now they have been changed by Americans."

"What are you asking, Moinette?" Mr. Greene said impatiently, pushing away his plate. "You and Antoine are so very French, circling around for hours not saying what you—"

"Let me bring coffee and tartes," I said, and stood up. "And an American."

Mr. Greene had heard a song about birds on branches, but he knew nothing of what I would do to get my son. Tretite sang the song about the birds in the trees, but now, in the kitchen, she glared at me for having bought a boy.

I found him on the street.

American planters who'd come south from Virginia or North Carolina wanted hundreds of hands to work new canefields, and every week, we saw coffles of slaves—mostly men, but women and children, too—walking behind wagons in chains or riding huddled under canvas. The tobacco land in Virginia was used up, the men said, and the slaves being sold off for sugar land. Their hair and faces were so dusty that no matter if they were African—they were golden, and thin from hunger, and if the planter needed money to continue his journey south, a few were sold off near the courthouse.

The American boy followed me into the dining room. His cheeks were mottled with silver tear tracks. I had deliberately not washed his face.

Charité had pointed him out—a small, dark boy, being pulled by a rope around his neck. He trailed a group of five men following a cart driven by a trader. Charité said, "Look how he cries. The man say he mought well kill him. Say he been crying ten days while they walk and he mought kill him for some quiet. You have money. I know you have money. Give that white man ten dollars. I hear him say he take ten dollars for some quiet."

Charité's basket of green beans and peppers was beside her feet. She put her hand on my sleeve. "I know you long time now," she said urgently. "You have money. Buy that boy, keep him a few weeks, you can sell him to Madame. She need a boy to deliver in town. Feed that boy. Teach him French words. I talk to her."

My hand was slick with lemon oil.

"I want that boy," Charité said to me. "He look like me. Look his face. Like mine."

"You want him for what?" I asked.

"For company. A little voice like that. Speak English to me like home." Charité pointed toward the square. "And you want money."

I shook my head. "Money for my own son."

"But you make twenty dollar on this one. Buy for ten. Everything buy can be sold again."

The trader pulled at his yellow beard with his finger and thumb, looked me up and down and said, "What? Nigger can't buy nigger. Yellow gal like you fetch a thousand yourself."

"I am a free woman of color." I swallowed the dust from the road and held out ten dollars. "Sell me the boy. Cash."

"He's ten. Works the field. Worth thirty-five at least."

I had expected that. Soap. Meat. Cloth. Bargains. "He's small. He can't work that much."

I pulled out ten more gold coins.

When the boy sat beside the fire, shaking uncontrollably from hours of crying, I rubbed a wet cloth over his head and his hair turned to separate black pearls. But I left his cheeks, dark as jet buttons, smeared with salt water. He said nothing when we asked him in English how old he was, but he held up each hand with four fingers spread wide.

"The trader knew it was illegal to sell a child from its mother so young," I told Msieu Antoine. "I need you to take me to the courthouse tomorrow morning. The sale papers are signed with my name."

Msieu Antoine motioned the boy back toward the kitchen, and then he pulled my arm to make me sit at the table again. "Moinette. You would trade this boy for your son?"

My eyes were level with the green flecks in his. His pupils. His irises. The watery film over my sight. "Traffic the way others traffic? That is the word. Conveyance of bodies and coins. I do not know this boy. And I do not know my son."

The boy David ate cush-cush near the fire. What if he ran? Where would we keep him? I rubbed the bracelet of scars around my ankle. No. Not a rope, either.

I put him in my room with Tretite, put a water jar in front of the door, and sat in my chair before the fire all night. My chair, covered with calico, smelled of my mother. I smelled like my mother. My cheeks rubbed the fabric, and the boy sobbed behind the door.

Jean-Paul was smaller than this boy. He was only two hands to the de la Rosières. Small spindle fingers that would have to begin by gathering cane trash and wood; then the hands would learn to hold the knife, sharpen it with the stone, swing it into the tall Indian grass.

It was July. This November, he would be hearing the cane knives sing, picking up the stalks left after the grown people moved on.

In the morning, David was silent at the table. Tretite said in French, "Why you buy him?"

I told her what Charité said, about his voice, his company, about selling him to Madame Lescelles.

Tretite frowned. "He not a bird," she said.

I asked him in English—"Where are your parents?"

"Die." He pulled his lips in so sharply he appeared to be eating himself.

"Your master?"

"Die."

I opened the armoire and got out the tin of Tretite's pralines, put four on the table before him, and said, "It is July. But Christmas for you today."

He didn't know his birthday. No one had written it in a Bible, like the whites did for their children.

Who would know when I was twenty-one? Until last year at Azure, I had never known my birthday. My mother always said fall, September because the pecans had only been small stars of green in the branches. The sugar broker had come to Azure for the crop in January.

I could have lied and been free long ago. I was small, but so was Msieu Antoine, and Charité. Who knew how old any of us truly were?

"Msieu," I said to him. "You know the date I was born. But you can write that I am twenty-one now. I am a slave. The day I entered the world is not important. But the day I am free . . ."

He separated the hair near his ears with his long fingers, again and again, before he said, "Very well."

We stood in front of the clerk at the Saint Landry Parish Courthouse. The clerk entered the documents into the conveyance book. Msieu Antoine had made a timely payment of the balance of my purchase back in 1815. There were no liens on my sale. I was now free. *Manumitted.* What a strange word. It didn't sound French or English.

Latin, then. Like the words we heard in church. Céphaline said Latin came from the Romans, and the Romans had slaves. Had they sung the song about branches in their hearts?

The ledger was so thick, the pages formed pigeon-breasts at the center. Page 142. July 20, 1818. I signed my name. Moinette, FWC. I didn't know what to feel. The ink dried.

I couldn't trade him. I thought I would take him to Rosière and move him forward with my palms on his shoulders and nod to Etienne and pull Jean-Paul to me by his hand.

But I couldn't even put a rope around his wrist.

He was haunted. Crescents of white showed under his irises. Rings of gray around his lips. Tretite fed him cush-cush and milk. I didn't touch him, didn't want to be tender toward him, because he was not mine. But I couldn't put him in the cart.

I kept him for a month. Charité came by nearly every day, with licorice from Madame Lescelles's store and cloth she had secreted away for a new shirt. I sewed the calico, set in the small sleeves, and then took him to Madame Lescelles.

She lived over her store. She studied him. She asked if he would work. We had told him what to say in French.

"Oui, madame. Work. Travaille avec Charité."

Her name had been Charity in Virginia. She smiled and waited for his hand.

Madame Lescelles gave me forty dollars. In the courthouse, I signed the boy over to her. Sold to Madame Jeanne Lescelles. The slave David.

The next day, David came to the door, holding the basket of figs. When he said, "Two for a penny," shivers climbed the back ladders of my ribs. Pennies.

"Where is he? You cannot have traded him," Mr. Jonah Greene said at dinner. "I cannot watch it occur. It makes me a participant, and I cannot live with that."

"Keep your voice down," Msieu Antoine said to him.

"I have arranged for a bond to be cashed," Mr. Jonah Greene said. "I will lend you one hundred dollars. I will only participate in the transaction for your son, and even so, I feel infected."

A week later, I signed my name on the third piece of paper: Jean-Paul, quadroon slave, 5 years old. Purchased by—

I hesitated. Slaves never had last names.

I looked up at Julien Antoine, whose fingers held down the edge of the page. Page 147. "Do I have a surname now?"

"You may add mine," he whispered. His chest rose and fell. The clerk was not looking at us.

"We are not married," I whispered back. "I am not your daughter. Not your wife."

"It cannot be defined," he said. "Pick up the pen."

I signed quickly, Moinette Antoine, FWC.

I didn't go to Rosière. Msieu Antoine had obtained the signatures from Msieu Laurent, notarized the papers, and filed them in the courthouse.

He brought Jean-Paul into the kitchen.

My son held nothing. No pecan shells, no feathers, no stones, no comb, no extra shirt.

"Maman," he said politely.

Only my name.

I could not embrace him. It felt as if I would hold a tame bird—wary yet pleasant. I smoothed his hair. His ears were like translucent shells attached to his skull, yet they were cartilage. When I touched one ear, he shivered.

"Take your bath," I said, turning his slight shoulders. Not angel wings. Child wings. He fit in the tin tub. He stared ahead, with a slight smile, somehow a flourish at the ends of his long, thin lips like a curl.

I poured out the water from his bath—the dirt of Rosière and the road to Opelousas—onto my earth.

Jean-Paul did not seem damaged at all—no ash ring of fear around his lips, no bruise of longing under his eyes. He never cried as if he missed anyone on Rosière. He gazed at Tretite's face closing in on itself even more, as if her tignon were pushing down her eyelids. By the third day, he whispered things to pull up a small laugh from her heavy chest.

She was like Emilia, like Sophia, like Fantine, all the other women who slid plates of food toward him. He wanted to amuse her.

He didn't stare at my face. He knew my face. He touched the skirts in my armoire, the curtains, the tablecloths, studying through the soft pads of his fingertips the sheen and nubble and texture. He touched the men's coats where they hung after I'd cleaned them. His eyes narrowed to new moons when he saw colors—not just sky and grass and leaf, but bark and moss and even sugar. Not white. Sparkling. Salt duller, grayer. Whites—all the permutations of white. Skin and bone and flour and salt and bleached muslin for the mosquito barres. Folds and pleats and seams.

He didn't want to amuse me. He stood at the doorway of each room I swept, and when I knelt at the pile of dust and leaves and hairs and thread, he pulled out the threads and put them in his pocket.

"We have new thread," I told him. "Look."

I bought woolen pants from Madame Lescelles but didn't bring him with me. I didn't want people to stare, to wonder, for me to identify him. Who the father? Take but one candle to light a room. Mamère closing her lips and staring them down.

Who do you belong to?

The rose burned on his forearm was paler now, grown larger, stretched from baby to boy skin.

At night, I told Jean-Paul: "You belong to me now. Your name is on the paper with mine. You belong to God, true, but you are mine."

He asked me nothing for weeks. He watched us all.

If I said, "Is the chicken good?" he answered, "Oui, Maman, the chicken is good."

If Tretite said, "Did you bring in wood for the fire?" he answered, "Oui, Grandmère, I brought in wood for the fire."

If Msieu Antoine said, "How is your cold today?" he answered, "My cold is fine today, msieu."

There was a glint of laughter in his eyes, like a thick darning needle under his long eyelashes. His voice was laced with polite cheer.

But when David came with the basket on his head, filled with strawberries and early onions, with okra and green beans, Jean-Paul's whole face changed. He put down his broom and sat on the back step, with molasses taffy or one of Tretite's tartes. David said, "I slept in your bed."

Jean-Paul said nothing. They chewed, and I saw the sides of their faces when they stared at the chinaberry trees in starry bloom.

That night, he told me, "He said he was dark from the sun."

"David?"

He nodded. "I see the biscuits. Lard and flour and salt and milk. All white. Not like cornbread. But she takes them from the fire and they are brown." He looked at my neck. "He lived here. Before I came."

"David slept here for a time. I bought him from a white man who treated him badly. Now he lives with Charité. She is his mother."

He lay on the mattress, one cheek mashed into the fabric. Finally, when he seemed asleep, he said, "You bought me. You could give me to Charité."

I left my chair and lay beside him. "No. I could never give you to anyone. I am truly your mother."

"Charité isn't truly his mother?"

"She is now. But she wasn't before." His knuckles were no longer soft and dimpled under my touch. They were hard little rock-bones. "Tretite isn't truly your grandmère. But she is now. You sometimes make your family."

He waited a long time again. "Sometimes you unmake a family."

"You miss Emilia?"

"I miss Francine."

He faced the wall. On the ceiling, a tiny puff of whitewash made a cloud when Msieu Antoine knocked a book from his bed.

Every day when Jean-Paul brought wood for the fireplaces, the boarders and lawyers and visitors narrowed their eyes. Then they would nod at Msieu Antoine and say, "You had this one hidden, no?"

"He and his mother were separated by circumstance," Msieu Antoine said smoothly.

They smiled privately or frowned openly; there was no more to say.

In December, when we went over household bills, he laced his fingers like a fence over more papers.

"Just as with you, he cannot be freed until he is twenty-one."

"But he is mine. He is safe."

"No," Msieu Antoine said. "What if you take ill and die? What if I am required to move? Then who does he belong to?"

"Move? Where?"

He only shrugged. He was not required to speak about everything.

Jean-Paul belongs to God, I thought. Là-bas, where I would be—I couldn't help him then.

"What are you planning to write?" I asked. He began with a blank piece of paper—the flat emptiness that held our lives.

I touched the edges of the contracts near me. Céphaline's voice—paper is made of wood fibers crushed and wetted and pressed and dried. They used to write on skin. Animal skin.

Write it on my chest. Burn it. My son. Don't take him away.

"He is a boy. He must have a trade. He needs a legal guardian and protector until his twenty-first birthday. You own him. But you have little to assist him, and if you leave his life, he is a slave for sale."

"No."

"If you died, he would become inherited property."

"No!"

"Who is the father?"

I studied Msieu Antoine's moustache, his nose veined with tiny spiderwebs on one side. "Everyone thinks you are the father."

"I know."

"That is convenient."

"It is someone from Rosière," he said. "We both know who it is."

"Does it matter?"

He shook his head. "But he cannot be assisted by his father, true? I am suggesting an indenture. I will be his guardian."

We stood at the courthouse again, and Jean-Paul came with us. He threw back his head to look at the ceiling, the fans, the lights.

So the first man to buy my son didn't examine him, of course, didn't pull up his lips to look at the gums, the way men did. Didn't push hard on the boy belly, as a stranger would have.

But I was afraid anyway, with a tremble like wet hair across my back, even though this was the only man who had ever been kind to me. I was an animal, and my skin reminded me that my brain controlled nothing.

Julien Antoine looked at me, not my son, and said, "This is not a sale, Moinette. These are indenture papers. They only state that he is under my care for a period of years. There is no reason to be nervous. This protects him, with my name."

He turned to the clerk at the conveyance book and said, "The boy is only six, after all."

This time, when I held the pen, my son watched my fingers.

My own father's name was unknown. My mother never had a last name. My first owner's name was Bordelon. I was not a de la Rosière. Now I was free.

This man, Julien Antoine, had brought us both here. People assumed this was his son. I had trusted him now with our lives. On page 156 of the conveyance book, I wrote his name: Jean-Paul Antoine, quadroon slave of Moinette Antoine, FWC.

We began by blowing on the embers of the fire Tretite banked each night. She slept in the kitchen now because her head hurt in the night, and she liked to sit up near the warmth. All those years, she said every morning to my mother, "Dorm bien?" Sleep well? And my mother said to her, "Tête bien?" Head well?

When I suggested we call Doctor Vidrine, Tretite said the pain was as if a scarf were inside, under her scalp and hair, and someone pulled the tie tighter and tighter. She said, "Let me quiet for a time."

Jean-Paul and I woke her with our combined breaths on the red jewels inside the ashes because he loved the color.

I learned about texture and color and waiting from my son. He had waited for me for too long, and he liked only to be alone with his own imagination and with gradations of tint and shade. When I hung the shirts, when I lit the candles, when I added the flour, he watched. Skin and bone, bleached linen and muslin.

Folds and pleats. He taught himself to sew on scraps of cloth.

Every night, I prayed for him and for my mother, while Jean-Paul traced the branches on his plate. My mother's smell was in the heated iron, her night-shining eyes in the inkbottles.

Every morning, we went out into the yard. Jean-Paul shook the bottles, which each glowed different murkiness in the sun. The white shirts moving their sleeves, the pocked surface of the iron. New boats made of palmetto leaf.

This yard and kitchen were his place.

I remembered days and nights in the clearing and my mother's house with a vivid clarity. And I stared at him when he wasn't aware of me, wondering if these were his days. The ones that would remain sharp, every outline—like a child's pinwheel blurring in a breath and then stopped, frozen for a moment so each slice was distinct.

When he was seven, he brought me three dolls for Francine.

He had made them of scraps of brown velvet, and he'd sewn on black button eyes and crude mouths of red thread, even a crooked line of white in the center for teeth.

"Why can't we take them to her?" he said.

"We cannot visit Rosière. It isn't allowed."

"You visited me before."

It was winter, and his skin was so pale, a lavender bruise on his cheekbone from wrestling with David, his eyes the last moment of day.

"I was a slave then, and so were you. I came when Msieu Antoine visited. But the de la Rosières do not want free people there, on Rosière. They will not allow it."

"But we can go at night. When they can't see."

I shook my head. "Too dangerous."

He shouted, "Danger is the fire. Danger is the knife. Emilia said that a thousand times."

"Danger is different for you now." I tried to pull him onto my lap, to examine the dolls, but he ran into our room and hid them in one of his secret places, all of which I knew, but none of which I ever touched.

When he was eight, he pulled my forearm to the candlelight and said, "What mark is this?"

His brand was the blurred rose, the two thorns.

I said, "My own brand." I would not show him the fleur-de-lis. He put his fingernail next to the three coffee bean scars from the curling iron. My anger felt like a hot scarf pulled from my throat, but I couldn't cry. He was a child. The purple marks from the nail on the boat had disappeared. My dried blood on my teeth while the boat moved north in the water.

"I made those marks on myself to help me remember my mother."

He asked what I knew he would. "Did she leave you?"

"I did not leave you because I wanted to. Msieu Antoine bought me, and I was impatient every day to come back for you."

"And now he is your husband. He is my father."

My mother had not lied to me. She had withheld the truth when it suited her, and me.

"He is our guardian. Like Tretite is your grandmother."

He pulled at his own brand. A polliwog. A kite. Nothing recognizable.

"You don't have one of these. Everyone else has them. Francine. Emilia."

"I am the only one with your exact blood. The rest I have given you." My needle was warm. The grooves in my fingertips were permanent.

"Did it hurt? When you made the three marks?"

Would he try it? To please me, or to better me?

"It hurt very much. I would never do it again."

He smiled faintly. I kept his hair short and combed down tightly. His forehead was square, not round like David's. He said, "You wouldn't have to."

The next week, he and David tried to carry wood from the shed to the kitchen, and both hobbled on the left foot. I was astonished that they'd both hurt themselves. "Did you drop something on your toes?"

They had marked themselves on the bottoms of their feet. When I made them take off their shoes, blue crosses were inflamed and red on their soles.

"How could you hurt David like this?" I asked.

My son smiled. "He said it didn't hurt."

David was impassive as always. He added, "I hate the fire. We use a knife. And Jean-Paul put the ink."

"Like the Indian who comes to the alley to bring the wood," Jean-Paul said. "He has the ink on his chin."

I rubbed salve onto their feet and made them sit in the kitchen. "Why would you put it there? Now you can't walk."

Jean-Paul looked at me as though I were foolish. "We're the same color there."

"A cross?"

"Two lines. Two of us."

When he was nine, his voice grew little barbs like thistle. Soft and downy and pricking.

"Looking in the mirror won't help," Jean-Paul said.

"Help what?" Tretite sat with him in the dining room. I paused on the stairs.

"His coat."

They had been watching Msieu Redmond, who always examined himself in the large entry mirror. I stayed on the steps, listening until he left.

"Eh, là. You stop."

"Won't help his sideburns either."

Tretite whispered, "Ti maman hear you."

There was silence then. I sat on the top step. Not "No, she won't," or "But if she does, she'll laugh, too." He didn't say these sharp-edged words around me.

"I like to make you laugh. Your dress shakes."

"Eh, là, stop now!" She laughed again.

"I used to make Emilia laugh. And Francine."

He had asked only once more if we would ever go to Rosière. I told him I didn't know. Etienne and his wife had passed me once on the sidewalk near the courthouse when I delivered letters to Msieu Antoine. The wife was blond and plump, whether with food or with child, her waist full under the bodice of her dress. Her face clenched itself tightly as a red fist. Maybe she knew me; maybe she hated anyone with skin like mine; maybe she assumed I was one of Jeanne Heureuse's girls and would unbutton my dress right there on the street for her husband.

Jean-Paul said softly, "Msieu Redmond pulls at his coatsleeves in front of the mirror as if that will help them grow. Every time. The mirror won't help. Pas magique."

Tretite only huffed a little now.

I carried the basket of linens down the stairs into silence. "Jean-

Paul," I said, holding out my hand. He smiled, the effortless, polite smile he used for every human.

He followed me to the hallway mirror. The men spoke inside the office; cart wheels rumbled outside. "We are the same," I told him. He was tall, like his father. His face was level with my shoulder. His cheeks were like old paper, his hair combed smooth and hard as black glass with pomade.

"We are," he agreed. His smile did not change.

If my own father were reckless and unknown, what had his blood given? Etienne's father was in Jean-Paul, the supercilious assessment and impatience that had passed down through his own son. His grandson. And Madame? Her white garden. Her blossoms.

Even Pélagie, his aunt—her judgment and calculations, her love of finery—she was inside my son.

"Your true grandmère refused to speak if she didn't care to. Even to whites," I said to him now. "She trusted no one. As you do not."

If my mother's eyes had been nightwater, his were twilight. I said, "Her blood, and mine, are in your tongue. You must be careful, because your words are often in your eyes, and anyone can see them."

His smile became thinner, curled more at the corners of his lips. He said, "It is too bad we are not marked with ears and fur, like the dogs of Msieu de la Rosière. Hunting dogs are always easy to tell."

I said, "Yes, they are," remembering my mother's lessons, how she had spoken with weight and seriousness in the clearing and the words seemed to knuckle against my skull.

"You are not a dog. You are going to be a man."

"A dog barks. A man speaks."

"A man who looks like you must speak carefully."

"There are no other men who look like me."

My heart rose behind its bone. "Yes, there are. In Paris. Madame Lescelles's son lives in Paris. There are men who look like you, and they go to school. When you are fourteen, you will go to Paris. Then you can speak as you wish."

But he continued to speak as he wished every day.

"You hear him," Tretite said one summer night, snapping green beans, her fingers still quick, her glossy chin rounder each year, like an apple resting under her lips. Her eyes were smaller, the apple seeds. Jean-Paul and David made a puddle in the yard, floating paper boats on the water. "If you were still in le quartier, you wouldn't see him to worry about him. He be in the field or the barn." She pinched off a dangling stem. "But you hear his mouth. Là. Too funny for a boy."

She was right. He couldn't be silent. He spoke in front of me now, because he had to. "Madame Richard has an egg in her throat. It moves up and down so fast that the chick must escape one day.

"That man's coat is the color of the slime in the horse trough. It was black and then green, and now it can't decide. There is no name for it."

"Oh?" Tretite said. "What other name beside dark green?"

He narrowed his eyes at her. "Moss. Pine. There is turquoise. A stone. Sometimes it is very dark. I have seen a ring with that stone. There is winebottle green. A man wore a coat that color one day. He was from New Orleans. The nice clothes are from New Orleans."

His eyes moved rapidly from me to Tretite. His voice was not false now. He was not cheerfully repeating anything.

When he was ten, he could not sleep in our room any longer.

He was nearly as tall as me. He had outgrown his pallet three times, and another rope bed wouldn't fit into the room. Though Tretite slept in her chair, Jean-Paul was too old to lie beside her when she did rest in her own bed.

He needed his own place for his treasures. Msieu Antoine had seen Jean-Paul's piles in the kitchen—cloth scraps and tea tins and cigar boxes for boats and sails. In the yard, Jean-Paul had wood and tins of paint and hemp for rigging.

They'd begun to make bigger boats, he and David. They'd even flooded a corner of the yard with water to test the boats, and the new neighbor next door, another lawyer, had complained to Msieu Antoine that they'd damaged his fence.

"A boy have to sleep in the garçonnière," Tretite said. "Have to be apart from maman. Have to learn his task." She poured bacon grease into the tin, and the molten fat turned white in the cold. "*Your* maman—

she teach you to wash and sew, but one night she say to me, How I know? Moinette go with les blancs, how I know what to show her?"

Jean-Paul's figure, squatting near the puddle, wavered and blurred. "Why are you telling me this?" I wiped my eyes, and the grit from the beans hurt.

"Let him work with David. Take the letters to the courthouse, the papers to the men. What you teach him here? Sweep and serve the table and watch you sew? That not a man." She stood up.

I went outside to the shed, a small brick building that kept our wood dry and my washpots and tools from rusting. I hadn't opened the shed for nearly a year, since Jean-Paul was old enough to haul things from here to the yard or kitchen.

Could it be made into a room for him? There was only a tiny window, covered with cobwebs. When I pulled open the door, someone was breathing inside.

Jean-Paul and David came running at my screams. "Maman! He won't hurt you! He won't!"

An Indian slept beside the wood, rolled in a blanket so dirty the leaves and ashes looked like fur. His face was covered with a black hat, but the light made him twitch, and he sat up abruptly.

Red trade cloth in my mouth. It was Joseph. From the ciprière.

His eyes were filmed with alcohol. Waxed black buttons. He peered at me and pulled himself up, holding on to the woodpile.

"Maman. We knew he slept here, but we didn't want to tell you." Jean-Paul's fingers pulled at my sleeve. "When he brings the wood, I give him half the money you give me, and food. He likes it here."

Joseph said nothing. "What do you do with the money?" I asked Jean-Paul.

"Buy candy with David. Or canvas for our boats. Paint." He did not say he was sorry. He curved his mouth. "He saw us sailing our boat on Bayou Carron one day. He showed us his pirogue. But now it is gone. Maybe it was stolen. But he cannot talk."

Joseph could hear. He didn't move his eyes from mine.

Jean-Paul said, "I never say anything mean about his clothes, and he never says anything mean at all."

"This is not a joke," I told him sharply, but he pulled my ear to his lips.

"He is not a pet. He has half a tongue. He showed me. The other half is gone. He is a fantôme, like Tretite said, from the woods. He will not harm us. He makes boats."

Joseph did not open his mouth. He walked out the back gate and down the alley, pulling his hat low over his forehead.

"Jean-Paul, this is not our house. It belongs to Msieu Antoine. He could become so angry about this, he might send you away."

"I belong to you," Jean-Paul said. "You won't send me away."

His voice was serene. Genial. He went back inside with Tretite.

Half a tongue. The alley was bare, no summer vines, just wooden fences and gates. Why had Joseph left the ciprière camp? Where was his sister? Had the white man cut out Joseph's tongue?

I leaned my back against the brick. Joseph and his sister had sold me for gold. Now he was one of the drunken bodies we stepped around in the alleys or the square.

And my son had been to Bayou Carron, where I had not thrown my life away. He was a child, but not a child. He was not mine every moment of the day, as I had been my mother's, in the clearing.

"Jeanne Heureuse dead," Charité whispered to me when she came to the back door with her basket of sweet potatoes. "Someone put the belt around her neck and pull. The other girl in the house say she hear a man call Jeanne English words. *Mongrel cur.* Then he disappear."

Sweet potatoes heavy in my fingers. Rough skin and dirty eyes. *Mongrel cur.* Who had said those words? Not mule. Not mulatto. All these years, I had never seen her. She looked like me.

"Who will bury her?" I asked Charité.

"Say her girl send the body back to New Orleans. Say a mama there and five sisters."

"All this time?"

Charité nodded, lowering her voice. "She the oldest, send to work Opelousas. Just her job."

All day I thought of her. How old was she? She owned one girl, sometimes two or three. Where would they go?

I cleaned the coffee tray. When the men left the office for the courthouse, Jean-Paul said, "Msieu Césaire has white goose wings growing from his cheeks, but the hair in his nostrils is still black. How is that possible? You told me our skulls are full of cartilage."

"Hush," I told him.

"He hates us," he whispered.

"Hush!" I said.

Msieu Césaire hated Mr. Greene.

He and Madame Richard and others tormented Mr. Greene in offices and dining rooms and courthouse halls. Msieu Césaire, the tiny man who had lifted my skirt with his cane, stared at Jean-Paul with baleful eyes. He cocked his head at Msieu Antoine to ask, "You buy that one or make him?"

His whiskers were like goose quills.

"I do not see you at Mass," he said to Mr. Greene while I left coffee the next morning.

"I worship elsewhere."

"You are a Jew."

"It is difficult to worship in Opelousas."

"In the original Code Noir, in 1724, the first article decreed that all Jews must leave the colony or become Catholic."

"I have read the article. It was written nearly one hundred years ago."

"This is a Catholic parish."

"This is an American state."

"The Code Noir was the law."

"The Black Code. But I am not black."

"You are a Jew. I don't do business with Jews, and my friends don't do business with Jews."

Msieu Antoine could not make Mr. Greene stay. "The fever, the people, the swamps, the intolerable heat. The utter intolerance and lack of ideas. It is preferable to you that these Creoles think you have fathered a slave than to believe I worship differently."

"There are others to do business with us."

"No. No. I cannot live this way. Never."

But we had to live this way.

"You and your son could accompany us to Paris."

I sat at the table for only the second time in my life. Accompany to Paris. Back when I was sixteen and thought I would swim home. Now this was my home. This brick building would never burn. My papers were in a metal box.

"I have no trade in Paris. We will run the boardinghouse for you and put the money in the bank. You will return in a year? You will decide then what to do?" My eyes were level with Julien Antoine's. His eyes were surrounded by a burst of lines, like etchings on a fine table.

"Yes, although it is doubtful given Jonah's feelings that we would return for long."

"Then we will make a pact. When Jean-Paul is fourteen, we will send him to school in Paris. Like the son of Madame Lescelles. Paris is better for sons who look like mine."

He was sleeping now in the shed. I crossed the dark yard, holding the poker. Joseph often slept outside, against the back wall of the shed, near the woodpile. But perhaps someone was with him—a trapper or a drunk. Tonight, no one was there.

Jean-Paul's mouth was open. He lay on the rope bed. A crate for a desk. A square of hemmed brocade over the tiny window. I sat in the chair until he awakened.

I never began with a word for a lesson, as my mother had. He began everything. He liked words but wasn't interested in writing. When he was a baby, I spent all my time imagining my absence, but now that he was half grown, I imagined nothing. There was only each day, the food and money and dirt there had always been.

He said when he was twenty-one, he would own a store. Tailoring and fabric and notions. He liked that word. "And I will marry Francine. She will sit behind the counter, like Madame Lescelles. With a tignon of purple. She loves purple. Like the wild iris in the ciprière."

The following week, after Julien Antoine drew up papers naming me the manageress of the property, I asked him about Jean-Paul. "He is indentured to you."

He was sorting outdated papers for burning. Upstairs, Mr. Greene was moving trunks. "I have given that some thought," he answered. "You don't know me at all by now? You think that I would be so careless?" He showed his palms to the ceiling. "The indenture will be nullified, Moinette. He is twelve years old now, oui? He needs a trade."

The circles of candlelight wavered on the windows against the blackness outside. "What kind of trade does a boy take when he loves cloth? Boats? Not coopering or carpentry or bricklaying?"

Jean-Paul was taller than me, but just as slight. His fingers moved the needle in and out of fabric as quickly as a bird dipping its beak into water, were narrow and long. His hair was a shelf on his head, combed from a side part, with only four wide waves toward his left ear.

The boarders looked at him with a mix of curiosity, when he took their boots in the evenings, and confusion when they happened to see him holding a bolt of brocade. He sewed in our bedroom, with the door propped open and his long table set up between the beds.

How did he know how to pleat the drapes perfectly to fit the brass rings? He stacked the rings and played with the colors of the cloth. He made boats from cypress brought by Joseph, hollowed out and carved and fitted with elaborate sails and riggings, which he sold to Madame Lescelles for her store.

The curtains and drapes she sold to wives who thought the décor had arrived from Paris. Green silk folds with appliqués of bronze leaves, slanted as if falling.

"Moinette," Msieu Antoine said, distracted by a box of contracts. "Men were unhappy with Jonah Greene and with me, for not marrying one of their daughters, for not drinking with them, for not being who we should have been. And you understand me fully."

I nodded.

"You should apprentice your son to François Vidrine, the upholsterer. He lives near Grand Coteau. I will have a message sent to him before we leave."

The second man to buy my son's body only glanced at his hands and nodded. He was French, old enough to have dark gray moustaches and an old-fashioned queue at the back of his head, the hair like a small tail.

The papers in the courthouse read: "Jean-Paul Antoine, age 11, quadroon slave of Moinette Antoine, is hereby indentured to François Vidrine, Grand Coteau, for the term of nine years, for the sum of $900, to be payable in equal installments each year."

A different book. So many pages. Slaves and horses and hogsheads of sugar. He was owned by me because I couldn't free him yet. Nine years. If Msieu Antoine came back in one year or two, and thought he should take Jean-Paul to Paris, he said it would be easy to cancel the indenture.

"I am going with Msieu Vidrine. The cousin of the doctor," Jean-Paul said. He sat near the trunk I had bought for him.

"You are to work for him. You are not sold."

"I am not free." He smiled.

"You are only called a slave because of the law. Words on paper, Jean-Paul. Do you understand? You belong to me."

"David is a slave. You bought him."

"Jean-Paul."

"When I am free, and I have money, I will buy Francine. I will marry her, and David will buy someone to marry, too."

He was still a child.

"When you are finished learning the trade, I will have bought this house from Msieu Antoine. He might not return here to live."

"My father." His soldier-coat eyes were fixed on mine.

"The house will be mine." I pulled my shawl tight around me.

He would be a free man of color, when he was twenty-one. He would have the bottom floor of this house for himself. His own window. His name painted. Chairs and sofas. Curtains. No one could object to curtains made by a free man.

He had filled his trunk with fabric and needles and clothes and his new boots, which he would save from the long, dusty journey on the cart. He had nothing when he came, I told myself. He has things he loves now.

When he turned to wave at me from the cart, his smile was measured and small as ever. Then he faced the road that led from Opelousas to Grand Coteau.

David was angry, his thin face clotted with held-in tears. "He had to learn a trade," I said, in the yard. "He will return."

Finally he said, "He told me you always said that when you left. 'I will return.' And you didn't come."

"I came when I could," I told him. His eyes didn't waver. I went back into my kitchen. My kitchen. Bricks and my windows, where the moonlight fell blue from the eastern sky three nights of each month.

Charité said, "He ask Madame Lescelles send him to Grand Coteau, work with Jean-Paul, and she look at him like he crazy. Tell him, your work drive the cart and deliver the goods."

The next week, Charité appeared with no basket, no sweet peppers, no madras, no candles. "Gone," she said. "Supposed to pick up tobacco and cigar from somewhere. Drive that cart and never come home."

Her tears smeared hot at my neck when she fell into my arms. She whispered, "He could put me on the cart. He could say, my mother ride with me today."

She stopped shaking and pulled away.

"Fourteen now. A man. I smell him grown, and I knew he would go," Charité said. Her eyes were nearly hidden in the roundness of her cheeks, and her arms were so wide now from good food that they flattened themselves against her sides. "I come on a cart. He come on a cart. I had him a few years."

She must have cried all night, because her eyes were smaller in the morning than in the afternoon. Madame Lescelles studied me coldly in her store. Someone had delivered the cigars. I bought three of them for Msieu Vosclaire, who had stayed at the house for months. I laid them on the clean desk in the office.

We kept it as an empty office, for men who needed to confer with someone in private or to write documents for court. The boarders ate in the dining room, but the office would not make a good parlor anymore. Parlors were for women who received callers. I received business. And the desk made me know Julien Antoine would return.

Two months later, Jean-Paul rode with Msieu Vidrine to Opelousas to deliver furniture, and he bounded off the cart and ran into the kitchen, not to embrace me but to lay his palms along my face.

"Feel this!" He had calluses from the needles and leather. "Here." He handed me a parcel. A simple dress, brown watered silk, the puffed sleeves ending in a spray of lace.

"Lace is worked by showing the absence," he whispered. "The empty space is the art."

He fixed me hard with his eyes and then spun to hold out his arms.

"David is gone," I said.

He knew. I saw the shift in the hollows that held nothing.

"You saw him."

He would have moved his muscles differently if he'd been surprised. His smile required many muscles. "He came to the barn where I work. He asked people where Vidrine's place was. He had cigars and tobacco in the cart, and he said we could drive north and sell them until we had enough money to take a boat to Ohio."

"Ohio?"

"Where everybody is free."

The dress was warming to my hands. I had forgotten how thin silk was against skin. Maybe David took the same road as Hervé Richard.

"Did you want to go?"

He straightened his cuffs. "Msieu Vidrine came out to the barn and saw the trunk full of cigars. He bought five." Jean-Paul looked past me at the fire. "Are those biscuits for me?"

Some days, I didn't want to rise in the morning. Tretite was awake before me, and blew on the embers and roasted the coffee. Her eyes were clotted with pain, and she moved as though blind, but I couldn't rise. The men's feet moved on the floors above my face. My ceiling. The sun shone on the chinaberry trees outside, their purple-star blooms, and the chickens groomed their feathers by the shed.

But I couldn't move. He wasn't mine. He might have gone. I would never see my mother.

All the coins and paper and fingers and the years of waiting and washing and then waiting. All the bones growing longer, and the hair, and the meat we ground between our teeth and the waste that left us to melt into the earth.

My own braids were so long, they wrapped around my head three times under the tignon. At night, my head ached from the weight. I was afraid to cut them. The *ni* is in the hair. Where was my mother's *dya*? The first time I cut Jean-Paul's hair, my fingers felt his skull. The African men's hair grew in whorls and curls. If we let Jean-Paul's hair grow, it would be long and wavy to his shoulders. He was a boy. I held his *ni* in my fingers, then kept it in a cloth bag under my bed.

Tretite didn't sing. She hummed. The words had been worn down to sound. Finally she stood in the doorway. "You only twenty-some years old. Too young to be tired. Get up and heat that iron for Msieu Vosclaire."

My hand moved into the air beside my bed. The absence of wrinkles. Clean white space. My family was an odd assemblage of animals. Not a herd.

Msieu Vosclaire stayed permanently in the far north bedroom. He worked all day as clerk of the court and drank one glass of wine while he read the newspaper at night. Then he went to sleep.

Joseph slept sometimes in the shed. He brought wood once a week. We left food for him. His mouth moved over the cornbread and meat, but I could only imagine the stump of a tongue.

Charité was not my sister. But she drank coffee with me and Tretite every morning at ten. She set her basket on the floor and rested her elbows on my table.

The American men spoke loudly in front of the house.

"It's run by a nigger."

"No, it's not."

"You've seen her. High yellow gal. I don't care how much the French like them, they're dirty. I wouldn't stay there."

"Vosclaire says it's clean."

"I'm staying at the other place. Eibsen. German."

But we had full rooms most nights. We cleaned the baseboards with a brush, swept the yard, washed the bedframes with boiling water in spring, oiled the hinges on the armoires.

It was clean. But at night, I was afraid. Men in the dining room and upstairs, some of them coming home drunk. One day, I asked Madame Lescelles, leaning on the scarred counter so thick with varnish it looked as if the marks swam under our hands, "Do you have a gun?"

She nodded toward her lap. The counter. She moved her fingers. Leaning closer to her as I'd ever been, I saw the rifle on the shelf under the counter.

"Do the Americans think about taking your money?"

She said, "They think about it all the time."

"Will you find one for me?" I said quietly. "A small pistol?"

She called the gun a derringer. In the silent house that night after I paid her, the gun was heavy in my apron pocket, the candles out in each room. I listened at each door for the sound of sputtering, so that no flames or carelessness could erase all our hard work.

I painted my name on the window in 1825.

Bricks and mortar. Wooden floors polished with lemon oil and soapy water that made me think of Félonise, her spindle fingers sealed to mine. My building, now that Julien Antoine was moving to Philadelphia to be with Jonah Greene. He sold the property to me for nine hundred dollars.

During his last few weeks in Louisiana, Julien Antoine wrote the sales transactions. I paid him three hundred dollars, with the balance of six hundred dollars due in exactly two years: May 23, 1827. Just as I had been paid for with part cash, part promise, when I was property.

The promise, the mortgage, was my son.

My own body couldn't be used as security, because if I were sold back as a slave, I couldn't own the building or Jean-Paul. A lawyer, Msieu Charles Drouet, was appointed to oversee the transaction and make sure the balance was paid on the property.

"You receive one hundred dollars annually, no?" Julien said, his fingers buried in his sideburns. "It is a safe mortgage. Jean-Paul is the only thing you own. And as well as you've maintained the property, you will continue to make money." He looked out the window. "I worry about leaving you alone, except we know Henri Vosclaire will be a steadying influence."

We had one last carriage ride together. "Are you ready?" I asked.

When we were far from town, the rented carriage stopped outside a thick woods near Bayou Courtableau. I knew what the livery driver thought when Msieu Antoine and I walked into the trees. He kept his face averted. The moss and bark and damp earth smelled strong. I had not been in a woods for years. I had eight rooms now. My wood, sanded and varnished and dead under my feet.

We came to a clearing and a small bayou, sluggish and black, with insects making dappled circles as they landed. Julien Antoine's fingers were firm on my wrist to guide me over a trailing vine. Suddenly my heart felt hot, behind my breastbone. The trees, where Hervé Richard waited for me, where lovers met and people hid and kissed. I pulled at Julien Antoine's hand, and his chest met mine. His coat smelled of lavender water. His sideburns brushed my neck. His wrists crossed behind my spine, held me tightly for a moment.

Then he sighed. "Give me the gun," Julien said. "You are afraid. You could marry, no? A man would be better protection than a pistol."

Surprise was bitter in my throat. "You are joking, true? I cannot by law marry a slave or a white man. Free men of color marry their own kind."

"I was not joking." He smiled. "I have been in Paris, where love seems more important than law and business, but that may be pure sentiment." He studied the small derringer. "Etienne de la Rosière would say this kind of gun is only useful for hunting a man. The men on the steamboats all have one. They are for gamblers and cheats."

"No one will be hunted unless he hunts me. I will not be hunted like Madame Pélagie."

The small pistol made a sharp report when he showed me how to pull the trigger, and the ball disappeared into a tree trunk. "You will not need to use it, I wager," Julien said. I flinched when the gun fired the second time. "You will only need to show it, unless the person is a fool, to put him into his place."

My place.

"You do not appear to know your place," Madame de la Rosière, the wife of Etienne, said to me one day when she saw me outside the courthouse.

I had gone to deliver a letter for Mr. Smythe, a lawyer staying upstairs while he partitioned an estate. He said a doctor had recommended Madame Antoine's as the best place for fresh coffee and comfortable rooms. He mentioned perfectly white shirts.

From my lemon tree in the back, we made lemon oil as Félonise had taught me. Each room was a still life; Pélagie had called her rooms still lifes, and I arranged books and flowers and objects. I looked at the men as collections of muscle, bone, brain, and organs, as Céphaline had appraised us all.

Every morning, Tretite tied grosgrain ribbons around the clean stacks of clothes and linens. Men liked the codes for their rooms. Green for Mr. Smythe. Red for Msieu Séjour.

My place was full of men who ate lunch or dinner, Tretite's roasted chicken or ham, her biscuits, her pralines. For all these years, they had smoked cigars and drunk fresh coffee until evening with Msieu Antoine, and even after the place was mine, they still lingered to talk courthouse business, since I was right across the street.

There was no liquor. No excuses for the people who hated me.

My place, according to Madame de la Rosière and the other wives, was underneath a trader or gambler or farmer. My place was with Jeanne Heureuse, whose house at the edge of town was dark. My place was inside one room, on one bed, under many men that the mesdames wouldn't dream of acknowledging in the street.

I held the letter for Msieu Séjour—the spidery ink handwriting had made me pause there, in the courthouse lobby, to think of Céphaline. Her pages and pages of notes. The bones and trees and birds. She had always whispered the names of the birds. The heron I had thought would lead me back to Azure in the tangle of watery skeins that was Barataria. The veins in her wrist, pulsing blue-green and moving under the skin when Doctor Tom bled her.

Madame de la Rosière swept past me with two other women, their wide skirts brushing the dusty floor. "Decent women—"

"This is not New Orleans, where they congregate at will."

"She could be whipped for dressing that way."

She had left Paris to marry Etienne when she was seventeen. Their money was joined. Their bodies were joined. They had two daughters, who were very small. He never came to town, and I was happy not to have to see him from my own window.

Eleven | NI

That winter, the wind blew and blew, every day, blew every leaf and piece of cane trash from the carts into our doorways and under our tables. Then frost rimmed the windows, grew itself furred on the chinaberry branches, and stiffened the sheets.

People could barely walk. My laundry blew down, and when we hung wet clothes inside, cinders from the fire leaped to burn two shirts, which I had to replace.

Madame Lescelles handed me needles and said, "Losing cane out there, all that frost and wind. Why I never buy land. Flood or freeze or blow away, all that dirt. But people still come here for provision. This don't fly away."

The dust gathered on my bottles of bootblack and wrapped soap cakes. The sky turned black with smoke and roiling ash from the sugar mills.

While Tretite slept and the men were gone, the only sounds were the creak of the shutters against the angry wind. Tretite had lost a tooth. It lay in a dish. Céphaline and I had touched the teeth in Doctor Tom's office. What if Céphaline had a son, with the man chosen for her? What if her son had her blue flame eyes, but he was an Auzenne who cared only for horses and gambling? Would she have loved him because he was her blood? Would she have sent him away?

But her own mother had loved her without reservation. Madame Bordelon would have died in her daughter's place.

Etienne's wife rode past in their carriage, her bosom trembling like flan, but never him. He had two daughters. No sons.

But Pélagie—what if she had borne a son by the husband or the brother, hated and hateful? She would have sent the boy away as soon as possible to boarding school. She would have had her window, in New York, somehow.

I had a window.

Jean-Paul had left the three dolls for Francine on his bed. Francine was fourteen, old enough to have children of her own, who would sleep in her bed.

Joseph slept in the shed. He ate one plate of food each night, and he drank himself insensible. He had nothing besides his clothes and his hat. It was easier to have nothing.

Jean-Paul sent no message. He merely appeared, the week before Christmas. He was cordial. Vague. A pleasant guest.

He hugged Tretite, he pressed his lips to my cheek, he sat at the table and ate the gumbo we made for him. Then he sat in the office and sewed, while I went over the ledgers. He said, "I worked on a sofa all week. Brocade. Gold and green. Not a good combination."

"We should go to Mass," I said, but we didn't move. I wanted to hear the chirp of small scissors, to hear him breathing.

"I hate the people at Mass when Msieu Vidrine makes me go," he said politely. "I cannot speak of their clothes or their stupidity. I cannot bear their self-satisfaction."

"Is Msieu Vidrine unkind to you?"

He shrugged. "No. But he speaks endlessly, about the work, the weather. It makes me tired to answer. Always he needs an answer. He says I must learn to be more pleasant and friendly. To him and the people who buy the furniture. On Sunday, we have to speak about the weather as well." Finally he looked up. "I want someone to listen. But you are not there."

His eyes so dark they were nearly purple. His brows fine and black as if painted on his forehead. I stood behind him and combed his hair down, while he let me. "Maman?" he said again.

Hair is dead. A collection of vines. Decorations for your scalp. Scalp covers the skull. Skull holds the brain. Where is the *ni,* inside these strands that lie sideways?

"My name reads Antoine, but he is not my father."

"No, he is not your father. Solely your guardian."

If I told him it was Etienne, he would see the man on his horse, riding his fields. Memory people. Would that make my son angry or fill him with the same melancholy as his father?

"I never saw my father," I said. "I didn't know who he was. Your father can do nothing for you." Then he turned around. His teeth were level with my eyes. "My mother always told me I belonged to her, not to the man who believed he owned me. And that was true."

One night, I dreamed of her, sitting at the table with me, our fingers working and our eyes not on each other. We were sorting rice, taking out stems and pebbles. She whispered, "Someone put white stones where they bury. Stones so many like God was laughing and lose his teeth. And they stick in the earth. A big God. Not my mother's god. Not the god from Senegal. Another one. From here only. Louisiana God."

I put a stone on the earth the following year.

I bought a piece of land, and a white angel.

Tretite died of pneumonia in the winter, and we buried her in the Opelousas cemetery, near the plots owned by the Lescelles family and other free people of color.

TRETITE. BORN 1765, DIED 1828. The mason carved a stone with those words, and an angel. A white gown. No more words. No Beloved Wife, Mother, Daughter. No last name. She was not really Julien Antoine's property. She belonged to herself now.

I was thirty years old. Jean-Paul would soon be fourteen, the age when he should be sent to Paris.

A window. A school. Perhaps a tailor in Paris. More money than I had been able to save. Passage on a ship, a place to live, necessities. Tretite's burial had been expensive. Her plot of land was my piece of earth. I washed dust from her white stone. The day she was buried, Charité and I were the only women to mourn her. All the women on Azure—were they buried now, too? My fingers rested on the carved indentations of Tretite's letters. My mother had no stone. Her name was Marie-Thérèse. Her body rested on the surface of the bayou. Dangerous to be so rested. No resting place.

When I left the cemetery, Msieu Césaire, shrunken and small as a child, stooped inside his fine black coat, was leaving his wife's tomb. Keeping my gaze on the trees, I let him go ahead.

The boardinghouse was quiet all Mardi Gras season, when everyone went to New Orleans. Every month, when it seemed that the numbers on the paper would be what I wanted, they danced in a different way before my eyes.

For the first time in my life, I was alone. Msieu Vosclaire, the other boarders, were not even a herd. Only a shifting school of fish, swerving around the furniture and into the dining room and up the stairs.

Charité asked me, "Why you never think of a man?"

"I think of one man. But it's only thinking. If I had a man, one more to cook for, to wash for, he might tell me to sell the house for something else. A farm. A boat. You know the truth. A woman cannot run a boardinghouse if she marries."

The days passed as though blurred. An old painting. I needed to find a girl to help but couldn't bring myself to look for a slave. To buy someone, even to find an indentured servant, would cost more money. The hundred dollars received annually for Jean-Paul would be traded for someone else.

He could come home. But he would learn nothing. All those beds to be made. The eggs. The still lifes of each evening. Two chickens cut up in a pot, with tomatoes and onions and herbs. The shirts flat and limp by the fire when it rained. The conveyance of crumbs. The coffee beans. Mamère.

Joseph came to the back door every afternoon, when he woke. He motioned with his head to ask whether he should bring in wood, his long black hair oily and straight around his shoulders. Where was his pirogue? Where were his woods? When he was a child, he lived in the trees, until we came. New animals.

Msieu Vosclaire was a creature of habit, with his paunch touching the table until he pushed himself away, and his one glass of wine at the desk. He wrote a letter each night to his sister in Saint Louis, Missouri, and then he left it for me on the dining room table. His were the last shoes to move over my head. The white envelope glowed in my candlelight. He tried to keep his promise to Julien Antoine, to make people aware that this was a respectable place.

But I was still sang mêlé. My hair. My skin. Even my money was not respectable.

One morning before dawn, when I went out past the shed to dump the ashes, a man put an arm around my throat. He held my hair at the back of my skull so tightly my head couldn't move. His words were English. "Whorehouses got plenty of whore money. Take me to it." He pushed a knife tip into the skin above my collarbone, and blood slid down my breast while he jerked me toward the back door.

The money was never in the house. I knew someone would try to find it there. I said, "Under the tree. The stone."

He said, "All that money for fuckin all those men. This one's free."

He pushed me to the ground. The ashes inside my nose, stinging my eyes. He cut my skirt from the bodice, cut the bodice in half, and tore off the cloth.

"Branded, huh—you ran away." The knife tip touched the fleur-de-lis on my shoulder. "Mongrel cur."

I had heard his voice somewhere. Then he pushed into me so hard that the earth went into my mouth.

He was a mongrel. Only an animal. A dog could bite me. My blood and skin all he had. He was not human. He would not kill me.

When he was finished, the smell of his tobacco hung over me. My teeth were grinding against the ashes, my eyes stung. He kept my hair clenched in his fist, a knot at the back of my skull, while he arranged his clothes.

Then he let me go, and I raised myself on my knees. I could see out of one eye. He wanted me to see him.

The trapper—his empty gums, his red face. He had seen me at the store and on the road. He thought I was Madame Lescelles's daughter. He spit tobacco juice onto my feet. Then he turned to dig up the stone.

The belt. Mongrel cur. He had killed Jeanne Heureuse.

I didn't have the gun. I felt bowls of mud on my knees. The ashes were for lyewater. The bucket was near the woodpile. The wire handle was cold. I said, "Sir. Sir."

He swung his beard around, and I threw the lyewater into his face. He screamed and fell to the ground, scrabbling at his eyes. He would kill me now. I ran into the kitchen, my hands before me, and felt my way to my room, to the gun beside my bed.

But he didn't follow me.

A sheet wrapped to my body, I went outside, where Joseph stood over the trapper, whose throat was cut. Joseph wiped the blood from the knife. He put the knife back into his boot.

The blood was hot and metal and steaming on the dirt. I could see half the world. The ashes had sealed themselves to one eye. Joseph dragged the body toward the alley.

No sound. No one had bothered to investigate the scream, and the night-morning was quiet. Only a horse, far down another street, hooves soft and steady.

I pushed my clothes into the fire, filled the tub with cold water, and cleaned the dirt from my teeth, the liquids from my legs, and rinsed my eyes again and again, but ash had burned my left eye, and I could see nothing from that side.

My boarders, two Creole brokers in town for business, were sleepy and pained from the rum they had drunk the night before. They barely acknowledged me bringing their shirts and hot water. They left with Msieu Vosclaire.

In the yard, the blood had turned black and hard as pebbles and burned saucers. But when I raked the dirt into the fire under my wash-pot, the smell of burning red made me sick.

Joseph came back toward dark. He sat on a dirty blanket nested against the back fence. "What did you do with him?" I asked.

He dug a small channel in the dirt with his knife and filled it with water. Then he floated a chicken bone down the bayou he'd made.

The body floated somewhere. Joseph's black eyes met mine. He took three dollars from my hand and left to buy drink.

That night, I finally shivered and cried near the windows covered with Jean-Paul's curtains. Me. Not Madame Eibsen or Madame Delacroix. Mongrel. All the men. Leave their seed. Ride me and then ride the horse, ride back to the house, to the woods to kill animals and sell skins. Skin. What if their sons, left by the mothers, sold or traded or just left, walked in the same woods and killed their fathers over the last raccoon? What if their sons sat beside them in a tavern and didn't like the sounds of their words and shot their fathers, stepping over their bodies when they spat and left? Left. Left and left, over and over.

My eye was so burned and blurred that I could not cook or wash. My hands were skinned. People believed me—the wind had blown an ash into my eye, tripped me up to scrape my face and arms and knees.

Msieu Drouet let me borrow two hundred dollars to hire a girl, as I couldn't run the house. A free woman of color in New Iberia had a niece who needed a trade, so a fifteen-year-old girl named Noémie was apprenticed to me for one year, for two hundred dollars, to learn washing, sewing, cooking, and cleaning. Msieu Drouet filed the papers in the court, the same day I received the payment for the year for Jean-Paul.

I sat up all night in the office, writing the sums in the ledger, holding my good eye close to the paper. All we were. Conveyance of numbers and crumbs and passages full of liquid.

But something had entered my blood and wouldn't leave. Not a baby. Not seeds. Something foul that made me burn and made me weak and made me faint.

I locked the front door.

The girl Noémie brought hot poultices for my belly. She was a nervous, kind child, with cinnamon-colored eyes and small hands, which she left hanging in front of her like a squirrel while she waited beside my bed. She said, "Should I let in boarders?"

"No," I said. "No one."

Noémie pulled up a chair. "You are so beautiful. My mother had heard of you. She heard you were married to a white man."

I shook my head no. Noémie whispered, "She said your beauty got you this house. A big brick house."

I closed my eyes and told her to get Charité from the store.

Charité brought a tea she mixed for monthly troubles. I told her it was fever. But this was a different burning, and my head filled with wiry boiled moss so that my thoughts were caught and tangled.

All the rivers and bayous led to the ocean, past walls of earth. The men built wooden walls and brick walls, and we moved inside them small as ants. Cages and chains. Then we went outside to gather pebbles and crumbs and bring them back. The birds caught seeds in their beaks and huddled in their nests. Léonide and Tretite could cook, but I had to lie down and lift my dress. Christophe and Gervaise could cut cane and move wood, but Jean-Paul had to drown.

The steam from the washpots used to dance with the smoke, if the air was heavy enough in the clearing. Céphaline said the ankle had to show. Her mother said a small ankle, well-turned, might be all the man could see. Peeking out from the skirt. The ball of bone a tiny head under the skin. A petite skull rubbing against the iron ring. The feel of that chain, every night, and I couldn't move. Twice I had wet myself in the morning. I had washed my clothes and gone to the fields with them wet, and the sun was so hot the steam flew from my hem, when I hoed the bad grass from the good grass. The bad women from the good women. The ball of bone. Why would men care about the ankle? What could they put inside the ankle?

"Impure contact," Doctor Vidrine said, his face over mine. "I hadn't thought you would—"

I turned my face to my wall. My whitewash. My plaster.

He took my blood, with the lancet. It ran dark into the bowl. Give it to me. He poured it into the washbasin. Infected. Impure. Inside the blood. But what came from my passage was white and yellow, not blood. Noémie rubbed onto my passages an ointment. She was not my blood, and she had to wash my blood. My gums bled. I swallowed my blood. Then he purged me with liquids. Bottles and jars. Cleaning solutions. White corrosive sublimate and new rum, he said. Expel from the habitat all remains of the disorder. Once or twice a day. Nothing left inside me. No blood. No liquids. My liquids flew into bowls and towels, my throat scraped raw, my gums swimming in blood, my eye swollen closed.

Half of their faces leaned over me. Jean-Paul. He came. He stayed and wiped my skin with cold water. He did not smile.

The third man who bought my son said nothing.

It had taken weeks for me to walk again. Around the gray floating scar, like a tiny cloud in my eye, I saw the man's boots. Were they shined with saliva?

We stood in the office of Msieu Drouet. He had lent me money to pay the doctor, to pay Noémie's mother, to buy food and candles and cooking oil and soap. I had mortgaged the building to him months ago, for security on the loan, and now the payment was due.

"You have written twice to Julien Antoine, three weeks have passed, and we have no answer. Clearly he must be traveling," Msieu Drouet said.

I nodded.

"You have one asset remaining, Madame Antoine. Your son has offered himself for security."

The indenture to Vidrine could be canceled, he said. If I sold Jean-Paul to Msieu Drouet's cousin, who owned a sugar plantation in Petit Pinière, twenty miles away, I would receive $750. Half due now, which we could apply to the mortgage on the house.

"They can use an upholsterer for their new plantation while they furnish the rooms, and then he can be trained as a carpenter. Valuable trades. If at the end of the year, when the balance is due, you wish to repurchase him, you may. That is written into the terms of sale."

"Don't lose the house," Jean-Paul said. "This time don't sell the curtains. I worked very hard on that color. Celadon. Do you know how many dyes I mixed? They were for your office."

"Your office," I said. "That is your office."

"Then don't sell my curtains. I'll make new ones when I come back." He smiled slightly, and then his eyebrows leaped higher. "I will return. Remember, when you used to say that?

"Celadon," he said, shaking his head. "The perfect color."

If the house were lost, he would never have his own table for cutting cloth, for draping coats and dresses and couches. With no house, I could only sew or cook for someone else. "For one year?" I whispered.

"Jean-Paul, quadroon slave for life, originally acquired from Laurent de la Rosière, sold by Moinette Antoine to Crespin Frozard for $750, on November 4, 1828."

Saint Landry Parish, Notary Book B, page 243.

Msieu Crespin Frozard didn't look at me or at my son. He walked toward his carriage, and Jean-Paul walked backward for ten steps, facing me on the steps in front of the courthouse, smiling wider now to let me know that everything would be fine this time.

Noémie's night breath rattled in her throat like dried gourd seeds. She was not my child. Her murmurs made me melancholy. I moved my bed to Jean-Paul's room.

I would not rent that room, with the south-facing window overlooking the yard, where the chinaberries were winter-gold balloons for mice. I spent the nights watching the moon cold and December blue, the shadows like black needles on the bare ground.

He had taken his trunk. What did he have? I didn't even know. His washbowl was white, but deep inside, I saw the faint black etchings. A boat on the little desk near the window. A junebeetle had steered it once, his thorny legs attached to the tiny tiller made of a translucent grain of rice.

My eyes hurt when I tried to sew. Only the blouse for Fantine, made of white ponds, was beautiful. My sewing was nowhere near Jean-Paul's, not fine like my mother's. I was only good for moving dirt and collecting money. Holding on to bricks. I could keep the bricks from burning, so Jean-Paul would someday have them.

The wind returned, and the house swirled again with ashes and leaves and fine dust from horse hooves. The dust coated everything, even when we kept the shutters bolted and the house dark.

Msieu Vosclaire said, "A shift in the atmosphere."

Msieu Césaire said, "Only God sneezing."

His valet said, "Some of that coffee there, eh?"

They sent a cart for me.

The Frozard groom said, "Didn't know who to send for. Boy a slave, the overseer said. Msieu Frozard, he in New Orleans. Then the cook say, That boy Jean-Paul tell me he not sold, he just loan. Say, Get the mother from Opelousas."

"Is he ill?" The road was rutted deep by wheel tracks, and my teeth cut my lip. Blood from inside the mouth tastes different. The wind pushed behind us, pushed the mule's tail along its side to make the skin tremble.

The groom was silent. "Bad off," he said. Then he looked ahead at the road.

Beef broth for fever, Tretite always said. Willow bark tea for headache. Ginger for stomach. I had packed these things hurriedly.

The groom pulled down the long road to the canefields, passing the barn, and then he turned his head away from me as if a stone had struck him.

Jean-Paul lay on a cane-cart, shaded with burlap over the frame. I bent over his face. His eyes were closed. His lips were hard as cypress. I reached out to move the burlap sacks covering his body and saw the blood. Pooled in the cart. Black. They had wrapped his thigh with sacking, and it was rusted brown, and already the dust from the wind clung to the wetness and his hair and his eyelashes.

The cook. Smell of meat. Smell of coffee in her tignon when she held my shoulders. "Why is he in the cane?" I shouted. "He is an upholsterer! He was not hired for cane."

She whispered into my ear, "He took them chairs out piece by piece to the barn, put on new cloth, but she never like the work. The colors. Then she go off to New Orleans, and the overseer tell that boy go in the field. Too much cane."

The overseer shouted toward the cart, "That who owned him? Tell her get him out of here before the others stop working."

I climbed up into the cart, tearing my dress hem. So much blood. His eyes closed. You belong to me. You belong to me. His neck warm. His throat still.

The groom stood close at my elbow and said, "That wind make the people angry all week. They work so hard, don't like how your boy smile all the time. Marques didn't cut him on purpose. That boy just don't move. Marques keep yelling at him go faster, stop smiling and move. All week I hear him. That boy don't answer no questions. Just smile. Smile and say something low. Like he ain't here. Then today Marques—he flail up that cane knife, and that boy don't move out the way."

"Her boy," the cook said.

The tall, sweet grass rose like a wall around us. I lifted his head to rest it in my lap. His neck bent. His spine. My fingers on his face.

Cloth smelling of coffee. The cook bent herself around me, a stranger, and said as if she couldn't believe it, "You his mother."

I took him home.

The cane knife had hit him in the thigh. A vein. The blood pooled at the bottom of the cart. The groom carried Jean-Paul, wrapped in sacking and a sheet brought by the cook. The overseer was a distant voice in the cane.

I took him home.

He lay in his room. Charité and Noémie's hands with mine on his skin. The passages. The swinging dangle. The sternum, where water pooled for one moment like a tiny bayou. The cut on his thigh like a tear in cloth. A vein. Wrist and throat and temple.

When the women were gone, I lay on the floor beside his bed. With the sharpened knife, I cut off my braids. My mother was gone. There was no *dya* to shift into another skin. My hair lay under his bed. Ropes. Reins.

I pulled the blade across my wrists, just where the scars were from the boat, and across the coffee bean burns. Blood welled up in a fine sting. I pulled again. But the tingle was only a burn. Not enough.

And no voice spoke to me. God did not tell me to stop. My mother did not speak to me. Jean-Paul's utter silence above, on the moss mattress, did not change.

Cut after cut after cut, threads of blood meshing, smeared with my palms, but I could not find my veins, because I did not have the courage. I lay on my back, my tears streaming past my neck onto the floor, my blood already drying so that it was a second skin.

Dis-rien, moi. Rien.

Say nothing.

The spoon came close to my mouth. She was not my sister. Charité. She said, "Crime against God, what you do."

The rag was wet on my arms. She was not my daughter. She was someone else's child. Noémie. But she bathed me because I had paid for her. Paid money to her mother.

Coffee. Sugar. All die. Tou-mort. The blue cloth. The dahlia plates. The peacock. His pheasant plate on the stand over the fireplace. My fireplace. His fireplace. His curtains. Tou-mort.

Nothing in my mouth.

Someone died for coffee? Where? Eggs and rice. Hera and Phrodite could have died in the rice. He died in the sugar.

She tried to give me broth.

Rien.

Rien.

Water. Who died for water? The rain fell on my roof and ran into my cistern.

Bricks. He died for bricks. Wood burns. Ashes and pig fat make soap. Someone dies for soap. Ashes. No ashes from brick. Even if I knocked this candle over while his body lay here, in the room where he would have sewed, and we burned to ash and bone—my hair burned to my skull, his hair combed over so neatly—the bricks would not melt.

I kicked at my own walls.

Screamed and screamed into my pillowcase, my face hot—fevered as a child. As when I burned with fever and my mother moved a wet cloth over me. My mother. So much better than me. Gone. My son. I pushed my face into the wet cotton. I will not breathe. I can die now.

"Madame!"

Maman. Noémie turned me over. Her hands were brown. She was not my child.

Twelve | DYA

"Did you have sisters?"

"No, petite." I held her small, pale hand in mine.

"Who taught you to sew?" Marie-Claire asked.

"My mother."

"Where is your mother?"

"Dead." We waited for a horse and cart to cross the street.

"Why do we not visit her?"

We walked through the dusty streets toward the cemetery. The ribbons I tied at the ends of Marie-Claire's braids were green as ivy.

"She is in Africa," I said. "I visit her in my memory. She is with her own mother, and her mother's mother."

"Where is Africa?"

"Across the water, petite."

One spring, when I was five or six, a violent wind rattled the tops of the trees on Azure, and when we went out, baby birds were dead everywhere, lying on the brick paths and in our clearing, their bodies only scrawls of bone and their eyes dull buttons still covered with skin.

When I cried, my mother said, "They see nothing, they feel nothing. They never live yet."

But I imagined them waiting, their beaks open, having heard and felt the larger wings in the nest that came and went, and then I imagined how they felt falling.

She was my daughter.

Marie-Claire was my daughter because I bought her, and she had no one else, and I was her mother, and would free her when she turned twenty-one.

She helped me wash the angels every month. Jean-Paul. Tretite.

I had washed them alone for five years. I sat on the earth beside Jean-Paul's headstone, and every time, the idea that he was under the grass hurt freshly behind my ribs. His femur. Thigh. His eyes. The soft spot on his skull, pulsing while he drank inside my dressfront. The smile that everyone knew was not a smile.

A few times, my fingers pushed into the dirt. The conveyance of everything we were into dirt. Then I touched the angel wings, gray in the moonlight.

But now when Marie-Claire helped me light the candles, the marble glowed golden yellow. Beloved son.

Marie-Claire was not a candle. Her skin was bright. She lit my rooms the best she could.

I had seen her sitting in a trader's cart in 1835. An American, the trader, a dirty man with a dark blond beard like sawdust clinging to his chin. He had been in the square for two days selling Indian blankets he said Opelousas people had sold him in the woods. It wasn't until the second day that the small head and shoulders moved above the cloth.

"Who is the girl?" I asked him.

She was about five. Lightest brown, pecan-shell, with curly hair matted and full of dried leaf specks. She sucked her thumb.

"They found her in the woods and sold her to me. Them Indians. I'm takin her to Baton Rouge."

"I'll give you one hundred fifty dollars cash for her now."

He squinted at my dress. "I can get more for her in Baton Rouge. Sometime they want 'em small. Buy 'em cheap, get 'em ready." He grinned at my breasts, covered with my shawl.

"Two hundred dollars," I said, coolly. "Cash."

When I lifted her off the wagon, she smelled like a wet dog. "You are ready now to be free," I whispered to her.

She didn't know her name. In front of the fire, where I bathed her, she answered the same to each question.

"How old are you?"

"Sais pas."

"How were you lost in the woods?"

"Sais pas."

"You must be five, petite. Someone must have called you by a name."

She shook her head.

"What did you do?"

"What they tell me."

"Where are your parents? Your mother?" She only moved her shoulders, but her eyes had not been sealed under skin, never opened like the baby birds. She had seen a mother sometime. She ate rice with her fingers, but she knew how to hold a spoon.

When she was finished with the rice and gravy, she lay before the fire in a clean blouse, which fell to her knees. She curled on her side, her thumb in her mouth, her cheeks pulling inward.

I sat for a long time, watching the rice she had dropped on the tablecloth. Rice was wet and soft when cooked, and it dried hard and translucent, and if you cooked it again, nothing would soften the grain. It was finished in that form. A seed.

I brushed the dried seeds from Jean-Paul's pheasant plate.

I bent my legs and knelt near her, asked her if she would be called Marie-Claire, and she nodded.

I said, "You may call me Maman."

I used to spit on Pélagie's floor every day. Manuel, the Rosière groom, always joked that the best bootblack was African saliva mixed with lead blacking. "Something in my spit make it hold and shine."

Sweeping and washing floors every day, back then, if I came back into a room to see a small clot of mud from Etienne's boots, or a tangle of reddish brown hair or green thread, I spit onto the floor and gathered with my cloth the dirt that would not be gathered dry.

My saliva stayed in the grain of the wood floor, and my dirt was outside, and even though the whites would not eat with me or look at me, their feet touched my spit, and when I bathed Madame de la Rosière and Madame Pélagie, I saw that though our skin hung and creased and gathered differently, they had two breasts, with tiny passages for milk, and under our dresses we were all the same.

The tiny passages for milk, even years after my breasts had no one to feed, still collected sweet-smelling moisture sometimes.

If I left the earth, and lay under a third stone angel, and my soul went là-bas to be with my mother and Jean-Paul and Tretite and the others I had loved, but no one left behind ever remembered me, the touch of my hand on skull, the tender part down the center of someone's hair—if no one remembered that I had saved coins and then the paper printed with ink worth much more, that I had paid for this house where my blood stained the floor in one room and was covered with a small Turkish rug—then my mother's words were nothing but sound formed around lye steam and saliva and evaporated in the wind of the clearing, and my own words were nothing but ink in trails on pressed treebark.

Only human animals remember us, aside from the words we leave behind on paper. Five years later, when Marie-Claire was ten, I bought Marie-Thérèse. Marie-Thérèse was dark as my mother, with glowing cheeks and fine hair in whorls along her skull. She was part of an estate being partitioned at the courthouse, and I stood near the group of men buying slaves.

Across from me was Etienne. He stared at me for a long time, while the bodies were being assembled.

I stared back. I was not owned but should never look at white people's eyes. He could have me arrested. But he could not meet my eyes. He dropped his own eyes to my breasts and then looked away.

My breasts, like any other woman's. Céphaline's had been small as biscuits. Pélagie's round and trembling pushed forward in her dresses. Fantine's cone-shaped, like anthills, and then plump when she fed her daughter and my son. And mine had grown large and veined after Jean-Paul's birth. When I left him behind, it seemed to me the blue veins would burst. How did blood turn to milk?

Etienne lifted his chin.

We had buttocks cleft in two. Toes. Collarbones. Angel wings—not shoulder blades. We were marked. Not marked.

He lifted his hand to bid for two men. Field slaves. Then he turned and left.

I waited for another daughter, watching her vacant stare.

The money was set aside. Sometimes, counting it at night, I held a coin and thought of my son's fingers pushing the needle through cloth or my own fingers sliding the first coin into my apron pocket here on this very street near the courthouse.

The boardinghouse was always full. Marie-Claire helped me now with the laundry, ironing men's shirts for Madame Delacroix's house, which was run now by her daughter, who, when she saw me every day, still called to her own slave, "The laundry girl is here for the shirts!"

I was not a girl, but a woman who had saved enough money so that if someone small were falling, someone with no wings, I would open my mouth.

I waited for the small girl, five or six, who sat in no one's lap, who was held around the wrist by a piece of rope.

Only our pelts were different, I told Marie-Claire and Marie-Thérèse. Our skin and fur. Everything else was the same.

Marie-Thérèse didn't listen in the same way. She was feral, like a cat raised out-of-doors who wasn't certain she wanted to be inside. She hid biscuits, buttons, pralines, and even eggs. She knew how to make a hole in an eggshell and suck out the liquid.

When she learned that inside the yolk was a baby chicken, Marie-Thérèse said, "I don't taste no feathers."

"What if we had feathers?" Marie-Claire said.

We hung up the sheets, the mended spots like moths in the sunlight.

"Sell your pelt," I murmured. The American trapper had said he'd skin us and sell the pelts. He'd traveled through the woods, killing and skinning, leaving his seed. Etienne loved the forest—not his own land, his wife, his daughters. He never knew his son. He had nothing now, perhaps.

I had my children. My memories of Jean-Paul, and now the laughter of my girls. The trapper tried to erase me, my skin and breath, but he was nothing and he left no one.

I had my daughters, my property, my memory, my history, my future. I had never wanted to raise animals, or crops in the earth—not sugarcane growing from green femurs to tall grass.

Inside my kitchen, in a dark cupboard, the cone of sugar hung away from the ants. Each morning, Marie-Thérèse took it out and cut large pinches with the sugar scissors, and put two or three pieces in her mouth, her fingers quick as birdbeaks reaching down for the sweetness.

Then Marie-Claire took the cone away from her sister and said, "Greedy pig. Cochon." She ground the rock-hard sugar into powder in a bowl for our baking.

I was forty-three years old, and all I wanted to do was sit down. The year was 1840.

You can taste one crystal of salt or sugar on your tongue. One. The ocean water dries, the cane juice boils, and they leave behind pieces of sparkle.

I remembered boiling the yard grass at Azure, trying to make it into sugar. I remembered the first time Jean-Paul saw sand, outside Emilia's door, and he put the pebbles in his mouth. I remembered my mother dropping one shard of sugar into my palm and studying my face.

I had left my mother behind nearly thirty years ago.

All I wanted to do was sit in my velvet chair by the fire and sleep.

The fire was enough sound for company. The fire was never silent. That was why old people always had a fire. Not just for the heat.

Every piece of cloth made me see Jean-Paul. Fine muslin for mosquito barres. Linen for the tablecloth. Fine soft calico printed with flowers for the girls' dresses. Pleats. Tucks. Sleeves. My fingers on the needle. Their fingers on the needle. We sat before the fire. They talked, the coals shifted, and I could cry silently without them ever knowing. I knew how to keep my nose from sniffing. I knew how to move the handkerchief—soft as an old tignon—up to my eyes as if sweat gathered there to sting.

I didn't want them to think my tears meant I was unhappy with them. My girls.

My blood now. My name after theirs. My daughters.

But water still moved inside me. Salt water. Céphaline had said the ocean took the water from the rivers, the clouds took the water from the ocean, and the rivers took the water from the clouds.

One night, I cried for her. For her voice, her fine brain that held all those words and patterns and numbers and the way she gave them to me because she couldn't keep them all for herself.

One night, I cried for myself. The girls had gone to sleep in our room, the door open a black wedge because they never wanted it dark; they wanted a slice of firelight and the glint of my needle.

But my hands rested on my skirt. By the end of the day of plucking chickens and rinsing clothes and cutting onions, the veins on the backs of my hands looked like green-blue letters. My shoulder was marked with a flower of France. My eye was marked with a floating scar. My insides were marked with poison. I was shrinking, the way women did as they got older, and my skin was thin as old parchment. My wrists and arms and hands scribbled with tiny dark bayous.

When the fire was only jewels, and the house was safe from burning, I let my head rest on the black velvet pad sewed for my chair. I couldn't sleep lying down but had to begin my rest this way, as my mother had, as old women did, with my body still convinced that it was working, watching, waiting.

Every month, at my son's grave, my daughters laid the only flowers he had ever loved: sewn blossoms, on scraps of cloth.

My own place was beside him and Tretite, my stone already ordered, my angel already carved by the mason.

At the outskirts of the cemetery, we passed the grave of Joseph, Opelousas Indian, died 1829. He had frozen to death one night in the alley behind my house. I had paid for him to be buried in a cypress box in this small piece of earth near the other graves of Indians. I tied red trade cloth to the small iron cross once a year, and it faded to pink.

"Why do the Indians wear blankets and the whites wear coats?"

"The Indians don't all wear blankets."

"The ones near Bayou Carron do."

"Why were you near the bayou?"

"You told us to take that package of shirts to Madame Delacroix."

"That's not near the bayou."

"Noémie's Eulalie said the water was so low we might find something in the banks. But all we saw was a dead dog."

"Why would you want to see that?"

"I thought we would find gold. From the pockets of a dead man who someone threw into the bayou."

"Marie-Thérèse!"

"Eulalie says bad men fight and throw one another in the bayou. But now the water is only black puddles. It smells."

"When the rains come, the bayou will flood again."

"Where does all the water go?"

"To the ocean."

"How does it get into the sky?"

"I don't know."

Marie-Claire had been silent all this time. Then she said, "Who told you to buy me?"

We stopped walking, and our reflections froze in the window of a tavern. "I saw you waiting there for me, petite, told myself you needed a mother."

"I had a mother," Marie-Claire said. "She died."

"I had a mother," I said. "She died."

"That's not fair."

"No."

We came toward my window, with my name in painted letters.

"My name was Jacinthe," she said.

"I know. One night when you were feverish, you told me."

"I don't know my mother's name."

"I know."

In our backyard were clean clothes walking in the wind, the empty sleeves reaching out for the laughing girls. Get the gravy out, you use this one. Get the rust out, this one. Get your monthly blood out, this one and cold, cold water.

"Who told you?" Marie-Claire asked, when I showed her how to erase her own blood.

"My mother."

"Every month? Forever?"

"For a long time."

She whispered, "For you, too? Even after you have a baby?"

I said, "Not anymore. Now I am finished."

The white shirts we washed for all the lawyers and clerks and planters hung stiff and starched on another line. Marie-Claire liked to whisper, "That one is like a ghost. Reaching out his arms."

She shivered. Marie-Thérèse would roll her eyes and say, "That's the shirt of Msieu the Boring Book Man."

Msieu the Boring Book Man was Mr. Johnson, the new court clerk, who lived in Msieu Vosclaire's old room. Mr. Johnson had never married either. He wanted to read his books when he was not eating. He spoke only to the other men. He ate his breakfast and walked across to the courthouse every day, and he paid me his board every month, and because he was a red-faced, red-haired man who was known throughout the parish, and who planned to live out his life here in my house, no one ever bothered me or my daughters.

Msieu Césaire had died. Etienne had gone to New Orleans with his wife, who hated Opelousas. He had sold Rosière to someone I never met.

Madame Lescelles had died, and her nephew inherited the store. But there were other stores now. Sometimes I wondered about Hervé Richard, who could have been in New Orleans or New York, but who would never be able to come back to Opelousas and see what had happened to me. He wouldn't see me with two daughters. "You will have your own child," he said that day, but these were my own children now.

Julien Antoine and Jonah Greene lived in Paris. They wrote to me once a year and sent fine handkerchiefs or lace collars. Then, after seven years, their words ceased.

My work was now to speak. I told my daughters of my mother's mother, on the boat, and I washed their hair, so like my own. I told them of my mother's muslin clouds and pink-sequined arms, while I sat beside their bed. I told them of her stitches, and Jean-Paul's thread, and I put pinches of sugar in their palms.

Marie-Claire was seventeen in 1847. She was old enough to be noticed by Eugène the mason's son, Eugène fils, but she could not marry until she was free. She could not be free until she was twenty-one, and then she would own her sister, until Marie-Thérèse was old enough to be free.

I had to live that long.

"You smell," my younger daughter said to me.

"Oui, Marie-Thérèse. I am ill."

"You are not coughing."

"No. I am ill inside my blood."

She skittered away. She was twelve. She would never think of anyone but herself, and I had to smile at the obstinacy of her own blood. Marie-Claire was obedient, thoughtful, the older child, who would be a mother forever. Marie-Thérèse was disobedient, watchful, and never thoughtful, and she would always taste and smell and touch what she wanted before considering anyone else.

She studied me gravely in my chair, from which I could hardly move.

Pélagie—her husband's brother had left her barren from disease. The trapper had left me with something inside my blood—syphilis, whispered Doctor Vidrine's nephew Gustave, who treated me now. Impure contact. But how did the fluid of seeds leave something inside blood that raced through every part of my body? How did my vision fail? There was no blood in my eyes. Only salt water bathing my irises. Lead in Céphaline's blood, and sweet smell on her breath.

Did the animals in the woods leave disease with one another? The alligators and birds?

I felt like a child myself, melted into my chair, my flesh loose and soft, my feet swollen, while Marie-Claire cooked.

She would be eighteen, then nineteen. Twenty. Twenty-one. I drank the broth she made, and waited.

I remembered—in the clearing, Mamère stirring the black clothes, stirring the bloodied clothes of Eveline. I pricked my wrist and waited until the blood had formed the shining button—not black, not red—laid the dried perfect circle on a plate and crushed it with the pestle. Powder. Powder that contained all my thoughts and measurements and my mother and father. Sang mêlé. My blood mixed with theirs.

I added a drop of water and waited. Stirred. Only a smear of dark moisture. Nothing else. Resurrection. That was what the God of smoke and words promised during Mass. Heaven.

Home. That was what the Ibo god promised. What had the Bambara gods promised my mother?

Where was Jean-Paul? Had he ever believed in me? He had not believed I would come back. What God did he love?

They had to be waiting for me. He was with my mother. Là-bas. Over there. Tretite and my grandmother, her breath stained indigo blue. Céphaline and Pélagie? Were whites in the same là-bas? Heaven. Were we separate? I would have liked to tell Céphaline about the body, to tell Pélagie about celadon and ocher and aubergine satin. I would have liked Jean-Paul to tell her. But là-bas—

My daughters brought me broth and took my soiled clothes and combed my hair. My skull ached under their touch. Marie-Claire combed for hours, and I shivered like a horse's flank when he is stroked. Marie-Thérèse watched.

"You will take care of her," I told Marie-Claire. "You will tell Marie-Thérèse the stories until she knows them."

"Of course."

"She has my mother's name. Every time I combed your hair I knew you had the *ni* of my mother."

"Oui, Maman."

"You will be the mother. Her blood."

"Oui, Maman."

"You will marry Eugène, and he will keep this house forever with you. He will not burn it."

"Maman. No one will burn it."

"Bricks cannot burn, but the floors. The doors. Watch the candles. Always watch the candles."

"Maman."

"Paper can burn. But the papers are in the courthouse. Mr. Johnson has already taken the papers."

The papers already filed in the courthouse on October 3, 1849, in the large book of Notarial Acts, read:

It being understood that the said Moinette Antoine is to emancipate the said mulatto girl slave Marie-Claire, 19 years of age, the said griffone girl slave Marie-Thérèse, 14 years of age, when they arrive at the full age of majority, or before that period if the law changes to permit it, and the said Moinette Antoine hereby promises to obligate herself, or her executors Monsieur Richard Johnson and Monsieur Charles Drouet, to pass an act of emancipation in favor of the said girl slaves at the shortest period that the same can be done by law, giving the said slaves all the prerogatives and privileges of free persons, as though they had been born free.

I copied the wording of the last part from the document I had finally read: Le Code Noir of 1724.

All Jews must be expelled from the colony of Louisiana. I thought of Mr. Jonah Greene, his bulb of flesh, the small cap I had seen him put on his head in his room. His church in his room, his murmured church words.

They were in Paris, with their own window, sitting in chairs before a fire with their shoulders touching or their knees.

I lay with my bed drawn close to the fire, inside my bricks, with my daughters nearby.

Every night, they slept in their large bed, their braided hair tangling with each other's outflung arms or tucked-close chins. Marie-Claire tried to inch away in her sleep, as she was grown now, her shoulder turned away from Marie-Thérèse, who began most nights still pressing her face to her older sister's spine. Then Marie-Thérèse would shift and lie facedown, separate, arms flat underneath her and toes pointed as if she dove all night through the air.

When I knew I would die, when the pain pulsed in every watery branch of my body, I asked Marie-Claire to buy the coffin. The coffin-maker refused to come. He said it was bad luck to measure someone for a coffin while they were still alive. So I measured myself but said the coffin was for a boarder who would take it to his plantation when he left town.

He was satisfied with this deception.

I wrapped myself in white linen, the shroud I had sewn many months ago and put aside, when I first felt little crystals shooting inside my heart. The girls knew nothing.

I left my daughters everything. Every brick and piece of wood and iron. Every ash and sliver of soap. I hoped they would love each other forever.

I laid myself in the coffin one night, in the kitchen where the man placed it. The fire burned low. The wood smelled sharp, and in one corner, I saw sap glistening from a wound in the pine.

I was inside a boat, a pirogue shaped to fit only one body, to take nothing down the river to hunt, to kill, to sell. Nothing of value. Bones and skin and ligaments and the brain swimming in the skull. The muscle of the heart hurting, not aching, as people always said: heartache. Broken heart. Foolish. It was a thick, tough, pulsing thing. The pain was in the muscle, just as in the leg or the wrist, from twisting wet clothes, from moving and moving and moving.

I couldn't let them send Jean-Paul down the bayou, toward the ocean, because I wanted to lie beside him. All those years. My place in the earth. But if we went là-bas, to be with my mother, there was water. Céphaline would laugh, she would have an explanation for the clouds, for rain, but I didn't have to listen now. I was old. I could imagine all the rivers and oceans, the fog so thick and moist in the mornings, and the sky as one place. The rain came from somewhere above us, and fed the rivers, and it never disappeared.

ACKNOWLEDGMENTS

Debts will always be owed.

I can't write anything without Richard Parks and Holly Robinson. At Pantheon, Alice van Straalen. Also Elaine Pfefferblit, Beth Kephart, Juli Jameson, Kate Moses, Dwayne Sims and all my Sims family, Revia Chandler and all the Aubert family, Kari Rohr, Eric Barr, Nicole Vines, and Tanya Jones, who helped me in many ways. My mother and father, who are never done, my neighbors who see the light on at 2:00 a.m., my relatives who tell stories—it takes a village to raise a book. In Washington, Louisiana, I was honored to share a house and stories with Susan and Robert Tinney.

I am immensely grateful to libraries and their staffs—the University of California, Riverside, library staff especially for years of friendly companionship. In the stacks, I found the story of a remarkable woman named Manon Baldwin in *Creoles of Color in the Bayou Country,* by Carl A. Brasseaux, Keith P. Fontenot, and Claude F. Oubre. I found recipes for cleansers and tonics in a book by a remarkable man, Robert Roberts, who wrote *The House Servant's Directory,* one of the first books written by an African American and published by a commercial press (in 1827). I found inspiration in *Africans in Colonial Louisiana,* by Gwendolyn Midlo Hall, and *Intimate Enemies: The Two Worlds of the Baroness de Pontalba,* by Christina Vella.

I owe my girls big-time: Gaila, Delphine, and Rosette.

A NOTE ABOUT THE LANGUAGES OF EARLY NINETEENTH-CENTURY LOUISIANA

During the 1700s and the first few years of the 1800s, Louisiana was a colony ruled at different times by France or Spain. Many native Indian tribes lived there, along with French, Spanish, Swiss, German, and Canadian officials, soldiers, farmers, and trappers, as well as Acadian refugees and Africans from a number of tribes brought as slaves to the Americas. Each group contributed words and phrases from their own language to the standard French spoken by residents who had emigrated from France. The result was Creole French, unique to Louisiana. In 1803 Louisiana became an American territory and in 1812 it joined the Union, but it would be years before English was widely spoken.

GLOSSARY

Attakapas—Indian people of the Gulf Coast and other areas of Louisiana; a former colonial territory in Louisiana.

Bambara—an African people, as well as the language they speak.

la barbe espagnole—Spanish moss, from the French for "the beard of a Spaniard."

barracoon—a barrack for temporary holding of slaves.

batture—the low-lying land between a riverbank and its levee.

besoin—French for "need."

blanc, les blancs—French for "white," "the whites."

blankitte, les blankittes—single and plural form of a Creole word used by slaves for whites.

bousillage—a mixture of mud, horsehair, moss, and straw used to chink walls.

bouton—French for "pimple."

bozal—Creole word for newly arrived African slaves.

cadeau—French for "gift."

chalan—French for "barge," a kind of boat often used in nineteenth-century Louisiana.

chênière—a wooded ridge or sandy hummock in a bayou or swamp.

cimmaron—a fugitive slave.

ciprière—Creole word for swampy uncultivated land with cypress trees in standing water.

cochon—French for "pig."

Code Noir—The Slave Code instituted by France in 1724 to regulate the discipline and commerce of Negro slaves in the colony of Louisiana. In 1806, under American territorial rule, it was revised to restrict slaves and free blacks more harshly.

corbateur—itinerant trader.

coureur-de-bois—a hunter or explorer of the woods.

Dieu—French for "God."

dya—Bambara word for the essence of one's spirit, which after death transfers to the next born in a family.

faro—Bambara word for water spirit.

fleur-de-lis—a stylized image of a lily, traditionally used as an emblem of French royalty, and by extension, France.

garçonnière—French for "bachelor apartment," often a room separate from a main residence.

grandmère—French for "grandmother."

griffe, griffone—male and female versions of the word for a person who is three-fourths black and one-fourth white.

Ibo—An African people, as well as the language they speak; used in nineteenth-century Louisiana to indicate African tribal origin.

jardin—French for "garden."

Ki—term used in 1800s Louisiana to indicate African tribal origin.

là-bas—French for "yonder," "over there"; used for "afterlife" by Moinette.

maman—French for "mama."

maringouin—Creole for "mosquito."

matelas—Creole for piles made of harvested sugarcane to prevent freezing; from the French for "mattress."

Mina—An African people, as well as the language they speak; used in nineteenth-century Louisiana to indicate African tribal origin.

mulâtresse—a woman who is half-black, half-white.

nègre—French for "Negro," a black person.

ni—Bambara for "soul" or "spirit."

octoroon—a person who is one-eighth black and seven-eighths white.

ouaouaron—Creole word for "bullfrog."

oui—French for "yes."

pas—French for "not."

père—French for "father."

petit, petite, petites—male, female, and plural forms of French for "child."

pigeonnière—French for "dovecote," a separate building.

quadroon—a person who is one-fourth black, three-fourths white.

le quartier—the slave housing area or street.

sacatra—a person who is seven-eighths black and one-eighth white.

sagamite—a gruel of hulled cooked corn.

sais pas—shortened French version of "I don't know."

sang mêlé—a person of mixed blood.

Singalee—African-Creole for someone from Senegal.

tafia—a cheap rum made of distilled sugarcane juice.

tignon—headscarf required by a 1786 Spanish law stating that women of color, free or slave, must cover their hair.

toujours—French for "always."

tout—French for "all."

A NOTE ON THE TYPE

The text of this book was set in Sabon, a typeface designed by Jan Tschichold (1902–1974), the well-known German typographer. Based loosely on the original designs by Claude Garamond (c. 1480–1561), Sabon is unique in that it was explicitly designed for hot-metal composition on both the Monotype and Linotype machines as well as for filmsetting. Designed in 1966 in Frankfurt, Sabon was named for the famous Lyons punch cutter Jacques Sabon, who is thought to have brought some of Garamond's matrices to Frankfurt.

Composed by Creative Graphics, Allentown, Pennsylvania
Printed and bound by Berryville Graphics, Berryville, Virginia
Designed by M. Kristen Bearse

4/4/06